I0676995

The Aries Appointment

KATHY T. KALE

The Aries Appointment

Copyright ©2015 by Kathy T. Kale

All rights reserved. No part of this book may be reproduced or transmitted in any form or by any means without written permission of the author.

This is a work of fiction. Names, characters, places, and incidents are either the product of the author's imagination or are used fictitiously. Any resemblance to actual persons, living or dead, events or locales is entirely coincidental.

Library of Congress Control Number: 2015902040
ISBN: 9780983686082

Published by:
Pollux Press
Fort Pierce, Florida
34981

Acknowledgement

My deepest thanks to those in both the literary and astrological fields who helped bring this book to fruition and endeavored to make it a better book. I am grateful to Mary DeDanan for her keen editorial insights, and to Ray Farrell, Luc Allan and Robert Block for their comments and corrections. Many thanks to my early readers: Joan Farrell, Claudette Wingell, Francis Kavanagh, Ann Marie Montgomery, Mary Ferguson, Penny Baehr, Ann Viljoen, Ann Huff, and Ron Griffin. Thanks also to Vicki Racine at Eye Design for the cover design, to Doug Perrine at SeaPics.com for the cover photograph 'Sea of Stars' (image: 0036784-DPE), and to Peter Hughes at Abbey of London in Stuart, Florida for the author photo. I shall always be grateful to Eugene 'Spiritweaver' Vidal who introduced me to the astonishing world of astrology, and to all those in the South Florida Astrological Association and the Florida Atlantic Chapter of the National Council for Geocosmic Research, for enlightened conversation and friendship over the years. I am thankful to my parents for their continual interest and enthusiasm in my projects, I appreciate the excellent company of my sons, and I cherish the love and support of my husband.

For Bill, who holds a different worldview

Prologue

SOUTH BEACH BABY SNATCHED

Miami Beach—Shock waves are rippling through the exclusive gated community of J'Adore Del Mar following last night's presumed kidnapping of six-month-old Sierra Rossario. According to Detective Daniel Kane, no ransom note was received, but police are certain the motive is money. Sierra is the only child of Good Food mogul and Fortune 500 entrepreneur Ciro Rossario, who has vowed to move heaven and earth to bring his daughter home. The infant is under medical care and in need of life-saving medicine.

According to Detective Kane, the mother, Tiffany Crystal (nee Jones) Rossario, was asleep in the family home and Mr. Rossario was in Mexico on a business trip when Sierra was taken. Mrs. Rossario, a former beauty pageant contestant and Miami Dolphin cheerleader, awoke to find the nursery empty, a second-floor balcony window screen removed and Sierra missing. How the kidnapper(s) breached the high security of the oceanfront estate is under investigation and police are following a number of leads. Detective Kane stated he was confident the infant would soon be found.

Miami Tribune Friday, May 4

Chapter 1

Four years later…

The appointment was set for four and Daniel Kane arrived on schedule. He'd booked the session online, but left the reason for it blank, which in my line of work wasn't unusual. I was sitting in my office staring at the planetary transits and trying to guess why he was coming, when he arrived in a noisy black Mustang. I stood up, smoothed down my long denim skirt, and went to the door.

I work out of my home, a Spanish mission house built in 1920, for which I sold my soul. It had Dade County pine floors, wide arched doorways, high ceilings, and big casement windows. I opened the paneled stained-glass front door and stepped onto the small front porch.

The loud engine died. Daniel Kane leapt from the car and jauntily crossed the lawn. He swept up the steps as if he owned the place. He was athletic and too good looking, with jutting sharp cheek bones and a golden tan. He shook my hand in a crushing grip. "Morgan Sterling, I presume."

He had come to my house. Exactly who was he expecting? I kept a blank expression. "I gather you had no trouble finding the place?"

"I can read a map," he said, as he appraised my house with the eye of a real estate agent. "I never get lost."

Lucky him. "Come in." I moved to the side allowing him to enter and then locked the door. I lived alone, which considering my work, was taking a risk. But I had a dog, I kept a cell phone in my pocket during working hours, had mace scattered throughout the house, and wore a rapid response call button on a chain around my neck. At this point it seemed like overkill. In the last four years I'd had no serious trouble—at least not from clients.

Daniel veered off course and stepped into the living room to pet Shiny, my graying, eight-year-old border collie who lay stretched out on the couch. She wagged her tail vigorously as Daniel rubbed her head.

"How can I help you?" I said.

Daniel turned and faced me. He was gangly, over six feet tall. He had long, wavy brown hair that touched his collar and bangs that were brushed to one side. He had a sharp nose, brown eyes so dark they looked black, and thick, long eyelashes. He looked vaguely familiar but I couldn't place him.

I felt pale and small standing next to him. I was a foot shorter, with drab ash blonde hair, bland light blue eyes, and bad eyesight. Taken aback by the intensity of Daniel's gaze, I removed my glasses.

He said, "I'm not sure you can help me. My sister thought you could."

"And your sister is?"

"Claire Quade."

Ah. Claire was my best friend. As soon as Daniel said her name, I saw the resemblance. They were both striking in looks and height. I knew Daniel had recently moved back to town, was a police officer, and thirty-five—two years older than Claire, and three years older than me. I also knew he was no fan of astrology. Which made me ask, "Why did you make an appointment? You didn't come for a reading."

His dark eyes widened with surprise. "The stars tell you that?"

"Actually, the planets."

"I'm going to be honest. I don't believe in astrology."

"You don't have to believe in astrology for it to work." I leaned against the wall and stared at him. "Given how you feel, I'm surprised you're here. Why are you?"

"You don't know?"

"I'm not a psychic," I said, much to my own chagrin. I was a fourth-generation astrologer in a family that had three genera-tions of psychics.

Shiny dragged herself off the couch and went to Daniel for more attention. She liked him. He bent down on one knee and rubbed her back. "I'm sorry for the secrecy. I don't want anyone to know I'm here."

"Or what? You'll be stoned to death? Burned at the stake?"

He chuckled. "And a sense of humor and everything."

"Free of charge," I said. Not that I found much to laugh about these days. I repositioned my glasses on my face. "Shall we get started?"

We went to the front bedroom, which I use as an office and I closed the door shutting Shiny out. The room was bright and rays of the afternoon sun slanted through the front windows onto an oversized desk. On the far side of the room sat an easy chair and couch that flanked a low pine coffee table. I flung a hand at the couch. "Please sit down."

Daniel didn't move. He was staring at my diplomas. I'd gone to the University of Texas and had an undergraduate degree in psychology and two master's degrees, one in clinical psychology and the other in neurobiochemistry.

"You have two master's?" Daniel said. "Are these fields related?"

I wasn't going to go into it. "One deals with causes, the other with effects."

Daniel frowned and looked puzzled. "Couldn't you get a real job?"

I laughed coolly. "I have a real job."

Daniel stepped along the wall and studied the rest of my diplomas. He pointed at the American Federation of Astrology diploma that granted me the title of professional practitioner. "Is there actually a school of astrology?"

"There are a few."

He blinked theatrically. His thick eyebrows formed a deep V that looked like horns, and I decided he had Aries blood in him. Also, strong Leo, given his dramatic flair and the hair, which resembled a mane. He gazed across the room, staring at my overstuffed bookshelves. "I went to the library and they had one astrology book. *The Idiot's Guide to Astrology*. I see there are more."

"You're quite observant. For a policeman."

He laughed happily. "Police detective." He adjusted his hair with a sweep of his hand. "I see Claire's told you about me. What did she say?"

That he'd been married and divorced multiple times, but I wasn't going to tell him that. "Why don't you sit down?" I gestured at the couch again. "The clock is ticking."

Indeed it was and ticking loudly. It occupied a shelf beside my diplomas. The transparent casing revealing spinning gears and turning wheels that kept humanity's idea of time, while the planets in the sky kept real time.

Daniel took my easy chair at the head of the coffee table, establishing his position. I had dealt with his type before. He had paid for the session and wanted to run it his way. It was both an Aries and Leo trait; they liked to lead. I grabbed his file off the desk and sat down on the couch. Without the data to erect a natal chart, I had drawn a transit chart for the start of our four o'clock consultation. I picked up my recorder. "I'll tape the session?"

He shook his head. "Please don't."

"Okay." He was afraid someone would find out he had come. I put the recorder down and picked up the chart, which showed the current placement of the planets. Venus and Neptune loomed large. With Venus, the planet of love, in contact with Neptune, the planet of delusion and confusion, in his house of marriage, I figured there was trouble with women; one of the three or four former wives.

He folded his hands and sat forward. He had fine golden hairs on his forearms and his veins stood out like ropes. "I'm here on account of a cold case. Four years ago a baby was lost and her mother has never been the same."

He paused and for one terrible moment, I wondered if he was talking about me.

He went on. "I mentioned it to Claire and she said to talk to you."

I was immediately alarmed. Had Claire found out what happened? But how? Only my mother knew, and she was miles away in Africa, not paying too much attention to my life. "Talk to me?" I said, in far too high a voice.

Daniel looked at me carefully, as if registering my distress. I took a deep breath as I was taught in yoga and tried to center myself. When I spoke again, my voice sounded normal. "Talk to me about what?"

"Astrology. That is what you do, right? I'm trying to find the abducted baby. Her mother is distraught. Tiffany can't function. I'm afraid she's thinking of giving up. She needs to know what happened to Sierra. Claire said you could look at a chart and tell. That you find lost wedding rings and wallets and could find a baby."

It wasn't so simple. The examples he referenced came from a book. In hindsight, everything was easy.

He went on. "For the record, I think its hooey."

A lot of people thought that. I looked at the clock and then the chart. It was just past four, which meant the transit chart could serve as a horary chart, which translated meant a chart of the hour. Ask a meaningful question and the sky would answer. My eye went to Venus and Neptune, which I guessed, besides uncertainty with women, could refer to a baby girl's uncertain fate. "Where was the kidnapping?"

"In Miami. South Beach. You may have heard about it. It made national news. Sierra Rossario was snatched from her crib when she was six months old. There was no ransom. Neither she nor the kidnappers were ever found."

I remembered the case clearly for my baby was the same age. At the time of Sierra's disappearance, my husband said it was the worst thing he could imagine happening: to have your baby taken and not know what happened to her. The following month I would learn worse things could happen. I shook off the memory. "Is there a new lead?"

"Tiffany wonders if Sierra is alive."

I took off my glasses. "Why?"

He looked pained. "She's been having dreams."

"What kind?"

He made a face to let me know that paying attention to dreams was akin to consulting the sky. "I don't know what she dreamt. When I mentioned the kidnapping to Claire, she said to ask you. That you would blow my mind." He looked at me expectantly, as if he was waiting for that to happen.

I laid the chart on the table. Some horary charts couldn't be read, and with Saturn associating with the 7th house, this was one of them. It was a warning to not get involved; the astrologer's judgment could be off. The sky was reflecting back my own uncertainty about correctly interpreting the chart. I said, "I'm sorry. I can't read this."

"I knew it! I told Claire as much! Too bad, for once in my life I'm right. I mean, how can you ask the sky a question and get an answer. Come on."

"Well, you can, most of the time," I said. My mother especially, was very good at it.

Daniel wouldn't leave it alone. "Don't take this the wrong way, but how can planets influence what happens on earth?"

"No astrologer thinks that. Don't take this the wrong way, but how can someone who knows nothing about astrology argue against it?"

He laughed. "Touché. Now you know how desperate I am. Believe me, I wouldn't be here if I had other options. You're my last hope, as dim as it is. You're all I've got." He paused and smiled with his eyes.

I could see he was used to getting his way with women. Claire said he married at the drop of a hat. The numerous ex-wives took him to the cleaners.

He shook a finger and the smile deepened. It created a dimple in his left cheek. "You're thinking about it. You're considering it. I can see that you are."

"So you're a mind reader?"

"Not at all." He folded his hands together and raised them to his heart in a plea. "I'm stuck. I don't know what to do."

He needed help. It was the astrologer's rallying cry. If I couldn't read the horary chart, I could always look at an event chart. "What was the date of the kidnapping?"

"May 3rd or 4th."

"A two-day spread? That's pretty broad."

"Sierra was taken during the night between 9 p.m. and 9 a.m."

A twelve-hour window. "I need a definite time. Can you pin it down more closely?"

He stared up at the ceiling for a moment, and then said, "I think around 8:40 on the morning of the 4th, Tiffany called 911."

I repositioned my glasses and noted the time on the chart, remembering bits about the kidnapping I had read. "The mother had been out drinking and slept in. When she woke up, she found the baby was gone. The father was out of town. He owns the Good Food grocery store chain."

Daniel was taken aback. He nodded at the chart. "You can see that in there?"

I looked at him. "I follow the news. It was a well-publicized case. There were no clues."

"Of course there were. There's no perfect crime. Not everything we knew was released to the public."

"What wasn't released?"

"I'll get the file, if you help me. I hate cold cases. Especially of kids. What if Sierra's alive and out there and longing for her mother as her mother longs for her? What about the bad guy who got away and thinks he got off scot-free? He could do it again. Maybe he has done it again. My job is to keep people safe. Fight crime. Stop evil."

He spoke with passion that belied the simplicity of his words. Was the world so black and white to him? I didn't have much time to consider it, as he went on.

"There's a reward. A hundred thousand dollars. You can have it all."

I removed my glasses and rubbed my eyes. I wouldn't take a case solely on the basis of getting a reward, but this was serious money. Helping law enforcement would also give me credibility. Before her exile, my mother was a police consultant, and helped solve numerous criminal cases. In her mind, that was the ultimate use of astrology. Solving this case would show her I was in her class. I might not have fifty years of experience, but I was good, and my certification was worth something, even if she didn't recognize it.

"I'm worried about Tiffany," Daniel added. "She's not strong. This is killing her. Even if we find out Sierra is dead, at least she'll know what happened."

I understood how a tragedy could bleed the life blood from you. "All right. Narrow down the time Sierra was taken and I'll look at an event chart."

The smile reached his eyes. "I'll get the case file from Miami PD."

I told him my fee to look at a new chart.

He looked incredulous. "You're going to charge me?"

It never ceased to amaze me how people assumed I'd work for free. "This is my job. It's how I put food on the table."

"I'm not getting paid," he said. "I'm doing this on my own time."

"I don't give away astrology, on principle."

He looked puzzled, scratched his chin with long fingers, as if trying to figure out the principle I was standing upon. Nonetheless, he pulled out his wallet.

I ran his credit card. After he signed his receipt, I walked him to the door. "Claire must be happy to have you back."

"It's me who's happy. My third marriage just ended. It's going to be one hellish divorce. I was glad to get away. What about you?" He looked deep into my eyes. "You're widowed?"

I broke eye contact, looked down at Shiny and nodded, afraid my voice would betray me if I spoke.

"Seeing anyone?"

Now I looked at him. "That's none of your business."

He smiled smugly. "Claire said you weren't." He put on his sunglasses. "I'll be in touch."

I watched as he swaggered to his car and hopped in. He was flirtatious, like his sister. He wanted my help and must have decided feigning interest was a sure way to get it. I typically ignored men like him. They were too reminiscent of my husband.

The sun broke through the branches and I shaded my eyes as I waved goodbye. Today was the spring equinox and it was warm for the first day of spring. Though I lived in South Florida, it had been a cold winter and I was still frozen in its icy grip. I felt I was living in the land of the dead, feeling nothing, if you excluded guilt, grief, remorse, hatred, anger, and bitter resentment.

A rattle of beer cans snagged my attention. To the south, Porter, an unemployed, unkempt, fifty-ish neighbor crushed a beer can with his foot. Shiny, standing by my side, noticed him and began barking.

Daniel was stopped at the end of the drive, waiting for a car to go by. Porter reached into his pocket, fired up a lighter, and tossed a firecracker our way. An explosive *pop* in the driveway made me jump and Shiny's tail shoot between her legs.

"Shut that fucking dog up," Porter yelled.

The engine of the car died. Daniel flew out, tore across Porter's lawn, and yanked his arm. "What was that? What did you just do?"

Porter, likely drunk, stumbled and lost his footing.

Daniel righted him with a grip to the shoulder. He whipped out his badge. "Was that a firecracker? Is that any way to treat a lady and an aging dog? Apologize."

Porter stared blearily in my direction. He swayed unsteadily on his feet and mumbled something that sounded like, "Damn bitch makes too much fucking noise."

"I didn't hear you," Daniel said. "An apology begins with 'I'm sorry.' You can say it here or down at the station. Your choice."

"Let go of me." Porter tried to wrench his arm free, but could barely move it. "I can light a firecracker."

"You can't throw it at a person."

"I threw it at a dog."

"Animal cruelty. Apologize or I'll take you in."

"You're crazy. You got nothing on me."

"I can hold you for 72 hours. Is that what you want?"

Porter glared at me. On the road, a UPS truck rumbled by. "I'm sorry," Porter muttered without remorse.

Daniel looked at me. "Do you accept his apology?"

"Yes," I said, with a mixture of amazement and shock. Porter, with his guns and firecrackers and temper, was the bully of the neighborhood. He'd lived here for twenty years and was the self-appointed king. No one stood up to him.

"This is your lucky day." Daniel released his hold. "Pick up your trash. Find the firecracker."

Porter half staggered through the hedge to my drive, head downcast, making no eye contact.

Daniel took out a pad. "I'm writing this up. Give me a reason to come back and that will be offense number two. You hear what I'm saying?"

Porter surged and came up with the charred red end. "Got it."

"Let's hope so."

Porter lumbered to his yard and Daniel burst through the bushes and came to the steps. "What's his name?"

I told him.

"Has this happened before?"

I couldn't tell how many times either the drunken neighbors to my south or the religious fanatics on the north let me know I was not welcome on the street. The drunk was the good one. "He gets like this when he's drinking." Which was most of the time.

"What's the problem? What did you do to him?"

"He found dog poop on his grass. I have a dog. Ergo I was trespassing."

"This happens again and you call me. I'll have a car here in two minutes."

I was impressed. "You can do that?"

He smiled proudly. "I'm a detective." He shot an imaginary gun at me with his index finger and thumb, before strutting to his car. He sped off in a manner that announced he wasn't worried about getting a speeding ticket.

Chapter 2

Across the street, a door flew open and my good neighbor, Jake, barged out and strode determinedly in my direction. If I was besieged on either side by malefics, the neighbor across the street was my salvation. Jake was forty-three and a good friend. He had a Pisces Sun and an Aries Moon, a difficult combination. He was sympathetic yet pushy, compassionate yet self-centered. Thanks to the Pisces, he had codependency issues, bad feet, and medical problems that were hard to diagnose. He hated exercise, but under doctor's orders had taken up walking and yoga. I'm sure his idea of exercising would be to have someone carry him up and down the stairs.

He climbed mine and embraced me in a suffocating hug that lasted too long. "Who was that guy? A cop?"

Nothing got by Jake. I had the sneaking suspicion he sat at home all day and watched my house. He was a day trader who depended on me for stock trading tips—which he followed only when it suited him. Consequently he was still in the market long after I advised he get out and he'd lost a lot. Now the market was rising and he was making money, just not fast enough for his liking. But that was an Aries Moon for you—they have no patience.

I disentangled myself and stepped back to give myself space. "You know I can't talk about my clients."

Shiny leaned against him and he patted her head. He took good care of her. Whenever I was gone for any length of time, he hung out with her. If he was bored, which was often, he took her to the dog park. He was a good friend, a good cook, and good company. He also had a healthy respect for astrology. He had taken my twelve-week introductory course, declared it too difficult, and hired me as a consultant.

"A cop for a client," he said, as he rubbed Shiny's side. "That's new."

"I never said that."

"You kind of did."

I decided to shut up and say nothing more that would betray a client's confidentiality. It was one of my cardinal rules and a professional requirement.

"I hope it teaches Porter a lesson," Jake said. "It's about time someone put him in his place."

"I hope it doesn't send him into a rage." Porter had a nasty temper. Most of the time it was directed at his wife, but these days she was around infrequently. When she was home, they fought like cats. Furniture was thrown, glass broken, obscenities screamed. All this I knew without wanting to. It was the nature of the close-knit neighborhood. We knew each other's business.

"We still on for yoga?" Jake asked.

"I can't make it. I have to work."

Jake couldn't hide his disappointment. "You work too much. What's that cop got you doing?"

I just shook my head. I didn't work too much. Jake worked too little. He followed the stock market hours, worked 9:30 to 4:00, and considered it a long day if he put in seven hours. I worked ten hours a day, prepping charts, meeting clients, and preparing lectures. I taught two classes a week on introductory and advanced astrology. But I liked to keep busy. Work saved me. It kept my mind occupied and away from dark thoughts. In my spare time, for fun, I read astrology books. If I lived long and studied for the rest of my life, I would never know all there was to know about the subject. I was surrounded by shelves of unread books. I knew I bought too many, but I couldn't help it. I was always online, searching for the irreplaceable one I'd let go, and finding others I had to have. And Daniel thought there was one!

"What about the protest on Saturday?" Jake asked with unmistakable petulance. For a grown man, he behaved like a child when he didn't get his way.

"I'm going." I usually worked Saturday mornings, but I had set this one aside for the "Don't Shoot Me" protest. There'd been another high school shooting, this time in Tampa, and we were objecting to lax gun laws. In my case it was too late, but this wasn't about me.

"Don't forget to make a poster," Jake said, pointing a warning finger.

I looked at my watch. "I should get back to work."

"I'll take Shiny to the park if you want."

"That would be great." I got her leash and walked them to the street. I lived in a quiet neighborhood in Coral Cove, half way between Miami and Orlando, a mile from the ocean. There were no sidewalks and the road was narrow, but there were few cars. The streetlights were widely spaced and at night it was dark enough to see the stars.

We parted at the road. They lazily lumbered down Sable Street and I returned to my office, sat down at my desk, and woke up my desktop. I grabbed my glasses and my Magic 8 Ball, closed my eyes, shook the black orb, and asked: Will I find out what happened to Sierra? *Cannot predict now.* Will I get the reward money? *Ask again later.* I tried a new approach: Should I proceed? *It is certain.*

I threw the ball down and faced the monitor. My astrology software was always running and with the app on my iPhone and iPad, I was never far from a timed chart. I typed in the data for the kidnapping and set the time on May 4th for 8:40 a.m.

I stared at the chart, which was a circle that represented the sky. Divide the circle in four and you got the angles: a cross inside a circle. On a clock, the angles corresponded to 12, 3, 6, and 9 o'clock. I was looking for a number of planets near the angles, which meant action. At 8:40 a.m. there were no planets on any angle. I played with the chart, changing the time, and watching how the planets rotated during the night. In the twelve-hour window there were two times when multiple planets were near the angles—10:50 p.m. and 3:45 a.m. I thought it was likely that Sierra was taken around one of those two times.

I studied how the planets were interacting with each other. Mars and Uranus were together, suggestive of a rash, sudden act. Venus was opposite Pluto, which could describe a girl's abduction, or worse. Saturn was opposite Neptune; the authorities didn't have a clue what happened.

Staring at the chart made me anxious. I consciously tried to relax my knotted stomach. I rolled my shoulders. Horary and event astrology were not my specialty. Both types of charts held a definitive answer to a specific question. There was no wiggle room, no avenue of possibility. I had done poorly on this portion of the certification exam. *Just let the sky speak*, my grandmother used to say when I was a child. But the sky had stopped speaking to me.

I closed the chart, opened a search engine, typed in the name "Sierra Rossario" and got thousands of hits. I grabbed my notebook and made notes as I read old news.

The early reports focused on the infant's disappearance and the distraught parents begging the world for help. There were more questions than answers and the same information was repeated over and over, with nothing new added as days went by. An upstairs window was left open; a baby was taken. Two weeks passed and then a child molester who lived nearby was picked up for questioning. Though he maintained his innocence, he had no alibi, and was charged with the crime. The police and press were sure they had their guy and he was routinely convicted in the pages of the *Miami Tribune*. Daily the prosecutor held news conferences anticipating this verdict. Unfortunately, the man was stabbed to death soon after his incarceration. He had not cracked. Police had no clue what happened to the baby.

Attention turned to hospital employees. After having a seizure at twelve weeks, Sierra had been seen monthly by specialists at Miami Memorial Hospital. There were extensive interviews with physicians, nurses, aides, volunteers, secretaries, custodians, but all for naught. The child had vanished.

Meanwhile, the FBI arrived. Off the record, agents called the police investigation "shoddy." They had a different theory. The mother was a party girl. The former cheerleader liked to drink and occasionally snort cocaine. With her husband always traveling, she was on her own. She frequently left the newborn with a nanny to go bar-hopping on South Beach. A multitude of photos showed Tiffany smiling happily in her skimpy Dolphin's cheerleading outfit, her long strawberry blond hair streaming out in an invisible wind. A favored photo appeared over and over:

Tiffany in a sheer pink slip, down in the grass on her knees, hands covering her face, the long hair tangled and awry. I knew from one site it was taken the morning of the kidnapping, though without context, she could have been puking in the grass after a long night of drinking.

Journalists were no kinder to Ciro Rossario, who, given his Mexican roots, Italian-sounding name, dark skin, and immigrant status, was painted as a possible drug lord or mafioso. In what looked like a mug shot, he appeared as a thug, with a massive head, dark skin, and black sunglasses which hid his eyes. Though now Good Food was a runaway success, four years ago, Rossario had been criticized. He was underselling his produce and losing money even if he was gaining customers. Some said he was growing too fast, opening too many stores, and borrowing money he could never repay. Unnamed sources speculated he was so deep in debt that kidnapping his own baby for an insurance payout was his only recourse.

Meanwhile, there were no breaks in the case. Like the police, the FBI was reduced to asking the public for help. Months passed and the kidnapping left the front pages, articles became shorter and shorter, and blogs more infrequent. But every year on the anniversary of the kidnapping, the tragedy was revisited, with no new news, and long fingers of suspicion still pointing at the parents.

I opened the astrology chart and was looking to see how it aligned with the news reports, when the phone rang. Daniel's sister was calling.

"I just got off the phone with Daniel," Claire said. "Did you like him?" She was a Gemini for whom siblings are of paramount importance.

"I did. But you're right, he's no fan of astrology."

"You'll change his mind."

"We'll see. Why didn't you warn me he was coming?"

"He didn't tell me. I think he was afraid he'd chicken out."

It was precisely for that reason, I required payment in advance. Keeping the phone nestled between my ear and neck, I stood up and stretched. I padded to the living room and sank down in the arm chair facing the fireplace. I looked for Shiny, momentarily forgetting she'd gone for a walk. I peered at the window. Sunlight was shining through the trees, blazing through the glass. I said, "Daniel seems anxious to find out what happened to Sierra."

"It was his case."

Ah.

"He was taken off it."

"How come?"

"He had a personal connection to the victim."

"To the baby?"

"The mother."

"Connected how?"

"They were once lovers," Claire said in a disparaging tone. "Tiffany led Daniel on, then dumped him for someone richer. She broke his heart. I don't know why he agreed to help her."

"He seems noble. Determined to catch bad guys. Purge the world of evil."

"Don't laugh," Claire said. "He's wonderful. You'll love him. He needs you, even if he doesn't know it. He's going through a rough spot. His job is on the line."

I was immediately on guard. "Why?"

"He accidentally shot his partner." Claire sighed audibly. "He was up in Jacksonville with wife number three. Jennifer. There's a skank if you ever saw one. She was running around on him, but that's nothing new. Anyhow, one night there was a robbery and the thief was running away and it was dark and Daniel shot him. Only it was the wrong guy. Never mind his partner recovered, Daniel was transferred. It happens. A lot. He's been moved all over the state. If you could help him solve the case, it would do wonders for his career. His whole life, all he wanted was to be a cop. If he lost his job, I don't know what he'd do."

Red flags were flying. Who had I agreed to help? How good a cop was he if he was always transferred? Was he the reason the kidnappers went free and Sierra was lost?

"Don't tell him I told you," Claire said. "He hates that I talk about him."

"I won't say a word."

"Daniel says you can have the reward money."

"I won't spend it yet."

"Speaking of money," Claire said, "I've got a new listing. A waterfront in Stuart asking 999." She was a real estate agent, one of the top in the county. I met her the week I moved to Florida, four years ago. She sold me my house. I never knew we'd become best friends, and that because of her, I'd return to astrology. If I had any inkling how close we'd become, I would have watched what I said—but I never thought I'd see her again. As it turned out, I see her all the time and talk to her nearly every day. She's taken all my astrology classes and I give her professional astrological advice—I tell her when to put a house on the market, when to hold open houses, and when to sign contracts. For this she pays me five percent of her commission.

I did the math of the new listing in my head and liked the numbers. "When do the sellers want to list?"

"ASAP. They're motivated, so we probably won't get the asking price, but close enough. Find a date soon."

"I'll get you a good one."

"Great." She paused. "There's one more thing. Kev *may* have you deposed."

Kev was Kevin, her soon-to-be ex-husband. I hated the nickname and refused to use it. "Why would Kevin do that?"

"He's an asshole."

Divorce seemed to be the rule rather than the exception in her family. She was embroiled in a contentious breakup, which might explain why she was so down on Daniel's ex. I said, "What does he want from me?"

"I gave you as a character reference and that makes you fair game. Kev's trying to paint me as some drunk loose vixen."

That was the Sun-Jupiter-Neptune-Pluto side of her.

"But you know me," she said. "You see the best in me."

"You have the Moon in Capricorn. You're responsible and hard-working."

"There you go. Concentrate on that. Kev wants half the commission from the Sewell Point sale. If he wins and I have to pay up, I'll need a second mortgage. With credit so tight, I might not get it. If I don't, I could lose the house. *My* house. Motherfucking asshole."

"He won't get away with it," I said, saying what I thought sounded reasonable.

"Yeah, you're right." She calmed down instantly, which was another Gemini trait. Their moods changed with the wind. "He's just messing with me."

"He is." And she took the bait every time.

She sighed audibly. "I feel better. I'm going to game night. Want to come?" Claire lived next door to a Club Med and had a membership that allowed her to use their facilities. They had a singles night every week and held a variety of activities. She competed in every event and so long as she didn't drink too much, she often won; whether it was ping-pong, darts, pool, cards, tennis, running, or beach volleyball, she played hard and played to win. She couldn't stand losing. "Tonight it's euchre," she said.

"I've got to work. But you be careful. Don't drink too much. Keep your wits about you." Claire had a bad habit of picking up men at these singles nights, and not all of them turned out to be single.

"You'd better come. You're a good influence. When I'm with you, I try to live up to your exalted standards. I take the high road." She paused. "Daniel's coming."

Was she gauging my interest? For her information or his? I stayed neutral. "Have a good time."

We said goodbye and I put down my phone. I grabbed my laptop and opened the astrology program. Later I would find a good time to put the waterfront house on the market; right now I was more interested in finding out what I could about my new client.

Specifically, I wanted to know when Daniel was born. I couldn't ask Claire, not after I drummed into my students the importance of respecting other people's privacy. Most people had no idea how much information a birth chart held. So I went to Facebook and pulled up Claire's page. From her I found Daniel and clicked on his page. He had top notch privacy settings, but his birth date was there for the whole world to see. April 1st, an April fool. As I suspected, he was an Aries. Like Claire, he was born in Miami.

I subtracted his age from the present date and erected his chart. Since I had no birth time, I set the chart for noon and placed the sun rising on the horizon. I gathered from his hair and manner that Leo was strong, and since he had no Leo planets I guessed that sign was rising, which meant, given a Miami birth, he was born between one and three in the afternoon. I also figured, with his multiple marriages, he had Jupiter, the planet of excess, configured with his marriage house, and at 2:30 p.m. it was.

I studied the placement of his planets. He had three in Aries, which described his passion—and his simplicity—get the bad guy. He had Mars in Cancer, which explained his job as a policeman. Cancer is the homeland and Mars is the guy who fights for it. If my time was right, his Sun, the center of his universe, and driving purpose of life, fell in the 9th house of law, which explained his moral fixation with good and evil.

I mentally noted his strengths and weaknesses. Then, how his planets aligned with mine, which would reflect how we'd relate. I saw mutual Moon and Venus contacts, meaning we'd like each other. Throw Neptune into the mix and there would be enchantment, possibly delusion. There were also difficult contacts, indicating trouble, and I was thinking about these when Jake returned with Shiny.

He waved through the window and I put down my laptop and went to greet them. Shiny came in wiggling all over and Jake handed over her leash. "Want to come over after yoga?"

"I can't. I've got to go grocery shopping. I've got the horary—"

"That cop's got you doing a horary? What was his question?"

Here was the Pisces, pushing boundaries. I kissed Jake's cheek. "See you later."

Chapter 3

I headed for the grocery store. I only had diet food in my house and thinking about Good Food had stimulated my appetite. To hell with my spring resolution to eat healthy and lose the five pounds I gained over Christmas. I was hungry and wanted real food.

I backed out of my drive, looking first as I always did at the back seat and the empty space on the passenger side that once had a car seat. Now it held a stack of cloth grocery bags. There were no cars in the street and I backed onto the road. I drove my grandmother's twenty-year-old, tan, standard-shift VW Rabbit that was slowly rusting away. She gave it to me when I went to Texas and it was supposed to bring me home. Then she died and I was on my own.

I headed for town. My neighborhood was outside of the city limits, though not what could be properly called a suburb. The streets were straight, the houses were unique, and the lots were one-half acre. There was a mishmash of architecture, old houses and new; nothing cookie-cutter here. True to the clichés, pink flamingos and garden gnomes graced the occasional front lawn and there were some fish and manatee mailboxes. The houses were painted in outlandish pastel colors of blue, purple, and green, and many sported Christmas lights that would never be taken down.

I drove east, radio cranked, one hand on the wheel. At rush hour, traffic was heavy, at least for a town of 90,000, though nothing like DC where I grew up, or Austin where I went to school. Ahead the light turned amber and the old truck in front of me gunned it. I stepped on the accelerator. I was ready to fly through the light when the pickup stopped abruptly. Too late, I hit the brakes. The car sailed forward. I closed my eyes, bracing for impact. It came. Metal screeched and glass crunched as I plowed into the pickup's back end. I fishtailed sideways as the pickup skidded into the intersection.

I stopped my car, jumped out, and raced to the pickup, heart pounding. Glass from a broken headlight glittered on the pavement. At least the truck seemed undamaged. My bumper was more skewed than ever, but since it was falling off anyway, it wasn't a concern. I reached the driver's door as it opened and saw a dazed and groggy lady. "Are you okay?" I asked.

She stepped out, tottering, but smiling beautifully. She was my height, and I guessed she was in her mid-seventies, but it was hard to tell. Her hair was long and shockingly white, not gray. Her cheeks were smooth and polished and her skin shone as if she were standing in a ray of light. She said, "I'm fine. And you, dear?"

"Fine."

"We should move the cars out of the intersection."

No one stopped to help. They were slowing down to gawk and then veering around us. There was a parking lot in a medical office across the intersection and we headed there. Now the shock of the accident was wearing off, I was worried about the expense. I decided to offer to pay to repair her car myself if she wouldn't notify her insurance company.

We parked and she was out of her vehicle before me. She moved quickly for someone her age. She bent down and peered at my bumper. "Looks like it took a beating," she said, playing with the rusted free end. "And you broke your headlight. I'm so sorry."

I looked at her truck, which appeared unscathed. "You don't seem to have much damage—"

She interrupted me. "Do you have a phone? I guess we should call the police. I've been instructed by my insurance company to report any collisions."

It was not an instruction I'd ever heard, but I wasn't going to argue with her. "What if I pay for the damage to your truck?"

"It's not damaged. I'm worried about *your* car."

"It's old. I won't get it fixed. I won't even notify my insurance company."

"They can be pricks," she said, surprising me with her language. "Last time someone banged into me, I lost my fender. Even though it wasn't my fault, my rates rose. I hate to think what will happen to yours."

"Exactly," I said, distracted by her statement that she'd been rear-ended before. How often did it happen to her? Now I was on the subject, I wondered if her brake lights were working. Did she even have a license? Maybe the accident wasn't my fault.

She was looking at me closely. "Okay, I have a suggestion. We forget the whole thing if you do me a favor."

Overhead, a crow perched on an electrical wire began to shriek. "What kind of favor?"

"See the bags of food in the bed? Could you carry them to my barn?"

I looked in the back of the pickup and saw three huge bags of dog kibble. "You want me to go to your house?"

The crow shut up as if it too were awaiting the answer. "You got it. I train dogs and I got the food on sale. A bag weighs sixty pounds. I don't know how I'll get them out of the truck. What do you say?"

"Where do you live?"

"On the other side of 95. Not far."

"Fine." I would take this necessary detour and then go shopping.

I got back in my car and followed her. Her brake lights were working now, though I was certain I didn't see them before. I was beginning to feel miffed that I was called into her service when she had no damage.

At least she didn't live far, only a few streets past the freeway, down a dirt road in a wood frame house about the same vintage as mine. I heard barking as soon as I parked. She released her dogs and four golden retrievers of varying ages loped my way, bounding and leaping, and seemingly out of control in a house run by a self-professed trainer. The dogs had long blond fur of similar hue and ranged in age from a puppy of about four months to a panting elder of at least ten. I sank down to my knees and greeted them all.

The lady watched. "You must have dogs."

"A border collie."

She held out her hand and I wiped the slobber on my slacks. When we shook, a shot of electricity ran up my arm, making the hairs on the back of my neck stand erect.

"I'm Judith Rendell. Nice to meet you."

"Morgan Sterling."

"I prayed for help and here you are."

I was instantly on guard, wondering if she was a religious nut who had somehow orchestrated the accident to get me out to this deserted place.

Judith smiled like a saint, as if she'd read my mind. "Don't worry. All is well."

It was too weird for me. "Where do you want the food?"

"The barn's over there." She pointed down the long driveway. "We can drive."

We got in the pickup and the dogs chased after us, tongues lolling out and looking like the happiest animals I'd ever seen.

Judith pointed out where she wanted the bags. Of course, in the back of the barn, against the far wall. It was heavy work, despite the wheelbarrow. In my profession, I did a lot of sitting and talking. I wasn't used to heavy lifting and was glad when the deed was done and my debt was paid. I could leave with a clean conscience.

Judith decided to leave her truck at the barn and we headed to the house on foot. The dogs ran around us, running into each other and into us. The sun had set and the twilight sky was quickly growing dark. We passed a flowering tree that emitted a vaguely familiar aroma. "What's that tree?" I asked.

Michelia champaca," Judith said. "It's the scent in Joy perfume."

It was my grandmother's fragrance and the aroma brought her back to me. I was inhaling the air when Judith said, "Morgan Sterling, what do you do?"

I braced myself for her response, which was typically never favorable from strangers. "I'm an astrologer."

She stopped walking and peered at me. "Marvelous." She clapped her hands. "Simply marvelous. You're in contact with the planets."

"I know what they mean."

"And you talk to them."

"I wouldn't say that."

"But you know energy work."

It wasn't a question. "What?"

"Your third eye is opened to the invisible realm." She tapped the space between her eyebrows.

"Well, no."

"Then you're in tune with the all-knowing mind of spirit. Astrology shows you the thoughts of God."

I exhaled heavily. We were not on the same page at all. "I look at astrology as a science."

"A science," Judith pinched her face in a frown. Then she waved a hand, as if to clear the words from the air. "Never mind. You must come to my class. It's here at the ranch. Every Wednesday at 8:00, 7:00 in the winter, though I'm getting ahead of myself. It starts in an hour. You're welcome to stay."

"I have to go."

"You can go shopping any time."

Had I told her I was going shopping? I didn't think so.

"Aren't you interested in knowing what kind of class you're dismissing?"

I thought quilting or macramé. Possibly dog training. But okay, I'd bite. "What kind of class?" I asked, as we began walking again and the dogs ran in circles around us.

"Intuition instruction." She shot me a deep penetrating look that seemed to reach into my mind.

I said, "I didn't know you could teach that."

"Of course you can. We all have a sixth sense."

Not according to my mother. "I'll think about it," I said.

"You do that," Judith said, smiling kindly and crinkling her eyes. "I have a feeling you'll be back. You've found what you need. You just didn't know it was missing."

I had nothing to say to that.

We reached my car and she waved at the sky. "The air is crackling with electricity. It's buzzing. There's something new. Do you feel it?"

Astrologically she was right, and I explained the significance of the day, without bothering to edit myself. "On the spring equinox, the Sun is at the Aries Point. It's at the intersection of the ecliptic and the galactic equator. It's moved out of Pisces into Aries, out of south declination into north declination. Only two days a year does the sun set directly in the west and rise directly in the east, and this is one of them. It's a new beginning."

"We're at the starting line," Judith said.

She was letting me know she knew exactly what I was talking about. In this regard she was like my grandmother. Subtle. It was a gentle warning not to underestimate her. Judith even reminded me of my grandmother, who had been taller but had the same shocking white hair and the same forgiving benevolent smile. To my grandmother, everything was amusing. Life was fun, a game; not a problem to study, but an adventure to experience. I thought if I had just a portion of her humor and awe, life would be easier. But alas, like the psychic genes, I was bereft in these areas.

Judith was studying me intently, eyes narrowed and brow wrinkled. I looked away, afraid she'd see too much. "Well, good night," I said as I opened my car door. "I'm sorry I ran into you."

She waved off my apology. "There are no accidents. Surely as an astrologer, you know that."

In this regard she was like my mother; nothing unforeseeable, unexpected, unknowable. "I'm not a fatalist." I said. "Goodbye."

She watched me drive out, staring at me, as I stared at her through the rearview mirror and nearly drove into the ditch.

I went straight home. Night had fallen and I was no longer hungry or desperate for high calorie food. I had a salad for dinner and was washing my dishes when the phone rang. My mother was calling.

Chapter 4

It was a long distance call, coming from an island in the Indian Ocean, nine thousand miles away. For five years my mother had lived in Moroni, the capitol of Comoros, serving as an advisor to the president. In a country with numerous coups d'état, her task was to keep him alive. With a seven hour time difference between Coral Cove and Moroni, it was three a.m. her time. I pushed the accept button. "Good morning, Mother."

"Good morning to you too."

"It's evening here."

"You woke me up. I had a bad dream. You're in danger."

Yes, *I* had woken her up. My mother was a text book narcissist. It was all about her. She was ruled by Pluto, the planet of power. She always had to have the upper hand.

"What's going on?" she demanded. "You didn't have another melt down did you?"

In her mind, my nervous breakdown reflected badly on her. In public I was to behave at all times like a perfect child. I said, "I'm fine. And, for the record, dreams don't tell you about other people. They tell you about yourself."

"Don't spout new age psychology to me. It's bunk. It gives astrology a bad name."

I don't know how many times I'd told her I didn't do new age astrology, which was centered on personal growth and development, and was as far as I could tell, an off-shoot of Jungian psychology, which was frowned upon in most psych departments around the country. For scientists, Jung was too much of a mystic. I followed the astrologic tradition of my grandmother: we looked at energy combinations, potentials, and possibilities.

My mother went on. "I know your degrees mean everything to you, but I'm afraid you can't learn much in school."

My mother considered herself a world scholar. She was her high school valedictorian, studied abroad for a year in Italy, got a scholarship to Harvard and dropped out after six months. She went to Cornell for a year and the University of Berlin for another. She never graduated and had no degree. She found higher education wanting, a waste of her time. Unlike me, she wasn't a certified astrologer, despite having worked in the field her whole adult life. I thought if I took the exams and became certified, she'd recognize my skill, but that was too much to ask. In her mind, like university, certificates were worthless.

"I saw Saturn on your Pluto activating your Mars," she said. "If that's not danger, I don't know what is."

I rolled my eyes. Four years too late she was tuning into my chart and alerting me to a perilous period. I turned on the faucet and filled Shiny's water bowl as I listened to the dire outcomes promised by an interaction of the planetary trio: rape, murder, death ... "So which is it?" she asked, after she exhausted her list.

I wondered what to tell her. I hated to be an open book, but she was too good of an astrologer to hide much from her. I certainly wasn't going to tell her about Daniel and his cold case. I made the mistake before of asking for her input. She made me feel inept. I didn't want to hear her say again how dismal I was at horary. As Shiny slurped thirstily, I offered an alternative explanation that satisfied the planetary combination. "I was in a car accident. It was minor. A fender-bender."

"Hardly sounds dangerous. What else?"

"A friend is going through a divorce. There's a power struggle. Her husband's lawyer may depose me as a character witness."

"Hmm. With Mars, I knew it had something to do with a man, but closer. Not some friend's husband's lawyer."

I tried again. "I had an altercation with my neighbor. He threw a firecracker at Shiny."

"That could be it."

Phew.

"Except it has to do with your work."

"I'm working hard. Saturn, Mars, and Pluto symbolize hard work on a deep subject."

She laughed theatrically and I could see her throwing back her head and crinkling her cold gray eyes. "You're in the wrong field. I hear the job market is improving. Why not go back to research?"

She said 'research' like it was a dirty word. My mother had no regard for science. She found scientists misguided and ignorant. She thought Descartes was a fool and made a drastic error when he decided science should study only the physical world and ignore ninety percent of reality. Not that she was spiritually minded. She was secular in a practical sort of way. She also knew why I couldn't "go back to research." In my last job, I had what I called a "brief mental breakdown" and it was on my record. There was no statute of limitations and I couldn't expunge it. I had tried to find a job in a lab when I moved to the coast and no one would hire me. Astrology was the only thing left I could do. I said, "My practice is good. I'm making a living."

"I hear Sylvia Stryker's daughter made an appointment with you."

Her sentence almost took my breath away. Sylvia was her long time friend. Had my mother finally recognized my skill, my diploma, and my four years' experience? Was she referring me to clients? As I searched for the words to thank her, she cut me off.

"Don't screw it up. Suzanne wants a wedding date. Tell her August 27th."

I quickly pulled up my schedule, typed in the name Suzanne Stryker, and there she was—coming on Thursday for a natal reading. I scanned the notes I'd prepared for her session. She was twenty and stated the reason for the appointment: *my mother made me.* I saw no signs of an impending marriage. I would have to look again.

"Are you up to it?" my mother asked. "You can turn her down. I'll warn you in advance, she's difficult. She can't take good advice and acts out just to upset her mother. Don't mention Sylvia approves the date or Suzanne will never agree to it. She's like you in that regard. Rebellious and hard-headed."

My mother didn't know me at all. I wasn't like that in the least. I also hated her cross-talk. I never spoke about my clients or their sessions behind their backs. My mother did it all the time. *And,* I *could* do a reading.

"Don't forget to look at the ingress chart," she said.

"All right."

"Tell me you've looked at it."

The ingress chart was set for the moment the Sun moved out of Pisces and into Aries and showed the tone for the coming year. "Not yet."

My mother offered a disparaging sigh. "The whole point of prediction is to know in advance what is coming, rather than after the fact."

"I don't do prediction."

"That's just stupid."

I didn't take the bait. There was no aligning our philosophical differences. She'd studied astrology in India, which, following the culture, believed in absolute fate. A good Indian astrologer could tell the day of your death, whether you would be happily married, successful in your profession, and have joy from children. In my mother's view, life was set in concrete and an astrologer could predict everything if they were competent enough. In her mind, she was *that* competent. Unlike me. She claimed I didn't have the chart of an astrologer. That I was wasting my time. I would never be any good. Period.

Well, I didn't believe in her determined world. I saw random meaninglessness. Hardly the mindset for an astrologer who was supposed to see order in the sky, but there it was. I changed the subject. "How's the weather?"

"I wish you'd quit asking. The rainy season is in full force and every day feels like a sauna. There's no air conditioning and the fans only work when the power is on. Which is less and less these days. It's hell on earth."

"You didn't like the cold here," I said, looking on the bright side. My mother couldn't come back even if she wanted to. "And you hate humidity."

"Don't talk to me about humid. Try living on an island."

"DC was built on a swamp."

"But it has air conditioning."

I changed tack again "How is the stock market?" Among her many talents, my mother was a solid economic astrologer and knew what the Dow Jones would do before it did it. She was my source of information that I fed to Jake.

"We're looking at a correction," she said. "If you've got money in stocks get it out mid-July. Mid-August is the bottom and you can jump back in."

"Thanks." I was awed by her confidence. And her success. She gave good tips. She didn't know it but she'd made Jake a ton of money.

"Let me know how it goes with Suzanne," my mother said, winding the conversation down. "If you change your mind and don't feel up to it, I'll talk to her."

"*I said* I'll do it."

"I'll hear a full report from Sylvia."

"I'm hanging up now."

She sighed out loud with what sounded like exasperation. "I'm trying to help. Why do you have to be so difficult?"

We both knew why. My Pluto was opposite her Moon and I brought out the worst in her. Her Mars was square my Mercury and she made me angry.

Through the silence, I heard chatter in the background. Almost three-thirty in the morning and my fifty-eight-year-old mother wasn't alone. My next words popped out of my mouth before I could stop them. "Tell me you're not with the president."

"Honestly, Morgan, you're such a prude."

"What about his wife?"

"Wives. *I'm* hanging up now."

I heard the thud of a heavy receiver and then the dial tone. I put down my phone, silently reaffirming my vow never to be like her. She might be single, fancy-free as she called it, but she played too loosely for my conservative Capricorn Venus. I played by the rules. I took love seriously. I didn't sleep around, have flings, one night stands, or trysts with married men.

I also took my work seriously. I wanted to solve this cold case. I wanted to show my mother I could apply astrology as well as she could. And, I wanted to find out what happened to the baby. Up until now I thought having your baby murdered was the worst thing imaginable. Now I wondered if having your baby disappear was worse. If Sierra were dead, her mother was living with unwarranted hope. If Sierra were alive, her mother was living as if she were dead. I knew astrology had the answer, if I was skilled enough to see it.

Chapter 5

That night the sky was clear and the stars were bright, with the milky river shimmering across the dome. There were shooting stars, one after another, as the earth passed through the debris field of a comet's discarded tail. I was lying on a lounge chair in the back yard with my elbows behind my head and Shiny beside me stretched out on the grass. I was picking out the constellations and making wishes on arcing stars when one zoomed toward me from the Praesepe Cluster in the dim constellation of Cancer. It came closer and closer, so bright it took my breath away and I had to sit up. When it reached me, I saw it was a lantern, held by a withered arm belonging to a hooded figure draped in a dark cloak. I leaned forward, squinting and screwing up my face, trying to see who it was, but the face was lost in the lantern's glare. I tried to stand up, but I felt paralyzed and I couldn't move. I was frozen. My helplessness left me so frustrated I screamed. It woke me up. I opened my eyes and found myself in bed. Shiny was on the floor, sleeping peacefully on her orthopedic cushion.

I didn't need a degree in psychology to interpret the dream. I was trying to make sense of the sky and I was stuck; I needed illumination that was just out of reach. Much was hidden from me.

There was a sense of déjà vu about the dream and I wondered if I'd had it before. The image seemed familiar and I knew I'd seen that hooded shadowed figure somewhere. I just didn't know from where. I took the dream as an omen: I needed help. I thought of my mother and violently shook my head.

In the morning I awoke to pouring rain that felt like it would last for days. Dark gray clouds hugged the ground and the rain left puddles and a sour, boggy smell in the air. But the trees were happy and overnight, barren deciduous branches broke out in buds.

The work week began and I saw clients and waited to hear back from Daniel about the time of the abduction. Wednesday came and when I hadn't heard from him, I began to worry that he had a change of heart, and was either dropping the whole idea or had found someone else to work with. I knew with Mercury about to turn retrograde, people were apt to change their minds.

On Thursday morning, dark and early, a some-time client and former student dropped by on her way to school. Annie was an elementary teacher and came in dripping rain. She had gray eyes the color of oak bark, and nicely styled hair that was prematurely gray. Clad in navy slacks and a beige blazer, she appeared over dressed for a teacher who taught eight-year-old special needs kids.

While thunder boomed and Shiny shook with terror, I made tea and Annie dried her hair with a towel and sought advice. She was forty, and she and her husband were in the process of adopting a child. She'd been trying to have a baby for ten years without success. After five *in vitro* fertilization attempts that went nowhere, she'd given up. Or her doctor had. He couldn't in good conscience take any more of her money and suggested she and her husband adopt.

They were working through a private company, which meant the adoptive parents were hand-picked by the birth mother. All potential adoptive parents had to create a book about themselves, which the birth mothers used as a guide to choose who would get their child. Annie and John hired a professional photographer to take pictures of themselves having fun. They wrote essays about their lives and hopes; their history—where they met and how they fell in love. Also, how much they wanted a baby. It was an impressive-looking book.

I helped them choose a good time to contact the adoption agency and was ecstatic when they were selected a month later by a tenth-grade Jupiter High School student. They'd met the mother and everyone liked each other and the terms were set. In exchange for the newborn, Annie and John would pay a monthly stipend and all medical bills. The baby was due in mid-August and once it was born, the mother had three days to sign the adoption papers. If she changed her mind, she could keep her baby, but she would have to refund the money she'd been paid.

I poured Annie a cup of tea. "What's up?"

Annie folded the tea towel and wrapped it over the oven door handle. "I don't know why, but I'm afraid Kolby will change her mind."

"Mercury's about to go retrograde," I said, getting out a carton of coffee cream. "If she changes her mind now, she'll change it back."

Annie added a splash of cream to her tea. "Will you look at a chart? She has a doctor's appointment this week. She mentioned a while back we could go with her and hasn't mentioned it again. I'm worried she's having second thoughts."

"Every expectant parent worries," I said.

Annie looked at me sharply. "How would you know?"

I saw my mistake and tried not to react. "It's what I hear. Let's look at a horary."

I grabbed my glasses and we went to my office. The sky was dark with clouds and looking as if it had been painted a gloomy gray. Rain fell in curtains and lightning forked as thunder roared. Shiny scooted under the desk, panting hard. It was where she liked to hide in a storm, and though it was awkward to have her there, I let her stay. I pulled over a chair for Annie and she sat down beside me, legs to the side to accommodate the dog.

I set the chart for 7:35 a.m. and printed it out and wrote the question: "Will Annie get her baby?" In interpreting a horary chart, the question is paramount. If I had asked: Will Kolby keep her child, I would interpret the chart differently and get a different answer.

I studied the chart. There were no astrological contraindications that prohibited reading it. Annie was represented by the 1st house and Jupiter. The baby, since it wasn't hers, was shown by the 11th and Saturn. Any sign of these planets interacting was evidence the baby would come to her.

I could hear Annie's hard breathing and tried to block her out. I opened my notebook, picked up my pen, and jotted down what I saw. There was no direct connection between Jupiter and Saturn; in fact, the two planets were opposite each other, which pointed to a problem. Luckily, the Moon was going to contact Saturn and then Jupiter, bringing the two planets together, which would seal the deal. "Kolby will go through with it," I said with atypical confidence. I had my mother check the adoption chart and she said it would go through. "You'll get the baby. Is it a girl?"

"Kolby thinks it's a boy." Annie said. "But she hasn't had an ultrasound." She clasped her hands to her heart. "Is it a girl?"

"I think so. Saturn rules the baby and it's in Libra, the sign of Venus."

Annie started hopping around. "I want a girl."

I stared at the symbols and random thoughts streamed in. The Sun was still in early Aries and just leaving Uranus, the planet of upset and change. With the Sun connected to the house of health, I wondered if the teen was having unexpected medical issues. "How is Kolby's health?"

"She's fifteen and four-and-a-half months pregnant," Annie said. "I'm sure she's been better."

"I meant physically. Does she have high blood pressure? Any heart or back problems?" These were all areas ruled by the Sun.

Annie shrugged. "She's a little overweight."

I sat back and looked out the window. The wind was blowing the rain at a ninety-degree angle. It was coming from the north, bringing a blast of cold air. I gathered my sweater around me and went back to the chart. "You can get out of the deal if you want to, right? If the baby is born with health issues, you can change your mind?"

"We're not going to change our minds."

"I know that, but does Kolby know? I'd call her up. Make sure she understands you're in it for the long haul. I think that's why she doesn't want you to go to the doctor's. She's worried the doctor will find something that will turn you off."

Annie blinked. "Find what? Is there something wrong with the baby?"

"No." The baby was ruled by an exalted Saturn, which bode well. "The baby's healthy. Just let the mother know you're there for her."

"We've backed off. We thought we'd give her space and not be smothering. I never thought about it from her point of view."

And that was the power of astrology. It gave objectivity. It allowed you to look at an event from the outside. I removed my glasses and laid them on my desk. "Kolby loves her baby. She wants it to have the best home and the best parents, and she picked you. She's afraid of losing *you*."

Annie put down her tea. "I'll call her." Then she had to go. School was starting and traffic would be backed up in the rain.

Chapter 6

By Thursday afternoon, the deluge ended and the sun came out and shone brightly in a bold blue sky. The world looked newly green, with the grass and leaves freshly washed and polished. I could almost feel the vapor streaming up from the sodden ground.

The puddles bothered Suzanne Stryker not one bit. She pulled into the drive splashing rain and muddying the sides of her late-model baby blue Lexus. She emerged from the car and the sun beamed down upon her, highlighting waist-long yellow blond hair that streamed down her back. As her name suggested, she looked striking. Tall and slim, she stood straight as if with regal bearing. Her knee-length silk dress was pink and cinched with a tight belt that showed a small high waist. She walked with power in high, high heels. I knew from my mother that her father was a congressman and she was apparently getting married on August 27th, even if I still couldn't find it in the chart.

Well, I wasn't going to make up what wasn't there, but I was still going to try to dazzle her with my reading in the hope it would eventually reach my mother.

I met Suzanne on the porch and was greeted by a radiant half-moon smile. She towered over me, but I thought if she removed her heels, she'd be about five foot ten. "Come on in," I said, with a wave at the door. I looked down at my clothes. She had dressed up and here I was in a pair of beige chinos and a flowered blue button-down shirt that was beginning to fray. Not that she seemed to mind.

"This is exciting," she said as she entered. "I always wanted my horoscope read."

She pivoted uncertainly in the hallway, circling on the point of the sharp stiletto. I nodded at my office, as I pushed Shiny away from her. "We'll go in here, Suzanne."

She made a face that did little to detract from her good looks. "Please don't call me Suzanne. Only my mother does. I go by Suzie."

"Suzie it is," I said, remembering my mother's warning about Suzie's rebelliousness, especially in regard to her mother. I gestured at the couch. "Have a seat. Mind if I tape the session?"

"Not at all," she said as she sat, crossed her legs, and smoothed out the fabric of her dress that rode up her thighs. She had a square face, round red-rouged cheeks, and sea-blue eyes that sparkled. Her long hair nearly reached the cushion on which she sat. I wanted to know why she hadn't booked an appointment with my mother and I came right out and asked. "I'm surprised you're seeing me and not my mother."

She lifted finely arched eyebrows. "I wanted someone my age."

"Sounds reasonable," I said, though I was twelve years older than she.

"Plus, my mother insisted I see an astrologer. You were the compromise."

"Great. I hear you're getting married. Congratulations."

Suzie waved a dazzling diamond that glittered on her wedding finger. It must have cost a fortune. My own engagement ring was a half a carat and likely still sitting in an Austin pawn shop along with my wedding ring. "It's beautiful. Tell me about your fiancé."

"His name is Elliot."

"How long have you known him?"

"Forever. He's the son of daddy's biggest campaign contributor."

"I see. And you grew up wanting to marry him?"

"Actually, I used to think he was a dick."

I was taken aback, but she was laughing so I laughed with her. "What happened to convince you otherwise? That he was the man for you?" I sat forward, minimizing the space between us, becoming more intimate: letting her know I was ready to hear a love story.

"Daddy lost his campaign and went into debt."

"I'm confused. What does your father going into debt have to do with you getting married?"

"There's no money for school, so I quit."

"How many more years do you have left?"

"One."

In any type of counseling, there's always the issue of subjectivity; of the therapist attempting to impose their values on the client. I was as guilty as anyone. School and degrees mattered to me. Maybe it was a response to my mother who said they didn't, so to me they mattered very much. "You're throwing away three years," I said. "And a piece of paper is something." She had a strong Saturn, which meant she needed to be competent in her career. She had to be looked up to as an authority, which typically required a good education. "Could you take out a loan and finish?"

"I'm an art major. What am I going to do with that? Mom says if I get married, I won't need a degree."

Hmm. And here I'd been led to believe she'd do the exact opposite of whatever her mother wanted.

"Anyway, I have a job. I'm a model."

I put on my glasses and looked at her chart. She had the Sun and Moon in the hidden 12th house that hated the spotlight. She would not be at home on a catwalk. She also had Mercury in Virgo rising, which ruled her profession. She would be overly critical, mostly of herself. I got the sense that modeling was beneath her; she had something important to say. Being looked at wouldn't be enough. "You're only twenty. You've got lots of time. Could you do modeling on the side, go to school, and wait to get married?"

"Your mother said I was getting married this summer."

I kept a blank expression, while inwardly fumed at my mother's interference. In my view, this was exactly how an astrologer was not supposed to work. The idea was to give clients options, point out blind spots, not declare the future as if it were fact. I said, "Suzie, what you do is up to you. It's certainly not up to my mother. Do you want to get married?"

"My agent said marriage will give me gravity. Mom agrees."

"Gravity? I don't understand."

"You know, influence."

"Gravitas?"

"That's it."

Sounded far out to me. "Do you pay your agent outright or does he take a cut of your pay?"

"Until I start getting jobs, I pay him a flat rate."

I didn't like the sound of that. And I didn't like her reason for getting married. But my seeing something and her seeing it were two different things. "Marriage is a big commitment," I said. "It's not something to take lightly."

She looked at me. "Are you married?"

"Not anymore."

"Divorced?"

"No."

"Oh."

When she looked sad, broke eye contact and stared at her hands, I realized I'd slipped and she'd jumped to the wrong conclusion. Rather than clarify, I moved on quickly. "How long have you and Elliot been together?"

She made eye contact again. "Six months."

That wasn't very long. I removed my glasses. "What does he do?"

"He's a musician."

At least he had a skill. "Did he graduate from college?"

"He got kicked out. Mostly he does drugs."

"Do you live together?"

"No." She sounded shocked. "Daddy runs on a platform of family values."

"How old is he?"

"Sixty-five."

"What? He's forty-five years older than you?"

"I'm talking about Daddy."

"Sorry, I was talking about Elliot."

"He's twenty."

"You're both very young. How will you live?"

"His parents have money." She wore a gold necklace with a round emerald which she ran back and forth on the chain by her neck. "Do you always wear your hair like that?"

I had it tied back in a ponytail. "Usually," I said, wondering if she was trying to change the topic, which showed avoidance and a subject she was reluctant to discuss. "What about you? I think you're too ambitious to let someone keep you."

"As I mentioned, I have a job. I'll be modeling."

"Do you like it?"

She shrugged, lifting one shoulder. "It's work."

"But do you like it? Do you like being in front of the camera?"

"Actually, I hate it. I feel like I'll never measure up, no matter how hard I work."

There was the influence of the 12th house, Virgo, and strong Saturn. "Does it make you work harder?"

"I work as hard as I can. Modeling is hard. Posing, smiling, doing what I'm told as the lights flash and the cameraman makes faces. I know I'm not a natural. Everything looks forced. You can see it in the pictures. Agh."

In my view, the point of astrology was to help a person align their life with their chart. A natal chart showed the innate promise of what was possible and what was not. It showed what to do to find happiness and success. Working against the chart brought misery and failure. "If you weren't a model, what would you do?" Part of the astrologer's job was to point out options.

"I don't know."

"Well, you're young. You'll figure it out. Just don't limit your options. Which is why getting a degree is something to consider. It will buy you some time." I returned to the chart and saw Mars in Taurus in her house of higher education. Mars is energy and the planet that motivates us to work and go after what we want. But in Taurus, Mars doesn't want to work too hard. I wondered if she had done badly in university. "How were your grades?"

She shrugged a shoulder. "I got by. Professors were pretty good."

I'm sure in her experience they were. She had Venus ruling her 9th house and her looks would have served her well. Nonetheless, Mars in Taurus was likely causing her problems. Since Mars also signified the man in her life, I wondered what was up with Elliot. "So, Elliot does a lot of drugs. It must zap his energy."

"You're not kidding."

In her chart, Mars ruled her 8th house of sex, which made me wonder if he was lacking energy in the bedroom department. "How is the sex?" I asked.

Suzie studied her lap and played with an array of bangles on her wrist. "Okay." She lifted her eyes. Her cheeks seemed redder. "Are your eyes that bad you need those thick lenses?"

"Yes, I have bad eyesight. You're satisfied in bed?"

Suzie pulled off the bangles, one after another. "They make new lenses you know. They're lighter, thinner. Then the frame doesn't have to be so thick."

"Thanks for the information. I'm surprised with the family values being so strong, and given this urge to get married so quickly, you're already having sex. You use birth control?"

She had all the bangles off. They sat in a pile in her lap. "We use condoms. I couldn't go to a doctor and get pills. It couldn't get out."

"You couldn't go to a clinic anonymously?"

She lifted a shoulder.

"I sense all is not well in that department," I said, and it wasn't a question.

"Is that what the chart says?"

It was mainly what she was saying without actually saying it. "Is there an issue with quantity? Like one person wants sex more than the other?"

"That's not it."

So, there was an *it*. I went back to the chart. Mars in Taurus might not perform well. "Do you think Elliot's drug use impairs his, um, performance?"

Her bright eyes opened wide. "You can see that?"

I took a leap. "He has a hard time getting aroused?"

Her face fell.

"Or, he gets aroused too easily? All the time?"

She finally helped me out. "It's over so fast. It's so frustrating."

"I see. Has he ever stopped doing drugs?"

"He's hooked. He smokes hash all day and does coke all night. He's never clean."

I searched carefully for my next words. "Does he try to satisfy you in other ways?"

"When he's done, he's done."

"And you want to marry him?"

"Your mother said I was *going* to marry him. My mother has already told people to reserve the end of August in their calendar."

I felt like a hammer had struck my heart. My mother interfered with my life endlessly. She tried to plan it for her benefit. I wasn't going to let her do the same to Suzie. "Tell your mother you're going to wait a while. Slow things down."

"I can't."

"Would Elliot be willing to wait?"

"Why would he? His dad is going to buy him a house and double his allowance."

"What would happen if you stopped having sex?"

"He wouldn't like it. The sex is fine for him."

"What if you told him you're not satisfied? Would he get clean?"

"Never. He'd find someone else."

"Then you'd have a reason not to marry him."

Her face broke into a smile that brought light to her eyes. "I'll put on the brakes."

"Sounds like a plan. If it feels right, do it. You're the master of your fate. What you do is up to you. It doesn't depend on the stars, your mother, and especially not my mother." I went on to explain her chart in layman's terms. "You're passionate, sensual, sexual. You need to be in a relationship and your happiness and success in life depends on it. But you have to follow your heart, follow your own path, not the path your parents made for you. You're attractive, and I bet you're a good model, but I don't think that's what you want to do with your life. I see you as more of a teacher."

"Teaching what?"

I looked at her 10th house, which was the house of the career. Mercury was strong in its own sign and interacting in good way with Saturn and Mars. "It's something practical, some kind of instruction. You tell people what to do, what action to take. Maybe an agent or a director?"

"Hmm. I never thought of that before."

"You'll figure it out. Pay attention to what opens up. You'll find the right job. And the right man. Don't be worried about change." Mars in Taurus could get stuck.

She shoved her bangles up her arm, as if rolling up her sleeves and getting down to business. "You're right. I'm going to slow things down. See what he does."

"There you go."

The clock chimed, marking the end of the hour and Suzie picked up her purse. "This was great. I can't believe I didn't want to come. I'm glad I did."

She wouldn't be the first to tell me that. "When you do the right thing, it feels right, and you know it. You can't have peace without being true to yourself," I said, speaking the words of my grandmother that were coming back to me from long, long ago.

We stood up and Suzie hugged me. I walked her to the door and watched her leave, hoping she'd tell her mother how successful the session had been. Take that, Mother, I thought, as she backed out of the drive.

Chapter 7

I had my advanced astrology class Thursday night, which meant I had a two-hour dinner break. I let Shiny out and she ran around the grass as I sat on the porch steps drinking in the sunlight. It shone through the queen palm fronds that flanked Jake's driveway, filtering through the leaves of the live oaks that graced my lawn. Up in DC it was snowing, and over in Texas there was record cold, but this balmy seventy-five degrees was typical for late March in Florida and I loved it. When I had to leave Texas, I closed my eyes and threw a dart at a map. I aimed for the ocean and got it. I didn't end up here by accident.

The neighbor to my north pulled into her drive. Maribel was a religious fanatic in her mid-twenties. She was a stay-at-home wife who was married to a youth pastor at a Christian church who vehemently opposed my business and had picketed me when I first moved in. "Astrology is of the devil," Joey had shouted, as did his sign. Although I would have tried to set him straight, I didn't have a chance. He would never look directly at me and made the sign of the cross whenever he saw me. Maribel wouldn't look at me either and never waved. Over the past four years we'd reached a mutual understanding of feigned detachment, which involved both sides pretending the other didn't exist. For this reason, I didn't look at her as she ferried groceries to her house. Instead, I clasped my hands together and kept my eyes on Shiny, who was watching squirrels leap through the branches.

I realized Maribel was in trouble when I heard a crash. I peered past the waist-high cocoplums that divided our lots and saw her writhing in her driveway. I jumped up, tore across the grass, and poked my way through the sharp hedge. She was twitching, her whole body shaking as if she were undergoing a horizontal death by hanging. I knelt down beside her. White foam streamed from her mouth and I turned her head to the side so she wouldn't choke. I tapped my pocket and found no phone. My hand went to my neck and I pushed the button on the rapid response alarm button twice to summon an ambulance.

Maribel was kicking her legs and feet, and her hands and arms were shaking. I put my hands on her shoulders to try to stop her movement. Her tongue stuck out her convulsing mouth and foam dripped from her lips. Her head was quaking and I moved my hands to her ears to keep her head immobile and to the side. Her skin was alabaster and her eyes had rolled backwards.

On the other side of the hedge, Shiny was whining and I shouted, "Be quiet," and she was. In the distance I heard a siren and prayed it was the ambulance. I stared across the street and Jake's car was gone. There was no sign of Porter. A car cruised down the road but did not stop.

As Maribel quivered on. I decided she was having an epileptic fit, which wasn't deadly, but there was action that had to be taken and I didn't know what it was. Prevent choking I thought, which I was doing, but I wasn't sure. I heard more sirens and quietly prayed I pressed the alarm the correct number of times. I had never used it before but I was pretty sure that one press brought a phone call, two brought an ambulance, and three brought the police. As I wondered whether to press it two more times, the siren got louder and a fire engine clanged down the street.

With the bells ringing and lights flashing, the truck stopped in front of Maribel's drive. A pack of firefighters spilled out and edged me out of the way. I backed up to the bushes, biting my knuckles, as the firemen did what I had done and held her writhing body still.

There were more sirens and an ambulance turned the corner. Maribel finally quit kicking. A fireman eased down the cloth of the light cotton sundress that had ridden up her legs. She wore cowboy boots that came to her calves. Her pale, stick thin arms went still. She was flat-chested and her bra strap rode down her arm, but no man was willing to put it back in place. Her eyes fluttered and focused. She sat up groggily as the ambulance technicians rushed across the grass with a stretcher.

"What happened?" she asked in a strong southern accent, as she screwed up her pretty face. She had big blue eyes, prominent cheeks, and a round face that was framed with bright blond hair with dark roots. This must have been the style for it was cut in a V-shape at the back and the hair by the nape was left dark. She always had white skin, as if she were afraid of the sun, but now it was the color of bleached plaster.

The firemen stepped back to make room for the emergency crew. There were more sirens and a police car came and then a sheriff's car. An EMT looked at me as if awaiting the answer to Maribel's question.

"I heard a crash." I said to Maribel. "You dropped your groceries. I think you had an epileptic fit."

Her mouth dropped open and she looked puzzled. "I never had a fit before," she said in the slow heavy drawl.

The EMT said, "It's what you had now, ma'am. The worst is over, but you should come to the hospital and get checked out. Especially if this is the first episode."

Maribel didn't object and the stretcher was raised and in one easy movement she was on it lying prone, her body covered chastely to the neck with a sheet as white as her skin.

"Is there anyone you want me to call?" I asked.

"Joey," she said, and then winced, as if she thought better of it. "Never mind. I'll call him. Will you get my purse? It's in the car."

I got her purse. She was in the back of an ambulance and she clasped it to her heart, as more emergency vehicles arrived. Another fire engine came and another cop car.

By now neighbors along the street were out on their lawns watching the spectacle. The ambulance doors closed, a siren started up again, and Maribel was swept away. I thought I might have to make a statement, but no one paid any attention to me. The officers headed to their various vehicles, chatting in small groups. The neighbors returned to their homes. I stood in the driveway looking at apples that had ended up in a puddle.

Once the emergency vehicles departed, I gathered the fruit and stuffed them into a Good Food cloth bag. Her trunk was open and I saw ice cream and milk. I couldn't leave her groceries there. I grabbed her remaining bags.

Our houses were similar, but mirror images. They faced due west and had glass front doors, only mine was made of orange and yellow stained-glass. Her house was dark. Her door had a shade and the blinds on her windows were closed. I hit the hall switch and stared at a stark living room. There was a couch, no carpet. There were crosses on the wall and the mantle over the fireplace was dominated by a portrait of Jesus with a red heart and raised stigmatic hands.

I went to the kitchen, dropped the bags on the counter, and turned on the light. Here on the walls were more crucifixes and framed biblical sayings: *Beware of Fallen Angels* and *Our struggle is not against flesh and blood, but against the powers of this dark world.*

I quickly put away the perishables, shut the door, and left. The house was too dark and had a bad feeling. Maybe it was my own sense of trepidation of being an intruder in a house where I wasn't wanted, or my fear that Joey would come home and find me there. In any case, I hurried home to my dog and my bright house of light.

I was climbing the front steps when I heard the rumble of a loud engine and saw a black Mustang turn the corner, red light whirling. Daniel zoomed into the drive and killed the siren. He jogged across the grass and came to the steps. "I heard the 911 call over the radio. I couldn't get here earlier."

"Everything's fine," I said, touched by his concern. "The neighbor had an epileptic fit."

"Maribel Cross," he said, patting Shiny's head. "Too bad it was the wrong neighbor."

I had no reply. In my view they were both wrong neighbors, but seeing Maribel so helpless showed her in new light and my dislike for her had vanished.

Daniel removed his shades. Today he was wearing tan dress slacks and a stark white blazer. "I've been in court all day," he said, as if to answer a question I hadn't asked.

"You want to come in?"

"I won't stay," he said, as he scuffed shiny shoes on the grass and leaned casually against the handrail. "I know you have class."

"Not until seven." I sat down on the top step.

"When I heard the address on the radio, it freaked me out. I should have warned you, we need to be careful. We could be stirring a bed of snakes. Whoever kidnapped Sierra is still out there. They won't like being poked. They could strike back."

It hadn't occurred to me before that someone might think they had covered their tracks and had gotten away with the crime.

"Are you still okay with this?" Daniel fixed his dark eyes on me.

"I've got security," I said looking at Shiny, who stood with Daniel, wagging her tail. "Did you find out what time Sierra was taken?"

"I'm going to Miami on Saturday morning to pick up the case file."

"No hurry? Is that it?"

"Look at you, you old task-master. For your information, I can't just go and pick it up. This is all on the down-low. My old partner's doing me a favor. He'll get me access to the box and I'll photocopy the reports. We won't have physical evidence. I can't break the chain of custody."

The sun went behind a cloud and the world instantly darkened. "You never mentioned Tiffany was an old girlfriend."

"It wasn't important."

"But you were taken off the case."

Daniel looked in my eyes. "The FBI thought I was too close. They said it clouded my judgment. It didn't. I knew they had the wrong guy."

"How did you know?"

He thumped his fist below his heart. "I go by my gut. It knows. The FBI called it irrational."

As did I.

"You know what?" he said. "I want to solve what they couldn't. Prove them wrong about me and their theories."

I agreed, but the thought was sobering. How could we solve a case the FBI couldn't, especially after all this time?

Shiny flung herself down on the grass, began rolling around on her spine, scratching her back. Daniel watched her with amusement and I took advantage of what I hoped was a light moment. "So what time were you born?"

He laughed artificially and turned my way. "Oh no you don't. My lips are sealed."

"On April 1st you'll be thirty-five. Happy birthday in advance."

"Did Claire tell you?" He pursed his lips and narrowed his eyes. "I told her not to."

"I'm an astrologer. I know these things."

He shook his head. "Impossible."

"All right. I found your birthday on Facebook. You should protect your private information."

His eyes brightened and he laughed again. "You're very sneaky."

"If I tell you what time I think you were born, will you confirm it?"

He rubbed his chin and a bristly five o'clock shadow. "Maybe. What time do you think?"

"I'd say you were born in the afternoon between one and three. Specifically, 2:30."

He hissed loudly. "Claire told you."

"I would never ask her."

"She promised not to."

"She didn't. Are you going to tell me?"

"The time on my birth certificate is 2:34 pm." He exhaled slowly as he stared off into the street. "I don't believe you figured it out." He scratched his brown mane. "How could you?"

I lifted my shoulders and raised my hands apologetically. "You've got to know astrology."

From the open window of his car, his radio cackled and a voice called out a code. Daniel glanced at his watch. "I've got to run. You want to get together Saturday afternoon? Look over the file?"

It was perfect. In the morning I'd promised Jake I'd go to the protest. "What time?"

"I'll call you when I get back to town. It's a date." He jammed his shades on his face and headed for his car.

"An appointment," I yelled after him.

Chapter 8

The advanced astrology class was held in my dining room. I had four students who sat across from each other in seats that weren't assigned but might as well have been, for everyone took the same seat, week after week, month after month, year after year. Besides Claire, there was Robert, a medical doctor; Trent, a stockbroker; and Portia, an author who lived in Vero Beach. They were students from my introductory class who wouldn't stop coming. They took their seats, got settled, and opened their notebooks. I passed around the evening charts and took my place at the head of the table, Shiny at my feet.

The room was small but open, and flanked on the south side by the kitchen counter. The east wall had french doors that led to a small, covered back porch. During the day the room was bright with natural sunlight and at night I turned the dimmer chandelier switch on full. Most of the furniture in my house came from garage sales and thrift shops, but I had nice stuff. There was a pine sideboard and an oversized rectangular oak dining room table that nearly matched the eight nicely carved maple chairs. The north wall had two high square stained-glass windows that shone in the late spring light.

We spent the next two hours discussing the spring equinox and the energy in play for the coming year. In mundane astrology, the main thing to watch was the influence of the three outer planets,

Uranus, Neptune, and Pluto, for these three set the major themes. We were currently moving into a Uranus–Pluto combination that would peak in two years and be felt on earth for ten years. The planets combined in some manner every 35 years or so, and with Uranus representing freedom, common people, the unexpected, the unusual, and all things shocking; and Pluto symbolizing power, big money, the personal unconscious, sex, and war; the interaction of the two planets was explosive. They came together in the late sixties in an era characterized by hippies, free love, the Beatles, psychedelic drug use, student protests, and the ending of a war.

In the early thirties, the two planets formed a ninety-degree angle, known in astrological parlance as a square, and a difficult aspect. In the US there was the stock market crash, an economic meltdown, and a buildup to war. Now, eighty years later, the planets were square again and the economy had crashed, we were in economic turmoil, and trying to end a war. Elsewhere on the globe there was the Arab Spring and oppressed people were fighting for freedom.

Since Mercury was turning retrograde, we reviewed that. In reality, Mercury didn't reverse direction, like a car went in reverse. It only seemed like Mercury was moving backwards. It was the same phenomenon as two cars going different speeds on a road—at some point the faster car would catch up to the slower car and pass it. Once this happened, it would seem to the fast car that the slow car was moving backwards, though this wasn't the case.

Given Mercury's orbit, it went retrograde three times a year, for about three weeks. When retrograde, all things the small planet ruled went awry. This included communication, cars, and computers. It was not the time to sign documents or decide matters of importance. Anything initiated at this time generally had to be redone. A Mercury retrograde period was the perfect time to redo, revise, and revisit.

The class ended at nine and everyone left but Claire. She accepted my offer of iced tea and I poured drinks. We went to the back porch and sat down on the rattan flowered sofa that faced the fenced backyard, which was dominated by a forty-foot flamboyant tree. Beyond the fence was a foreclosed property thick with oak, cypress and palm.

Claire crossed her legs and sipped her drink. She was beautiful. She had shiny brown hair that curled lightly and favorably framed her face. She had a golden complexion and skin that looked like it was buffed with fine sandpaper. She had Daniel's bright eyes; the same dark brown with brilliant whites tinged with blue that betrayed good health; she did triathlons for fun. She was tall and favored string sandals, tight jeans, and hundred dollar t-shirts. Her toes and fingernails were always painted and her eyebrows were always waxed. Given her profession, she had to look good. She swallowed iced tea and put down her glass. "I'm afraid you're going to be deposed. Kev's lawyer is preparing the paperwork. He wants to question you under oath."

Her divorce case was beginning to stress me out. "What does he want from me? What do I know?"

"Who I was with last summer and when."

In the summer, while Kevin was screwing around, Claire had her own tryst. She found out about his first, kicked him out of the house, and filed for divorce. Then he found out about hers and now they were having a war of epic Uranus–Pluto proportions. I said, "Why don't they ask you?"

Claire batted her long lashes. "I admitted to having a brief affair." She sipped more tea. "I may have fudged the date."

I blinked. "You lied to them?"

She stared off into the yard. "I never thought Kev would go this far. He must really hate me. He wants to hurt me. He knows how much I love my house. He'll do anything to take it. If that means painting me as a whore, he'll do it."

And he could. I knew what Claire was afraid of. Her August tryst was unexpected and unprotected and she was terrified she'd acquired an STD. She asked me to run a horary and I did. I didn't think she had picked up anything, but recommended she be tested. She was, and it took six months to get a definitive answer, which came last month. She was clean.

"Does it matter if you were with someone?" I asked. Thanks to my practice and numerous clients who went through divorces, I knew the state's laws. When it came to divorce, Florida was a no-fault state, which meant the courts would not lay blame. Infidelity was only a concern if a paramour received marital wealth or property. "Who cares about the date?"

"They do. They're saying I squandered shared assets."

"On what?"

"They don't have a clue. They're fishing. That's why they want to talk to you."

"When?"

"Likely mid-April."

"In the midst of a Mercury retrograde? No way. There will be a glitch. They'll call me back. It will never end. You've got to delay until May."

Claire sighed so loudly, her bangs lifted. "I'll try, but they're getting suspicious of my requests and I'm running out of excuses."

Just like I found Claire good times for optimal real estate sales, I found good times for her to meet with Kevin's lawyer—times when her energy was stronger than his, and the rulings more likely to go in her favor. "Try hard," I said. "I'll find a good time in early May."

Claire's phone buzzed. She silenced it with a push of a button. "Speaking of times, did you find a time to sign the waterfront contract?"

"With Mercury going retrograde, the window is small. Do it tomorrow morning at 7:37."

"That soon?" Claire drained her drink and left to go prepare the paperwork.

Chapter 9

Friday started with a last-minute appointment. A new client, Crystal Jones, booked the session overnight and paid twice my going rate to secure an early hour. She used a prepaid bank card that could not be traced, which wasn't that unusual. Some people were embarrassed by the fact they were seeing an astrologer. Daniel was a case in point.

I got up early to look at her chart and it was immediately obvious that she was going through a difficult time; hence, I gathered, the reason for the last-minute session. She was three months younger than I, which meant that like me, the outer planets, Uranus, Neptune, and Pluto were currently active in her life. Her Sun was in the last degree of Taurus, conjunct the Pleiades, the weeping sisters; any planet at this degree gave something to cry about. Throw in a difficult transit from Neptune, which knew no boundaries, and there could be grief without limits.

She arrived at 7:55 in a BMW convertible, accompanied by a driver in a suit who opened her door. I saw immediately she was sick, just skin and bones, and wondered how I could have missed such a blatant health crisis.

I hurried to the door to greet her and catch her in case she fell. She wore huge dark sunglasses that hid her face. A white tracksuit hung off her skeletal frame. She had shoulder-length strawberry blond hair that looked dry and in dire need of deep conditioning.

She wore flip-flops and walked carefully, gripping the arm of the driver who escorted her up the walk.

"Good morning, Crystal," I said in greeting as I nodded at the driver.

He started to speak, but she silenced him. "Gomez, I'll see you in an hour."

Gomez tipped his hat, called me "ma'am," and returned to the car. He pulled silently out of the drive.

"Come in," I said.

We went to my office and I directed her to the couch. She had bony hands with raised blue veins and ragged fingernails. Big green eyes dominated her gaunt ashen face.

I sat down in my chair and handed her a chart. "Have you had a reading before?"

She put the chart on the table without looking at it. "No."

Some clients were interested in looking at the astrology and knowing the source of the information, and others weren't. I filed her in this latter category. I said, "I'll tape the session?"

She nodded.

I turned on the recorder. "May I ask why you came for a reading now?" Though I figured she was having a medical crisis, she had not put that on the form, and had left the reason for the consultation blank.

"I'm going through a rough time. I can't sleep and when I do, I have nightmares. I'm being treated for depression, but the drugs aren't working."

Just depression? She looked like she had been undergoing lengthy chemotherapy, which was also symbolized by Neptune. "Are you ill? Under a doctor's care?"

"Not anymore. He wasn't helping. Nothing's helping."

She didn't say, *helping with what.* I looked at the chart. "I can see you're going through a very difficult time. You're confused and may feel like you've lost everything that matters." Neptune was called the planet of confusion, delusion, and illusion for a reason.

Her face lit up and I could see that if she gained weight, she would probably be beautiful. She had a plucky smile that showed her gums and nice white teeth. "You can tell what happened?"

"In general, yes. Specifically? No. The good news is, the situation is going to change for the better." Uranus was about to make a pleasing aspect to her Jupiter, signifying unexpected luck.

"You're kidding? Really?"

I studied the chart. Like me, transiting Saturn was hitting her Pluto, which ruled her 5th house of romance and children. Her progressed Venus had been hit with the previous solar eclipse. Venus was love, and in her case, ruled the home. I said, "What happened? Was there a crisis in the family? Did someone close to you get sick or die? A lover? A sister? A child?"

She started to cry. "Sick and die? Is that what you see?"

She was sweating and a bad odor fell upon me like a shadow. I looked at Crystal Jones and it hit me, who she was. Add thirty pounds, put on a cheerleading uniform, grow her hair eight inches, brush it out until it shone with a bright luster, and she could be dancing at the Love Hate Lounge without a care in the world. "You're Tiffany Rossario, aren't you," I said, handing her a tissue.

She blew her nose, sobbing as she nodded.

I turned the recorder off, removed my glasses, and waited for her to compose herself.

She pulled herself together quickly. "I should have told you the truth. I've never been to an astrologer before and I didn't know what to expect. Daniel told me about you. He said he was going to talk to you, and get back to me, but it's taking so long, and I can't wait. I need to know what you've found."

I was determined to appear stoic, but inwardly I was captivated. Here was a woman who had experienced as devastating an event as me. How did she get through it, I wondered, as I said, "I'm waiting on more information. Daniel should have it by Saturday. How did you find me?"

Tiffany was wearing a gold necklace with a crucifix and absent-mindedly twisted the chain. "Daniel wouldn't tell me your name. He has to control everything. But he said you were the best and I knew he'd moved back here, so I figured you were local. I called up the American Association of Astrologers, told them I was looking for an astrologer in Coral Cove, and you're the only one. They gave me your website and I made an appointment. I got tired of waiting on Daniel."

"How does he control everything?" Not that it was pertinent, but I was curious.

"He has to be the boss. Be in charge all the time."

I nodded without expression. An Aries was like that. Throw in Leo rising and he would feel it was his birthright to run the show. "Crystal... can I call you Tiffany?"

"Of course. I'm sorry." She wrung her hands together at her throat. "I was worried if you knew who I was, you wouldn't see me. Can you really look at the chart and tell what happened to Sierra?"

"I'll try, but to be honest I've never found missing people before."

"I know you probably think I'm a wreck. So impatient. You'd think after waiting all this time, I could wait, but—"

"It's okay. I understand. Don't worry about it."

She rubbed her nose with her hand, sniffling.

Kathy T. Kale

I said, "I hope you know, what happened wasn't your fault."
As I knew full well, Saturn connecting with Pluto could mean
crushing guilt.

If possible, Tiffany's pale face blanched whiter. "Of course it's
my fault. I left the windows open. It's killing me. Why didn't I
just close the windows? Why couldn't I do that one simple thing?"

"You have the right to leave your windows open. I leave mine
open all the time. You can't blame yourself for wanting air."

"I feel like I'm being punished."

"By whom?"

"God."

"Oh."

"I don't know what to do to turn it around. Get on His
good side."

"Pray?" I offered.

She laughed, only it sounded like a cry. "I pray all the time.
Or I did. And things went from bad to worse. I give up." She
sniffled loudly. "I give up."

In graduate school, when I was getting my first degree, I helped
lead a year's worth of group therapy sessions and knew that people
who lost their faith often became despondent and depressed. I
looked at her crucifix. "Have you spoken to a priest?"

"Please. I stopped going to church. How can I believe in a God
who would let this happen?"

It was an excellent question and I found myself nodding in
sympathy. My heart hurt for her. It occurred to me that not
knowing what happened was worse than knowing the worst. I
said, "It sounds like you're having a crisis of faith. Your old beliefs
were shattered and you have nothing to replace them with."

"You could say that, yes."

74

"You have to stop blaming yourself. Sometimes shit happens. It's no one's fault. There's no one to blame."

"Not in this case." She pointed to her heart with her broken nails. "Leaving the window open was like giving the kidnapper an invitation to the nursery."

"That's just wrong. You were the one who was violated." I was hearing a typical messed-up victim-aggressor response pattern. The kidnapper was the one to blame, not her. I repeated it wasn't her fault. "Most people put the baby to bed, go to sleep, wake up, and the baby's there."

"Not me," she said.

"You didn't hear anything?"

She was chewing on a nail and dropped her hand. She wore a loose wedding ring and an engagement ring with a huge pink diamond that would dwarf Suzie's. Tiffany twisted the gem back and forth. "I didn't. I had the baby monitor on and by my ear. The waves are loud, but that never stopped me from hearing Sierra before. I wasn't drunk and passed out, if that's what you're asking. I hardly drink at all. The news reports about me partying in South Beach were from ten years ago when I was cheerleading."

"The news reports seemed overly sensational," I said.

"Ciro and I were tried in the press and declared guilty. We were accused of staging the whole thing. Supposedly Ciro needed money and I needed freedom. As if I could harm my own child."

"Impossible," I said, speaking as a mother.

"It was as far from the truth as it could be. We had money. Ciro's business was doing great. Though after the kidnapping, there was a cloud of suspicion. We were investigated by the IRS. Forensic accountants combed through everything. Ciro's reputation suffered and the company took a hit. Of course, nothing panned out, but the damage was done and investors slunk away. I'll say right now for the record. I wasn't screwing around. I had no lover. That's not me."

I knew the press could spin the truth. There was the influence of Neptune again. Tall tales. Neptune was also bad dreams. "You mentioned you're having nightmares?"

She sniffled and wiped her nose, picked at her nails. "I dream of Sierra all the time. She'd be four now. I can never really see her, but I know she's crying. She says, 'Mommy, don't go. Please don't go. Come back.' I dream it over and over." Tiffany rubbed her eyes. "What do you think it means?"

"Are you planning on moving?"

"No. No way. I've kept her room."

"Okay, maybe 'go' in a figurative sense, as in, forget her?"

"How could I?" Tiffany went back to chewing her nails.

I was at a loss. "I'm sorry. I don't know what the dream means. I hope it means she's alive and she's telling you not to give up."

Tiffany dropped her hands to her lap and wrung them together. She stared at the table and said, "I almost have given up. I've been thinking about taking out the boat and driving until I run out of gas. I'm at the end of my rope. I used to have a life. I used to be happy. I had friends, I was active in my church. Ciro and I were the golden couple. We threw huge parties and organized fundraisers. Ciro was expanding Good Food, which *is* good food, and he was seen as a visionary. He could pick up the phone and call the governor. He was invited to the White House. Then Sierra was taken and everything fell apart. We became pariahs. There was a hostile takeover attempt of the company. We were ostracized by our friends. We lost everything."

That was Pluto and Saturn for you, and I knew it well.

"I made a deal with myself," Tiffany said. "I'll pull out the stops. I'll try one last time to find her. Four years ago, when the cops gave up, Ciro and I did what we could. We hired three PIs and none of them got anywhere. The police said they'd reopen the case if new evidence came to light, but none has. I was about to give up, when I thought of Daniel. He agreed to give it one last try. He called you and here I am."

She was handing me her life. I had to get this right. "I'll do everything I can. You gave me your correct birth data?" I asked. When she nodded, I added, "I'll need Ciro's and Sierra's as well."

"I'll get them for you."

I would look at the three charts separately and then combine them, progress them, arc them, look at the transits, and try to deduce from the natal horoscopes what happened, and what was likely to come of it. In the meantime, I had to find a way to help her through the misery. I learned in school three things were needed for happiness: meaningful work, something to love, and hope. I focused on the first. "What do you do with your time?"

"What do I do?" Tiffany looked at the ceiling. "What do I do?" She seemed to be asking herself. "I wait. I do nothing."

She needed something to make her feel useful. I had astrology. "The days must seem endless."

"And the nights."

"Could you volunteer? Help a group that you're interested in?"

"Nothing interests me."

I knew how that went. "What about helping a candidate in the next election?"

"I don't care what happens."

I could relate. *Act as if*, was the advice I gave myself. "What about helping an organization for lost children?"

She blinked her big green eyes. "Is there one?"

"I'm sure. Someone put photos of missing kids on the tax instructions."

For the first time in the hour, her eyes lit up and shone like emeralds. "And milk cartons."

I went on, encouraged. "I bet a lost children group would be happy to have someone with your social skills. Maybe they have ideas about searching for Sierra you haven't thought of."

Tiffany sat forward. She was engaging. She thought it was a great idea.

The clock chimed, signaling the ending of the hour. Our session was over and we never started on the astrology, for which I apologized.

"I'll come back," Tiffany said, and her flat tone had changed. "I'll get the birth times." There was excitement in her voice as we made an appointment first thing Monday.

Chapter 10

S aturday came and I went with Jake to the protest at the
farmers' market that began at ten. I wanted to drive myself
because Jake planned to go out for lunch with the gang and
I had to meet Daniel. But Jake promised to run me home when
we were done, so I had no excuse not to ride with him.

As Jake parked in the library lot, I checked my phone. Daniel
was picking up the case file from Miami and had promised to let
me know when he got back. Not yet. I put away my phone. We
got out of the car and Jake handed me a poster. "I didn't think
you'd make one." The sign read: *Guns DO kill people*. His billboard
said: *Shoot the NRA*. I shoved the sign under my arm, adjusted
my sunglasses on my face, and followed Jake to the library where
about ten people milled around a rickety card table. I checked
my watch. We were early—it was almost nine-thirty.

I turned and stared at the water, glinting in the morning sunlight. The market was on the Coral Cove inlet and the sun had
cleared the palm trees that dotted the shoreline. It was going to be
hot. According to the thermometer on the library, it was already
seventy-nine. I wished I had brought a hat.

I'd joined the group a month ago in an attempt to follow advice
I routinely dispensed: get involved, help your community, work
on behalf of a greater good. *Act as if* you care and maybe you'd
begin to. For me it wasn't working, yet.

Jake slapped a sticky name tag on my t-shirt and introduced me to my fellow protesters, who apparently forgot they'd met me at the anti-Monsanto march in February. I guess I was a person people didn't remember, and I went along with the game that we were meeting for the first time. Jake offered me a bottle of water, which I accepted. He was already red-faced and sweating and we moved into the shade to escape the sun's bright rays. I told myself, this wasn't so bad, I could do it. The air smelled sweet. Someone was frying donuts and brewing good coffee. A reggae band played and the beat was good.

An enthusiastic woman of about fifty bounded over and kissed Jake's cheek. Her name tag read Lizzie and she held a clipboard in her hand and a pencil in her ear. She tapped a page with her finger. "I'm looking for volunteers."

I turned and checked my phone again. Nothing. It was getting on ten o'clock. Would this protest never end? When was Daniel going to let me know when to expect him?

"What about you?" Lizzie asked, with a tug on my sleeve. "You want to be VP?"

I was taken aback. "VP of what?"

"The group. The Coral Cove Warriors who fight social and environmental injustice."

"Lizzie lives in West Palm," Jake explained. "She's started groups across the state and needs local talent. I agreed to be the secretary."

"I'm too busy," I said.

Lizzie furrowed her brow and looked at me intently. Then her eyes popped open wide. "You were a victim of gun violence, weren't you."

I gasped audibly. How could she see it?

Jake came to my rescue. "That's not it. Morgan *is* very busy. She works too hard."

Lizzie smiled and looked interested. "What do you do?"

I swallowed hard. "I'm an astrologer."

"Oh." She backed away, before brushing Jake's arm. "Thanks, man, you really helped us out." She threw me a tepid smile before going to join the gang.

"You could be VP," Jake said, when she was gone.

"I'm not sure this is my group," I said.

"Give it a chance. It's for a good cause. You have to do something besides work. That's what you always told me."

A middle-aged man in a straw hat came over and said we were going to march through the market. Jake lifted his sign a few times to show he was all for it. I looked at my watch. Time was crawling. "I'll stay here and hold the fort."

"Oh come on," Jake said. "Live a little."

"You go." I fanned my face. "It's getting hot." Not that I minded.

"I'll give you my hat." He took his off and helpfully positioned it on my head. It buried me like a sack. He had a big pumpkin head.

I returned it. "I'm fine. Really."

"I don't want to leave you alone."

"I'm fine," I said again with as much exasperation as I felt.

"All right then."

He went off with half the crowd, tottering on his bad feet. I stayed under the library's portico, sipping water. I put the sign down on the ground by my feet. I wasn't good in groups. I didn't socialize easily and wasn't comfortable mixing with strangers. I blamed this on my childhood, being an only child raised by a mentally disturbed mother.

I leaned against the library, feeling the cold stone on my back. The remaining protesters at the welcome table were trying to engage the market-goers who were hurrying by, trying to avoid eye contact. "Want to stop insane people from getting guns?" one protester shouted. A shopper replied, "No."

The protesters grumbled amongst themselves. What was wrong with people? Why didn't they care?

I stood apart, glad for the shade and my sunglasses, which allowed me to avoid making eye contact with both the protesters and wanna-be shoppers. I wore dark clothing, which was probably a mistake in this heat, but since the accident, it's what I wore. Like a Catholic in mourning, all my casual clothes were black. For work, I tried to be more cheerful.

Someone with the nametag of Lester came by and asked me to pick up my sign. "It's hard to read down there," he said in a helpful tone.

I sighed—I'm sure far too loudly and stooped down and picked it up.

"This your first time here?"

I nodded. I wasn't going to remind him we'd met last month.

"Glad you came out." He looked at the street and wiped sweat off his brow. "You could try to talk to people. Explain that guns really do kill people."

"I've got my sign."

"Okay then."

He left and I went back to my wall. A little later the marchers returned and Jake took refuge beside me. I checked my watch. Ten-forty-five. I told myself to stop watching the clock. It only made time move slower.

The minutes inched past. We made it to eleven o'clock and the halfway mark and the protesters were returning to the market to march and once again I declined. "I feel like I'm having heat stroke," I said.

The marchers left and I pulled out my phone. Still no message. I tucked the phone in my pocket and then noticed a man on the far sidewalk gawking.

Daniel.

He lowered his shades as if to see me better. He held up his hand and stopped the traffic so he could cross the street. He swaggered toward me dressed in khaki shorts and a bright yellow collared t-shirt. He was unshaven and sweaty and smelled like musk. "So this is what you do in your free time."

I shrugged. "Lunatics with guns are on the loose. Someone has to do something. Did you get the case file?"

"I did. I'm not sure you picked the right place to protest. This isn't a sympathetic crowd. I'm sure most are NRA members. They're probably all packing."

I shrugged again. I couldn't really argue with him.

He surveyed my comrades. "Pretty poor turn out."

"There's more. They're marching through the market."

"You didn't go?"

"Thought I'd hold up the library. How'd you find me?"

He tucked his sunglasses in his breast pocket and peered up at the sky. "We have drones. We know who's out rabble-rousing and exciting the locals."

"You're kidding." I followed his gaze and saw an endless, clear blue sky.

He elbowed me. "Of course I'm kidding. Claire told me where you were. But we do have drones up there. We know who's here. You can't hide from the police."

There was loud chanting behind him and he turned and looked. My fellow protesters were returning. They'd formed a line and were chanting: *Guns kill, guns kill, guns kill.*

As I watched them approach, Jake broke rank and jogged across the road—nearly getting hit in the process. He hopped up on the sidewalk beside me and faced Daniel. "Can I help you with something?"

"No."

I put a restraining hand on Jake's sleeve and made introductions.

The two men looked at each other. "Oh right, he's your *client.*" Jake said with undisguised scorn.

"Another neighbor," Daniel said. "That's some street."

"If the cops did their job, we might know peace," Jake said.

I tried to break it up. "That's enough."

"I'm sorry," Daniel said to me. And to Jake, "Excuse us. We're having a private conversation."

"Give me a minute," I said to Jake.

Daniel followed me to the corner. "Want to blow this pop stand? I've got something to show you."

"What's that?"

"I'm not going to whip it out here. Let's go for lunch."

My savior. "Wait here."

I crossed the portico and went to Jake. "I'm sorry. I have to go. Something came up." I picked up my sign and handed it to him.

He looked sullen. "How will you get home?"

"I'll give the lady a ride." Daniel had snuck up behind me. "Don't worry about her."

Jake opened his mouth, but I didn't let him speak. "It's work," I whispered, as I patted his arm.

He shrugged it off.

Chapter 11

The Tiki Bar was a five minute walk away. Perched precariously on the edge of the waterway overlooking the inlet, the place was an outdoor restaurant covered with a thatched roof made of coconut palm leaves. It was almost 11:30 and we got a booth. I sat down facing the entrance. I expected Daniel to sit across from me, but he edged me over and sat down on the bench beside me.

"Here's what you're looking for," he whispered. "Well, parts of it." He plopped a manila folder he'd brought from the car onto the table.

The waitress appeared and he slipped the file onto the seat beside us. She was Janet and we ordered drinks. He got a beer and I asked for lemonade. I wasn't much of a drinker—especially not this early in the day.

The waitress left and the file resumed center stage. Daniel laid his forearm across it. "This is confidential, so you can't tell anyone what you see. It could mean my badge. Consulting with an astrologer." He shook his head as if at the foolishness of it all. "Agreed?"

"Fine." I reached for the file. "I met Tiffany."

He gripped the folder, maintaining possession. "Did you go behind my back?"

Was he used to people maneuvering around him? "*She* found me."

"I never gave her your name. Why didn't she tell me? Why didn't you?"

He was acting like the control freak Tiffany said that he was. "I'm telling you now. She came for a reading yesterday. She looked me up online. I want to help her."

Daniel relaxed his grip and I took the folder. "Keep me in the loop," he said. "She says anything pertinent, I need to know."

I wasn't sure how that aligned with my requirement of confidentiality, but I wasn't going to think about that now. I opened the folder. On the very top page was a black and white picture.

He tapped the grainy photograph. "That's a still from the security cam,"

I picked it up. It showed the back of a figure, more of a blur than a shadow. I could see a baseball cap and possibly shoulder-length hair. It could be a woman or a man. The security cam mostly caught shrubs and flowers. The figure had a long stride and carried a towel over one shoulder.

"We think Sierra's under the towel," Daniel said.

She didn't appear to be struggling. Whoever was carrying her knew how to hold a baby. "Where was the picture taken?"

"In the South Beach gated community where Tiff lives. She has a mansion on the ocean."

Tiff now. Like his sister, did Daniel have the same annoying habit of shortening names?

He went through the file and pulled out pictures of the house. A wrought-iron fence and a tall double-sided gate enclosed a yard with trimmed shrubbery, stately palms, and manicured grass. There were pictures of the nursery, with pink gauze curtains, a mahogany crib with a matching changing table that had a box of mid-sized diapers on the shelf. I'd had a nursery set much like it, only mine was white and made of pine. The memory of it brought tears to my eyes and while I wiped them away, they didn't escape Daniel's notice.

"Everything okay?"

I turned the photo over and put it down. "The room looks so empty and sad."

"I know. Tiff hasn't touched anything since Sierra was taken. Except put bars on the windows."

"A house like that and there's no alarm?"

"There is. It was armed, but it didn't matter, since the upstairs windows were open. The downstairs was locked tight, but the second floor was unsecured. The upstairs bedrooms have balconies and we figured the kidnapper climbed up from the outside. It can be done, I know, because I did it."

I remembered Tiffany's crushing guilt. "There was no window screen?"

"It was removed. There were no fingerprints, so we assume the kidnapper wore gloves. Obviously, he took them off, as there's no evidence of them in the photo."

"Okay, so we're looking for someone who has gloves and knows how to hold a baby. How did he get in and out of a gated community?"

"We don't know for sure, but a twenty-foot wall on the south side was likely breached. It was lined with a row of bougainvillea, but these had been recently trimmed. There were trellises, which made a handy climbing apparatus." He looked at me. "I know. I climbed it too."

"What's on the other side?"

"A road."

"A wall that high would be a hard climb with a baby."

"It was a hard climb without a baby."

"So, someone athletic. What about a get-away car?"

"The road leads to a public beach. The kidnapper could have parked there, climbed over, and back."

"You think there's just one person?"

"That's all the camera picked up. That doesn't mean more weren't involved. Someone could have been waiting in the car."

"There were no tire tracks?"

"Nothing we could use. The road is tarmac."

"No other cameras picked him up?"

"None. He was in and out."

"Sounds like he knew the place."

"I thought so too."

"Where did the towel come from?"

"He must have brought it with him. It wasn't Tiff's."

"Why do you think there was no ransom note? You steal a baby from a guy this rich and you'd expect there'd be one."

"Exactly. We thought the kidnappers would get in touch, but they didn't."

"Is that usual?"

"Depends on the kidnappers' goal. If they wanted money, there'd be a note. If they wanted to keep her, probably not. If there was an accident and she died, ditto."

"What do you think the chances are of getting her back alive?"

Daniel exhaled slowly. "Not good. The first 48 hours are critical. After that, chances drop quickly. We were late to begin with, already behind the curve, and we did what we could. We organized a grid search of the gated community and the beach.

We pulled in bloodhounds. We talked to every home-owner at J'Adore Del Mar and we put a road block on A1A for the day. We questioned everyone. Came up with nothing."

I started going through the pages. The file wasn't very thick. "Is this everything?"

"I brought what I thought was important."

"I'd like to see everything."

"Fine."

A missing person's bulletin showed a picture of Sierra Rossario that almost stopped my heart. Taken in a photography studio, she was sitting up with her legs crossed, beaming at the camera. She looked about four months old. She had wispy brown hair, round brown eyes, and pink chubby cheeks, no teeth. She wore a pink dress, bare feet. Her arms were out, as if she was waiting to be picked up, her face full of love for whoever was reaching for her.

One night, it would be someone bad.

"Cute kid, huh?" Daniel said.

I nodded, suddenly choked for words. I could almost feel the little arms around my neck and smell the sweet baby breath. I never got around to getting a professional picture taken of my daughter.

"Everything okay?" Daniel asked, swinging his head sideways to look at me closer.

I put the bulletin down. "Fine," I said, though there was a frog in my voice. "I just find it all so sad."

"Here's a before picture of Tiff." Daniel passed me a photo. Tiffany was sitting at a table in a flower garden looking drop-dead beautiful. Her hair, on the reddish side of blond, was gleaming. Her big green eyes were shining, as were her peaches and cream skin. Unnatural white teeth beamed from a sly smile that seemed to whisper: fuck me.

"She doesn't look like that now."

"I know."

I turned the photo over. In ink on the back were the words: *Back yard*. I looked at Daniel. "Whose back yard?"

"Uh, well, mine."

So. "Any photos of Ciro?"

Daniel rooted through the file and came up with one that I had seen online. The mogul was in sunglasses looking like a thug.

"He was born in Mexico City," Daniel said. "He came to the US illegally when he was a boy and gained citizenship when Reagan granted the illegals amnesty."

He pulled out another picture of Sierra. This one was time-progressed and a computer projection of what Sierra would look like now, at four—a miniature Tiffany, with a clear complexion, big round eyes, and long straight auburn hair. She had her mother's looks, her father's coloring.

Janet reappeared and Daniel closed the file. He smiled broadly at her as she passed out coasters and drinks. She took our order, one hip jutting out, elbow on her pelvic girdle. Daniel was going to have a hamburger with fries and another beer. I ordered the blackened redfish salad.

When she left, I said, "Who did you think was behind it?"

Daniel rubbed his chin. "Initially, I thought it was connected to Ciro's business. He needed money he couldn't get from a bank and borrowed money from bad people."

"Bad people?" I asked, eyebrows arched.

"Loan sharks. Ciro's not a good judge of character. There's something off about him. I never liked the man."

"Could it be he married your ex-girlfriend?"

Daniel cracked his knuckles. He lifted a shoulder. "Maybe."

"How was your breakup?"

He exhaled slowly. "Quick."

I looked at him. That wasn't much information. "Go on."

"I got transferred. She met Ciro. Not necessarily in that order."

"Then you were transferred back?"

"Right. When I first met Tiff, we were both in Lauderdale. I was sent to Gainesville and then to Miami. By then, she was married to Ciro and living in Miami. I was on duty the morning she called 911."

"How did Ciro feel about that?"

"As you could imagine, he wasn't happy. But Tiff was relieved she knew someone she could call any time."

"But you were taken off the case."

"Right. My lieutenant thought I was too close and I couldn't be objective. That was just wrong. I would have done whatever it took. It's imperative you start looking in the right direction and don't get distracted."

"And they got sidetracked?"

"They started focusing on a child molester when there was no evidence. Ciro was putting on the pressure. Miami PD had to find someone." He paused, guzzled his beer, wiped his mouth with the back of his sleeve, and went on. "I feel responsible. Only there was nothing I could do once I was off the case. I really need to make this right." He looked at me intently. "I told you what I got. What do you have? Claire told me two possible times for the kidnapping."

I let him change the subject. I took my phone out of my purse, pulled up the astrology app and checked my notes. "My guess is either 10:50 p.m. or 3:45 a.m."

Daniel sighed loudly, as if in pain. He rooted through the file, found the grainy photograph of the suspect, and turned it over. On the back was a time stamp that read: May 3, 22:53 hr.

The photo was taken at 10:53 p.m. "How long would it take to get from the bedroom to where the photo was taken?"

"It's across the street, so I'd say around five minutes."

Which gave a time of about 10:48 pm. I tapped the information into the astrology app and pulled up the chart. I liked it. Multiple planets were near the angles: Venus, Mars, Jupiter, Uranus, and Pluto.

"What do you see?" Daniel slung his arm on top of the bench and moved closer to get a better look at the phone. "What do those lines across the center of the circle mean?"

"They're aspects. They show how the planets are communicating. Who's talking to who. And, the nature of the interaction."

"What?"

I tried to explain the concept of aspects. "Planets in set geometric patterns are linked. We want to look at the arc separation of two planets. If they're 90 degrees apart, or at right angles to each other, that's a square. It's a difficult aspect. The two planets are butting heads. Planets that are 180 degrees apart are in opposition. Like the word suggests, they're complete opposites. They want opposite things. That's also a difficult aspect. Then you have a trine, an easy aspect. These are planets 120 degrees apart. They effortlessly help each other. Planets that are sixty degree apart are in sextile. They also help each other, but more effort is required. Then you have planets that are together. They are conjunct. Depending on the planets, the aspect is easy or difficult."

Daniel rubbed his chin. "I'm lost. Can you cut to the chase?"

"Good aspects denote help, ease, and cooperation, and generally a good outcome."

"And the bad aspects show the opposite?"

I smiled at him. "See, you're getting it. Difficult aspects show resistance, hindrance, and conflict. Usually a struggle. But there's a lot of energy associated with them. They make things happen."

Daniel screwed up his face in a frown. "*But what does it mean?*" he said in a cranky tone.

I interpreted the wheel, pointing out planets as I spoke. "Mars conjunct Uranus is a sudden act. I don't think it was well-planned. Jupiter conjunct Pluto can mean luck in kidnapping, and possibly protection against murder. Jupiter is Sierra, and she's in her own sign of Sagittarius, which is good. But she's retrograde, which isn't. I think she's in a weak position. She's square the Mars and Uranus, which means something unexpected, or a loss of luck. But she's trine Saturn, which means help from the authorities. Or, whoever took her isn't entirely evil. Mercury, the planet of information, is conjunct the Sun, which in horary is a bad combination. There may be a problem collecting physical evidence. Or maybe with logic."

Daniel scratched his forehead. "Is nothing certain? I hear a lot of waffling."

"Astrology has limits." At least the way I understood it. "The planets are symbols. They can mean many things. The art is to put together a story that makes contextual sense." Which was much easier done in hindsight. "I can tell you, the most potent piece of information here is Venus."

"Why?'

"It's on the angle." I pointed out the cross within the circle. "Venus represents the kidnapper. She's attacking Sierra. We're looking for a woman."

"We are? Why?"

"Venus represents women. She's in Gemini, so she could be a young woman, a teacher, or a communicator." I paused abruptly. "But Mercury is also important. The two planets are connected. Two people are involved."

"How do you know?"

"It's complicated. Short version, Venus is in Mercury's sign and vice-versa. That's called a mutual reception. It connects the planets, but not in an overt manner. One planet is obvious, the other not so much. Mercury is hidden in the background."

"I don't remember anything about a hidden person."

"It's someone you don't know about. Hidden in that sense. Like you said earlier, someone waiting in a get-away car, or a job that was done for hire. We have Venus ruling the 6th house, which is the house of servants, workers, even policemen. We're looking for a domestic worker."

Daniel retracted his arm and sat back on the bench, hands on the table. "What about a nurse?"

"Did Tiffany have home health care?" I remembered reading the baby was under medical care and in need of medication.

"No home health care," Daniel said. "Bryan, my partner, thought a worker at the hospital where Sierra was born was involved."

In a chart, hospitals were shown by the 12th house, which was unconnected to Sierra's attacker. "Nope. No one connected to the hospital."

"Just like that? You rule it out?"

"I thought we decided it was someone familiar with the gated community. We're looking for a domestic worker. We can't ignore Mercury, which is someone young, a student, or a teacher. It's in Taurus, so it could be someone who works with money or with the earth. Perhaps a landscaper."

"They have those at the J'Adore Del Mar."

"Add Venus and it could also be a day-care provider, driver, or housekeeper. Even a policeman."

"What about a security guard?"

"Exactly."

Daniel blinked. "The FBI went after the sex offender. Could it be him?"

I studied the chart. I'd give the 8th house to a sex offender, represented by Cancer and ruled by the Moon, which was unconnected to Venus. "Nope. He wasn't involved."

Janet was back with heaping plates and moving too animatedly for my palate. She bent low to place Daniel's plate and I was surprised her boobs didn't fall out of her tank top. She addressed him when she said, "Need anything else?"

"We're fine," he said, with the smile that showed his dimple.

And Janet departed with a blatant sashay of her hips.

I stole a french fry from Daniel's plate. It was smoking hot and crispy. I looked down at the greens on my plate and hated my diet.

Daniel picked up his hamburger and grease dripped down his fingers. He paused before he took a bite. "We looked at workers in the gated community. No one was suspicious."

I removed my glasses and picked up my fork. "What about at Ciro's work?"

"We looked there too. You'd never find a happier bunch of employees."

We ate in silence, digesting food and information. Daniel stared at the water and I stared at my phone. *Let the chart speak*, my grandmother used to say. She thought it communicated in code. Crack the code and the sky spoke. The skill wasn't so much in breaking the code, but in grasping the correct nuance of meaning. *The sky will help*, she said, but then she thought the whole universe was alive and could bring aid. It wasn't my world-view, or my experience.

We finished and the waitress returned and picked up Daniel's empty bottle. "Another?" she said, batting her eyelashes.

"You can bring the bill," he said, dismissing her.

She cleared the plates and took her time bringing the bill. While we waited, Daniel chomped on my ice. "So, where are we?" He pulled out his notebook.

I grabbed a napkin and made notes that I would transfer to my notebook at home. "We're looking for someone opportunistic, athletic, who can climb, knows babies, knows the gated community, and isn't working alone. The motive was either money or someone who wanted a baby. There are at least two people, one is a woman."

Daniel scribbled notes and then paused. "Can you tell if Sierra's dead or alive?"

I sighed heavily. "It's hard to say." While the kidnappers seemed clear to me, what happened to Sierra was not so evident. I pulled up the chart and pointed to the planet of death. "Pluto is in her house and stands for death and kidnapping. But Pluto also represents rebirth and transformation. She could be dead, or alive with a new identity. Either is possible."

The waitress was back and slid the bill on the table in front of us. "Have a great day," she told Daniel with a provocative wink.

We reached for the bill at the same time and he got it, but not before I saw that Janet had scrawled her phone number on the back of the ticket.

"It's on me," Daniel said as he pulled out his wallet. "For your invaluable input."

"Are you calling astrology invaluable? That's a step up."

He laid a stack of bills on the table and smiled the dimpled smile. "Let's see how it works out." He shot me a long, lingering look.

I glanced away, fumbling with my purse. I was definitely getting a vibe from him, but I was set on keeping my distance. I wasn't a one night stand and I wasn't looking for a relationship. Daniel didn't have to seduce me in order to get me to work with him. I was all in. We solve this and he would prove his worth as a detective, and I would prove mine as an astrologer who could rival my mother. It was a win-win for us both.

Chapter 12

We drove home and I had my first experience riding in a police vehicle, even if it was an undercover car. A police scanner sat on the front console beside the gear shift. There was a hand-held radio next to it and on the floor behind me, a portable red light that went on the dash. Now off duty, the equipment was idle and Daniel had the radio on and tuned to the oldies' station. It was cranked so loud, there was no way we could talk.

When we got to my house and pulled into the drive, I saw the front door open and Jake sitting on a rocker on the porch. Daniel turned off the radio. "What's he doing here? Should I arrest him for trespassing?"

I unclasped my seatbelt as Shiny roared down the steps. "He looks after my dog when I'm out."

"He seems to think he's more than a neighbor."

"He's not." Though I had tried to make myself clear to Jake, where we stood, I wondered if he got the message. As much as I hated to, I got out of the car knowing I had to go over it again.

Daniel leaned toward my open window. "I'll call you once I check my schedule. You can come over and examine the entire case file at your leisure."

"Okay."

"I'll draw up a list of domestic workers."

"Try to get their birth dates."

"Birth time and everything?"

I knew he was kidding and flashed him a wave before walking to the house. Jake stood up as I climbed the stairs. I should never have given him the key to my house. I wondered why Daniel wouldn't go.

"What's he doing?" Jake asked, dismissing the car with a flap of his hand. "Getting ready to arrest me for trespassing?"

"He's joking. He's got a bad sense of humor. Come on in." I snapped my fingers at Shiny and she bounded up the steps. Jake did a lot for me and I didn't want to upset him. He gave me the freedom to leave for long hours and not worry about her. I liked having an advocate on my side, a benefic to oppose the two malefics. Whatever I said couldn't cause offence, and a Pisces was offended so easily.

He held the door open, like the gentleman that he was, and we went inside. I closed the front door and we went to the kitchen where I poured two glasses of iced tea. We took them to the back porch and sat down side by side facing the garden. I took a long sip. The sun had moved around to the front of the house and the flamboyant tree cast a long shadow. I put down my glass. "We need to talk."

He chewed on a cube of ice then swallowed heavily. "Here it comes."

"What comes?"

"Why you chose him over me."

"Jake, I'm not choosing anyone. He's a client. I don't get involved with clients. I'm helping him. Period."

Jake looked skeptical. "What about me?"

"You're my friend."

"That's it? You said you needed time. I gave you time. Have you been stringing me along all this time?"

I stared at my glass. "Jake, I meant, I needed time to get over what happened."

"Which was what? What was so tragic you still can't talk about?"

I reached for my glass. "Stop asking me about it."

"I waited. I told you I would."

"I didn't think you were serious. An Aries Moon doesn't wait."

"Why do you have to bring astrology into everything?"

"It's who I am."

"Why can't you be normal?"

What do you say to that? "I tried. It didn't work."

"Try harder. When did you write me off? When Dick came on the scene?" He flung his hand at the street. "Or when you put our charts together and shook your head."

It was true, we had no romantic synastry together, but I didn't need the planets to know that no sparks would fly; no links would bind; no passion would burn. You can't make love happen. "It's best like this. We're good friends, right?"

"Wrong. Tell me the truth. Is that what you're looking for?" With a jab of his thumb he gestured at the road. "Someone who goes around threatening to arrest people?"

"It's a case." Though I hated to breach client confidentiality, I was backed into a corner. "It's a kidnapping. A baby was taken. The mother is dying from grief. I'm trying to help her."

"What's her name?"

I shook my head. "I've said too much already."

"This is bullshit. I don't believe you. I don't believe half the things you say." He stood up and sighed as if deeply aggrieved. "We are *not* friends."

He stormed through the house and stalked to the door, slamming it behind him as he left, leaving the floor shaking beneath my feet.

I was stunned. What things didn't he believe? I was as honest with him as I could be. Certainly I told him more than half the truth. He exaggerated everything. Jupiter with Neptune could do that; there were no boundaries, no limits.

I took the glasses to the kitchen and dumped them out, then went to the front door and stared across the street. Jake had lowered the shades on his front door and on the windows facing the street. He was letting me know he was shutting me out. What happened here was no longer his concern.

I felt sad and alone, and I patted Shiny's head, which was hanging. It wasn't only me who lost a friend, it was her. Somehow I had to make things right.

Chapter 13

I woke up Sunday to the shrill ring of the phone. I groped on the nightstand, squinting at the bright screen. Mother. I grabbed the phone and sat up. It was four a.m. I pushed the "accept" button.

By way of hello, she said, "What were you thinking, telling Suzanne she didn't have to get married, that she's too young, she can wait."

My whole body tensed. The bedroom faced east, the curtains were open, and a last quarter moon hovered low in the sky. I frowned at the shadows in the yard. "Hello to you too, Mother. Suzie's not sure she wants to get married."

"Of course she does. And she is. The astrology doesn't lie. She'll wed in August."

"I don't see it. Mercury's retrograde all month, Mars is in fall, and Jupiter is stationing. It's a terrible time to get married."

"If you check her *dasa* and *bhukti*, and the transits to her *navamsa*, you'll see. For that matter, look at the Capricorn ingress, the next eclipse, her Jupiter–Venus midpoint, and the upcoming tertiary progressions. It's all there."

I rolled my eyes, wondering if she was just throwing out words, or if she actually used all these methods. Like my grandmother, I only used two. "I looked at the secondary progressions and transits and didn't see anything."

"Which is why you'll never be a good astrologer."

"That's all Vivi used."

"Right. And your grandmother used the tarot, frankincense, and dreams, and still considered herself an astrologer."

My mother had a point. Vivi was in tune with the universe and proudly used everything at her disposal. According to my mother, Vivi couldn't draw an accurate chart—which back in her day was drawn by hand using tables. She was sloppy at math and through necessity was forced to rely on non-astrological techniques. Unlike my mother who used straight astrology, period.

"Suzanne is getting married and that's final," my mother said, bringing me back to the present. "Call her and right what you have wronged."

"He's a drug addict."

"No worse than a professor."

I let the slight pass. My mother was no fan of my husband, Andre. No matter what I did, I could never live up to her standards. Everything I did was flawed. No wonder I grew up cautious, insecure, and afraid. Or, what Andre called in one of his critical moments, neurotic and joyless. I said, "You don't know Elliot. You don't know who Sylvia wants her to marry."

"I know exactly who. The son of one of the wealthiest families in Lauderdale. Do your job. You don't get to pass judgment on fate and you can't stop it."

Though my mother behaved like she was the ultimate authority of the universe, I stood my ground. She might be able to manipulate me, but she wasn't going to manipulate my clients. "I won't encourage it. That's just wrong."

"Fine. You do that and I'll go around you. *I'll* talk to her. As for you, you will have seen my last referral."

That left me speechless. She had never given me any referrals. In her mind, I would never make the grade. Suzie had picked me.

"I don't care if you do have a certificate," my mother added. "You don't know astrology."

"I'm helping the police." The words just jumped out of my mouth.

There was a long silence. "What police?"

"A detective."

"Ah. That's the Mars–Saturn–Pluto you lied about. What's the case?"

I closed my eyes, as if doing that could make her go away. "A kidnapping."

"Cold?

"Yes."

"Give me the data and I'll look at the chart."

"I want to do this on my own."

My mother snorted derisively. "I have experience. I worked with the police. *And* the FBI. *I* know what I'm doing."

"We're making progress."

"Are you now. How old is the baby?"

"Now? If she's alive, she'd be four."

"What a coincidence. Holly would be four."

"I don't see your point."

"You're rubbing salt in a wound. Are you sure you want to get involved?"

"I'm already involved."

"Can you be objective? Even if you get this baby back, it won't help you get back yours."

"I know."

"I thought you had problems doing horary. You hate to pin yourself down. The kidnapped child could be fine, or, she could be dead. Maybe's she lost, maybe she'll be found."

I winced at her mocking impression of me. I felt cold and gathered the blanket around my shoulders. "I can do it," I said, with a confidence I didn't feel.

"Can you? In your state of mind? Have you forgotten your nervous breakdown? You haven't handled what happened well at all. For instance, why does Suzanne think you're widowed?"

"I didn't say that. She jumped to conclusions. Anyway, as far as I'm concerned, it's true."

"Until he rises from the dead and comes knocking."

"He's in Paris. He's gone."

"People don't stay gone forever."

I stiffened, wondering if we were still talking about Andre. "Some do."

"You know what they say. Never say never."

"Are you coming back?"

"I detect anxiety. Do you not want me to come back? Have you told people *I'm* dead?"

"No."

"I guess I should be thankful for small mercies."

"Is there anything else? I'd like to get back to sleep."

"Fix it with Suzanne." She hung up abruptly, without bothering to say goodbye.

But that was my mother. She was single and twenty-seven when I was born, unplanned, unwelcome, and unwanted. Now the distance helped, as long as I stayed off her turf. She hated me doing astrology.

I was too unnerved to stay in bed and I got up and went outside to see the cloudy sky. The moon was rising higher, but no stars shone. At least it was Sunday, which was the one day of the week I allowed myself coffee.

I drank it on the front porch; a double espresso with whipped coffee crème that gave me a buzz. I loved coffee and all through college I'd been a big coffee drinker. I gave it up when I moved to Florida. My grandmother thought caffeine wrecked the reception of celestial energy and counseled drinking herbal teas. My mother called that hogwash and consumed coffee from dawn to dusk. I limited myself to Sundays, hoping to better commune with the sky. So far it didn't seem to be working.

The sky turned from black to gray as I finished my coffee. My Sunday ritual involved watching the morning news shows and taking Shiny to the dog park. Typically, around eleven, Jake would come over and we'd go together. But as I stared across the street at his dark house with the shades drawn, I knew I would be going to the dog park by myself.

Which is what happened.

At noon I ate a healthy feta sandwich with lettuce, alfalfa, and cranberries. I washed the plate still hungry, and then distracted myself by preparing the coming week's charts. I was looking at Sierra's when my phone rang. Suzie was calling. I picked up and she was crying.

"I did what you said. Elliot and I broke up."

When had I told her to break up with him? "I thought you were going to slow things down."

"I tried. Then he broke up with *me*."

Now she sounded more angry than upset. "What happened?"

"I told him I wasn't satisfied. Guess what? He's not satisfied either."

"Did he say what was wrong?"

"I'm too uptight to smoke pot."

"I wouldn't call you uptight. I'd call you ambitious."

"I miss him," she said in a trembling voice.

"What did your parents say?"

"God, I didn't tell them. They'll kill me. I told my mom you didn't give me a wedding date and she was on the phone to your mom. I can't say we broke up. I don't know what to do."

"Maybe we should get together and talk about it."

Susie sniffed loudly. "Okay."

"Everything will be fine. You have to believe that." This was more advice from my grandmother, coming out of nowhere. "Don't worry, things will work out for the best."

"I don't see how. I never thought he had a problem with me."

"That's the thing. We see only our side of things. I bet he misses you too."

The sniveling ceased abruptly. "Why do you say that?"

"It's chemistry. Reactions don't happen in a vacuum. If one person reacts, so does the other."

"Really?"

"Yes. Come tomorrow. Any time after five."

Chapter 14

Tiffany was back on Monday morning and looking better. Her hair was washed and may have been trimmed. She wore jeans and a white button-down shirt that didn't show her skeleton. She sat down and faced me, looking like a brand new woman. Such was the power of hope.

"Do you mind if I ask you some questions about the kidnapping?" I said. "I'd like to hear your impressions about what happened."

"Of course," she said, and there were lights in her eyes and excitement in her voice. "Daniel told me there was a breakthrough. We're looking for two people, a domestic worker, one's a woman. I don't know who they could be."

He stole my thunder. Not that it bothered me. I had an 8th house Sun and didn't mind being in the background. In fact, I preferred it. "Tell me about the people who worked for you. You've got the driver. Did you have a nanny? A cook? A maid?"

"It wasn't Josefina." Tiffany's hand went to her neck and she slid her cross back and forth along the chain. "She was my housekeeper and beyond reproach. She worked for Ciro before we were married. He found her though a housekeeping referral company. She'd been vetted and had no criminal record. She was indebted to Ciro. He sponsored her to become an American citizen. Ciro helped her brother and mother immigrate. Josefina would have done anything for us. She was as upset as we were at what happened."

"Did she live on your property?"

Tiffany's hand dropped to her lap and she studied her fingers. They were unpolished and bitten to the quick. "She lived in the city. She was going to night school, getting her GED. She wanted to make something of her life."

"Was she married?"

"I don't think she was interested."

"So, no children."

"I don't think that's what she was looking for."

"Did she babysit?"

"A few times. We didn't go out much. Only when necessary and mostly for Ciro's work. He liked to stay home too, especially after we had Sierra."

It was the same for me, especially after working all day. I looked forward to being home at night. I made myself focus. "But you trusted Josefina with the baby."

"I trusted her with my life." Tiffany folded her hands and placed them in her lap. "She was like a sister to me. The thing was, *I* wanted to look after Sierra. It's as if I knew, or some part of me did, that I wouldn't have much time with her. I couldn't stand to leave her."

I knew how she felt. It was hard to drop Holly at daycare and go to work. But I didn't have a choice. Andre bought a house that was falling apart and it was either pay up and fix it or foreclose. It was in his name, he bought it before we met and he didn't want a black mark on his record. It was old and needed everything and was costing us a fortune to repair. There was no way I couldn't work.

Tiffany was looking at me expectedly and I moved on. "What about your driver?"

"Gomez has worked for Ciro for ten years. Like Josefina, he was vetted. He was our driver then, as now."

"Did he drive you around when Sierra was an infant?"

"We only went to the doctor's. He's really Ciro's driver. Now, Ciro insists I use him. He doesn't want me driving alone. He says I need a body guard to keep away the press." She lifted her hand and pressed a palm to her throat. "*I* think the real reason is that Gomez is supposed to watch me. Make sure I don't take out the boat, or anything."

At least Tiffany's husband knew how vulnerable she was. "I hope you'll call me if you get an urge to do that."

She lowered her eyes and her hand. "I feel much better."

"That's good to hear." I moved on. "Did you have a woman gardener?"

"Our gated community employs a service. Their workers come and go. They don't seem to be able to keep them. But that has nothing to do with us."

"Are the workers legal?"

"I wouldn't know. A lot of them are Hispanic, but so is Ciro."

"What about the security company? Do they employ women?"

"Of course. You can't discriminate in this day and age. I mean, I don't know any of them. I don't pay attention. Why would I? I'm sure the FBI checked them out."

"They did. What about neighbors?"

"They were checked too. No red flags. We know our neighbors, we used to socialize with them. They're professionals, not criminals."

"How about Good Food? Any disgruntled employees?"

"Ciro says no. He pays people well. He grew up poor and knows what it's like. He has a low turn-over of employees. He invests in people. He doesn't try to rip them off or take advantage of them. He thinks it's good for business and it is."

"What about the pediatrician? Did you have any suspicions about his office?"

"Not at all. I told the detective that, but he was convinced it was someone at the hospital. The doctor has an office at Miami Memorial and we were there every month, but I only saw the office staff. Daniel didn't think it was the hospital either, but once he was taken off the case, he had no say."

"What was Sierra's health condition?"

"She was eight weeks early. She wasn't due until January and I went into labor in November. My water broke, we tried drugs to stop the contractions, but I was allergic to them. I had an emergency C-section."

"Were there complications?"

"She had some respiratory problems but they didn't last. She weighed three pounds and was eight inches long. You could hold her in the palm of your hand. She had no fat and you could see the blood vessels through her skin. She stayed in NICU for six weeks and came home the week before Christmas. By then she weighed five pounds and was eleven inches long."

"I thought she was on medication."

"She had a seizure when she was three months old. Which was equivalent to her being a month old, according to her pediatrician. He didn't go by her birth date, but the day she was due—her gestational age. He put her on Dilantin as a preventative. He didn't know if she'd have more seizures, but since she'd had one, he didn't want to take any chances. She's probably not on it now."

Tiffany was talking in the present tense, as if Sierra was still alive.

"I lost a baby before her," Tiffany said. "I always felt Sierra was a gift. Compensation for the loss."

"I'm so sorry."

"Harry was premature, born at 27 weeks. If I could have carried him for one more week, he would have lived. One week, that close, but no. I was devastated. I thought I'd never get over it. Then I had Sierra. I thought God was trying to make up with me after taking Harry." She made a disapproving hiss. "Hardly."

"I know it's hard to wrap your mind around the reason why bad things happen," I said. It was something I wondered about endlessly. If I had been doing astrology, I would have seen the horrific transits that were so clear in hindsight. There were some great ones too, which would have muddied the waters, but the bad ones alone called for caution. Even my mother, who had just moved to Moroni, missed them. If she alerted me to what was bearing down that day, I never would have left Holly. I would have stayed home. But I didn't know. Sometimes I wonder if the planets had extracted revenge because I'd abandoned them.

Tiffany coughed lightly and I shook off the thought. I couldn't remember where we were, so I said, "Why was Daniel taken off the case?"

"It was high profile. There was a lot of pressure to find the kidnappers. Miami PD put their best detectives on it."

I wondered what that said about Daniel's competence. "He said he was removed from the case on account of your history."

"That's right. The captain thought he was too emotionally involved and claimed he couldn't be objective. I pleaded with the captain to let Daniel stay on, but a month later he was transferred, again."

"How long have you known him?"

"Seven years. I met Danno when he was with the PD in Lauderdale." She slid the cross along its chain, smiling at the memory.

Was Danno her pet name for him? Did he have one for her besides Tiff? I kept these questions to myself.

She went on. "I was in college and cheerleading for the Dolphins and one Sunday he was working at the stadium. He waited for me after the game and we went out for coffee. We fell in love immediately. Then he was transferred to Gainesville."

She'd glossed over quite a bit. "How long were you together?"

"Six months. We were going to get married."

"What happened?"

"I didn't want to give up cheerleading and move to Gainesville. He was nice. I loved him. But he had his issues. I'm not saying I don't have mine, but he's got baggage. His ex-wife wouldn't leave him alone and he'd jump through any hoop she threw. Plus he was far too close to his family. He had all these siblings and parents who always needed him. I thought they were trying to keep him from me because they didn't like me. After his first marriage turned out so badly, they were worried for him. They thought we got engaged too quickly. *Claire* thought so. Those two are far too close. If she could, I think she'd have him for herself. She didn't like me. Any chance she could find to get him away from me, she'd take it. And he always went. He never said no. I wasn't first in his book. When the phone rings and you're making love and he leaves, it tells you something."

"He does seem close to his family."

114

"That's not all. He hates to be alone. He doesn't give you any space. And he's jealous. He's got a bad temper." She paused, she was getting animated. She inhaled deeply and when she spoke again, her tone was flat. "Not that it matters now."

I was taken aback by the long litany of complaints and wondered if she was more bitter than she knew. Though in all fairness, I could think for hours about Andre's endless shortcomings. I said, "So you had issues and you grew apart."

"We had a fight at a party and he stormed out. He left me there. I'd say the relationship came to an abrupt end."

"What did you fight about?" I was too nosy for my own good.

"Mostly his family. Plus I wanted a baby."

"And he didn't?"

She shrugged. "Not like me. It was something I really needed."

"You don't want another baby?"

She looked at me with horror. "Are you kidding? Bring another baby into a world like this? Forget it."

I could relate. I felt the same.

"The thing is, I know he would do anything for me. I always knew it. I could pick up the phone and he'd answer and he'd be there." She smiled her plucky smile. "And he is."

"He wants to find out what happened to Sierra."

"Do you think you will?"

"I'm hopeful."

She sighed loudly. "Me too. I hate not knowing what happened."

"I can imagine."

"Just waiting and waiting." Tiffany clasped her hands together. "It's hell."

"You have to find something to do, to pass the time."

"I did!" Tiffany sat forward. "I did what you said. I called the National Center for Missing and Exploited Children. I'm going to volunteer. Help them out."

"That's fantastic."

"I have a meeting with them tomorrow. I don't know what I'm going to do, but I'll do something. I'm actually excited."

The clock chimed. Our session was over and we made another appointment for the following week. Then I walked her to the door and handed her over to Gomez. I wasn't sure if I'd learned much about the abduction, but I'd learned a lot about Daniel.

***

At the end of the day, Suzie arrived just after 5:00. She must have come straight from the salon because her hair was newly coiffed in pleasing ringlets, her skin was glowing, and she smelled like flowery shampoo. She wore a white halter that showed off a large diamond necklace. For someone recently heartbroken, she looked quite happy.

"You look nice," I said, as we sat down on the rockers on my porch. "What's going on?"

She shifted her position to get out of the sun. "Elliot and I are back together. We have a date tonight. We're going out to dinner."

I hated the relief that I felt. Over the shrieking of mockingbirds I asked, "What happened?"

"I called him. You were right. He missed me too. I'd only been thinking of the bad stuff. There's a lot of good." She was eyeing her ring that glinted in the afternoon sun.

"Tell me the good stuff," I prodded.

"He writes songs for me. He sings to me in bed. He buys me jewelry." She dropped her hand to her lap. "He's honest. He doesn't run around. He trusts me and lets me do what I want. He supports what I do."

I put a lot of weight on fidelity. In my view, the opposite was a deal breaker. Still, in her case there was the downside, and while her decision was best for me, I wasn't sure it was best for her. Though I hated to, I reminded her of her frustration. "What are you going to do about the sex?"

"I'll live with it."

"What about talking to him? Address the problem head on. They say communication is the most important factor in marriage."

She pulled a bangle off her wrist and raised her eyes and looked at me. "Will you talk to him?"

I drew back and the rocker creaked. "No. You have to. No matter how hard it is."

"What if he came to you? You could bring it up."

"No."

"He wants to see you. He's really interested in astrology. He wanted to know all about my session and all about you. He wants me to make him an appointment."

"Really?" I wondered if she'd told her mother this.

Suzie smiled. "When can he come?"

"I'll read his chart, but that's it. I will not talk about sex."

"If it comes up, you will, right?"

"I can't see it coming up."

"It might." She jumped up and threw her arms around me, dousing me with the scent of her shampoo. "You're the best. Thank you."

I got out my phone, checked my schedule and we booked a tentative appointment for Elliot on Saturday. Then she had to go.

She reached the bottom step when she stopped and whirled around. "Next Thursday I'm having a shoot. I'm going to have a makeover the day before."

"Sounds like fun," I said.

"Do you want to go? I have a two-for-one coupon at the spa."

"Me? No." The last time I had a makeover, I had my drab hair dyed bright blond and chopped short. It was a shock to me and everyone who saw me later at the funeral home. I hadn't got my hair professionally cut since. These days I cut it myself at home. Looking in the mirror, I divided the two sides in half and took the scissors to it.

Suzie mistook my silence for concession. "It'll be fun. We'll go at the end of the day and be out by 9:00."

"Next Wednesday?"

"I know you don't have class and no one goes to these things alone. We'll have a massage, a facial, do our nails. Get a pleasing cut. Advice on eye-wear. You could do something with your eyebrows. You have an interesting look, but you could tweak it. Come on. What do you say?"

I made an effort not to touch my face. "What's wrong with my eyebrows?"

She started to laugh. "Seriously? When did you last have them done?"

Done? "I don't get my eyebrows done."

"There you go. What about your hair? When was the last time you got it cut? By a professional."

"A few years."

"And your glasses? How long have you had those?"

I wasn't going to answer. "I get your point."

"Leave it to me. I'll get you in order."

"Why do you care if I'm in order?"

"Because I'm going to invite you to my wedding and I want you to look good."

I watched a pair of squirrels chase each other across the lawn and wondered what my mother would say to this. Her clients loved her and she became friends with them. It was turning out the same for me. "All right," I said. "I'll go. *And* I'll find you a good wedding date." One at least that was better than my mother's.

Chapter 15

Tuesday was the first morning of the season when it was warm enough to have breakfast on the back porch. The sun was rising and golden rays streamed through the flamboyant leaves warming my face. Birds flew across the garden, singing for joy. I sipped black tea, which had roughly the same amount of caffeine as coffee, but without the additional toxins. I was reading the paper, and as usual, the news was dire. As if it didn't understand the difference between spending and debt, Congress was about to renege on paying its bills. I flipped through the pages, glancing at the headlines, and noticed a classified ad: Judith Rendell was holding a "nature meditation" on Wednesday. I was thinking about that when I heard a knock on the door. Shiny stood up and I threw the paper down. There were still twenty minutes before my first appointment.

I hurried to the door and saw my neighbor Maribel. She was decked out in a white turtleneck and wearing a black tunic that looked like a nun's outfit. It was warm and humid, and she must have been hot. She held a pie wrapped in cellophane. "I just wanted to thank you for helping me the other day," she said in her thick southern accent as she smiled sweetly.

She wore no makeup, but then she didn't need to. She looked pretty and sweet in an innocent kind of way, if you ignored the blatant dye job of her hair. It was naturally dark brown I assumed, with the top layer colored a uniform white blond. She obviously wasn't content with the way the good Lord made her. I said, "You don't have to give me anything. Anyone would have done what I did."

She had round bright blue eyes that looked startled and I wondered if she was afraid of me. "Not anyone did something. You did." She lifted the pie higher. "Please accept my peace offering."

"Thank you," I said, quietly lauding her bravery to cross into enemy territory. I took the pie. I was no cook and definitely no baker. "I'll return the plate."

"It's a peach pie. I cut the sugar and added honey, so it's a bit more healthy, but not much." She smiled shyly. "Not that I'm saying anything about your weight or anything."

"No offense taken," I said, looking down at my waist, and my belt that suddenly felt tighter.

Maribel gestured over her shoulder. "I'll go home. I don't want to disturb you. I know people are coming over."

"You're not disturbing me. I'm glad you came. I like knowing my neighbors." I lifted my eyes, glancing to the south and Porter's. "Well, some neighbors anyway." I waved in the direction of the kitchen. "I made tea, would you like some?"

"No thank you. I should go." She took a step backwards and then paused, her pretty face screwed up in a frown. Venus was obviously strong in her chart and given her religious fanaticism, Jupiter had to be compromised. She said, "Can I ask you something?"

"Sure. Ask away."

"Do you worry about going to hell?"

I would have burst out laughing, except I saw that she was serious. There were so many responses I could have made, but all I managed to say was, "No."

"Eternity is a long time to burn."

"I don't think I've done anything that egregious," I said, trying to make light of her statement.

"Father Barnabus says most astrologers don't realize what they do is evil. All you have to do is repent and you'll be forgiven."

If this was what she believed, her picketing of me made sense. I wondered what I could say that would make her see it from my point of view. The only thing I could think of was, "I'm afraid I don't agree with Father Barnabus."

"It says in the Bible that all fortune-tellers are in the service of the devil."

I shifted the pie in my hands. "Astrology isn't fortune-telling, and I don't believe in the devil."

Maribel seemed genuinely shocked. She pursed her lips and narrowed her eyes. "You see, that is his greatest power. You don't realize he exists, which allows him to tempt you."

I saw how desperate she was for me to hear what she was saying, as if she was genuinely worried the devil would win my soul. "I'll have to think about that." I wasn't raised with religion. I had no idea people thought the devil was real.

She warmed to me. I could see it in her eyes, which suddenly became animated and brighter. "It says in the Bible there are two spiritual powers. God and the devil. The devil is as real as God. Joey says you're a vortex for the devil. You bring him here. He fears for you. He says—" She paused then and bit her lip, as if swallowing her words.

I was stunned and prodded her to continue. "Joey says what?"

"We have been trying to have a baby and God has not blessed us with a child. Joey says with the devil so close and strong, God stays away."

I had a number of clients who were trying to conceive and had been able to help a few. "Have you seen a doctor?"

"What for? I'm healthy."

"There could be a physical reason you're not getting pregnant." If I knew her chart, her 5th house would shed light on the nature of the problem. Lacking that, I threw out possible explanations. "You could have blocked fallopian tubes. Your immune system could attack Joey's sperm. You could have a hormonal imbalance. It might not even be you. He could have a low sperm count. His sperm could be sluggish. There could be genetic reasons. Chromosomal issues."

She seemed taken aback, though even when she frowned, she looked pretty. "You're quite knowledgeable, for… an astrologer."

"I have two masters. One in clinical psychology, the other in neurobiochemistry."

Maribel looked astonished. "I would not have guessed that. My goodness, you are turning out to be a surprise."

"As are you." I couldn't fathom anyone suggesting astrology was evil or the work of the devil. "You seem like a very sweet person. You'd make a good mother. Talk to your doctor."

She folded her hands together. "I can't. Joey says it's up to God and that would be interfering with His will."

"What if God put doctors here to help you?" I remembered a Christian dating site advertisement I'd seen on TV. "Doesn't God help those who help themselves?"

She looked at me puzzled. "You know God?"

"Not really. Next time you go to the doctor for a checkup, mention you've been trying to have a baby. The doctor can help you."

"How?"

I fell into my teacher role and explained basic conception. "To get pregnant, a sperm has to fertilize an egg. There's only a three or four days a month when the egg is receptive. You have to have sex during that time and do all you can to maximize your success."

She looked down at the floor. "What about the rest of the time?"

"Then sex is just for fun."

"Are you joshing me?"

"No. Do you have regular menstrual cycles? Can you predict when your period will come?"

Her eyes rounded at the word "predict" as if it were a swear word.

"Watch your cycle to figure out when you're fertile. For now, assume halfway through the cycle, about two weeks after your period, you'll produce an egg. That's when you want to have sex."

"Oh my." She raised her hand to her throat. Without meeting my eyes, she said, "You are very forward. I must go. I just wanted to bring you the pie." Without another word, Maribel bowed her head, rushed down the steps, and slipped through the sharp, dense cocoplum bushes without looking back.

***

Wednesday night I considered going to the nature meditation, but ended up going to yoga. I waited and watched through my living room window for Jake to exit his house and then contrived to leave at the same time. I had to win him over. I hadn't realized how much he meant to me or how much I missed him.

I waved to him as I jogged to my car dressed in my yoga sweats and carrying my rolled up mat. He ignored me. For someone so lumbering and out of shape, he managed to get into his car first and shoot down his drive and roar into the road before me, without bothering to check if he was going to run into me, which he almost did. I had to brake hard and my brakes screeched, but he never slowed down.

I couldn't catch him. I lost him at the first light.

Yoga was held at the Coral Cove Community Church that was on the intracoastal waterway, not far from the library and the Saturday morning farmers' market. The CCCC was a non-denominational church with a large ballroom that was used for church brunches, dance classes, recovery meetings, and yoga. The teacher, Hyacinth, was forty and looked thirty. She was setting up her music as I walked in, searching for Jake. He was in the back and I strode toward him. He was stretching out, slapping his thighs on his mat in a warm up, purposely ignoring me.

I rolled my mat out beside him. "Is this place taken?" I asked, as I threw down my towel."

"Yes," he said in what sounded like a growl.

I sat down and followed his lead, stretching out my legs and wiggling my toes. "I'm sorry, okay."

"You strung me along." He stood up and went into downward facing dog.

I did the happy baby pose. "I didn't. I thought we were friends."

"You knew how I felt." He straightened up and did a low lunge.

At the front of the room, Hyacinth clapped lightly, applauding his initiative, when he was only trying to get away from me.

"You said you weren't ready," he added. "Now apparently you are. Only not with me."

"I'm helping the police find out what happened to an abducted child. It's work. You know that's a boundary I won't cross."

"So you said. Which is why I stopped taking your class."

"That's why?" I distinctly remembered him saying astrology was too complicated.

He lay on his back, with his knees to his chest and rolled sideways stretching out his spine. "Just go lie somewhere else. Pun intended."

I did a half lotus. "Can't we be civil? We live across the street. Would you like to come over after class for a beer?"

"Oh, you got beer now? Did you buy it for *him*?"

"I don't have beer. I'll buy some for *you* on the way home if you want one."

"I don't. I don't want anything from you."

"I miss you. Shiny misses you too. She rests her chin on the window ledge and stares wistfully across the street at your house."

"Bullshit."

It was indeed.

Jake stood up and began rolling his mat. "I don't miss you." He shoved the mat under his arm. "We're done. You can tell Shiny that for me. I don't care if you're gone all day to your fucking workshop and she shits all over the house, or if she's lonely and howls at the door and Porter gets his gun and shoots her. Maybe your boyfriend can look after her."

"He's not my boyfriend."

But Jake was already stalking away. He might have a placid Pisces Sun, but he had the temper of an Aries Moon. He marched to the front of the room and unfurled his mat before Hyacinth.

I lay down and let out a long sigh. I wasn't that surprised by his coldness. Mercury was turning retrograde in my 11th house of friends, which meant I could expect a turnaround in that department; things would get worse before they got better. Mercury was also opposite my Pluto, which meant I could bring out the unconscious shadow in friends; or friends could bring it out in me.

Seven o'clock came and Hyacinth clapped her hands and started the class. "Good evening everyone. We'll begin with the salutation to the sun. *Surya Namaskar.*" She loved calling the poses by their proper names.

The class passed quickly as it always did and by the cool down the tension had left and I was feeling as loose as jelly. We ended with a guided meditation, during which I usually fell asleep. As the symphony played, Hyacinth's melodic voice instructed us to follow a glowing ball of light through our body, opening up the tight places.

Send the light from the soles of your feet into the far reaches of space. See the light shine a path through the darkness. Feel the warmth in your heart and know you are connected to the universe that is calling out to you. See the ball of light…

I saw it arc tightly, banking a 180-degree turn and come zooming toward me. It looked like a shooting star and shone with the light of a sun in a midnight sky. It streaked my way, came close and once more I saw the lantern held by the hunched figure in the hooded dark cloak. I recognized the image. It was a card from the major arcana of the tarot: the hermit. The hood fell back and I saw my grandmother. I blinked. "Vivi," I said in my mind, "is that you?"

"It's me," she replied in her soothing kind voice that could comfort the entire universe.

"I miss you."

She smiled benevolently. "I am here. Just remember."

"Just remember? Remember what?"

She didn't answer. She was holding something under her cape and was staring down at it. I tried to get closer to see what she had, but it was hidden from view.

She raised her head and looked at me only she wasn't Vivi anymore, but Judith, the dog trainer, whose pickup I'd hit. And Judith said, "Remember meditation on Wednesday." She clapped her hands loudly and the vision cleared.

I felt movement around me, opened my eyes, and realized I was in yoga. It was Hyacinth who was clapping, bringing everyone back. "I'll see you all next week," she said.

I sat up, blinking in the bright light, and rubbed my eyes. I shivered and my skin had goose bumps. My grandmother saw dead people, but I never could. Why had she come? What did she want me to remember? And what did Judith have to do with it? I looked around, remembering Jake. He was already gone.

***

The next evening, Claire arrived early to class. I was sitting on the front porch with Shiny waiting for my students and watching Jake's blacked-out house. He was going out of his way to let me know he was finished with me. He was leaving at lunch time and I yelled, "The market's going to have a correction," but he didn't take the bait. He jumped into his car and sped off. He hadn't come back and I wondered where he was.

"What's on your mind?" Claire asked as she came up the walk and plopped down in a long ray of weak sunlight. A front was moving in and the temperature was dropping quickly. "You're a million miles away. Did you get the subpoena?"

"Not yet." I pulled the edges of my sweater together. "Were you able to change the date?"

"I tried." Claire removed the Coach bag from her shoulder and laid it on the porch. "Kev's lawyer refused to go along with it. The judge agreed we'd asked to reschedule too many times."

"Shit."

She sat down beside me. "Now the tide has turned. This week all the rulings went in Kev's favor. They're making me hand over my bank statements and tax returns."

"That's standard, isn't it?"

"There's a problem." Claire bent her knees, bit her lip, and rubbed her chin. "The money I paid you. Kev's saying I spent it on a lover."

Overhead, gray clouds scuttled past. "You wrote the check out to me."

She swung her head and raised one eyebrow. "The judge hates two things. One of them is gays."

I blinked. "Me?" I laughed, mainly with dismay. "But it's not true."

"As I have come to learn, it's only the appearance of truth that matters. They'll take a speck of truth and twist it. We're best friends. Why can't we be lovers? Why couldn't I shower you with monetary gifts?"

I felt cold, despite my heavy sweater. "You could, but you didn't. I'll take a lie detector test. I declared what you paid me on my taxes. We consult. That's it."

She rubbed Shiny's ears. "You've convinced me. I hope you can convince them. Now, if you were dating Daniel…"

I clicked my teeth and shook my head.

She raised her hands. "Just kidding." She stared across the lawn. "I hear things are heating up. You're going to his place for dinner." She flicked her eyebrows up and down.

"It's work," I said firmly.

"He likes you. He's a good guy."

"I have rules." I didn't want to talk about Daniel, not to my best friend, especially not to his sister. "He's got a top secret file I need to see. It's very hush, hush. I don't know why he can't just let me have it. I won't show anyone."

"Because he wants to see you."

"He's a colleague. Off limits. Period. Full stop."

"I warned him you had strict boundaries. That's one of the things he likes about you."

I tried to shift the conversation away from me. "Where's he been all week? We're progressing so slowly. I feel bad for Tiffany. She's a mess. A walking skeleton. She's more than half dead."

"Really." Claire's eyes opened wide. "Daniel didn't mention that. I guess that's why he agreed to help her. He has a big heart. When his first wife, Melissa, got sick, who do you think she called? Him. They'd been divorced for five years, he'd remarried, as had she, and he's the one who took her to chemo. Never mind that she was living here and he was in Gainesville. He came down and took her."

"Where was her new husband?"

"She had divorced number two by then. He wouldn't lift a finger to help her. He was rich and she took him for half of everything in the divorce, so I understand how he felt. Then she died and left everything she had to Daniel." Claire looked at me, one eyebrow raised. "He didn't tell you?"

"No."

"I'm not sure how much money was left after her medical bills were paid, but he got the house and it's worth a fortune. Too bad Natalie didn't see that coming. She was wife number two. She might not have been so quick to flee."

"How long were they married?"

"Under a year. That was the longest. His marriages don't last. They start out the same way and end the same. He picks the wrong people. Natalie didn't like all the attention he was paying to Melissa, and found someone else. Natalie filed for divorce, which she tried to stop once she learned about his inheritance. If he hadn't been transferred, I'm sure he would have stayed. He hates change. When he commits, he commits."

"What about wife number three?" I asked, wishing I wasn't so interested.

"That would be Jennifer. She's in Jacksonville. They got married after they'd known each other a month. It was a record, even for him. She asked for a divorce on Christmas Eve. I don't think she realizes that under Florida law the assets he had before he was married aren't divisible property. She won't get her hands on it."

"Does he have a pre-nup?"

"Are you kidding? He's sure whenever he falls in love, that this is it; it's going to last. He won't 'cheapen' things by bringing in lawyers." She raised her fingers and made quote marks. "He never expects things to end badly. Live and learn is not his motto."

From the distance, there was a low rumble of thunder. Shiny got up and wiggled into the narrow space between us. "When will his divorce be final?" I asked.

"Who the hell knows? He's waiting on Jennifer. He won't do anything and as far as he knows, she hasn't done anything."

"Maybe they'll get back together."

131

"They better not. You know the best way to get over someone is to find someone new. I'm talking to you here."

"I'm not listening." I put my hands over my ears.

Claire fixed me with her intense stare. "I was talking to Daniel and I realized you know everything about me, but I know next to nothing about you. Why is that?"

"I have an 8th house Sun and a Scorpio Moon."

That didn't appease her. "It's little stuff, like what your husband's name was, how long you were married, what he died from, why you moved here, or why you left DC."

I was instantly on guard. I was careful not to talk about my past. "How did you know I lived in DC?"

She made a face, forming deep frown lines. "Is it a secret? Daniel ran your car registration."

I swallowed hard. I couldn't believe it and I didn't appreciate it.

"Don't worry. He does it with people he likes."

"Isn't that illegal? An abuse of office?"

"It's routine in his line of work. He just types your name into a data base and sees what comes up. Speeding tickets, drunk driving charges, and the like."

"That's hardly fair."

"Maybe. But you know all about him. You looked at his chart."

"It's not the same thing."

"He didn't find anything."

That was a relief. For once I was glad I had taken Andre's last name for the duration of our short marriage. We were married less than a year and I hadn't found the time to legally change my name, so it was easy to revert to my maiden name after the incident.

"He said you didn't even have a speeding ticket," Claire added. "Though how could you in that car? I'm telling you, you should let Mike set you up with a new one. He'll get you a great deal."

Mike was another brother. "Let's wait until you sell the waterfront. How is that going?" I was desperate to change the subject.

"The sellers signed the contract. I've had a few buyers in for looks."

"Do you want an open house?"

"I'll let you know."

Our conversation ended as another student arrived. Trent, the stock broker, joined us as big fat drops of rain began to fall. We got up and went inside and the topic of conversation changed to Wall Street. "There's going to be a correction in August," I said, passing on my mother's prediction. "Sell in mid-July."

Chapter 16

On Friday night I put on old jeans and a faded t-shirt, grabbed Shiny and my briefcase, and headed to Daniel's for dinner. I deliberately dressed down. As I made clear to Claire, this was work, period. I couldn't imagine that Daniel was as taken with me as Claire insinuated or desired, but that was beside the point. I didn't like him checking into me and I was going to tell him that. My only concern was to find out what happened to Sierra.

Shiny loved going for rides and started dancing when I grabbed my car keys and her leash. She'd been Andre's dog and mostly indifferent to me until he was gone. One of the first things about him that caught my eye was how kind and thoughtful he was to his dog. If only he had been that considerate of me, things may have turned out differently for us. My grandmother said you could tell a lot about a person by how they treated their pets. She had a small terrier named Roxie whom she adored and my mother used to kick.

We went to the car. The front had rolled through and the clouds were gone and the sky was clear. It was April Fool's day and the temperature was in the low eighties. It was also Daniel's birthday, but I hadn't bought him a present; I was going to stay detached and professional. With Venus in pleasing aspect to Pluto, it was a good night to delve deep into a dark case. It was a good night for sex too, but I wasn't going down that road. I opened the passenger door, Shiny hopped in, and I rolled down her window. Across the street, the blinds on Jake's windows and front door were down, but at least the slats were open. He was out, his car was gone. Not wanting to, I wondered where he was.

I drove east toward the river and one of the most coveted zip codes in the county. We arrived ten minutes early and I drove around the block, not wanting to seem too eager. At seven on the dot, I pulled into a long driveway and drove up to the house. I parked behind a bright red pickup that was next to the Mustang and let Shiny out. The house had a white picket fence and was built on the top of a long slope and faced the river and the barrier island beyond. At the end of a long dock, a mid-sized boat rocked in the water. The sun was setting and the sky was a deep blue and the water looked black. Shiny was running around the grass smelling the flowers when Daniel emerged from the house. "You found the place."

The house address was well-marked and the road was old and famous. "Not a problem," I said, as Shiny raced toward him and I climbed the steps. A big wrap-around porch surrounded the sprawling one-story house that was painted a muted mint green. Daniel opened the screen door and we went inside.

The house smelled great and I was instantly hungry. I tried without success to identify the spices as I followed Daniel through the living room. It was sparsely decorated, the space of a bachelor. There were white tile floors, a black leather couch set, and glass tables set in black metal frames. Two large speakers flanking a fireplace belted out a Bob Seger tune and the supporting walls seemed to vibrate. Daniel grabbed his iPod and turned down the volume.

The floor plan was open and in the kitchen a pot boiled madly. "What do I smell?" I asked.

"Me," Daniel said, wiping sweat off his forehead. "I'm late. I was taking my long run. I went twenty miles. Dinner will be a while."

"What's a short run?"

"Anything less than ten. What's in the briefcase?"

"Work."

"On Friday night?"

"We have a baby to find. Where's the file?"

"In good time." He went to the stove and lifted the lid off the pot. Over his shoulder he said, "Anything else you want to say?"

"Why did you run my car registration?"

He turned around. "Habit, I guess."

"It's a violation of my privacy."

He picked up a spoon and held it in the air. "You're very mysterious. I like that. I'm talking about today. Anything special about it?"

He was incorrigible. "Happy birthday."

A smile split his face. "Did you get me a present?"

"I'm going to help you solve your case."

"But my birthday's today."

"Then, no."

"You could give me a kiss."

"That's not happening."

"Okay, later then. Put down your briefcase and get a glass of wine."

I promised myself I would have just one. I dropped my briefcase and sat down on a stool at the island and watched him open a chilled bottle of white wine and pour two glasses. He handed me one.

I took a sip. It was fruity, cold, and good. "Nice house," I said, staring past the black couch and out the wall of windows that overlooked the intracoastal.

"Full disclosure. My dead ex-wife left it to me."

I didn't tell him I already knew this. "What are you cooking?"

"Lobster étouffée, mushrooms stuffed with crab, and a salad."

"Sounds fancy."

"It is my birthday. And I love to cook." He shrugged. "Actually, I like to eat. That means cooking."

That had been another of Andre's draws. He liked to cook too. It was how he relaxed. He'd done all the cooking in our house, and having to assume that job after he was gone was a burden I still wasn't used to and didn't like.

"You never told me how you and Claire met," Daniel said as he stirred the bubbling sauce.

After being accused of being mysterious, I decided to be out front. "We met at an open house. I was on my way to meet a realtor and I got lost. I saw Claire's lawn sign and stopped to get directions." I didn't add that after I introduced myself, she asked if Mr. Sterling was in the car and did he want to come in for punch and cookies? Which was when I spontaneously lied: he can't, he's dead.

"Claire said you were looking on the bad side of town."

He knew the story. I wondered if he wore his cop hat when he was off duty and was checking our versions to see how they stacked up. "I didn't know any better. I'd only been in Coral Cove a week. Claire sorted me out."

"She knows how to sell. I'll give her that."

I couldn't disagree.

"Not only houses," he added, after a while.

137

"No." She'd pushed me back into astrology, but I didn't think he was talking about that. Claire was also likely trying to sell me to him.

"So, now you two collaborate," he said. "What exactly do you do for her?"

"I make sure her actions are aligned with the stars."

He laughed as if I were joking.

"She's a success," I said. "How many other realtors do you know who work with an astrologer?"

"None. But how did she know you were an astrologer? When you met, you'd been working at a university. You had abandoned astrology."

That was all true and must have come from her, because I hadn't told him. What I didn't know at the time was that I had burned my bridges behind me, and that even a minor nervous breakdown precluded any hope of finding another research job. But I kept this to myself. "She wanted me to sign a contract at the exact wrong time and I refused."

"What's the exact wrong time and how would you know if you'd given up astrology?"

Was Daniel more astute than I thought? I warned myself to tread carefully. "If you look on any calendar you can see the moon phase. You don't want to start anything in a dark Moon. Things are winding down then. It's better to wait."

"A dark Moon?"

"Like now. The period before a New Moon, before the Moon meets the Sun and gets lost in its light and you can't see it. That marks the start of a new monthly cycle. When the Moon overtakes the Sun and moves far enough away so that a crescent Moon is visible, then you can act."

"Did you learn this in graduate school or astrology school?"

"Astrology school. Though I grew up knowing it. My grandmother taught me the constellations when I was a kid. She used to say, when I was lost, to look to the stars." As I spoke the words, a shiver went up my spine, and I wondered if that was what my grandmother wanted me to remember. To look to the stars? I gazed out the window at the darkening sky.

"What are you looking at?" He followed my gaze.

"The stars are bright without a moon." I pointed at the window. "That's Regulus, the heart of the lion. It's one of the four royal stars of Prussia."

"Maybe some day you'll teach me the constellations." He looked at me with a slightly seductive smile.

I put on a blank face. "Maybe."

"Okay, then," he said, as if he could feel the chill I sent his way. "You could set the table if you feel like doing something."

"I feel like looking at the case file."

"You're no fun, you know that? Set the table and then you can look at it." He pointed to two china plates sitting on the counter with utensils wrapped in cloth napkins. He nodded in the direction of what I took to be the dining room. "And light the candles." He gave me a lighter.

The dining room was to the right of the living room on the south side of the house, also facing the water. Here were more floor-to-ceiling windows and the ever-present river. There was a long rectangular table that looked like it was made of plastic and I set the plates at the far opposite ends; one of us would have to eat with our back to the water. I turned on the lights of the chandelier and left the candles as they were. I wasn't going to send the wrong message.

I returned to the kitchen, where Daniel was cracking crab legs. "You'll find what you're looking for in the box by the couch."

I grabbed my wine and went to the living room and put the glass on the table. Shiny stayed with him. She was always underfoot when Andre cooked. I worked the lid off a cardboard box marked in black magic marker: Rossario, Sierra. The box was half filled with a stack of file folders. I took them out and rifled through them. The biggest was from the FBI and I scanned that first. The focus of the Feds' investigation was Ciro and Tiffany. Their cell phones, and the landlines in their house and Ciro's office had been tapped. Having learned nothing after three months of listening, the FBI decided the couple was very careful. They concluded the perpetrators were most likely members of a Mexican cartel and the child was most likely dead.

The child molester Huey Garson was a flash in the pan. He was arrested without evidence and the FBI privately concluded he was innocent, while publicly flaunting his guilt. As for the police investigation, the FBI was not impressed. Nonetheless, there were pages of interviews with nurses, doctors, cleaners, and staff at Miami Memorial Hospital where Sierra was born and where her pediatrician worked.

As for the staff at J'Adore Del Mar, the head of the security department and landscaping company had been intensively interviewed. There was a list of personnel for both, but only the guards on duty the night of the kidnapping had been interrogated. Both Tiffany's driver and housekeeper had been interviewed and were cleared of suspicion.

There was no physical evidence, no fingerprints or footprints. The kidnapper left nothing in his wake. The towel had been analyzed endlessly, but the resolution from the neighbor's security camera was too low to be of much help. That the kidnapper brought it with him showed planning and premeditation.

Daniel came in with Shiny, brandishing a spoon and looking domestic in an apron. How apropos for a Cancer Mars. He said, "Find anything new?"

"I think we should focus on the female employees at the security and landscaping companies."

"I'm already on it. I set up three interviews at Castle Security in West Palm Beach tomorrow afternoon."

I waited for him to invite me, but no invitation was forthcoming. Finally I said, "I'm free tomorrow afternoon." I had a morning consultation with Suzie's fiancé, but that was it for the day.

Daniel winced and made a face. "I should go on my own. I'd rather not have to explain you."

That was just unfair. He couldn't ask for my help and then take over and proceed on his own. "I should go. I might have some insight."

He scratched his head. "From astrology?"

"Sure. You'll get the women's birthdays, right? I'll look at their charts."

He looked skeptical and rightfully so. Without a birth time, the chart wouldn't have the critical angles, or the precise position of the fast-moving Moon. The chart would provide a measure of character, but nothing definitive.

"I thought you needed a time," Daniel said. "I'm not going to ask anyone that. No way. There would be no explaining it."

"I'll do a solar chart. Set the time for sunrise. See if any birth chart matches the chart of the kidnapping."

He stared up at the ceiling and I could see he was warming to the idea. When he lowered his eyes and looked at me, he said,

"All right. But I'll ask the questions and you keep in the background. Deal?"

I grunted my assent, not liking the deal at all. "Who are the women?"

"Three security guards who worked at J'Adore Del Mar at the time of the kidnapping. None was on duty that night, but we have to start somewhere." He swirled his spoon in the air with a flourish. "That's tomorrow. Now? Dinner's ready. Are you?"

I was starving and surprised to see my wine was gone. I returned the files to the box and replaced the top. I grabbed my empty glass and followed Daniel to the dining room where pots on hot plates were smoking. The table setting had been rearranged and now the plates lay across the width from one another, the chandelier was off, and the candles were alight. Daniel pulled out a chair and I sat down.

He went around to his place and we began dinner with a toast. "To us," he said.

"To solving the case," I clarified, as Shiny lay down by my feet.

"And that." He lifted his glass.

We filled our plates and I picked up my spoon and tasted the stew. It was delicious; salty and laced with onions and garlic in a rich heavy sauce. My diet would take a serious hit. I took another spoonful and noticed Daniel looking at me closely, eyebrows raised. I wondered what he was waiting for.

"How's your food?" he said.

I swallowed the bite. "Delicious."

"Just delicious?"

"Very delicious. The best étouffée I've ever had." Not that I ever remembered having it.

He pointed his spoon across the table. "Tell me, is your married name Sterling or is that your maiden name?"

"Why does it matter?"

"I'm curious. Did you take your husband's name or keep your own?" Thank god he didn't wait for me to answer and continued without a beat. "My wives took mine. Even when we divorced they kept it. Even when they remarried."

"What about wife number three?"

"We'll see what she does." He paused and threw back more wine. "What was your husband's name? Where did you meet? Why did you leave DC?"

I broke a steaming homemade roll in two. "Didn't they teach you in police school to ask one question at a time?"

"In police school they teach you to watch out for questions that people don't want to answer and try to avoid."

"That's what they teach psychologists too." He was staring, waiting, and I threw him a bone. "I met my husband in Austin. I left DC because I got a scholarship at the University of Texas. I left the family business. It was a bookstore. I was supposed to go back when I graduated and never did."

Daniel looked satisfied and resumed eating. After a moment, he said, "What did your father say when you didn't go back?"

My father now. At one time it was a sore subject, but no longer. "I don't know. I don't know my father."

"I don't believe that."

"You can believe what you like, but I never met him. I don't know his name. I know nothing about him."

"You have a right to know. Ask your mother."

"You don't think I did? She hates him."

"Why?"

It surprised me how easy it was to say. Perhaps because I'd said it all before to Andre, it was no longer the great secret I had to keep to myself. "All my mother will say is that my father betrayed her. He's no good. I'm better off not knowing him."

"I wonder what he did," Daniel said, swirling his wine.

"I don't know. Maybe she got pregnant and he promised to marry her and didn't. Or maybe he was married and promised to leave his wife and wouldn't. All I know was that there was some great betrayal that was beyond forgiveness."

Daniel looked shocked, as I guessed he might. He came from a big family and both his parents were still alive and living in his childhood home and having family dinners every Sunday that Claire couldn't miss.

"What about your mother?" he asked.

"She's an astrologer. I come from a long line. My grandmother was an astrologer and her mother before her."

"Why did you go to UT?"

"I got a scholarship to study math. My calculus teacher told me privately he hoped I wouldn't follow in my mother's footsteps and become a fortune-teller. He claimed astrology was bunk because astrologers didn't know about the precession of the equinox and I believed him. Overnight, I abandoned astrology. I never thought I'd go back."

"But your undergraduate degree is in psychology."

"I found math too cold. I liked biology and really liked behavioral psychology, which is actually close to astrology. I got a master's in clinical psychology and thought I would be a counselor."

"What happened?"

In truth? I met Andre who thought soft science was a waste of time. I was about to graduate and didn't want to leave him. He had a friend who was a professor of physiology who hired me as a PhD research assistant. I said, "I was interested in the association between mood and neurotransmitters and I met a professor who was studying the brain and wanted someone with clinical experience."

"Why didn't you finish?"

I wasn't going to tell him about my meltdown. "We did a lot of experiments on rats. I thought it was inhumane. I wanted to work with people. When An …when I was on my own, I decided to move and start over. I had enough course credits to get a master's and I did. I came here and met Claire. She wanted to learn astrology and there was no one in Coral Cove to teach her."

"Surely you'd make more money working as a psychologist."

"Surely. But when I moved here I needed to find work right away. I didn't have time to get certified by the state. That meant studying, taking an exam, and waiting for the results. Only then could I look for a job. Claire got me going immediately. She sent all her friends to me. She found six students to take a class."

"She's hard to say no to."

"That's why she's so good in sales."

"I thought it was because you gave her such excellent astrological advice."

He said this with a smile and I had to laugh. He was smarter than I initially gave him credit for. "Well, that too."

"What happened to the bookstore?"

"It closed after my grandmother died."

"When was that?"

"I was a senior in college." I didn't add that I had promised to return when I graduated to help her with the store, and I was glad I didn't have to keep my promise. Instead, I went to grad school, met a professor, got married, and had a baby.

"What was the bookstore called? The Occult? What is that? Black magic?"

I looked at him. He knew much more about me than my lack of speeding tickets and DUI convictions. This was much more than the simple checking Claire had alluded to. At least he hadn't found anything, which I was thankful for. I finished my wine and answered his question. "The bookstore was called the Occultarium. It's the opposite of a solarium. Not a room that holds light, but a room that holds hidden knowledge."

"Was your grandmother a witch?"

"What? No. She was a psychic. And an astrologer. A very good one. Why would you call her a witch?"

"She held séances. She communicated with the dead. The FBI was watching the store. They were also watching your mother. Did she advise presidents on astrology?"

"No," I said, suddenly feeling hot. Daniel had checked me out to the extent he'd run my name through the FBI? I was glad I hadn't taken my husband's name. Morgan Sterling had no nominal tie to Andre LeCuyer.

"Who did she advise?" Daniel asked as he stabbed lettuce.

"High level politicians. Not presidents, though she wanted to. She thought Reagan was getting bad information and would have counseled him differently."

Daniel refilled my wine. "I can't imagine a president listening to an astrologer."

"Yet it happened. You may not realize it, but you use astrology all the time."

He sat back as if affronted. "Before I met you, I did not."

"Let's see, the Sun is now in Aries and in the northern hemisphere that means it's spring and it will soon be time to plant. Good luck planting your flowers in January when the Sun is in Capricorn and it's going to freeze. Or, look at the Moon. When the Moon is full, the tides are higher and since our blood is ninety-seven percent water, we're also affected. There are more hospital room visits, more domestic abuse. Emotions are out there."

Daniel was listening carefully. "I'll grant you there's more crime at a Full Moon."

"There you go. The great thing about astrology is, you can see it in action. Astrology was the original science. All you have to do is observe it. Two thousand years ago, when a royal baby was born, astrologers used to watch the sky. They noted that babies born with the Sun in Aries were great warriors. They were brave, headstrong, impulsive, and always ready to fight."

"Sounds like me."

"Because you have an Aries Sun." I paused and took a sip of wine. "Babies born with the Sun in Taurus were quiet, cautious, and wanted to keep the peace. They didn't like going off to war, which was a good thing because they were terrible at fighting. Where they excelled was farming and cooking."

"Sounds like me too."

"Because you have a Taurus Moon."

"You know my chart off by heart? You must have studied it."

I put down my glass. "It's my job. I remember charts."

He rested his elbows on the table and leaned forward. His plate was clean. "What else do you know about me?"

I pictured his horoscope in my mind. "You have the Mars in Cancer; you're fighting for the homeland. Also your family."

"Why am I so bad at marriage?"

His wives were ruled by Uranus which was opposite the Moon and Jupiter. I picked my words carefully. "Off hand, I'd say your women don't have as deep an emotional connection to you, as you have with them."

He gazed into my eyes. "Tell me more."

"Your Venus is in Pisces. You're idealistic when it comes to women. Maybe you don't see them for who they really are."

He thought about that for a moment. "What about kids?"

Neptune was on the 5th house cusp. "There's more idealism there." But the house was ruled by Jupiter which stood with the Moon, and both were opposite Uranus, signifying trouble.

"But?" he said, as if he could read my mind.

"But, Neptune is there and it's slippery. It's not the planet of the real."

"So kids won't happen."

"I didn't say that." I tried never to speak in absolute terms.

"The doctor did." Daniel grabbed the wine bottle and reached over and refilled my glass and then his own.

I waited for him to finish and to explain.

He put the bottle down. "I had mumps when I was 17. My mother apparently neglected to get me vaccinated. I guess that happens when you're the third son. The mumps infected my groin. The doctor said I'll probably never have children. Of course, that's what I want more than anything."

My Scorpio Moon was taken aback by his honesty. Shocked, really. But there was Jupiter ruling the 5th with his Moon; and he would want kids very much. Need them.

"I'm honest about this. Up front. I don't mind adopting. I just don't think I'll ever have any of my own."

Why was he telling me? But now I knew the issue between him and Tiffany.

"I'm an open book," he said, as if he'd heard my unasked question. Then he added, as if an after-thought, "Morgan Spica Sterling. What does Spica mean?"

I closed my eyes. I thought I'd purged my middle name long ago. I left it off my driver's license and my tax returns, but it was still on my birth certificate. If he found it, that meant he had dug deeply. I said, "It's a star." The jewel of Virgo. "I don't use my middle name."

"I can't call you Spica?"

"No."

The light was dancing in his dark eyes. "Spike, then."

"Danno, I'm warning you."

His eyes narrowed and the light in them went out. "No one calls me Danno."

"I'm pretty sure Tiff did."

"All right, truce." He held up his flattened palms in surrender. "Truce."

"Now it's your turn. Tell me something about yourself you never told anyone. A secret."

I leaned back in my chair. That was a demand I wasn't up to.

"Come on. I trusted you. Let's see if you trust me."

The one thought that came to my mind, I pushed away. I would never tell him what I had done that filled my sleepless nights with guilt and crushing remorse. "I can't think of any."

"Try."

I drank more wine, swallowing my words. I wasn't going to say anything more.

"Well?" he prodded.

If he wasn't going to give up, my only recourse was to throw him off course. "All right. I did something I can never undo."

"What?" He leaned farther forward. "I won't tell anyone. You can tell me. You'll feel better. Confession is good for the soul. It's like opening the closet door and shining a light in the darkness and seeing there really are no monsters."

"Sometimes there are. Ask Tiffany."

He straightened, swirling his wine glass. "Did you kidnap a baby?"

I looked at him. "No."

"Did you kill someone?"

"Don't be crazy."

"Okay, you're going to make me guess." He bit his lip and looked at the ceiling. "You robbed a bank."

"I'm not going to say anything more."

"How bad can it be? Something you can never undo. You had an affair when you were married and now your nameless husband is dead and you feel awful."

"No."

"Just no?"

"Just no."

"Okay. You killed your husband. But it was an accident."

"I didn't kill him."

"How did he die?"

"I've had enough of this."

He held up his hand. "Fine. Don't trust me. I told you my most personal secret. I trusted you, but you won't tell me what you can't undo."

"Getting the mumps isn't doing something. And, Mr. Honesty, I doubt I'm the first one you've told."

"You're right." He jumped up. "Are you done?"

I was relieved he let it go. "Dinner was delicious. You're an excellent cook. Thank your Mars in Cancer."

"I've got dessert. A caramelized flan."

Any further thought of my diet disappeared. I would worry about it tomorrow.

I helped him clear the plates. He put them down on the floor for Shiny to lick. He had left a portion of his étouffée for her.

He brought two glass bowls out of the fridge, drizzled liqueur over the top, then fired up a blow torch and set the liqueur on fire. While it flamed, we returned to the table and dug in as the interrogation resumed.

"What's your mother doing in Africa?"

Had I told him she was there, or had it come from Claire, or from his own independent nosing around? I took another sip of wine and knew I was over my limit. I had to keep my mind; watch my thoughts and my words.

"She is in Moroni, isn't she?"

I was certain I hadn't told him that. "She's an advisor to the president."

"How does she advise him?"

"On how to stay alive. People are always trying to assassinate him. Is she still on an FBI list?"

"That, I wouldn't know. Do you miss her?"

It was the FBI who told my mother the IRS was looking into her returns and she might have trouble with a congressman who was about to be indicted on corruption and tax evasion. Thanks to the tip, she escaped before any legal papers were drawn up. She would be arrested if she returned.

"Is that silence a yes or a no?" Daniel asked.

"I talk to her all the time. I miss my grandmother more. I was closer to her. I never said goodbye."

"Did she die suddenly?"

"Yes. I was in Austin. She was dead a month before I knew she was gone. I'll never forgive myself."

"How could you not know?"

"My mother never told me."

"What?"

"They weren't speaking. They had a falling out when I was in middle school."

Daniel looked horrified. "What happened?"

"That I don't know. Something bad. Up until then we all lived together above the store. We moved out."

"You have siblings?"

"No. I'm the only one. My mother and I moved out. My grandmother got pneumonia and when she was in the hospital, something happened. I don't know what. I was never to talk to her again."

"But you did."

"When I could, yes. Not as often as I wanted. My mother forbade it. Her feud was supposedly my feud. My grandmother was supposedly screwing us both. How? I don't know." I knew all the questions Daniel was going to ask, because Andre had asked them before him.

"I can't imagine not talking to your own mother."

If he knew how they were together, he would be able to. They fought like cats and armadillos.

"So she never met your husband."

We had circled back to there. "My grandmother? No. I met him after she died."

"I'm talking about your mother."

"She did meet him." She didn't like him. He was a professor of immunology and she found university education pretentious, but I wasn't going to say that.

"Did she come to your wedding?"

"No."

Daniel was taken aback, shaking his head with disbelief. "No?"

I got married in France, but that was another thing I didn't want him to know. I figured as long as he didn't learn my married name, he could do all the checking he wanted, and would never find out what I wanted to forget. If he did learn my married name, he would know everything; all the lies I'd told to keep the past buried.

"Well?" Daniel said.

"She was already in Africa and couldn't make it," I said shortly. I'd had enough of his interrogation. "What about you? Did your parents come to all of your weddings?"

"Of course. Everyone came. It's expected."

Daniel opened a new bottle of wine and refilled my glass. I'd lost count how many glasses I'd had and it was enough. I was feeling lightheaded, a little woozy, and loose-tongued. I didn't like to talk about myself like this. Daniel had pried more out of me in one evening than Andre had learned in almost four years.

Bob Segar began playing again on the iPod. The music selection was repeating itself. Daniel jumped up and changed the playlist and a slow Emmylou Harris ballad began to play. I wondered if the music was supposed to set the tone and decided it was time to leave.

We cleared the table. Daniel offered coffee.

"I'll be up all night."

"That's all right. I'm not doing anything." He raised his eyebrows.

"I have to work in the morning. I hate to eat and run, but I need to go."

He put down his wine glass and took my hand. An electric shock shot up my arm. "Maybe I can help undo whatever it was that you did."

He held onto my hand. His skin was hot, radiating heat. "You can't."

He tightened his hold on my palm, his grip, solid and hot. "You can trust me, you know."

He was so close, I felt his wine-sweetened breath on my face. "I do trust you."

"It can't be that bad."

I turned and stared over his shoulder down at the lights on the road and the dark shadow of the water beyond. "I sold something that didn't belong to me."

"What?"

I sighed deeply. In my mind, it was theft. That I was in a bind, desperate for money, broken with loss and not thinking straight, was all beside the point. I'd committed a criminal offense. That I only realized it after the fact, when it was too late, mattered not.

He ran his thumb lightly across the back of my hand. "It can't be as bad as you think."

"It is."

"What did you sell? Drugs?"

"No."

"Kids?"

The absurdity made me laugh. "No."

"Your body?"

"A book." I just spat it out.

He closed his eyes and made a face. "A book."

"A rare astrology book."

"Hardly seems serious. Who did it belong to? The bookstore? Your dead grandmother?"

I wish. "My mother."

"What did she say?"

I looked at him. "Are you kidding? She doesn't know. If she finds out, she'll never talk to me again. I'm trying to find it and buy it back."

"Any luck?"

"None at all."

"Tell your mother what you did. It's just a book."

"A very valuable book. I didn't know how valuable it was until after I sold it. I'm worried it's her retirement fund. She's counting on it and it's gone. I feel terrible. I don't know what to do."

Daniel squeezed my hand. "Everything will turn out. She's your mother."

He was foolishly optimistic. "Exactly. You don't know her."

"When did you sell it?"

"Four years ago this fall. I sold it to pay the down payment on my house."

"How much did you get?"

"Fifty thousand."

Daniel whistled. "A book is worth that much?"

"At least double that. I just didn't know."

He raked his hair with his hand and stared up at the ceiling. "Who would know?"

He was dazed by the price of the book, not what I'd done.

"All right. I'll help you find it." He lowered his gaze and looked into my eyes. "We'll get it back. Don't worry about it."

I realized he was still holding my hand. I could smell his sweat and it smelled good. He was going to help me. The relief at spilling my secret was immediate and immense. The world didn't end. I wasn't arrested or reviled. The officer of the law wasn't eyeing me with hate and scorn. In fact, I realized with some shock, the opposite. I extracted my hand and stepped back. "I have to go."

His face loomed dangerously close and I wondered if he was going to kiss me. "You don't have to leave."

"Yeah, I do." I grabbed my belongings and ran out of there.

Chapter 17

I went home and couldn't sleep. I felt light-headed and light-hearted. I counseled clients that confession was good for you, and it was. A burden the weight of a boulder had lifted from my chest allowing space for my heart to swell. Years of anguish and worry fell away and I felt warm and good. Which was bad. I exhaled slowly and stared out the window at far away stars. I wasn't ready. I didn't want this. I was supposed to be fine on my own. Now, I felt like a caught fish being played. I was hooked, filled with an illusion of freedom, as the line slowly shortened. Maybe this time the catch would be okay.

No, screamed my mind. I knew my chart well enough to know that things didn't end well. And Daniel was dangerous. I don't know how he did it, but he got to me. I thought he was a medi-ocre investigator and he surprised me. I didn't like him digging into my past, of knowing what happened in DC, or suspecting things I could never admit to. I may have admitted one secret, but it wasn't the only one, and it wasn't the worst. Lies spoken could never be unsaid. Deceit could never be undone. It would stand between us always, like a wall. Nothing could ever happen.

At some point I fell asleep, and awoke to the screech of the alarm, which I hated. I got up tired to a day that was overcast and humid. Clouds were low and there was no sign of the sun. I took Shiny for a walk, ate breakfast, and went to my office to prepare for Elliot Robinson. If his father donated large sums of money to Suzie's father's political campaign, my guess was my mother also knew Elliot's father. One way or another, whatever happened in the session would likely get back to her. I had to be good.

Elliot was late. By 10:10, I wondered if he was coming and checked the transits. Suzie said he wanted a reading, but with Neptune ruling the 7th (me), and the Sun getting ready to oppose Saturn (fear, depression), I didn't think he was happy about coming. Just as I was about to give up on him, he materialized, shooting up the drive in a quiet, black Maserati. He dragged himself up the porch steps reeking of pot and peering through bloodshot eyes and not looking at all like someone who couldn't wait to have his chart read. He wore oversized blue jeans that scraped the ground and hung low on his waist, showing the band of his boxers. A navy untucked button-down shirt with half the buttons undone revealed a bare chest. He had brown hair that might have been blond if he'd washed it. He was sprouting facial hair as if he were trying to grow a beard, without success. Other than the car, the wealthy background my mother so extolled was not in evidence.

He apologized for being late and seemed sheepish as he did so, though he offered no explanation. Nonetheless, here he was and I took him to my office. He sat where I told him to sit and stared at the beginner's chart I handed him. I began by saying, "I get the feeling you don't want to be here."

"Suzie wanted me to come. She said there's something you wanted to tell me."

Of course she did. That wasn't going to happen. "Actually, it's the reverse. This is your session. You get to talk to me."

"I have nothing to say. I don't believe in any of this."

"That's fine. You're not alone. Do you have a problem with Suzie coming?"

"She can do what she wants."

Good answer. "If you want to leave, you can. I'll refund half your session."

He looked at the clock, trilling his fingertips on the coffee table. "It goes till eleven?"

"That's right." I wasn't going over-time, just because he was late.

"All right, read my chart. Suzie will want to know what you said."

I did my job. I ran through his chart, explaining what his Sun, Moon and the chart ruler wanted, and what stood in their way. I pointed out a Venus–Neptune contact, which was a talent for music. It was also a limitless desire for pleasure, which made him laugh. "Well called," he said.

"With that combination, you need to set limits. Establish boundaries. Push yourself."

"I'm not so good at that."

"Neptune also rules drugs. With Venus, likely recreational. You could go overboard there."

"You think?"

I fanned the air by my face. "Do you use every day?"

"Yep."

"I'm not here to judge. When you get into something, you forget how it was when you weren't in it. You might like the old normal. Have you tried cutting down?"

"Nope."

Okay then. "I hear you're getting married."

"According to you. You're the one planning it."

"Not me. It's up to you and Suzie to decide whether and when you'll marry."

"Your mother picked the date."

I silently cursed her. "My mother's not always right."

"According to Mrs. Stryker, she's never wrong."

"Well, Elliot, everyone is wrong at some point in their life. And you do have a say."

"Let's get it over with. That's my thought on the matter."

I hated his lackadaisical attitude and his reluctance to take charge of his life. I decided to push him, get him to react. "You're not worried you're too young?"

"Because I'm younger than Suzie? Did she say that?"

That provoked a mild response. I said, "I'm not at liberty to discuss anything Suzie and I spoke about. In the same vein, I won't mention to her anything we speak about."

He sat back in the chair, drumming his fingers on his thighs. His jeans were worn out and ripped at the knees. Or maybe they were new and he bought them this way. He said, "I just want her to be happy."

Another good answer. "Then you'll make a good husband. After you marry, what will you do for money?"

"My dad will double my allowance."

"That's all right with you?"

He lifted a shoulder in a half-hearted shrug. I wanted to shake him.

"Where will you live?"

"My parents are buying us a house."

"Don't you want to achieve something on your own?"

He looked at me with his lazy, bloodshot, bleary eyes. "This is okay."

"So, basically, you're selling yourself out." I gave up on the subtle approach and was determined one way or another to snap him out of his lethargy, wake him up, get him to take charge of himself.

He remained slouched in his nonchalance, pressed back into the chair. "I'm not selling out. My parents like her and want to see me married. I love Suzie and she loves me. Why not do it? We're great together."

"Great how?"

"You know." He lifted an elbow.

Okay. I should have expected that. What else could he say? While it was Suzie's duty to discuss the topic with him, it was my duty to see if he recognized a problem. I said, "How often do you have sex?"

"Every day. Every other day. Something like that," he said, proudly.

I took a sip of water. "And how long would you say the whole act lasts?"

He looked at the clock. "Ten, fifteen minutes."

Hmm. "Is that all, um, penetration?"

"What?"

"As in the physical act of union. A literal conjunction. You and her being together as one."

He scratched his head. "Maybe not that long."

"How long?"

"I never thought much about it."

I glanced at the chart. The 5th house of sex and romance was ruled by Mars, which was in Taurus, a sign that it hated, and the sign opposite to where it wanted to be. It was square the Moon, which ruled the first, which made me think the problem was physical, though it could be emotional, or related to his mother.

"What do you see?" he asked.

"Mars square the Moon."

"Is that bad?"

"Do you enjoy sex?"

"Of course."

"Is it satisfying?"

"I believe great was my word for it."

"Great for you?"

"Yes." He was getting a little riled, as Moon square Mars was apt to do.

"And for her?"

"I guess."

"You guess? Does she have orgasms?"

His face turned bright red, again betraying the Moon's relationship with Mars, the planet of blood. "I guess."

"You can feel it," I said. "During a woman's orgasm, the vaginal wall ripples with waves of contractions. There's a pulsing."

"I know," he said, looking at his hands.

"Women typically need prolonged stimulation. It doesn't happen immediately."

"I know," he said more stridently.

The clock chimed. Our time was up. This typically happened; at the end of a session, I'd reach the topic of interest. I said, "As a neurobiochemist I know that cannabis has vascular side effects. It blunts the reflexes, constricts the wrong blood vessels and relaxes others that need to work. It acts as a depressant. Viagra can help."

He was pulling out his wallet. "I don't need medication. How much do I owe you?"

I told him and he counted out the cash.

"You can go to a clinic. Pay in cash. That way there won't be a paper trail."

"I'm fine." He shook my hand.

"It was nice to meet you," I said.

He practically ran from the room, took a flying leap off the porch, jumped into his coupe, and tore out of the driveway, tires screeching.

I watched him turn the corner. Now it was up to him. I gave him information and he could do with it what he wanted. I liked him and I wondered if he smoked pot to have better sex and when that failed, whether he smoked more to shut himself down. Quite a shame, because according to his chart, he was a great musician, and could make something of his talent if he tried. Which made me think of well-meaning meddling parents who enabled their children's irresponsibility and hindered their growth. Unlike mine, who let me know from an early age I was on my own.

Chapter 18

An hour later, Daniel arrived. He jumped from the Mustang, rearranged his hair with a shake of his head, and crossed the lawn smiling to himself. The sight of him simultaneously made my heart flutter and my knees weak. He'd seen me worse than naked and he was still smiling. It was a warning if there ever was one. I opened the door as he climbed the steps, admonishing myself to keep cool, and reminding myself of my code. I didn't get involved with clients. And I didn't sleep with married men. No clients, no married men, I repeated in a mantra as I stepped onto the porch.

Shiny brushed past me and ran to him. He sunk down on one knee to pet her. "Ready for your first interview?" he asked.

"Let me grab my iPad."

He rubbed Shiny's head and she leaned into him. "I looked into the recovery of rare books. I need the name of the book and the author. Also a copy of the bill of sale, a copy of the certificate of authenticity, and anything else you might have."

"I'll have to find it."

"You know the title and author, right?"

"Of course." I had it written on an index card in my office. I went and got it.

Daniel frowned at the card. The title went on for four lines. "Send it to me in an email so I get the right spelling. Then I'll list it on ILAB."

"What's that?"

"It stands for the International League of Antiquarian Booksellers. It's a Swiss organization that runs an online data-bank for rare books. Within that site is a list for books for sale and stolen books. If anyone lists your book, you'll get an email alert. Who knows, it could be listed now."

It gave me a ray of hope, to imagine that I could actually undo what I did.

"We'll look for the buyer too, so get me his name and any other information you have about him as soon as you can."

I walked down the steps and knelt beside Shiny. "Thank you."

He smiled into my eyes. "My pleasure. You're helping me. I'll return the favor."

"Only I'm getting paid."

He held my gaze. "We'll work it out."

He winked then, or maybe it was a blink. Whatever it was, brought back the light-headedness and then a stern silent admonishment to focus on work. I tried to block the scent of his sweat as I put Shiny in the house. I recognized the smell: it was a scent of sex. *Focus on work*, I told myself, as I waited for him to open the car door. *Focus on work.*

The sky had cleared, the sun beamed down, and traffic on I-95 was light. Just before noon we stopped at a hamburger joint in Jupiter and sat on opposite sides of a booth. The waiter came and took our order. Daniel wanted a cheeseburger with fries and iced tea and I ordered the same. So much for my diet.

Daniel handed me a piece of paper. "Here's the information you wanted."

I unfolded the paper. On it was scribbled three names and three birth dates of the women we were going to interview. "Well done," I said.

"Claire didn't know how this would help. She said a birth date without a place and time was too imprecise."

And she was right.

"She said you didn't have to go in person. You could just look at a chart. It would tell you if someone was capable of kidnapping or not."

He was exactly right, but I wanted to go. I wanted to see him in action, make sure he asked the right questions.

"You could wait in the car," he added. "You don't have to come in."

I needed a reason to be more involved, and I found one. "Without the time, I won't know the houses. Since the first house shows appearance, I might be able to figure out what sign is rising from the way these ladies look. I have to see them."

"That just seems so wrong."

"It worked with you. It will also let me know where the Moon is, and what planets are on the angles. I want to know if any angular planets were active the night of the kidnapping."

"Which means?"

I paused while the waiter brought our drinks. When he was gone, I said, "The natal chart shows the sky the moment you were born. It freezes the planets in time. But the planets don't stop moving, they keep going. Those are the transits; where the planets are in real time. As they move, they impact the natal chart."

"Meaning?"

"Transits activate the natal planets. They come to life. If a natal chart shows an innate tendency toward violence or rash action, I want to know if that tendency was in effect when Sierra was taken."

"I'm confused."

"Luckily I'm not."

"Is this what you teach in your class?"

"This is pretty basic, actually. In class we apply this method and others to real charts."

The waiter came with our food and we began to eat. Daniel put down his burger, took a drink, swallowed and said, "Just remember, let me ask the questions."

"What if I think of something you don't ask?"

"Tell me after."

"Won't that be too late?"

He picked up his drink. "I know what questions to ask. And I don't want to introduce you. Or, I might introduce you, but I won't say what you do." He took a healthy sip.

"*Fine*," I said, too testily.

Daniel put down his drink and leaned across the booth. "Look, my lieutenant doesn't know what I'm doing. This is an unofficial inquiry. I have no authorization and you *really* have none. You aren't a police officer. This isn't an official case. You're not supposed to know anything about it. I don't want to introduce you because I don't want anyone searching for you online and finding out who you are."

"All right, fine," I said more gently. I knew I was lucky that he agreed I could come in the first place.

"If someone finds out I've reopened the case, there could be trouble. It could mean my badge. I'm kind of on probation."

I waited for him to go on, to tell me about the shooting in Jacksonville, but he went back to his burger.

"When my mother worked with the police, they acknowledged her help," I said. "They considered her a consultant. They asked her to sit in on their interviews and allowed her to ask questions."

Daniel laid down the half-eaten burger. "That may fly in liberal and progressive DC, but this is the south. I'm sorry to disappoint you, but no matter how good you are, the police here will never acknowledge your help." He grabbed a french fry and dragged it through a mound of ketchup. "Though I do."

Well, I wasn't doing it for acknowledgement, and the truth was, Daniel had softened his anti-astrological stance considerably in the last twelve days. He recognized my help and I thought he needed it. "I'll be quiet," I said.

Lunch was fast and we were back on the road in forty-five minutes. From Jupiter it was a short hop on I-95 to the West Palm headquarters of Castle Security. Daniel had set up three thirty-minute interviews to run consecutively, and as we drove, I familiarized myself with the three birth charts. Without knowing the houses and just looking at the aspects, the three women looked innocuous to me. I knew that even with a birth time, even with activated natal planets, it would be impossible to say with certainty a suspect committed a crime. Since the nature of astrology was symbolic, one thing could mean many things. This was where free will came in. You got to choose how to use the energy.

We reached the Okeechobee exit and almost immediately pulled into a small strip mall. Castle Security was on the far end and had a banner in the window announcing the name. I put away my iPad and Daniel parked. "Ready to work your magic?"

"It's science," I said, as I unclasped my seatbelt.

We crossed the pavement in radiating heat and I guessed it was about 85 degrees under a cloudless sky. The sun beat down with white intensity. We entered Castle Security and the air conditioning was off and the place was stifling. Daniel mopped his brow as he strode to the counter. A fat aging man with a wisp of hair on his head looked up. Daniel quickly whipped out his badge and hid it just as fast. The man beckoned us to the back. He opened a door on the right and a woman dressed in a dark pantsuit stood up and he introduced Molly Lambert. We were waved into a small room across the hall and he turned on the lights. "You can use my office."

It had a window AC unit that was loud and cold. He left and Daniel introduced himself to Molly without mentioning me. He flashed his badge again and there was no way she had the opportunity to read his name. "Thank you for coming," he said, as we all sat down. He took the managerial chair, Molly took the chair opposite, and I took the chair in the corner where I could see them both. Daniel took out a small recorder, and I got out my iPad.

"This is an informal inquiry," he said. "You can call me Daniel." He smiled the rakish smile that showed his dimple and Molly returned it.

She didn't mind being taped. "I just hope I can help."

She had brown hair pulled back in a ponytail, a round face, pudgy cheeks, and weighed about one hundred and sixty pounds. I knew from her birth data that she was my age. From her looks, weight, and demeanor, I guessed she had Cancer rising, like me. Moon people were eager to help and had a tendency to gain weight. Her Moon was in Sagittarius, which made it all the more likely. She had Mars in Cancer, like Daniel. With Cancer being all about safety, and Mars representing the military and the police, I knew

Mars was connected to her work. I tweaked her chart, changing the time, moving Mars closer and further from the horizon to see how it interacted with the house of the career.

At the same time, I listened to Daniel's questions. He was running through Molly's history and she confirmed she had worked for the company for ten years, but had not been on duty the night of the kidnapping. She'd been at J'Adore Del Mar for only three weeks when Sierra was taken. Soon after, her husband got relocated and they moved to Palm Beach. She asked for a transfer, which she got, and hadn't been back to the gated community since. She'd never seen Tiffany or Sierra. She hadn't been interviewed by the police at the time of the kidnapping because she hadn't been working the night in question. She had two children herself, one had been Sierra's age and was now five, and she couldn't imagine living through that hell. She would do everything she could to help find the missing child.

"Has there been a break?" Molly asked, clasping her hands on her lap. "Do you think she's still alive?"

I looked at how the transits stacked up against Molly's chart and her progressed planets. There were no violent aspects in her natal chart and none had formed around the time Sierra was taken, which led me to believe she wasn't involved.

"There hasn't been a break," Daniel said. "I'm tying up loose ends. Looking at the cold case one last time." He crinkled his nose, as if drawing her into his conspiracy. "Did you hear any gossip on the job? People talking? Pointing fingers?"

"Everyone was shocked. We're the security company. We're responsible. We're supposed to keep people safe."

"Was there any backlash from the incident?" Daniel asked. "Did anyone lose their job? Was there an internal investigation?"

"Nope. No one lost their job. The manager looked into it and found no evidence of any wrongdoing. I like my job. We're treated well. We get good health care and a good pension. People don't come and go. We're in it for the long haul. To our bosses, that's important. Especially seeing it's a security company. We're checked out. We have our fingerprints run before we start and every two years after that. I want to keep my job. I don't take shortcuts. There was nothing untoward that night. All the visitors' cars were checked in. The on-foot patrol filled out their reports. No one came or left anonymously. There's camera footage at the entrance. It was all above board."

Daniel sat back in the chair. "What do you think happened?"

"I think the mother was lax. She was drinking too much, not looking after her baby. She should have locked up her house before she passed out. She was as much to blame as anyone."

"She wasn't drunk," I said, coldly.

Molly turned and looked at me. Daniel glared and I winced and clamped my mouth closed. Molly said, "I'm just saying what I heard."

"Much of what was reported in the paper about Tiffany was untrue," I said.

Daniel cleared his throat. "Do you think anyone could have come by boat?"

"No," Molly said. "There were eyes on the beach. Video cams. No one came that way. I heard the kidnappers climbed the south wall. It's about twenty feet tall, but there was a trellis for bougainvillea. The vines were recently trimmed. Maybe landscaping had something to do with it."

"Why do you think that?" Daniel asked.

"Because of the timing of the trimming. The trellis was exposed. It was like a ladder."

"Were you suspicious of anyone in landscaping?" Daniel asked.

Molly shrugged. "Honestly, I never paid them much attention."

Daniel leaned forward and hit a button on the recorder. His interview was apparently over. "Thank you, Molly. If we need anything further, we'll be in touch." He gave her a piece of paper with his number and his first name. "Don't hesitate to call me if you remember anything."

"Ahem." I raised my hand and got Daniel's attention.

"Is there something you would like to add?" he asked, raising his eyebrows in a sign that I should shut up. Nonetheless, I asked a question he'd neglected to. "Was there anyone working with you who wanted a baby and couldn't have one?"

"No. There were only three women working security at Del Mar and we were close. We still are."

"Anyone in landscaping?" I asked.

"That I wouldn't know." Molly paused and looked up at the ceiling. "There was a lady in the health club. She was a fitness trainer, married to another trainer. He was real buff. I heard they wanted a baby and there was trouble in that department. It was funny because he looked like such a stud."

"Do you know their names?" I asked.

"I have no idea. I just saw them through the glass window of the gym."

"Do you use towels on your job?"

"Excuse me?"

"Like a hand towel or a bath towel?"

"No."

"You don't have one in the guard house or in your car?"

"I have one in my car. It's old and ratty. I use it to clean the kids' hands."

"Thank you."

Daniel thanked her again and escorted her to the door. When she left, he closed it and turned around. I raised my hands. "I'm sorry."

He walked toward me, filling me with the scent of his musky sweat. He pulled a rueful smile. "I liked it that you stood up for Tiff. I've learned to let what people say about her go. Next time, *try* to stay in the background. If I neglect to ask something you want to know, write it on a piece of paper and pass it to me."

"Yes, sir," I said with a formal salute.

He went to the desk and sat down. "Did you get anything from that?"

"I think we need to track down the trainers. I didn't see anything in the police file about them. They would have towels."

"I mean, did you get anything from the astrology."

Oh. "I think she had Cancer rising. I don't think it's her."

"Me either."

There was a knock at the door. The next guard had arrived and Daniel jumped up.

He interviewed the other two women and I sat as instructed and said nothing. The stories were similar. Both had children. Neither were working the night of the crime; an all-male crew was on duty. They were both long-term workers and liked their jobs and did them well. No mistakes had been made, though a baby was still taken. After the kidnapping, the manager of the gated community removed the trellis and added a barbed wire fence in addition to the concrete wall. The bougainvillea had grown back and no more egregious crimes had been committed in the gated community since. Both believed landscaping may have been involved. Neither remembered a trainer who couldn't get pregnant.

We finished at 4:30 and headed back to Coral Cove. The classic rock station was playing and Daniel was humming along. Occasionally he'd glance my way and smile. I wondered what it would be like to kiss him.

But he wasn't thinking about me.

"I think we're making progress."

I had to agree. "Two weeks ago you thought astrology was stupid."

He chuckled. "That's not what I'm talking about. We're making progress on the case. We're eliminating suspects."

"And adding new ones."

"I have the feeling we're going to crack the case. You feel it?"

I didn't. I guess that's what happened when you lacked the psychic gene. I said, "I hope so." There was a lot resting on it.

"I go by instinct." Daniel took one hand off the wheel and thumped his abdomen. "The gut never fails."

"That must be hard to explain to your boss."

He pulled a repentant smile. "I'll say. You'd be even harder to explain. Why I got an astrologer."

"I don't think you *got* an astrologer."

He glanced at me, eyebrows raised. "I'm working on it."

I didn't like what his words did to me, or the heat they brought to me, and I was glad when his phone rang. It was his brother, Mike. Daniel listened for a moment and then said, "Sorry. I'll be there soon." He hung up and threw his phone on the dash. "I forgot I was supposed to help Mike build shelves. I've got to fly."

He picked up his light and placed it on the dash. He pushed a button and a siren screamed. As we flew down the highway I recalled Tiffany's complaint that when it came to Daniel, his family came first and took precedence over everything and everyone. Even the case. Daniel didn't work Sundays. He went to church and then to family barbecues at his parents. Tomorrow they were celebrating his birthday. As if we had all the time in the world, we had to wait until the following weekend to interview the landscapers and find the trainers.

He dropped me off at home and sped away, without looking back. I should have been glad he could leave effortlessly, but I wasn't. It was like he took a part of me with him when he went. Already I missed him. He was going out of town for a few days, undercover. I didn't know when I would see him next.

I took Shiny to the park, lamenting my sorry predicament. So much for staying aloof. The question was, for how long could I keep control? I'd been alone so long, I'd forgotten what it felt like to have someone in my corner. I liked Daniel, a lot. Given our Venus–Mars connection, and mutual Moon–Venus aspects, how could I not? He liked me too. The planets never lied. I wasn't the only one with these feelings. Only Daniel seemed more in control. How could that be? According to Claire, he fell in love at the drop of a hat. I warned myself to slow down, do nothing rash. We had a case to solve; he had a divorce to get. I might not be able to control my feelings, but I could control how I responded to them. I walked home repeating my mantra: No clients, no married men, no clients, no married men…

Sunday night for dessert, I finished Maribel's pie, which says a lot about how my diet was progressing. It was delicious, a creamy tangy mixture of peaches, lemon, and apple, all enclosed in a flaky crust. I washed out the plate, wishing I could cook. I went outside, saw Maribel's minivan in the drive and no sign of Joey's four-door. I figured it was safe to venture into enemy territory and went next door to return the plate.

The sun was just setting, but Maribel's house already looked dark. As I climbed the front steps it occurred to me that she might be out with Joey. I could leave the plate, which was the easiest thing to do, but also the most cowardly. Although I found her attitude about astrology astonishing, she'd alerted me to the nature of the serious religious opposition to it. If Maribel and Joey thought I had the power to summon the devil, I could appreciate their trepidation at having me as a neighbor. What I found shocking was how little Maribel knew about the physical world, and how much she thought she knew about a fantastical world. I wanted to bring her down to earth and help her realize the baby of her dreams. Looking past the crucifix, I raised my fist and knocked.

A few moments passed before Maribel opened the door. She smiled as if delighted to see me. I thrust out the pie plate. "I wanted to return this."

"That is so kind of you." She placed the plate over her heart and beamed at me.

I peered down the dim hallway. "The house looked dark. I didn't know if you were home."

"I was praying." She lowered the plate and tucked a strand of dyed blond hair behind her ear.

"Sorry to disturb you." I backed away.

"No, that's okay. I'm glad to see you."

"Joey's out?" I said hopefully.

"He's ministering. He works so hard. He feels like his job is never done."

"That must hamper baby making."

Maribel averted her eyes and looked at the carpet. "Would you like to come in?"

"Okay," I said, with hesitation and uncertainty, and when she seemed less than pleased, I added, "But I can just stay a minute."

She led me to the living room, which faced south and was a more functional design than mine given the southern declination of the sun in the winter. Not that this room was bright. The blinds were closed and the room was dark. She waved at a pink couch covered in plastic. "Have a seat. Can I get you anything?"

"I'm fine."

"I was going to get some iced tea. We don't have alcohol."

"I'm not much of a drinker. I'll take a glass of water."

She got the drinks and came back and sat down beside me.

I thanked her for the water. "Can I ask you something? Why is it so dark in here? Why do you keep your blinds closed?"

"It's easier to pray. You don't get distracted by what's going on outside."

"You can't pray all day."

She shot me a sharp look, as if that was exactly what she did.

"I like the light," I said. "It's what I like best about my house. Sunlight pours in."

"Joey says it's the light within that counts. Though he's not one for the sun. He gets real sunburned. Plus he thinks the sun fades the furniture. He feels it's our duty to protect what God has given us."

"So, he would say the sun has an effect on earth," I said, jokingly.

She saw my point and stiffened her spine, sitting upright. "Father Barnaby said only God knows the future. Astrology is a false idol."

I took a sip of water. "I would say to Father Barnaby that if I know it's going to snow in the winter, that's not really knowing the future. It's knowing the world in which I live, and the cycles of which I am a part."

Maribel stared at her knees. Her lips were pursed and her hands were clasped tightly together. She was so tightly wound, so afraid of everything, that I felt sorry for her. She said, "Sometimes I don't know if I'm talking to an angel or a devil. You seem like a well-meaning, good person. You make me so confused."

"I don't want to confuse you. I think people have the wrong idea about astrology and if they knew what it was about, they wouldn't object to it so much."

"The Bible says it's evil."

"I don't think it says that." I had done some research on the internet since we had last spoken. "The three wise men were astrologers. They knew from the sky that there was going to be an important birth. Astrology is a science that tries to understand the cycles of time. You could look at astrology from the point of view that God made the planets and the sun and the moon, and astrology is only trying to understand the mind of God." Which was a philosophy most akin to my grandmother's.

"Father Barnaby says astrology is the devil's tool."

"You know what my grandmother said?" I didn't wait for an answer. "Christians are the real devil worshipers. They created the devil to scare people and take their power."

Now Maribel looked disturbed and crossed herself.

"I'm sorry I said that." I stopped myself from going any further. I was far afield of my objective of helping her conceive. I changed the topic. "Did you check the length of your menstrual cycle?"

Maribel stared at her glass. "I believe it's every five weeks."

"Okay, so you ovulate around day eighteen. When was your last period?"

A red blush bloomed on her cheeks. "The middle of March."

I counted the weeks on my fingers. She was coming into her fertile time. "Now's the time. Give it a try."

"When Joey comes home from ministering, he's so tired." Speaking on Christian ground, she was able to look at me.

I smiled at her. "Wake him up."

"But he must come to me."

"Why?"

She seemed shocked I could ask such a question. "That's the way that it works."

"You can't have a sex drive?"

She looked at her glass, picked it up, drank her tea and choked on it. Brown rivulets ran down her nose. I wondered if she had started to cry, but she was laughing. "You are of the devil."

No, my Sun was in Pluto's house and concerned with sex. I couldn't get away from it. Not that I mentioned this. "Call it what you will, but both men and women have urges. It's natural. Why do only men get to act on it?"

Maribel wiped her nose with a tissue. "The purpose of sexual intercourse is reproduction."

"Right. You know your fertile time. Go for it."

"I can't *go for it*. I'd scare Joey away. I have to wait for him."

"Help him out. Make the wait time short. Do you have sexy lingerie?"

She was taken aback. "Of course not. I have my long flannels."

"Go to bed, say you're hot, and take them off."

"I would be naked. He would be horrified. He would admonish me to hide myself, lest I tempt him."

179

"So, he can be tempted."

"That is of the devil."

"I thought God wanted you to procreate."

"There you go again. Twisting everything."

"I don't see the objection. You're married. You're having sex to make a baby, only you're doing it at the right time. How is that confusing or of the devil? I call it doing God's will."

She put down her glass. "You are the most surprising person I've ever met. You are either a high angel or a low devil, and for the life of me I don't know which one you are."

"I'm neither. I'm just human. I'd like to see you happy. I think it's okay to think and learn things and question what you've been told. God gave you a mind. Doesn't He want you to use it? Knowledge isn't of the devil. You want a baby and there are things you can do that will help you."

"You sound logical, but what you say is backwards. We are to have faith. Not to question."

I finished my water and put down the glass. Outside I heard a door slam and we looked at each other in fright.

She jumped up, raced to the front window, and then covered her mouth with her hand. She went white, like she'd become a ghost. "It's Joey."

"I'll go out the back." And like a fugitive, I slunk away, sneaking along the side of the house and waiting until he went inside before I crossed the cocoplums.

Chapter 19

Monday morning, I was expecting Tiffany and got her husband Ciro. He arrived in a forest-green Ferrari and when he emerged from the car, I recognized him immediately. I thought he'd brought Tiffany, but the passenger seat was empty and he was alone. He was short, square, and chunky, but walked quickly and with purpose. He was dressed in a black pinstriped suit and wearing his trademark sunglasses. With jet-black hair and a facial shadow, he cut a dark figure.

He seemed delighted by my surprise and waved off my concern that he hadn't given me time to prepare. "I am not here for a reading," he said in a thick accent. He reeked of after-shave.

"Oh. Is Tiffany all right?"

He smiled tightly, showing teeth bereft of cosmetic dentistry. He lifted his glasses and I looked into brown eyes staring at me with the penetrating gaze of Scorpio, which I recalled, was rising in his chart. "She is fine. She wanted me to see you. I have an appointment in town later and was in the neighborhood and she gave me her slot. I hope that's okay."

After hearing so much about him, I was interested in meeting him myself and I waved at the hallway. "Please come in."

A few minutes later we were settled in my office and I had his chart open on my laptop. I learned he was not a man accustomed to prevarication, for he got straight to the point. "I'd like to know what's going on with my wife."

I gave my standard spiel about client confidentiality.

"I'll pay you," he said. "Handsomely."

"Sorry, but no."

He sat back and crossed his legs nonchalantly. He had a burgundy tie that matched a hanky that was expertly folded and fanned out above his breast pocket. He said, "What surprises me is why she comes so often. I thought an astrology reading was a one-time deal. It is not as if your birthday changes from year to year."

He spoke slowly and I didn't know if that was a language thing or if he was carefully choosing his words. In any case, I was on guard. I replied, "We spend a lot of time discussing the case."

"Does she see Detective Kane when she comes?"

It occurred to me that Ciro was jealous of his wife's former fiancé. I said, "Not to my knowledge."

"So, possibly?"

Did Tiffany see Daniel after she saw me? The thought made me tense. Their relationship was finished. Wasn't it? Acutely aware of Ciro's intense stare, I said, "Ask Gomez."

"Oh, I have."

"And?"

Ciro smiled. "She stays in Coral Cove all day."

I kept a blank expression. "She comes here for an hour."

"I know."

"Does Gomez know where she goes?" I tried to sound casual, but my words came out staccato and sharp.

"He takes her to the beach and drops her off. She tells him to go run errands. As if he has errands to run here. I wonder if she's meeting someone."

"She could be taking a walk," I offered, hoping it was so.

"Or meeting Daniel."

I hated the notion. Though it was true he was gone long stretches of the day, often incommunicado for hours. Was he with Tiffany? Had he been playing me? Was I fooling myself? God, I hoped not. "It's over between them." I said with a certitude I didn't feel.

"Is it now."

"She said you had a strong marriage. All you had was each other."

Ciro gave a faint smile. "She said that, did she?"

My words cheered me. "That's almost a direct quote." Then I inwardly winced, realizing I'd betrayed a client's confidence.

"I don't want to lose her," Ciro said. "She'd be a hard woman to get over."

I tried to move the conversation forward. "How long have you been together?"

"Ten years. Married almost that long." He found it necessary to explain. "It wasn't a shot gun wedding. When you know, you know."

He got that right. "How did you meet?" I was always curious to know how people found each other.

"At a party in the Everglades. It was a fundraiser to get money to clean up the environment. It was in the middle of nowhere and she needed a ride home and I was happy to oblige." He raised his hands. "Now here we are."

"Here you are. I think you must have a strong marriage."

"Why do you say that?"

"To survive what you went through." After my own crisis, my marriage died instantly.

"What happened brought us together. At least I thought it did. And perhaps it has." He stared out the window. A garbage truck was coming down the street with a high-pitched whine and Shiny was barking.

"Do you blame Tiffany for keeping the windows open?" I asked, as the truck barreled by.

"Did she say that?" Frown lines appeared on Ciro's forehead.

I held up my hands in appeasement. "She did not. Any questions I ask in regards to her are coming from me. If you don't wish to answer, that's your prerogative."

Ciro looked at his hands. He wore a thick bold wedding band and a huge heavy watch. "I blame myself for being gone. That's who I blame. If I were home, it wouldn't have happened. I knew she slept with the windows open. I like them open too. But she's a sound sleeper and I sleep lightly. She was attuned to Sierra though. She'd wake up in an instant if Sierra cried. If a car backfired out front, Tiffany would sleep right through it."

"Which tells us whoever grabbed Sierra got her out of the house without her crying."

"Unless they knocked her out with smelling salts or some other drug. She wasn't struggling in the video. For all we know she was dead then."

He said it so coldly I shivered. "Do you believe that?"

"I have braced myself for it. I know the odds are not in her favor. I know I did all I could to find her and came up short. From my perspective, it's as if she were dead."

I put on my glasses and stared at his chart. Neptune and Jupiter were together in his first house and both were opposite Saturn, which bespoke of a dearth of hope and optimism. Also a spouse who might be depressed, or a burden.

"I deal with reality," Ciro said, as if he felt a need to explain himself.

"After Sierra was taken, you concentrated on your business?"

"I had to do something."

"How long have you been in the country?"

"Since I was a boy. I am sensitive to pesticides and had asthma as a child. I found it hard to breathe in Mexico City and my parents came here, illegally. Now look at me." He shrugged broad shoulders. "Living the American dream. It was never my goal to have so much material wealth. My aim was to get healthy food on the grocery store shelves that people with allergies could eat without incident."

"Let me just say I love your stores. I shop there all the time. Your business is doing well." I had searched Good Food online and had scanned the financial reports. According to all in the know, the stock was currently "a buy."

"Running a business I can do. Want to know my secret?"

No true Scorpio gave away good secrets. "Okay."

"I treat people well. I respect them. My customers and my employees. Everyone." He took the burgundy hanky out of his jacket breast pocket and wiped his nose, then stuck it back in a manner that retained the fan shape. "Tiffany said you wondered if a disgruntled employee was trying to settle a score."

"You could make enemies without meaning to," I said, thinking of a particular neighbor. "Without wanting to."

"At the time, all my local employees were questioned. They were invited to report anonymous gossip. We announced the reward money. We received many tips, but none panned out. I don't think it was anyone from the company. I try to be a good boss. I believe in the law of karma. What you do, comes back to you."

"It's hard to see how a kidnapping fits into that," I said.

"You have hit the hammer on the nail," he said. "What did I do to deserve to lose my child? How can this be?"

"What's your answer?" I was on the edge of my seat, breathlessly waiting. "How do you explain it?"

"When there is an upset of this magnitude in the relationship between cause and effect, there must be a God who overrides cosmic law. Who deliberately intervenes."

"A not-very-nice God."

"Exactly."

"That's a terrifying notion," I said. "Don't you think it might just be an accident?"

"I don't believe in accidents." He looked at me sharply. "And you do? How can an astrologer believe that? Doesn't that hamper your ability to predict the future? All these random events popping up all over the place?"

"It would hamper it. But I don't predict the future. I don't even try."

"I thought that was the purpose of astrology."

"Not at all. Astrology describes the quality of any given moment of time."

"Hmm." Ciro scratched his forehead. "After Sierra was taken, I consulted a *curandera*. Do you know who that is?"

"No," I said, feeling the session slipping away. Usually I was the one who asked the questions and had the answers.

"It's a person analogous to a shaman. A healer. A seer."

"What did this person see?"

"You. She said an astrologer would bring insight to the matter."

I felt a chill all over.

Ciro went on. "I thought she was mistaken. I didn't know any astrologers and frankly, I saw them as charlatans. When Tiffany told me about you, I thought it was fate, a cosmic appointment. You had come to save us."

I raised my hands in protest, not liking the burden he'd placed on my shoulders. Maybe they had found the wrong astrologer. I said, "A cosmic appointment?" I shook my head to make clear where I stood on the matter.

"Yes, a cosmic appointment," Ciro said firmly. "Like the *Appointment in Samara*. Have you heard that story?"

The foreign name jogged my memory and an old book, much like the one I had sold appeared in my mind. It had black and white pencil drawings. "I know the story."

"Tell me."

Was he testing me? "Okay. One day, in a crowded market in Baghdad, a poor servant ran into the grim reaper, who raised a skeletal finger and pointed at him. The servant was so horrified by the encounter that he ran home and begged his master for his fastest horse. The master agreed and the servant took the horse and rode all day to Samara where he thought Death couldn't find him. But that night the servant awoke to find Death standing over him. The servant had one question: 'Why did you point at me this morning?' To which Death replied, 'I was shocked to see you. There you were in the market in Baghdad, when it was written we had an appointment in Samara tonight.'"

Ciro was nodding. "You do know it."

"I don't believe it. I don't think anything is written in stone. Or in the stars."

"Yet, the *curandera* knew you were coming."

I took a deep breath, wondering how to answer. Ciro raised a hand. Sunlight glinted off his wedding ring. "We will not answer this age-old question in this hour. Regardless of our beliefs, the kidnapping was no random event. It was well planned and well executed. That is not to say things may not have gone wrong, but it was no accident. Sierra was the target. The kidnapper, he, she, or they, breached my house the very week I made the Fortune 500 list and the extent of my assets were announced to the world."

"Which indicates the motive *was* money and not someone who wanted a baby."

"Yet there was no ransom note."

"It doesn't make sense."

"I have faith you will figure it out."

"Daniel has made solving the case a priority."

"Do you think he is capable of it?" Ciro asked. "He seems full of bluster. Not much action."

"I think he'll surprise you."

Ciro considered this as the clock chimed. Then he looked at me through narrowed eyes. "Are you and Daniel a couple?"

I stiffened and sat up straight. "No! He's a client. There are rules."

Ciro got out his checkbook. "Forgive me. Of course." He clicked the end of a pen. "Do you think Tiffany will be all right?"

I took off my glasses. "I'm not really at liberty to talk about her."

"If you suspect she's in danger, or veering off-track, would you tell me?"

He was seeking independent eyes to watch his wife in case she strayed, or felt an urge to take out the boat and not come back.

Which put me in a bind. "Tell you what. I'll look out for her. If I see any warning signs, I'll call you."

He inhaled deeply. "I would be most grateful." He reached into his checkbook, extracted a business card, and laid it on the table. "Here is my personal number."

I picked up the card. "I like Tiffany a lot."

"She likes you too." He sat forward. "I will see you on Friday evening then? You'll conduct your interviews and come to dinner?"

I nodded, hoping to hide my surprise. I knew Daniel was working on a schedule, but dinner was news to me.

"Tiffany is so excited," Ciro said. "It's been years since we've had guests over for a meal."

"I look forward to it," I said, hating how my heart raced at the invitation and the thought of another night with Daniel.

Ciro scribbled a check, ripped it out of his book, and placed it in my hand. "Thank you for an enlightening hour."

I looked down at the check. Ciro had paid me five times my regular rate. I held it out in protest. "This isn't my fee. We didn't even get to your chart." I felt uneasy taking the money, especially after he'd offered to pay me "handsomely" for spying on his wife.

Ciro slung his hands in his pockets. "Keep it. What I call fair payment for your service."

As I was thinking how to respond, he stood up. I followed suit. Then he kissed me goodbye, a light brush on each cheek. His after-shave no longer smelled so strong. He squeezed my hand. "Until Friday."

He left and my reservations about him left too. He was obviously a man used to wielding power, but for a businessman, he was philosophic and reflective. I'd thought Tiffany chose him over Daniel because of the money, but now I wasn't so sure. Ciro surprised me. He had more faith in me than I had in myself. I promised myself to do all that I could not to disappoint him, to be *the* astrologer the *curandera* saw.

Chapter 20

On Tuesday morning, Annie dropped in on her way to work. The weather had changed, a front had blown in during the night, bringing pounding rain. She shrugged off her raincoat on the porch, kicked off her sensible heels, and followed me to the kitchen. She threw her oversized purse on the counter and pulled out a photograph. "We went for the ultrasound yesterday. I saw the baby." She thrust the photo at me. "It's a girl."

Of course she was. With Venus in Pisces exalted, she would be pretty. I couldn't take my eyes off the Polaroid. There was a grainy black and white background, but the baby's face was in color, a pink shade of peach. She was sucking her thumb. I remembered how exciting it was; how a picture on paper made the baby feel real. "She's beautiful," I said.

Annie teased the photo from my hand. "She's twenty-four weeks old. Due August 15th."

I got out two mugs and poured tea. The baby would be a Leo, one of my favorite signs. I passed Annie a steaming cup.

"Sixteen more weeks, if all goes well."

I looked at her. "If all goes well? Is there a problem?"

"You were right about Kolby's health. She gained too much weight and has high blood pressure. Eclampsia. She's on a diet. I told her, no matter what, we won't change our minds."

I blew on my cup. "There you go."

Annie looked sober. "I don't know. I get the feeling Kolby might change her mind."

"Did she say something?"

"No. But she didn't want to give me the ultrasound picture. We only got one. I think she could give up a boy, not a girl. I'm worried she wants to keep her."

I remembered a hiccup from the horary chart. Jupiter was opposite Saturn, suggesting problems. But the Moon would bring them together, which meant the adoption process wouldn't go smoothly, but it would end well. Annie would get the baby. "You have to think positively," I said, which was one of my grandmother's favorite sayings. "See yourself going to the hospital, picking up your baby, and bringing her home. Pick out her name. Make her yours. Stake your claim."

Annie exhaled long and loudly. "That will only make it harder if we lose her."

"You can't think that way. If the sky says you're going to get her, you'll get her."

"Right," Annie said. "I'll hold that thought."

The clock chimed, announcing the quarter hour. Annie grabbed her purse and kissed my cheek. She had to go.

***

Wednesday was the day of the makeover, and true to the nature of Hermes' day with Mercury retrograde, I wanted to back out. From nowhere came the irresistible urge to go to Judith's ranch for intuition training. The last thing I wanted was to sit in a beauty salon and be fawned upon. As if she sensed my change of mind, Suzie insisted on picking me up.

She was late and drove like she was in the Daytona 500. With the windows down and the radio blasting, she babbled away. "Relax," she said. "Don't look so nervous. It's going to be fun."

I didn't answer her, and I seriously doubted it. The last time I'd been to a hairdresser was the day of the "incident." One fine sunny Saturday morning I woke up with an over-whelming compulsion to get my hair cut. It was so out of character and so far out of left field, I still wonder about it today. It was like an order I couldn't disobey. I called an upscale shop a colleague recommended and there was a last-minute cancellation. And that was how I came to be at the beauty parlor getting my drab hair dyed and not at home with my daughter the day she died. A few days later at the memorial service, there I was, standing in front of a small grave sporting a new shocking look that left friends and colleagues speechless. Andre's parents, jet-lagged from an overnight flight from Paris, didn't recognize me. Since then I'd done nothing to my appearance. I didn't cut my hair, didn't shave, didn't pluck my eyebrows. Just the thought of it filled me with an anxiety I could barely contain.

Suzie stopped at a light and looked at me. "Well, are you going to ask?"

"Ask what?"

"You can't tell?"

"You look happy."

"Satisfied. Elliot went to the doctor. He got a prescription of Viagra. Problem solved. You did it."

I waved my hands in front of my face, warding off the very suggestion. "I didn't do anything."

She laughed. "All right. I won't tell on you. But thank you." She took both hands off the wheel to put them together in prayer.

The light turned green and I pointed to the road and she dropped her hands to the wheel.

"Only now all Elliot wants to do is have sex. He takes a pill a day and it never wears off. I'm exhausted."

I looked at her. With her hair blowing out the window and a sly smile on her face, she looked both satiated and satisfied. For a moment I was jealous, I wanted what she had, what I had lost.

"We want to get married right away. You have to find a date in May. We can't wait."

"That's fast. Can't you continue as you are? See how it goes?"

"Our parents want a church wedding. We're not supposed to have intercourse." She rolled her eyes.

"You don't have to announce to the world what you're doing."

"We're supposed to take marital classes. As it is, the priest has to rush them for August, which he didn't want to do. We figure if we get married now, we can skip them altogether."

"Maybe the classes are a good idea."

She dismissed the suggestion with a flip of her hand. "Find something in May."

"I'll look." I already knew the transits then were a lot better than those in August. It wouldn't be hard to find a better marriage chart than the one my mother had found.

The spa was on the intracoastal waterway, a few doors down from the library. We were the only clients in the small shop and outnumbered by employees two to one. The makeover started with a massage and my girl Rachel was from Thailand. She had amazingly strong fingers for someone who looked fifteen. She kneaded my skin like it was bread dough. "You are so very tight," she said, over and over.

An hour later, Rachel steamed my face, polished my nails, and waxed my eyebrows into high arcs that gave me a perplexed expression. "Relax, relax," she said, as she washed my hair and massaged my temples.

The hairdresser Marek stepped in. He was from Poland, obviously gay, and unhappy with my hair. "You are what? Fifty-year-old woman? Please. Who would wear such a stringy mop. Scissors." He held out his hand and Rachel passed him a pair.

"I want to keep it long," I said. "Nothing extreme. Just a trim. Half an inch."

Marek waggled a finger. "No, you have no say. You, I can tell, have no idea. I think blond highlights to soften the darkness?"

"No!" I shrieked so loudly he jumped. "No highlights."

He held out his hands as if to hold me back. "No highlights."

"She's very tense," Rachel said, from the background.

Marek began cutting and before I knew it, hair of varying segments lay in piles on the floor. At least he was fast, his fingers flying. He turned my chair away from the mirror when I complained he was cutting too short.

"Be quiet. Is good."

Then he was massaging in mousse and blow drying my hair with a round brush until my scalp burned. When the final touches were done, I was to close my eyes and turn around and when I opened them: "the duckling will be the swan." I did as instructed, was whirled around in the chair and when I opened my eyes and was facing the mirror, I didn't recognize myself. But then I didn't have my glasses on.

As I searched for them, Marek shook a finger. "No, the spectacles you will not wear again." He clucked his teeth in disapproval and thrust a mirror in my hand. "Now see."

I drew a sharp breath of surprise. Up close up, I didn't look like myself. He had somehow managed to make my dry mousy hair look good. It was cut in layers to my shoulder and flipped upwards, which somehow gave it body.

"I wish I had your hair," Suzie said, from the adjacent chair.

Marek whipped off the cape. "Now you will go to the spectacle shop and buy small lens that will show your face and not look like big black fence post on your nose."

Which was how I ended up with new glasses.

Suzie dropped me off at ten. She'd had a great time and wanted to get together soon to go clothes shopping. I put her off, told her I'd check my calendar, and let her know.

"It's all right," she said, as I opened the car door. "It's okay to look fabulous."

I smiled like I believed her, but it was an ominous sign. In my mind, looking good meant something bad was about to happen. Statistically of course, you couldn't correlate the two, but experience was hard to contradict.

***

In Thursday night's advanced astrology class, I focused on politics and the ominous fiscal battles looming in Washington. With some in Congress threatening to default on the debt, we looked at how the transiting planets hit the US chart, and decided it wasn't possible. We were having a Saturn return, which meant that Saturn had gone around the ecliptic and was returning to its natal place in the US chart. Given the double dose of Saturn, we were encountering a hard reality. With Saturn in charge of the country's second house of money, it was time to be fiscally responsible. Law-makers wouldn't agree to default.

What I hadn't factored into the class was the effect of my make-over. In a grim re-enactment of the funeral, my students seemed more enthralled by my appearance than my material, and it was difficult to keep their attention. While they stared intently at me, I got the distinct impression they were looking, not listening.

When everyone but Claire had left, we stood on the front porch and she peered at me bug-eyed. "You'd never know you were the same person."

I turned red instantly. "It wasn't supposed to look so drastic."

"You mean great. Has Daniel seen it?"

"I didn't do it for him."

"I'm guessing that's a no. Wait till he does. *Oh la la.*" She fanned the air as if it had suddenly become too hot.

Which it had.

"I hear you had a nice dinner," she added. "He took you to West Palm Beach." She looked at me closely. "Are you really able to look at suspects and guess their rising sign? When you covered rectification in class it was so complicated. You had to know at least ten life events and at least a general time. When Daniel told me what you were doing, I wondered if you were looking for an excuse to be with him."

"No," I said too stridently, trying to ignore her raised dubious eyebrows. "Relating appearance to the rising sign and ruling planet might not be precise, but it's something. He doesn't have much."

"He has you."

I just shook my head and scowled deeply.

She raised her hands. "Just joking. I know what you're like. No mixing business and pleasure. Keep away from clients. Every year

I hear your class on ethics and boundaries. No crossing lines. I'm surprised Daniel has complied. That's so not like him."

"He's still married," I said, more disturbed than I liked about Daniel's uncharacteristic control.

"That's never stopped him before," Claire said. "It must be you. He said as much. You bring out the best in him."

I felt the heat on my cheeks again and went off topic. "How's the waterfront listing?"

"Getting traffic. We may need an open house. Do you think I should do it in this Mercury retrograde?"

"Mercury is in Aries, so people are active. You could hold one now, if you don't mind waiting for Mercury to turn direct to have an effect. Someone who saw the place now could decide to buy it later."

"Find me a date."

"Will do."

"Speaking of dates, did you get the subpoena?"

"I did."

"Do you have to bring the laptop?"

"I do."

"Shit. Do you have a beer?"

I got her one from the case I got for Jake, who was still ignoring me. I poured myself a glass of water, grabbed the subpoena, and we went to the back porch.

"You've got to change the date," I said, begging. The hearing was set for a week from the following Tuesday at 2:00, and there couldn't be a worse time. "Mars is activating the Uranus–Pluto square, and things will get nasty."

"I can't ask. The judge has forbidden further changes to the schedule."

"You never told me the second thing he hated."

She frowned into her bottle. "Astrology."

"Wonderful."

She chugged half her beer, then put the bottle on the table and wiped her lips. "Kev wants to parade you in front of the judge to show him how stupid I am."

"Great."

"That's why they want the laptop. To look over your astrology charts. You know what's there, right?"

There was a horary file with all the charts that showed the best times to sell real estate and see lawyers. There were also charts dealing with her personal life, notably whether or not she had contracted an STD. "I'll delete the charts that have anything to do with you."

"They'll ask you under oath if you've tampered with anything related to the case. I know you. You can't lie."

She'd be surprised. "Okay. What if I get my laptop and go clean the dining room."

Claire took my hand. "You're a good friend." She squeezed my fingers. "I won't touch the real estate charts. You have to be able to prove I paid you for work."

"Got it."

I brought my laptop from the dining room and put it down on the coffee table and left her alone. She owned the software, she knew how to delete charts, and I left her to it. I cleared the glasses from the dining room and returned the jug of water to the fridge. I wiped the condensation off the table and polished it with a dish towel thinking about the ethics of what she was doing. I was possibly helping her commit a crime, but I had so little faith in the legal system, I didn't think it mattered. She paid for the house and Kevin was a no-good cheating loaf. With a clear conscience I returned to the porch. The laptop was where I'd left it, and Claire was sitting with her feet up on the table drinking her beer.

I sat down beside her. She leaned toward me. "Morgan, this has to go well. If the judge isn't convinced you got the money for legitimate work, I'll owe Kev half of what I paid you. I don't have the money. The house is under water and I can't find a bank that will refinance. Bottom line, I'm fucked if the judge rules against me. You have to convince him that astrology is legitimate. Otherwise I'll lose my house."

"I'll do everything I can," I said, staring out into the backyard at the shadows shifting on the grass. Astrology was hard to defend when someone was disinclined to be open-minded or unable to entertain what my grandmother called "real magic."

"I'm counting on you," Claire said.

Chapter 21

Friday afternoon, I rescheduled my last two clients in order to be free by 3:30, which was the time Daniel was picking me up for our jaunt to Miami and dinner with Tiffany and Ciro. Full of apologies, he told me about the trip first thing in the morning. I didn't mention Ciro's visit or his suspicions, and my own awareness of the invitation. I hadn't seen Daniel all week and I preferred to hear how much he missed me.

When he pulled into the drive and jumped out of the Mustang, there was a catch in my throat, as if it were suddenly hard to breathe. My heart was racing and the light-headedness was back. Despite the cloudy day, I broke out in a sweat. I wiped my damp hands on my jeans and regretted not dressing up. Self-conscious about my appearance, I had dressed down, and wore blue jeans and a short-sleeve tan sweater. In contrast, Daniel looked like he was going to a wedding and wore pressed black slacks and a navy blazer with gold buttons over a crisp white dress shirt. He looked great and smelled better. Had he put on cologne for me? It smelled of musk, like sex.

"Ready?" he said.

I was ready to throw my arms around him and tear off his clothes. Instead I shoved my hands in my pockets. "Let's go."

I put Shiny in the house and we left.

It was an overcast day and Jake was taking advantage of the clouds and out cutting his lawn—during a waxing moon, which was the growth phase and the exact wrong time to cut anything. I would have reminded him, but he was whipping around on his mower and ignoring me. At least he had opened his curtains and blinds, which I viewed as a step in the right direction.

"Trouble in paradise?" Daniel asked, staring at Jake.

I strode to the car. "It's all good."

Daniel didn't say anything about my new look. As we drove down the street, the air in the car grew thick with tension. I decided if he wouldn't say anything, I would. I opened my mouth, but he started speaking first.

"I got your book listed on the ILAB website. As far as I can tell, no one wants to buy a copy and no one has one to sell."

I sighed inwardly. "It's a rare book. There might only be one in existence."

"I didn't get any hits on the buyer either. He's not American."

That didn't surprise me at all. He could barely speak English. I had a hard time understanding him.

"As soon as you can, get me all the information you've got and I'll add it to the site. Page numbers, photographs, a copy of the bill of sale, letter of authenticity. It all helps."

Which meant opening a dark closet and having to face what I preferred to keep buried. With little enthusiasm, I said, "I'll do it."

"Sooner rather than later."

"Does Claire know about the book?" I wondered how much he told her. Would he help anyone look for a rare book, or just me? How much did she know about our dinner conversation?

In answer to my question, he shook his head. "I don't tell my sister everything."

We neared the corner and had to brake as a family of sandhill cranes marched across the street. It was a family of four, parents with two kids, though they all looked the same.

"Big birds," Daniel said.

I said, "I got my hair cut."

I felt him looking at me and turned my head. He winked. "I know. Claire told me to prepare myself. Tried and failed." He shrugged. "I like it."

"It's different."

"You're different. It suits you. You're not as tame as you used to look."

As I rolled my mind around that, he went on.

"I need to tell you something," He reached forward and turned down the radio.

"Sounds serious," I said.

"I have to go to Jacksonville. There's a hearing at my former PD."

He was looking at me closely, as if assessing my response. Since Claire had already told me, I merely nodded.

"I shot my partner. It was an accident, but there's going to be an official investigation. It's routine," he added, looking like it was anything but. "Whenever there's a discharge of a firearm there's an investigation."

"Okay." I wondered why he was going into such detail.

"It could go badly."

"Why? If it was an accident?"

The third bird stopped in the road and stared through the windshield at us. The bird behind it, stopped too. Daniel said, "Buck is a top-notch detective. He's good at his job and well-liked."

"What does that have to do with anything?"

"He blames me. He's saying it was deliberate."

That came as a shock and I didn't know what to say. I looked at the bird looking back at me. "What happened?"

"It was night and he was far away. We were chasing a suspect who robbed a liquor store. I mistook him for the suspect. I didn't shoot to kill. The bullet went below his knee. He may limp for the rest of his life."

"Sounds like an accident to me. Why not talk to him? Tell him what happened?"

"I'm forbidden to discuss it with him. We're not supposed to talk. And I don't want to talk to him." The last words came out in a snarly rush.

"Maybe you should."

"He's screwing my wife."

Ah!

Daniel shot me a long look. "Buck and I spent hours together working cases. I told him my suspicions about Jen. He told me it was all in my head. While he was screwing her."

I didn't know what to say to that. On the road, the sandhill cranes were moving on.

"If I'm found guilty, I'll go to prison."

I gasped.

"I thought you should know. That's one reason this case is critical. If I—"

"You don't have to explain. I get it. If you solve the case no one else could solve, your lieutenant will realize how good you are. He'll fight to keep you."

Daniel exhaled and smiled his dimpled smile. "I like how you think."

It struck me like a blow how much I hated the thought of losing him.

"Claire doesn't know," he added. "Well, she knows about the shooting. Just not how serious it is. Or about Buck and Jen. Let's keep it between us, okay?"

I nodded, remembering Claire's face when she first told me about the shooting. Like it was nothing.

The cranes reached the other side. Behind us, a horn tooted loudly. Daniel looked in the rearview mirror. I turned around and saw my neighbor, Porter, in his rusting red truck that belched black exhaust. Daniel popped the light on the dash and hit a button that turned on a siren and made the red light flash.

Porter slunk low in his seat.

Daniel hit a switch that unlocked the doors.

"We're going to be late," I said. I didn't want a confrontation now.

Daniel checked the new running watch Claire had given him for his birthday. "All right." He turned off the siren, put on his signal, and we drove to the corner and made the turn.

On the road I focused on the case and got myself up to speed about Avery Hector whom we were going to see. According to Daniel, she was a landscaper at a company called Go Green that had a contract at J'Adore Del Mar four years ago. She was one of five women employed by the company at the time of the kidnapping and so far the only one Daniel could locate. After the economy crashed, J'Adore hired their own landscapers and stole Avery away from Go Green. Our appointment with her was at five. Then we were going to the gym to see what we could find out about the married personal trainers. Daniel had called the gym but got nowhere. After that, it was dinner at the Rossarios'. The time was open, we could show up whenever. Gomez the driver would wait for us, so we would have the opportunity to speak to him as well.

Traffic outside of Fort Lauderdale was heavy and the fast lane on the Turnpike was slow with aging drivers maintaining the 65 mph speed in each lane, which prevented anyone from passing. Daniel, impatient, finally said, "Screw this." Once again the siren and flashing red light came on. The lane in front of us cleared immediately.

"Is this legal?" I asked.

"We're late."

We made up time and ended up at J'Adore del Mar on schedule. At the front gate, the security guard took our ID and made us fill out a lengthy sign-in form. If security had at one time been lax, it was lax no longer.

Avery was called and we were told to park at the gate and she would take us to the landscaping office where we could talk. A few minutes later a heavy-set, forty-ish woman appeared in jumpsuit driving a golf cart.

We sat in the back and Avery drove down wide windy roads without sidewalks that were bordered with pink and white impatiens, shaded by tall trees, and surrounded by golf-course-looking grass. Even in the gated community, the houses were nearly invisible and hidden behind high fences and locked gates.

Her office was a small white brick building in front of a series of metal garbage containers. In the heat, the odor was heavy and flies buzzed. Inside it was freezing and a window air conditioner droned loudly. We sat at a round table in what looked like a lunch room. "I don't know how I can help you," Avery said.

Daniel took out his digital recorder and I got out my iPad. I pulled up Avery's birth chart and tried to decide what sign was on the horizon from her appearance. Her turquoise jumpsuit was tight, though clean and perhaps pressed. She had graying hair that was pulled back in a loose ponytail. She was tanned, quite wrinkled, and earnest. I decided either Saturn or Capricorn were strong and stared at the chart as Daniel began the interview.

"Do you know Tiffany Rossario?"

Avery folded her hands on the table. "I know who she is now. I didn't know her then. I feel bad for her. I hope you find out what happened to her child."

"There don't seem to be many children in this community," Daniel said. "There's no playground, no basketball hoops, no sidewalks."

"It's not a retirement village. Children live here. At least there are no rules forbidding them. You see them at the pool or the club house."

"Do you have access to the houses?"

"Not the houses. The grounds. We have a master key for the pedestrian gates."

"Do you have a regular schedule?"

"For the private homes, yes. The residents don't appreciate being disturbed."

"So, any landscaper has access to any home?"

"To any gate, yes. However, the pedestrian entrances aren't always locked. There was some question back then as to whether the Rossarios' was. In any case, the residential fences are eight feet. That's the bylaw. You can climb them, especially at a corner. They're not that hard. The real security is in the perimeter fencing. That was supposedly impenetrable. Until... well... until..."

Looking at her chart, I decided she had Saturn in Virgo near the horizon that was making pleasing contact with Venus in

Taurus in the 4th house. Taurus was the gardener, and Saturn gave her premature aging and her acceptance of rules and bylaws.

Daniel was breezing through his questions. "How often do you cut people's grass?"

"Every week whether it needs cutting or not."

"Do the residents see you? Do you see them?"

"The mowers are loud, so I don't think you can miss them. But no, I never look in windows. I ignore residents and they ignore me."

Mindful I was supposed to be quiet, I ripped a page out of my notebook and scribbled: *Children????* I passed the note to Daniel, who asked the question.

"Do you have children?"

"I don't. It's not my wish, but that's how things turned out."

I grabbed the loose page and wrote: *adopt?????*

"You didn't want to adopt?" Daniel asked.

"No. We have cats. My husband and I. They're like children."

"The security office wondered if a landscaper was involved," Daniel said. "There was specifically a question about the timing of the pruning of bougainvillea on the south wall."

"They're pointing fingers for their own lapse," Avery said. "Did they also mention two security lights were out on the wall? There was a camera there, but it didn't pick anything up because there was no light. Whose fault was that?"

I grabbed the loose paper again. *How does camera work?* I didn't have a chance to pass it to Daniel.

Avery said, "Why don't you just ask me the questions yourself? Are we in high school?"

Definitely a Capricorn–Saturn influence; she was acting out with authority. I looked at Daniel and he nodded. "How do the cameras work?" I asked.

"They don't run continuously. Motion acts as a trigger, but there has to be light. As for ground patrol, the bikes were always broken and the streets weren't patrolled to the extent security wants people to believe. The guards sit in their house by the front gate playing on their computers. They insisted they get WiFi so they could check incoming vehicles, but we know what they do."

"Did any security guard look suspicious to you?" Daniel asked.

"No."

"What about on the landscaping crew?"

"We're all vetted."

"There were four other women landscapers working for Go Green," he said. "Do you know what happened to them?"

"They lost their jobs during the reorganization. There were cutbacks. The company went bankrupt. I was lucky Del Mar picked me up."

"Who decided when the bougainvillea was cut?" Daniel asked.

"The foreman made the schedule. It wasn't fixed, he went by the weather. Did the kidnapper take advantage of the pruned bougainvillea? Perhaps. Did he stake out the joint? I don't see how. Everyone lives behind high fences. When you cut someone's grass for an hour, that's hardly scoping them out. Would we know if someone left a window open? Hardly. Besides, everyone here needs a security alarm. That's a bylaw too. If Mrs. Rossario locked her windows as she should have done, this would never have happened. Rules are in place for a reason."

I hit save to retain the chart, confident I had found my rising sign. Capricorn reveled in keeping rules.

"Are all the landscapers legal?" Daniel asked.

"Legal and bonded."

"Is there a sailing or fishing club?" Daniel asked.

"No. Some residents own boats, of course."

"Have you noticed boats trolling out front? Could they watch a house? See windows open, night after night? Could they land if they wanted to?"

"No," Avery said. "Part of the guards' job is to stop boats that get too close. They call the Coast Guard on any loitering vessel. The beach is typically clear. Especially at night."

"Do you know a married couple who were trainers at the time of the abduction?"

"A married couple?" Avery looked up at the ceiling as if looking for the answer. Finally she said, "No."

"They were trying to have a baby, unsuccessfully," I offered.

"Still no."

Daniel turned off the recorder. "Thank you, Avery. I appreciate you taking the time to talk to us."

"I wish I could be more help." Avery stood up. "I'll drive you back to your car."

"No thanks," Daniel said. "We're going to the gym."

Outside, in the fading light, he looked at me full on. "Passing notes didn't work out."

"Nope."

"Next time, just jump in."

"Thank you."

"Did she do it?"

"No."

"I agree. She wouldn't still be here if she did." He checked his fancy watch. "Let's hit the health club."

We followed signs that took us off the main drag and down a lighted path to a brick building called "The Club" that was overlooking the Atlantic and lit up like Christmas. A notice on the front door announced the library was open on Wednesdays and there was a bridge tournament on Saturday. We went inside. Ahead was a beachfront restaurant with the health club to the right.

We walked through a vestibule to the gym. It had glass windows on three sides, one of which overlooked the pool. Beyond that was a patch of grass dotted with palm trees and seagrape, and then a wide sandy beach ending at the shoreline, where waves were crashing.

A perky clerk at the counter smiled brightly and handed us heavy, plush towels. Daniel laid them down and pulled out his ID. "Can I see the manager?"

"He's not here right now. I can give you his business card." She reached under the desk, pulled out a card, and handed it to Daniel.

"How long have you been working here?"

"This is my second day."

Daniel tucked the card into a pocket "I'll call the manager."

I picked up a towel. It was white, oversized, lush, and thick. I unfurled it to gauge the size. It was a bigger towel than the one in the grainy photograph. It occurred to me as I threw it over my shoulder, that it may have served a purpose other than covering an infant. I tried tying two corners and while it was hard to do, it was possible.

Daniel was looking at me puzzled.

"Maybe the towel was used as a sling." I remembered seeing pictures of my mother with African women who held their babies in cloths tied around their mid-section. A cheap lightweight towel was like a cloth. I demonstrated what I meant, using my purse as a prop. "You tie the towel around your neck and waist to hold the baby. It frees your hands." I waved them in the air.

Daniel snapped his fingers. "Which would explain how the kidnapper climbed with a baby."

It made sense to me.

I undid the towel, folded it back up, and laid it on the counter. It was getting on to seven o'clock and the sun was heading for the trees. Daniel wanted me to see the south wall and the site of the suspected breach.

We walked past a line of black metal fencing broken by double-sided gates and then reached the wall. Four bright security lights shone white phosphorescent high beams on high concrete. Sharp glass daggers pointing skyward were embedded on the top. The bougainvillea was red and about five feet thick in diameter. It was so dense the barbed wire behind it was not visible.

"They're not taking any chances," Daniel said. "Management learned from their mistakes. No way could you climb this now."

"It would be hard to climb with a baby," I said. "Even if she was secured by a sling."

"It would be hard, but doable."

I looked to the east where the sky was growing dark. I heard the ocean, which lay behind the gated fence of the corner house. There was no open access to the beach. In all likelihood, the kidnapper entered and exited via the wall.

"Seen enough?" Daniel asked.

I had.

Chapter 22

We headed to the Rossarios' estate. They lived five houses from the wall on the ocean side, which meant the kidnapper did not have far to go to make an escape. It also explained why only one security camera picked up the kidnapper. It took two minutes and eighteen seconds at a quick pace to reach our destination. We knew because Daniel timed it on his running watch. A kidnapper could be in and out quickly. Someone was familiar with the layout.

The Rossarios' yard was completely enclosed in an eight-foot high wrought iron fence with spikes on top all draped with honeysuckle that glowed orange in the security lamp light. The flowers were blooming and the air carried the scent of strong perfume.

Daniel got out a small, bright flashlight and examined the fence. When we reached the gate he rattled the two sides and peered at the keyhole lock. "Pretty flimsy security," he said. "You could pick this lock in a second."

"Tell Ciro."

"I don't think one tells Ciro anything." He nodded at the house. "You'll soon see what I mean."

"I met him on Monday. He came to see me."

Daniel straightened and faced me square on. "What did he want?"

"I think to check me out."

"Did he ask about me?"

"I can't talk about my sessions."

"He doesn't like me. I'm pretty sure it was *him* who tipped off the FBI about Tiff and me. Which got me taken off the case and conveniently transferred and out of the way. It was a black mark on my record."

"And you're still going to his house for dinner?"

Daniel lifted a shoulder. "Forgive and forget is my motto. Move on." He narrowed his eyes. "Did he say something?"

I broke eye contact, wondering how much I could reveal without betraying a confidence. Ciro didn't appear to have complete trust in Tiffany, or Daniel for that matter. "I can't talk about it. But, I'd watch yourself. I don't know what's going on with you three, but it's obvious there's unfinished business."

"You want to know what happened?" The snarly tone was back. Daniel took my arm and we moved into the shadows of a queen palm trunk. "He stole her from me. I took her to a party and she left with him."

Was this the same story I'd been hearing about? "Was the party in the middle of nowhere in the Everglades?"

"She told you?"

Christ, I had broken a confidence again. "I can't say anything."

"Here's what happened. We had a fight and I left. When I went back, she was gone. She'd left with Ciro."

"You can't blame her after you abandoned her."

"Except I came back. She should have known I would. I was just so pissed off."

"So you broke up."

"I got transferred to Gainesville. Ciro wanted me out of the way. He's got money, he's got high-up connections in the PD and they do favors for him."

"Yet you'd still help him?"

Daniel turned his back on the house. "I feel responsible. It may have been me who got Ciro into trouble with the FBI."

I blinked.

He sighed. "I didn't know the FBI agents would take me seriously. I mean they were discounting most of what I said. Checking out Ciro's Mexican roots was something they had to do anyway, but I may have egged them on. They went looking in the wrong direction even though it was clear early on he had nothing to do with it."

I looked at his face and saw the anguish in his eyes. "Is that why you feel it's your fault the kidnapper got away?"

"I tried to take back my statements but the agents wouldn't listen. When I was taken off the case, it was almost a relief."

I stared up at a seagrape and its heart-shaped leaves that shimmered in a light ocean breeze. "His stock took a hit. His phones were tapped for months. His baby disappeared without a trace."

"I feel terrible, okay. I'm trying to fix it."

"I wish you'd told me earlier."

"I've never told anyone. I didn't think I ever would tell anyone."

I looked into his eyes and I knew what he was talking about. Acts undertaken in times of madness weren't easily spoken. "Let's make it right," I said.

He took a breath, exhaled loudly, and echoed my words.

With that out in the open, we returned to the Rossario entrance and Daniel leaned on the buzzer. An intercom hummed. "The pedestrian gate is open," Ciro said in his heavy accent. "Come in, please." Though polite, it sounded like an order.

"Ready Spike?" Daniel said.

"After you, Danno."

The pedestrian gate was a gate within a gate. It had a knocker-type clasp that lifted and had holes for a padlock that was not in evidence. Daniel lifted the clasp and pushed it open. "Ladies first." I stepped through without needing to crouch.

The oversized front glass door opened and I realized I was severely underdressed. Despite her anorexia, Tiffany was decked out in a floor-length forest-green sleeveless gown that was low at the neck and showed the bones of her rib cage. Ciro was laden with jewels and wore a navy suit and white tie. He stood proprietarily close to his wife.

Tiffany stepped forward and took both my hands, "Look at you. You look fantastic."

"I'm way underdressed."

"I'm overdressed. I felt like wearing something nice. It seems like old times, you know." She looked me up and down. "Only I wasn't talking about your clothes."

"I got new glasses," I said, as my cheeks burned.

"And a fitting do. Love the cut," she said, with a pat to my head.

I smiled at the compliment and looked at the two men. They were standing an arm's length apart, both with their arms crossed in a defensive posture. "Hi Ciro," I said.

He opened his arms and kissed me, on each cheek, and then patted my arm as if we were old friends. "I'm glad *you* could make it," he said. "Come on in." He ushered us into the vestibule.

The floors were of buffed amber wood and the walls had cherry wainscot. Oversize portraits hung in the entrance hallway and a

216

grandfather clock rose toward the second story. A grand curved staircase with sconce lighting led the way to the second floor. Despite the strategic light, the house seemed dark. No windows were open and the air was dense and heavy. No breeze blew. Though immaculate and stately, the house seemed sad, as if too bore the sorrow of what had happened.

The driver appeared in the hallway and bowed. Ciro waved at the living room. "You may talk to Gomez in there. Take as long as you like."

Ciro and Tiffany left and Daniel and I went to the living room. We sat down on opposite ends of the couch. Gomez took the easy chair. He was wearing a suit and tie and polished shoes. "What would you like to know?" he said in an accent that matched Ciro's.

Daniel looked at me. "Take it away, Morgan."

"Thank you." I turned and faced Gomez directly. "How long have you known Ciro?"

"All my life. He was best friends with my older brother in Mexico City. He came here and then helped my family immigrate. He gave us all jobs. We are indebted to him. I would never do anything to hurt him."

"What does your family do for him?"

"My brother works as a store manager. My sister is an accountant in the head office."

"Where were you the night of the kidnapping?"

"At home. Ciro was traveling in Mexico. Tiffany was here. Once she had the baby, she seldom went out. If she needed me, she was to call. She never did."

"Do you have children?"

"*Si*. Twins."

"How old?"

"Six."

"Do you know other domestic employees who work in the gated community?"

"A few. I am mostly at the office, not here."

"When's your birthday?" I asked.

"May 26th." He told me the year.

He was 35, a Gemini, which explained why he liked to drive. "Did you know Josefina?"

"Of course. She was the housekeeper."

"Did you drive her around?"

"She had a work car for errands. Ciro allowed her to take it home. She was going to school. This way she could drive and not take the bus."

"Tiffany says Josefina was beyond reproach."

"That was my impression also. Ciro helped her and her mother and brother become citizens. He gave back the help he got himself."

"Did he give Josefina's family jobs?"

"They lived in Texas and there are no Good Food stores there. They moved here just before the kidnapping. When I say here, I mean Okeechobee, which also has no Good Food store."

"You met them?"

"Just her brother, Rique. One time. He came to the house to see Josefina."

"About what?"

"I think money. I overheard them talking. Josefina didn't have what he wanted and refused to ask Ciro."

"When was this?"

"After Sierra was born, but before Christmas. Tiffany needed diapers and the stores were busy with holiday shoppers. Rique said he hated Christmas."

"Oh. He went to the store with you?"

"I drove him to town."

"Where was he going?"

"I don't know. I dropped him at the intersection of 8th Avenue and 11th Street."

"What's there?"

"The train station?" Gomez offered.

"Little Havana," Daniel said.

"Miami Memorial Hospital is there," Gomez said, as if he was coming to Rique's defense.

"Was he going to the hospital?" I asked.

"I don't know. It's possible. You should ask Josefina."

"It's a seedy intersection," Daniel said. "The drug capital of Miami. Was he there on a buy?"

Gomez raised his hands. "I really can't say. He was a nice guy. He had a son and a baby on the way. We talked baseball. He was a Rangers fan and trash-talked my Marlins. The Rangers were—"

Daniel cleared his throat and stopped him. "Do you know any workers at the health club?"

"Some. If Ciro was having dinner there, I'd hang around. I met some of the trainers and the life guards."

"There was a married couple that worked in the gym around the time Sierra was taken. Did you know them?" Daniel asked.

"Barbie and Boris."

I blinked at Gomez's recall. "You met them?"

"Yes. They didn't work here long. Barbie's car broke down on the road one night and Ciro told me to stop and change her tire."

"Was she happily married?"

"I couldn't say. She had a nice car. A black Mercedes."

"Someone mentioned they wanted to have a baby and couldn't."

"I wouldn't know."

"Would the club's health insurance pay for fertility services?"

"That I can tell you. Absolutely not. Club employees don't get health benefits. There's a lot of grumbling about that."

"*In vitro* fertilization isn't cheap," I said, remembering the expense that Annie and her husband incurred. Even with health insurance it still ran into the tens of thousands of dollars.

"I know Boris had another job," Gomez said. "He was a bouncer at a sports bar on Calle Ocho."

"Little Havana again," Daniel said. "Was he Cuban?"

"He was foreign," Gomez said. "I don't know where he was from. Not Mexico."

"Was he into drugs?"

Gomez lifted his shoulders, relaying ignorance.

"There are a lot of Cuban mafia in Miami," Daniel said. "They run drugs. Mostly cocaine. Its importation, distribution, and protection."

"I don't know anything about that," Gomez said. "His wife said he was a bouncer."

"A bouncer with a wife who drove a Mercedes," I said.

Daniel looked at me. "Anything else?"

I shook my head.

Daniel thanked Gomez for his time.

We went outside. Ciro and Tiffany were sitting on a low slung wicker couch facing the water. He had his arm draped around her shoulder, jeweled hand near her throat. He nodded at the love seat beside them and Daniel and I sat down. The smell of the ocean was strong, the rote of the sea was loud, and the breeze was blowing. Off to one side, a glass dinner table was set for four. All around us, candles in hurricane glasses flickered mightily. A quarter moon was high and shining on the water from between the horns of the bull. Ciro offered drinks. I asked for wine and Daniel got a beer.

"How did it go?" Tiffany asked, as Ciro poured wine.

"We got a couple of leads," Daniel said. "I want to talk to Josefina's brother."

"I can give you her number," Tiffany said. "Why do you want to speak to Rique?"

"No one has questioned him before," Daniel said. "I understand he was here at your house. Did you ever meet him?"

"No," Tiffany said. "He lived in Okeechobee with his mother. I met her. She had diabetes that was causing some health problems. They were originally from Juarez and with Ciro's help, Josefina moved them to El Paso after the drug war heated up. He works in the sugar cane fields. Josefina went to live with them when she left here. I don't think he had anything to do with it."

Ciro handed us our drinks, nearly dropping Daniel's in his lap. Ciro resumed his place and his proprietary hold.

"Rique came here around Christmas time," I said. "Did Josefina tell you?"

Tiffany stared up at the night sky. "I think his mother was in the hospital. At one point she nearly had her foot amputated." She shook her head and lowered her chin. "Wait. No, it was his girlfriend."

"What was wrong with her?"

"I don't know. Josefina never said. She was reluctant to share family problems and I wouldn't pry."

"Does any of this matter?" Ciro asked sharply.

"It might," Daniel said, equally sharp. "Was she anxious to leave your employ?"

"Josefina didn't do it," Ciro said. "Move on."

Tiffany took his hand in a gesture I thought was meant to calm him down. "Josefina was relieved to leave. We had no need for her. There was nothing for her to do. We hardly ate, our days of entertaining ended quickly, and it was hard for her to be here. She was moping around and finally I asked her if I found her a new job, would she take it. She said if I didn't need her she'd move to Okeechobee to be with her family. I called a friend in Belle Glade and got her a job as a cook."

"This is all in the police report," Ciro said hotly.

"I don't recall reading about anyone moping around in the report," I said lightly, trying to lower his heat.

"You're right," he said in his normal tone. "Police reports are dry reading."

"Was Josefina athletic?" I asked.

"She wasn't overweight," Tiffany said. "Did she work out? No. She had a lot of energy. She liked to keep busy. She was no couch potato. If you're asking if she could climb a wall, the answer is no."

"Do you know when she was born?" I asked.

Ciro laughed out loud. "I have her employment records and will get you her birthday. It's not her, though. She worked as my housekeeper before we were married and I have known her for over a decade. She came from a reliable company that had her thoroughly checked."

"Do you know any of the trainers at the gym?" Daniel asked, addressing Tiffany.

Ciro answered. "Do you have anyone specific in mind or should we just throw out names?"

Daniel looked appropriately chastised. "A married couple."

"That's helpful," Ciro said.

I broke in. "Barbie and Boris. We're trying to find their last name."

Ciro picked up his phone. "I'll get it for you." He excused himself, went to the doorway, turned his back, spoke for a moment, and returned. "Gomez will contact management. Do you think this couple is involved?"

I waited for Daniel to answer and when he didn't, I said, "Someone in the security office told us Barbie wanted a baby and couldn't have one. Boris was apparently a bouncer in Little Havana and Daniel thought he might have cartel connections."

Daniel broke in. "I'm not saying he does, I'm not accusing him of anything, but it's something to check that wasn't checked before."

Ciro gave him a hard look. "I see. Just to be clear. You're not accusing people for no reason."

Tiffany took his hand and smiled at her husband reproachfully. She said, "The couple is long gone. There was a shakeup soon after the kidnapping. J'Adore was worried about a lawsuit and getting a bad reputation and didn't like the police hovering around. A wave of employees left. Everyone from the pool and health club got transferred."

Ciro looked at Daniel with narrowed eyes. "Your partner, Detective Parker, was furious. He felt J'Adore was interfering in the case, trying to scatter witnesses far and wide. You were off the case by then."

"Yes, I was *taken* off the case for no reason," Daniel said. "Transferred to Gainesville."

I put down my glass and tried to stop the two men from butting heads. "I love Gainesville. I guess I just like college towns. Can I see where you think the kidnapper gained entrance to the house?"

"Sure." Daniel put down his beer.

Tiffany stood up. "I'll show you."

The three of us went to the north edge of the porch and I stared down at the sand below. The first floor was elevated and a staircase led from the porch to the beach. I looked up and saw the railing on the second story balcony. Tiffany pointed out clips spaced along the frame of the balcony doors that were used to keep hurricane panels in place. "Daniel got up to the second floor using these," she said.

"You never removed them?" I asked.

Ciro joined us. "We have bars on all the windows now. And doors. No one can get in."

"Would you like to see Sierra's room?" Tiffany asked.

I said, "Sure."

Daniel said, "Why not."

"This way," Ciro said.

We got a tour of the house, which must have been over eight thousand square feet. There were windows and glass doors everywhere, and the view of the ocean and garden would have been spectacular if not for the heavy black bars that covered the windows and awkward gates that stood sentry by the doors.

Upstairs, on the second floor, there were six bedrooms, with two facing the water: the master bedroom and the nursery I recognized from a photograph in the police file. Sierra's room was unchanged and looked the way it did the night she was taken, except now the windows were closed and fortified with bars. But the crib was in place, as were the colorful bumpers and stuffed toys on the toddler bed she would by now have already outgrown.

I felt overwhelming sadness as I surveyed the room. The hope and happiness of another infant had been extinguished in a horrible second. I picked up a small teddy bear and wondered who had it worse: Tiffany or me. I knew there was nothing I could hope for, whereas she lived with the fear of too much hope.

I walked to the rows of windows and looked out onto the balcony. Beyond was the ocean I could see but not hear, with the windows locked tight. It was a shame to live so close to the beach and have to shut yourself inside. I remembered Tiffany saying that she was claustrophobic and felt responsible for the crime because she liked the breeze. Now she was trapped; a prisoner behind bars of her own making.

After the tour, we went downstairs for dinner. I helped Tiffany carry the food from the oven to the porch. We were having almond-crusted pompano with pasta in a white sauce and three different types of salad—all from Good Food. According to stylishly written name tags atop of dinner plates, I was sitting beside Daniel facing the water and opposite Tiffany. Daniel got to face off with Ciro.

"This is the first time we've had friends over for dinner in years," Tiffany said as she cut into her fish. "We used to have people over every week." She smiled warmly at her husband, who seemed to be bristling. "You remember, darling?"

"I do," he said, as he shoved a large forkful of fish in his mouth.

As did I. I remembered what it was like to be a part of a couple who had friends and used to entertain. Andre liked to cook and we had numerous Saturday afternoon barbecues. It was not the way I was raised, and being social was new to me, but I had begun to enjoy it. It was a life I saw myself living into eternity that ended up lasting almost four years.

Gomez arrived midway through the meal with a strip of paper he gave to Ciro, who passed it to me. On it was written two names, Barbie Cramer and Boris Shanksky. There was a dash by his name and the note, Ocala Fine Time Gym. He had located at least one of the trainers. There was also a cell number and address for Josefina Garcia. I passed the strip to Daniel, who tucked it into a pocket.

"Success?" Tiffany said.

"Success," Daniel answered.

"Ciro comes through," she said, and she gave his wrist a squeeze, which seemed to make him happy.

"Yes, some of us walk our talk," Ciro said, as he wiped his mouth with a white linen napkin and narrowed his eyes at Daniel.

Worried Ciro would start talking about hot air and bluster, I changed the subject. "How is the volunteering going?" I asked Tiffany.

She smiled brightly, showing her gums. "I agreed to host a fundraiser for the National Center for Missing Children at the Hard Rock Café. We're lining up a band."

"I'll come," Daniel said.

Ciro glared at him. "It's a thousand dollars a couple."

"Sign us up," Daniel said.

Wait. I wasn't going. "You don't even know when it is," I said to Daniel.

"Whenever you can come," Tiffany said. "Check your schedule. I need your help."

"What kind of help? I won't do free astrology readings. And I won't call anyone on the phone. I hate that."

She laughed, as if I were joking. "Help me sell tickets for the raffle. It's a way to meet people. I'll introduce you. You can give away business cards. Advertise your services. Once the party starts, we'll let the hostess take over."

"Um…" I was stuttering. Making faces. Conflicted. I hated these kinds of things.

"Come on," Daniel said, looking at me with hopeful eyes. "It'll be fun."

"Maybe she doesn't want to go with *you*," Ciro said.

I smiled at Daniel. "I'm in."

He winked at me, no mistaking it this time.

We left soon after dessert, which was raspberry parfait. Daniel waved off Tiffany's offer of a ride, and we walked under the starlit sky to the car. The wind had died and the shadows of the leaves seemed painted on the pavement. "Well, that was awkward," I said, as we walked down the middle of the empty street.

"Awkward?" Daniel said. "That was nothing. I was expecting much worse. I think Ciro got out his best behavior for you."

"You two need to get on the same side."

"I'm trying," Daniel said.

I smiled at him. "I know. It must be hard." It was one thing I needed to learn, how to forgive and move on.

"It was easy with you there," Daniel said. "Everything is easier with you."

I looked into his eyes. I knew what he meant. I felt the same about him.

The drive home passed in a flash as if time was acting strangely. The music played and we sang along as car lights blazed by. At home, he pulled into my driveway and parked. He must have run around the car, for when I went to open my door, there he was, offering his hand.

I took it.

He pulled me out and didn't let go. Or maybe that was me. I held on too long. He moved into me, or I moved into him, I don't know which. Then I had my arm around his back, and he had his arms around me. Then his lips were on mine and he was kissing me. Or I was kissing him.

His skin was soft, his tongue was urgent and his hands were strong. I felt his heart beating through his shirt, though perhaps it was mine. The scent of his sweat engulfed us; sex in the air. It was dark, yet light danced in his eyes and shimmered on his face. The surrounding space seemed electric and vibrated to the sound of frogs and crickets that rang out all around us. And we were a part of it, pulsing with the rhythm of life and the hunger of a touch. Then my phone rang.

The sharp chirp was followed by loud silence. It was as if the electricity in the air died, a current broke, and the frogs and crickets were all murdered. We looked at each other. I dropped my hands.

Daniel held me tight. "Don't get it."

I didn't want to. "It could be my mother. An emergency. A suicidal client." I glanced at my watch. Just after eleven. It rang again and I yanked it from my purse and saw the caller ID. "Claire." I answered the call.

"Are you with my brother? I'm trying to call him and he's not answering."

"He's here," I said trying not to moan. I passed Daniel the phone.

Daniel listened, his eyes widened. "I'll be right there." He returned my phone. "I've got to go. My brother had a heart attack."

Chapter 23

I didn't get much sleep that night. Try as I might, I could not get the taste of Daniel out of my mouth, or the weight and warmth of his body off my mind. So much for the free will to ignore feeling. The situation was not helped by the fact that he could go to prison. For what? Attempted murder? Intentional wounding? Prison must have been in the realm of possibility if he felt compelled to bring it up. Why did he have to tell me? Before I even had him, I was petrified of losing him.

Not that I could have him, I reminded myself, when the excitement settled down. There was the case, his sister, and boundaries; I was determined not to be just another woman who flung herself at him. There was also his marital status, not to mention mine, which raised numerous problems. I would have to find a lawyer and likely contact Andre. The thought of actually talking to that goddamned fucking piece of shit whose guts I hated and would hate for fucking ever blew away my warm fuzzy hopeful feelings. Just thinking of him twisted my heart in knots. A short review of a long list of righteous grievances left me seething with renewed anger. He was a lying, cheating prick who screwed me every way he could and ended up with everything. Because of him I lost my baby. Holly lost her life. I'd kill him before I'd talk to him.

The thought surprised me. The intensity of my rage was shocking. I thought I was getting better. In the last few years I got tired of hearing the tape playing repeatedly *ad nauseam* in my mind and I thought I'd finally managed to control it, to stop it. I was unpleasantly surprised to find it shrieking still.

Because of Andre I lived a lie, pretending to be widowed. For all I knew, he could have divorced me. Who knew how French laws worked. We married in Paris and I had no idea what my status was in the US. I guessed the time had come to sort it out.

Daniel was still married too, which was easy to forget, given that the philandering Jennifer was hundreds of miles away. He was off-limits. I'd heard too much heartache from clients awaiting lovers to leave their spouse. I would not be that person. Nor would I be my mother who had no qualms seducing unavailable, taken men. I could put my feelings aside, I didn't have to act now. If it was meant to be it would happen.

Wait! That fanciful thought stopped me short. I didn't believe anything was meant to be. Nothing was ordained. Which meant I could lose him. A thought which only made me want him more.

Dawn was breaking, and I was thinking of getting up when the alarm rang. Only it wasn't the alarm, it was the phone. I groped for my glasses, surprised to see it was 8:00 a.m. At some point I must have fallen asleep. I answered the call.

"You sound sleepy," Daniel said. "Have a late night?"

I shot upright in an instant. "How's your brother?"

"Patrick only thought it was a heart attack. Turned out to be gas. He'll get out later. I thought I'd go to Ocala to see Boris. Are you doing anything?"

Pining for you, I thought. "Going to Ocala," I said. We had to talk, settle matters from the night. Forget the pining. We had to make the boundaries clear.

"I'll pick you up after lunch."

He appeared at one-fifteen, decked out in faded jeans and a baby blue polo that brought out the bluish tinge in his dark chocolate eyes. "Ready to go?" he asked, as he rubbed Shiny's back, paying more attention to her than to me.

In the car, he babbled about Patrick and the hospital and I waited for him to finish before I said, "We need to talk." We were heading north on the Turnpike and I turned down the radio.

"I was afraid you'd say that."

"What happened last night, can't happen."

"Well it did. You wanted it, I know you did."

I turned and stared out the window at the trees speeding by. "Now is not the time."

"What? The stars aren't right?"

I looked back at him. "It's too fast. We're working this case. We have to focus."

"I can tell you, I've never been so focused on a case. So anxious to solve it. Put it behind us."

The words made my heart sing, my thoughts stumble. I closed my eyes to clear my mind. Then I said, "You're still married and I'm, I'm…" I stammered. I wanted to tell him the truth.

"Yes, a widow. Four years now. At some point you have to move on. Four years is not a rebound."

I didn't have it in me to undo the lie. I threw the ball back in his court. "From what I hear about your divorce, no one's filed any legal papers."

He bit his lip and ran his hand through his hair. "Jen is dragging her feet."

"Maybe she changed her mind."

He rapped his fingers on the steering wheel. "I don't care. I haven't changed *my* mind. If she won't file the paperwork, I will." He glanced at me, eyebrows raised. "Okay?"

"Do what you're going to do, but in my mind you're married. I won't be the other woman."

He nodded at the highway. "I'll take care of it. In the meantime? Hands off." He lifted his palms off the wheel.

I pointed at the road, unsure of how I felt that he didn't protest more.

It was a two-hour drive to Ocala and we hit rain as we reached Highway 4. The gym was on the south side of town, in a tin-like building that had no windows. Unlike the facility at J'Adore Del Mar, there was no pool and no floor-to-ceiling windows with a view.

Daniel hadn't spoken to Boris and we didn't have a birth date. "We'll ask for it," I said, keeping up the pretense it might be helpful. "Does he know we're coming?"

"I called the gym this morning and learned he was working from noon to nine. I wanted to surprise him." He parked the car and we got out. Across the roof, he reminded me to let him ask the questions.

The gym smelled of dirty socks and mildew. Rain plonked loudly on the metal roof. For a small town, it was packed, with every machine taken. There was one trainer on the floor, which meant it had to be Boris. He looked like he'd stepped out of a seventies Schwarzenegger movie. He was ripped and wore a red muscle shirt that showed huge shoulders, arms the size of tree trunks, and a neck as thick as my head. His dark hair was cut in the style of a prince with bowl-shaped bangs that covered a backwards-sloping forehead. He wore white knee socks and short shiny green Adidas shorts that revealed furry legs. As he watched a row of men with weights, he uncapped a water bottle, tipped back his head and guzzled, emptying the bottle. He tossed it on the floor and then went to spot a man lifting a barbell.

I was intimidated by his size, but Daniel marched over to him, whipped out his badge, and said, "We need to speak with you."

"I'm busy," Boris said, in a heavy accent.

"Would you like to come down to the station?" Daniel didn't mention the location of the station.

Boris helped lower the barbell to the ground. "Two minutes." He stomped to a door, yanked it open and beckoned us into an office the size of a closet. He closed the door, leaned against it, and folded his arms, making his biceps pop. "I am working. What is the problem?" He spoke in a thick eastern European accent that may have been Russian.

"I've reopened the Sierra Rossario kidnapping case from four years ago," Daniel said. "I understand you worked at J'Adore Del Mar."

"So?"

"We heard you were trying to have a baby at that time."

"Bullshit. Who said that?"

"Is it not true?"

"Do I look like a guy who tries to have a kid? I have kids."

"What about Barbie?" I asked.

Boris turned and looked at me. "Who are you?"

Daniel moved in front of me, practically using his body as a shield. "She's with me. Where is Barbie?"

"Vero. She prefers the ocean. She does not care if she could make twenty thousand more working here. That's her nature. Someone else can make the sacrifice."

"How long have you worked here?" Daniel asked.

Wait a minute. I had to interrupt. "Does Barbie have children? Did you try IVF?"

Boris screwed up his face in a frown and looked at Daniel. "Who is she?"

"She came for the ride." Daniel turned his head and glared at me. "Can you wait outside?"

I stayed put. "Where are you from? What kind of name is Shanksky?"

Boris leaned into my face. "It's my name." His nostrils flared. "Why don't you go to the gym? Get on a treadmill. Turn that flab to muscle."

I felt myself turning red and hated it.

Boris turned to Daniel. "But you, now you work out. Where do you train?"

"On my own," Daniel said, looking obviously pleased.

I rolled my eyes.

"What can you press?"

"One-eighty."

"I think you must run. Long distance?"

"The marathon."

"Time?"

"Two hours, fifty-one minutes, eight seconds, was my record."

"Impressive. Been to Boston?"

"Twice. I've done the Iron Man twice as well."

Boris nodded up and down. "Remarkable."

I interrupted their love fest. "When's your birthday?"

"What?" Boris scowled, showing small, sharp teeth.

He looked like a Scorpio. "I'm guessing November."

"Why would you guess that?" Boris took a menacing step toward me.

Daniel held up an arm, blocking Boris' forward movement. "For the record, would you mind stating the date of your birth?"

"Yes, I would mind. That is personal information I do not give. I know my rights. Am I a suspect? Am I under arrest?"

Daniel held up his hands. "This is nothing official. We're trying to tie up loose ends, that's all."

"Then we are done." Boris flung open the door and rudely gestured at the exit.

We left the building, but not before I quietly retrieved the water bottle he'd thrown.

The door closed behind us with a bang and we went outside. The rain had let up. An odd drop fell here and there. Sidestepping the puddles, we crossed the parking lot. Daniel said, "It wasn't him."

I stopped walking. "I can't believe the questions you didn't ask."

"What did you want to know?"

"Did they try IVF? If so, where did they get the money? How long did he work as a bouncer? Was he in the mafia? How old are his kids? How long has he been married to Barbie? Does she still want a baby? Did they break up? Did something come between them, like a kidnapping? Where's he from? Why won't he give his birthday?"

"He didn't do it." Daniel resumed walking and I hurried to catch up to him.

"There's something suspicious about him. He's hiding something." I pulled the water bottle out of my purse. "Can you check it for prints?"

Daniel stopped walking. "You've got yours all over the bottle."

"Can't you subtract mine?"

Daniel reached into his pocket and pulled out a hanky and a plastic evidence bag. Using the cloth, he took the bottle and slipped it into the bag. "I'll have to take your fingerprints." He raised his eyebrows.

"Go ahead," I said, confident he would find nothing on me if he ran my prints.

As I walked, I pulled out my phone and examined the current transits. Neptune was in the 7th, representing Boris and Neptune was drugs. "How come he's so big? Is he on steroids? They shrink the gonads, you know. That could explain infertility."

"He works out."

"He got to you. He flattered you." I mimicked the strong accent badly. "You run so far. What big muscles you have. You're so smart for a policeman."

We reached the car and Daniel unlocked my door. "Police detective. Are you jealous he noticed I work out?"

"I found him very unattractive."

"For the record, I think you look just fine."

My rollicking boil simmered down. "Thank you."

"Boris isn't guilty. He's not the guy in the photo."

"It could be Barbie. Maybe he was waiting in the getaway car."

"We'll talk to her. My gut says they're not involved. My money's on the other one. Josefina's brother. Feel like going to Okeechobee tomorrow?"

"I thought you had church."

"And a barbecue. I'll sneak out early."

"I'd rather go to Vero and see Barbie."

"Something's up with Josefina. The number I got from Tiff isn't in service. I called her boss and she hasn't worked for her in years. Josefina lasted one month. Out of the blue she didn't show up for work and hasn't been seen again. It smells bad."

I had to agree. "Okeechobee it is."

***

Sunday afternoon Daniel was late. He promised to slip away from his parents by 1:00 at the latest, but when 2:00 came, I was afraid he'd chosen his family over me, as Tiffany said he would. I was waiting for him on the steps of the porch with Shiny when the next-door neighbors came home.

A car door slammed and Maribel and Joey got out. They were all dressed up; back from church I suspected. He wore an ill-fitting brown suit and tie, and she was in a girly pink dress with a high neck and long sleeves, despite the hot weather. It was April 10th and the temperature was expected to reach 90 by mid-afternoon.

They were with friends, another couple, who were similarly dressed in clothes that covered their skin. The man was clutching a Bible. They stood under the shade of an oak tree, deep in conversation, when Daniel roared into my drive. Immediately, a weight on my chest lifted. I was quietly appalled by how happy I was to see him.

He made his apology while patting Shiny. Claire had tried to prevent his escape, but he prevailed. He wanted to use the facilities and went inside, closing the front door with a bang.

The foursome on the grass looked over. A moment later, Joey burst through the hedge and stormed toward me. He reached the steps of the porch and yelled, "Stay away from my wife." His spit sprayed everywhere.

Shiny started to growl and I put my hand on her collar. "I was trying to help. She had an epileptic fit."

"Because of you. You brought the devil. She was fine before you arrived."

The front door opened and Daniel flew out. "Excuse me, sir. Step away from the porch. Move away from the lady."

"She's no lady. She's the devil."

Daniel whipped out his badge. "Move, now," he said sternly. "I won't ask politely again."

Joey took a few steps backwards. "You should arrest *her*. She's promoting ungodliness and willful fornication. She's a danger to society."

Daniel was on the grass in an instant, twisting Joey's arm around his back. "I don't know who you are, but that is no way to talk."

"The Bible warns about people like her."

Daniel looked at me. "Who is this?"

I nodded in the direction of his house. His wife and friends had disappeared.

Daniel dropped Joey's arm. "I want you to go home. Now. If you cannot speak civilly, you are to keep quiet. If you give Morgan any more trouble, if you say one more word about the devil and fornication, I will arrest you for harassment. I will get a judge to issue a restraining order that will keep you off this street. Do you understand?"

Joey looked sullen and hung his head. "It's my God-given duty to call out the devil in all his disguises."

Daniel pointed to Joey's house. "Go. Now. Not one more word."

Joey pursed his lips, set his jaw, but did as he was told. He marched across the grass and through the cocoplums.

Daniel came to the porch and watched Joey enter his house. "What did you do to him?"

"He thinks astrology is the devil's work."

"What does it have to do with fornication?"

"I told his wife how procreation works. She wants a baby."

Daniel made a face. "If he gives you any more trouble, call me."

"Should we go?" I wasn't going to cause any trouble for Maribel.

I put Shiny inside and we left, driving west on Route 70 at ninety miles an hour toward Okeechobee, the town on the north side of the lake, where Josefina lived with her mother and brother. It was a two-lane highway with intermittent passing lanes. We passed field after field of sugar cane that stood tall and green in the afternoon sun. The radio played, belting out oldies from the seventies.

As we drove, Daniel informed me that Josefina's phone had been out of service for years. He passed me a scrap of paper. It had Josefina's birth date and place. She was born December 26th in Juarez, Mexico. She was 36 and a Capricorn.

I entered the data into my phone and looked at the chart. She was born near a New Moon, with the Moon also in Capricorn, and depending on the time, closing in on the Sun. Mercury was also there, as was Venus, and this was one Capricorn gal. It explained her ambition and her desire to better herself. She would be responsible, hardworking, dependable, and reliable. All the attributes Ciro gave her, she had in spades.

"What do you think?" Daniel asked.

"She's not domestic. Her career was important to her. I don't think she was interested in being a mother or a housekeeper. I don't think she'd steal a baby."

"What if she was looking for easy money?"

"She would follow the law." I put away my phone. "I'm far more interested in seeing Boris's chart."

"I told you, he didn't do it. I've got a sixth sense about these things. I know."

I was beginning to understand why Daniel was frequently transferred, shuttled from one police department to another. Successful prosecutions depended on hard evidence and not gut feelings.

We reached Okeechobee in forty-five minutes and hit a stop light. The speed limit dropped as we drove into town. Daniel had entered Josefina's last known address into the GPS, which gave directions to a row of dilapidated bungalows on a lane parallel the highway.

"Turn right, now," a feminine voice in a British accent ordered from the GPS, and Daniel turned right onto the access road and pulled up the drive of the first bungalow. He parked beside a Buick that was the same vintage as my Rabbit.

We got out of the car and walked to the house. The grass was weedy and long. The house needed paint and the front windows were covered with cardboard. Daniel pulled out his badge and rapped loudly on the front door. From inside, a television roared. Loud barking came from the back yard. Daniel pushed on the door and it creaked open.

An old woman was shuffling to the door. On the couch sat two kids, a boy and girl. They glanced at us quickly, before turning back to the television. The woman let out a stream of Spanish, and I was surprised to hear Daniel respond in kind. I caught the name Josefina and the old woman stopped talking and shook her head.

A door slammed and a good-looking muscular man entered the living room, pulling on a white t-shirt. He whispered something in Spanish to the old woman, and she called the kids. The boy turned off the television and the three of them went through the kitchen and out into the back yard.

The man was my age, maybe a bit younger, with straight brown hair swept rakishly over the brow. He had deep-set almond eyes and thick lashes, a pink-bow mouth, and a shadow of facial hair. From his looks, I knew his Venus would be strong. He held out his hand and shook mine. "*Hola*!"

Daniel raised his badge. "Are you Enrique Garcia?"

The man dropped my hand and his eyes drifted lazily over to Daniel. "Who wants to know?"

"I'd like to speak to Josefina. Are you her brother?"

"Got a search warrant?"

"Sir, I don't want to search the place. I just want to talk to your sister. Tell me where she is and we'll leave."

"I don't have to tell you nothing."

I tried to help out and said in my nicest voice, "We were talking with Josefina's former employer, Tiffany Rossario, and she mentioned that she got Josefina a job in Belle Glade and we're trying to find her."

"Where's your badge?" he asked, his gaze wandering across my t-shirt.

"I'm not a policeman."

"You his lady?"

I felt my cheeks burn. "No."

He lifted his chin. "Why are you here?"

Daniel elbowed his way in front of me. "She came for the ride." His next words came out in a volley of Spanish. I left them to it and went outside, where the dog was still barking.

The woman and kids were sitting on the back stoop and the dog, an emaciated black pit bull, was chained to a tree, straining on his leash. I hate to see animals chained up and walked toward it, hand out.

The old lady said something in Spanish, and I said, "*No Español.*"

The boy said, "Look out. He bites."

I reached the pit bull, crouched down, and held out my hand. The dog smelled my hand, then lowered his head, and I patted it. I moved closer and he leaned against me, nearly knocking me over. "He doesn't bite. Look, he's friendly." I threw my arms around him and he licked my face with the sweep of a rough long tongue. "What's his name?"

The boy said something that sounded like Bubalito.

I called his name, but the dog paid me no mind. He was watching a squirrel. I turned to the boy. "What's your name?"

"Juan. She's Isabella."

"Is that your grandmother?"

"Un-ha."

"And your dad inside?"

"Un-ha."

"Is his name Rique?"

"Un-ha."

"Where is your Aunt Josefina?"

"In heaven."

"She's—?"

"With Jesus."

"I'm sorry." A heavy pall fell upon us. Seeking to lighten the mood, I said cheerily, "Where's your mom?"

"In El Paso." He looked at his sister. "Her mom's with Jesus too."

Great. I moved on quickly. "What grade are you in?"

"Third. She's in pre-K."

"How old are you?"

"I'm eight and she's four."

He was apparently used to answering for her. "When's your birthday?"

"March 15th. Hers is January 1st."

The squirrel was gone and Bubalito came to me, cropped tail, wagging mightily. There were scabs on the skin beneath his short fur. He wore a spiked collar that was too tight for his neck. I undid the clasp and took off the collar.

"No," Juan said. "He'll run away."

The dog wasn't going anywhere. "This is too tight. Look what it did to his fur, how it bunched up his skin. You shouldn't choke him." I loosened the collar as I spoke. "Treat him right and he might be your friend."

"*Con un perro?*"

"Yes, you can be friends with a dog," I said, as the grandma sniggered. I wondered if she knew more English than she'd let on. But I had no time to think about it, for Daniel appeared. His cell phone was out and he was snapping pictures.

Behind him, Rique was raging, "This is a violation of my rights. You have no right to be here." He had his own cell phone out. "*I'm* calling the cops."

I put my hand on Daniel's arm. "Let's go."

"I'm not finished."

"Daniel," I said, in a low voice that my mother used to use with me when she'd brook no objection. "We need to leave." I was afraid Rique would make good on his threat and get Daniel in trouble with his lieutenant. "We're sorry for the intrusion."

243

"I'll be back with a search warrant," Daniel said, as he shoved his phone into the clip on his belt and stalked past Rique.

I smiled at Rique. "I'm sorry about Josefina."

His hard look softened. "Friends with a dog?"

"They make good company."

"No, a man makes good company." He raised his eyebrows.

From the doorway, Daniel barked, "Morgan."

"He's a nice dog," I said.

"He's a fighter," Rique said.

"No, he's not."

"Morgan!" Daniel shouted again.

"Dog fighting is illegal," I said sharply, and went to the door.

Daniel stalked to the car. He paused at the Buick and peered in the window. He threw open the passenger door and grabbed a towel and tossed it at me.

It was white, frayed on one end, and streaked black with grease stains. It was the size of a tea towel, too small for a baby sling. I threw it back at him. "This is a rag."

He threw it on the hood, got out his phone, and snapped a photo of the license plate. Then he marched to the Mustang and wrenched open the passenger door. I got in and he slammed it shut. He stormed around the car, threw himself inside, and spun the tires, spraying dirt, as he reversed out the drive. "Guy's a fucking liar," Daniel said, as we turned onto the main drag. "I hate fucking liars. And assholes who neglect their pets. I'm calling animal control on him."

I looked over at him, shocked by his outburst. Up until now in trying circumstances he had been nothing but polite. But this was the negative side of Mars square Pluto. As Tiffany noted, Daniel had a temper. He exploded easily. Many criminals had Mars square

Pluto, as did those in law enforcement. The difference was in how Mars square Pluto was used. Daniel used the aspect to keep the law, whereas criminals used it to break the law. I wondered if he'd found out what I learned and I told him. "Josefina's dead."

"What?" Daniel returned my stare. His face was red and a line of sweat beaded his forehead.

"According to Juan," I clarified.

"Dead?" He pounded his fist on the steering wheel. "God damn it."

"Can you find out what happened to her?" I asked.

"That's step number two. First, I'm going to run Rique Garcia's photo and figure out who he is. He's been in prison. Did you see the tattoo on his wrist? Of course he knows his rights."

"He didn't have to talk to you."

"He would, if he didn't have something to hide."

"Or, if you spoke to him politely. He knows his rights and he knows you violated them. He's probably the only source of money for grandma and the kids."

"What? You want me to leave him alone because he's the sole breadwinner? No way. If he's guilty, he's going down. Did you see how he looked at you? What a prick."

I wondered if Daniel was jealous. Rique had been flirtatious, but it was innocent banter. I was amazed Daniel was so affected, though Tiffany had warned me about it. It was simultaneously disturbing and flattering. I wasn't used to men fighting over me. I brushed my bangs off my forehead and stared at my reflection in the window. A nasty thought hit me: was Daniel prejudiced? Maybe in his line of work he profiled suspects, lumped them together by race with no regard to individuals. I didn't like that at all.

"I am going to find out what he's done," Daniel said to the windshield. "And then I'm going back. He's hiding something."

"Is it because he's Hispanic?" I asked.

Daniel sent me a scathing look. "Of course not."

"You're usually so polite."

Daniel took an audible breath and ran a hand through his hair. "I don't know why he couldn't answer a few questions."

"Maybe it's how you asked. You catch more flies with honey than with vinegar."

He looked at me. "Is that what you call it?"

I shrugged. "I don't think he had anything to do with it."

"He had everything to do with it. We found our man."

"Hardly."

"He was on drugs."

"No he wasn't. He was in great shape."

Daniel looked over at me. "You noticed?"

"No. He's not nearly in as good a shape as you."

"That's right," Daniel said. "He's not."

He took me home and dropped me off. He had to go to his brother's and help move furniture. I didn't like the sudden chill in the air, but I didn't know how to warm things up.

"I'll run Rique's license plate and we'll get his birthday," Daniel said, tapping his fingers on the steering wheel as I opened the door.

Was he throwing me crumbs?

"I don't know when I'll get it. I'm going out of town next week. You won't be able to reach me."

The chilled air turned to lead and pressed down heavily on my chest. "Where are you going?"

"I can't say."

"When will you be back?"

"Friday."

"Can Claire reach you?"

"She knows how to get in touch."

"Will you be safe?"

"Sure," he said, not sounding convincing at all.

It struck me then what a dangerous job he had. I'd always known it, but it hadn't really registered. There was no guarantee he would make it home. The lead weight vanished, replaced now with impending emptiness. I wanted to kiss him, give him something to take with him in case I never saw him again. And have him kiss me, in case he didn't come back.

But he roared off, without looking back, showing way more self-control than I could muster. Was I really that easy to leave?

Chapter 24

The weatherman promised a rainy week and for once the forecast seemed correct. Though I tried to keep busy, I couldn't get Daniel out of my mind. I saw clients, studied their charts, listened to their stories, but as soon as they were gone, he was back. Tiffany hadn't mentioned how hard it was to care about someone you could lose at any moment.

Killing time, I did my taxes and went shopping with Suzie. She wanted to go to the mall and check out the spring sales and I went with her. I had found her a good wedding chart in late May, which was way better than my mother's. As we went through racks of dresses in Macy's, I explained the reasons for my choice. "On May 28th you're having a Venus return, which is like getting a double dose of Venus, the planet of love. On the same day, transiting Jupiter is trine your Sun and Moon, which is a marriage blessed by the gods."

Suzie liked the sound of it. "Will you tell my mom?"

I held up my hands. "No. You have to tell her."

Suzie held an orange sundress in front of me. "You could explain it. Why August is no good, when your mother said it was." She replaced the hanger, pulled out another. "I didn't know astrology was so subjective."

"It's not. I don't know what my mom sees in August."

"I may know."

I looked at Suzie with my nice eyebrows raised.

She grabbed my elbow and dragged me to an alcove, out of sight of a hovering sales lady. "August is a slow news month, right? Washington shuts down. The president goes on vacation to the East Coast. Look at the attention Chelsea Clinton got when she married. She stole the headlines."

I scratched my head, not liking it at all. Had my mother picked her date on the basis of the president's vacation schedule? "Where are you getting married?"

"In the Hamptons. At Elliot's dad's golf club."

"Do you think the president will go?"

"He'll be invited. I'm not sure he'll come. Depends how many donors show up."

"The wedding sounds like a political fundraiser."

"That's why I like your date."

I stared at the rack of sundresses and felt cold as I caught an inkling of wheels turning within wheels. Of course my mother would have her own reasons for selecting a terrible day in a terrible month. It was a date more fit for a hurricane than a wedding and she was counting on me to sell it. "Give your mom the May date," I said.

The so-called rebellious Suzie looked worried and I was worried too. Who knew what these mothers would do. I was already bracing myself for the fallout.

***

Thursday came and after class I walked Claire to her car. "Have you heard from Daniel?"

She shook her head "He's on a black op. Radio silence."

"He said you could reach him in an emergency."

"I can call the chief of police." She narrowed her eyes and looked at me sharply. "Is he in trouble?"

I was taken aback by her intensity. "Not at all. How would I know? I haven't seen him. I'm sure he'll be fine. He can take care of himself." I told her all the soothing words I'd been telling myself all week.

Claire wasn't buying it. "He can't take care of himself. He's hopeless on his own."

It wasn't what I wanted to hear.

She furrowed her brow. "Is something going on with you two?"

I drew in a sharp breath. "No! I'm thinking about our case. We can't work on it when he's not here."

She opened her car door. "Right."

No, wrong! If she only knew.

"How is the case going?" she asked.

With that invitation, I spat out the question that had been bothering me since Sunday. There was no right way to say it, so I just asked. "Does Daniel have a problem with Hispanics?"

Claire dropped her briefcase and leaned against the car. "His best friend from grade school is from El Salvador. Daniel took Spanish classes so he could speak to Marco in his native language. He's not a racist. Why would you ask?"

I looked up at the sky. It was streaked with clouds and there was a ring around the Moon, a harbinger of rain. "There's a suspect from Mexico. I don't think Daniel is treating him fairly."

"Is this the brother of Tiffany's maid?"

I wondered how much Claire knew about our "secret" investigation. "Yes. Rique. He's a nice guy."

Claire looked at me head on. "You liked him?"

"Not in the biblical sense."

"Good looking?"

I hiked a shoulder. "Maybe."

"There you go. Daniel is sensitive when it comes to women."

I had no idea what she meant and just stared at her.

"After what happened with Jen. And Tiffany. I could go on. And now, here's you and this so-called good-looking guy."

I was about to shake my head in protest, until it occurred to me she might have a point. Transference was a common occurrence in counseling and I saw it frequently in clients. Feelings associated with one situation were unconsciously transferred to an unrelated, but similar situation. Daniel's unwarranted emotional reaction to Rique was most likely his emotional response to the infidelity of his ex-wives. An inappropriate response to a stimulus was the key indication of the unconscious process. "You could be right."

Claire smiled her winning smile. "I know my brother."

"Any idea when he'll be back?"

"None whatsoever."

"Do you worry about him when he's gone?"

She looked at me closely. "You *are* worried about him. I knew it." She smiled a devious smile. "That's how it starts. That's the beginning."

I didn't tell her I was way past the beginning.

She gazed down the dark street. "You get used to it. I think the force thinks he's expendable."

"The Force?" *Star Wars* came to mind.

"The police force. I doubt they send their best detectives into harm's way."

I hadn't thought about that before. That was another reason Daniel had to prove his mettle.

"He loves his job and danger goes with it." Claire picked up her briefcase. "When he's gone it's like living in the gloom of a cloudy day. Then he appears and the sun comes out."

That was it exactly. "I could use some sun," I said.

"Me too. I'm tired of the rain. Depresses the hell out of me. Speaking of which. Ready for your deposition?"

It was five days away. "I don't think I'll ever be ready." I couldn't wait for it to be over.

She opened her car door. "I'm counting on you."

***

On Friday the sun came out and Daniel came back. He called during lunch to see if I was free to go to Okeechobee after work. "I got a search warrant for Rique's house."

"What about Barbie? I thought we had to see her." I was surprised how quickly he slipped into business as usual.

"We'll see her tomorrow. I'm worried Rique will abscond. I'll pick you up at five."

He came early and pulled into my drive the same time as Hyacinth pulled into Jake's. She got out of her car dressed in her yoga outfit and Jake opened the front door. I waved, and at least Hyacinth returned it, but from Jake, nothing.

Daniel looked smug. "He moved on fast."

He had. I had gone to yoga, trying once more to mend fences, and it was obvious to me they were a couple. He got over me fast, but still had no desire to talk to me. Not that it bothered me at the moment. The sun was shining and my world was all right. "How was your week?" I asked, drinking in Daniel's presence, soaking up his scent.

"Long. I missed you."

I turned my back on the sun. I wasn't going to say I missed him too. What an understatement that would be. "I'm glad you're back."

"When I was gone, I heard the chief came down and was asking about astrology."

I drew in a sharp breath. "Asking what?"

"I didn't ask. I didn't want to look too interested. Maybe someone complained about you. Molly from security, or Avery from gardening. I can't impress upon you how important it is to be careful. Word gets out about you and I could lose my job. No one holds astrologers in high esteem at the PD."

It was so different from what I remembered in DC. My mother was revered. "I'll be careful." I didn't want to be the one to make him lose his job.

He looked at his watch. "Shall we go?"

As we drove west toward the ball of the sun, I put on my sunglasses and lowered the visor to block the glare. "How did you manage to get a search order when no one knows about our investigation?"

"I said it was on suspicion of drugs. With a name like Rique Garcia? No questions asked."

"Is that fair?"

"He stole a kid. He has to pay."

I looked out the side window. "We don't know he did anything. Are you sure you're not mixing him up with someone who stole a girlfriend?" I turned my head to look at him. "Could it be you're mad at Ciro and taking it out on someone who looks like him?"

Daniel tapped his fingers on the wheel. "For your information, Rique's a convicted felon."

"What did he do?"

"Forgery. He got a ten-year sentence and served six months. Want a birth date?"

I got out my phone and tapped in the information. Rique was a Gemini and had four exalted planets. His Mars was in Capricorn, which made him responsible and a hard worker. He had Pluto in its own sign of Scorpio, Mercury in its sign of Gemini, and Jupiter in its sign of Sagittarius. I said, "It's a nice-looking chart."

"Meaning he'd get away with the crime?"

I turned off my phone. My battery was getting low. "Meaning, he wouldn't stoop to it. He's willing to work for his money and not take the easy way out. What did he forge?"

"A check for two hundred dollars. He told the judge his grandmother was sick. Yeah, right."

"Tiffany told us his mother has diabetes. And he got ten years? For that piddling amount? Obviously someone saw the injustice given he didn't serve his whole sentence."

"What injustice? Don't do the crime if you can't do the time."

We reached a passing lane and Daniel sped up to pass a line of transport trucks. I said, "If I forged a check for two hundred, how much time would I get?"

"Twenty to life. I'd throw the book at you. You know better."

"You'd make a lousy judge."

"No, a lousy judge let him out to commit a kidnapping."

"Under his sick mother's nose? From a house where his only sister worked and a patron who helped him become a citizen? I don't think so. Did you find out what happened to Josefina?"

We reached the end of the passing lane and Daniel cut off a pickup in order to get back into the lane. "She was hit by a car in Okeechobee two months after the kidnapping. I'm not sure if it means anything or not." He turned off his turn signal.

"What happened?"

"She was running across the street. Could have been running from something. Except she had her arms full of grocery bags and eyewitnesses said she likely couldn't see the car. It was late. Dark. A hit-and-run. They never found the driver."

The sun went behind a cloud and the sky went dark. I flipped up my visor. "And you wonder why Rique is mad? He gets ten years for writing a bad check and a killer gets away."

Daniel shrugged. "The police don't catch everyone." He tapped the brakes and slowed down. "Are you hungry?"

"I could eat."

He was pulling into a roadside barbecue. "Ask me about Isabella's mother."

"Ask what?"

"Okay, I'll tell you over dinner."

He parked in the lot of a place called the Juicy Pig, which sported a sculpture of a pink pig with a roast outlined on its side. I got chicken and he got brisket and we sat on a small porch at a picnic table eating thick sandwiches and drinking lemonade as the sun sank into a bed of clouds. Between bites, Daniel said, "Juan's mother is in La Tuna federal penitentiary outside of El Paso. She's serving a twenty-year sentence for manslaughter. Isabella's mother put her up for adoption."

I put down my sandwich and wiped my mouth, surprised by the news.

Daniel smiled a big smile, obviously proud of his detective work. "I got Isabella's birth certificate from vital records. She was born in Miami General Hospital and her mother, Gabriella Hortez, planned to give her up."

"Why?"

"I can think of a hundred reasons, starting with the father being a class one jerk. Maybe because she was sixteen. Maybe because she wanted to finish high school."

I took a sip of lemonade, which was cold and slushy with chunks of ground ice. "She must have changed her mind."

"No. She died. Convenient huh?"

I swallowed hard. "You think Rique killed her?"

"He didn't want her to give up the baby."

"How do you know?"

"I got the hospital records. He was banned from the place. He wasn't allowed anywhere near Gabriella. They weren't married and he had no say what she did with the baby."

"Why not?"

"Fathers don't in this state. It's all up to the mother. Even if she's underage. She gets to decide."

I liked that, though, in our male-dominated society I was surprised. "It doesn't seem fair."

"Typically, I'd agree."

"How did Gabriella die?"

"A complication of childbirth. Handy, huh?"

"What complication? Eclampsia?"

"How do you know?"

I put down my sandwich and wiped my fingers with the napkin. "It's high blood pressure. It's not uncommon." I knew Kolby, the pregnant teen who was giving up her baby, had got it. "It's associated with weight gain. It's not something you give someone deliberately."

"Well, luckily for Rique, Gabriella died the day after Isabella was born and before the adoption papers were signed. Once she was dead, the adoption was null and void. Rique was back in the picture. The baby was his."

"You have to give him credit for wanting his baby," I said.

"Any man would fight for his kid." Daniel said. "I'd never let someone else raise mine."

Except Daniel couldn't have any.

"I'm looking into the adoption agency," Daniel said. "Little Angels. It closed down a few years ago, but I found a social worker who worked with the mothers. Maybe she can tell us more about Rique and what happened."

It sounded like a plan.

We finished our food, got back on the road, and reached Okeechobee at dusk. As soon as I saw the house, I knew Daniel was right to worry. The old rusted car in the front yard was missing, the house was dark, and the front door stood ajar. From a distance it looked like Rique, his mother, and the kids had fled. "Son of a bitch," Daniel said as we turned onto the access road.

We went into the house. He turned on the living room light and the bulb blazed. Rique left in haste, without bothering to disconnect the electricity. He'd left the couch, but the television was gone. I heard a dog's mournful howl and went through the house into the yard. Rique also left his dog.

Bubalito yelped happily as if he remembered me. I unclasped his chain and he ran around in circles. There was a bowl of food filled with fire ants that I dumped by a tree. I washed out the bowl, filled it with fresh water, and Bubalito lapped thirstily. I wondered how long he'd been alone. I didn't think long.

I sat down on the back step and Bubalito bounded over and leaned against me. I patted his back and slung an arm around him. In that instant I decided to take him home.

I heard Daniel stomping around the house and wondered what he hoped to find. It seemed pretty obvious to me what happened. Rique was spooked, but that didn't make him guilty.

Ten minutes passed before Daniel came out. "Son of a bitch left his dog? Now do you see what an asshole he is?"

"He knew you'd be back."

"He hasn't been gone long. I talked to the neighbor. He was here this morning. I put out an APB. That's an All-Points Bulletin. I hope he hasn't made it to Mexico." Daniel sat down on the steps beside me and Bubalito went to him, nuzzling his hand. "I'm surprised he's got a nice dog."

"Maybe he's a nice guy."

"He's a kidnapper. That's why he ran."

"Or, he didn't trust you. You told him you'd be back and he believed you. For good reason. You could arrest him for nothing and he knew that too."

"Guiltless people don't flee," Daniel said, stubbornly.

"You could send him back to prison."

"Where he belongs. He's guilty. We found our man."

"You scared away your man. At least you've got Barbie and Boris."

Bubalito flopped to the ground. He was panting rank hot air, but smiling, as a dog can do. I rubbed his belly. "I'm going to keep him."

"That's a bad idea. I'll call Animal Control. They'll come pick him up."

"No way. I won't let him go to the pound."

"You've already got a dog."

"I can have two."

"It will be expensive. Vet bills. Shots. Heartworm pills."

"It's not so bad."

"All right. I'll take him."

"What? You're never home."

"I hate to be alone."

"You can't have him. I'm going to call him Bob. Come here, Bob."

Bob came to me and I encircled his broad shoulders with my arms. I lay my face on his back and looked at Daniel. "You could come over and see him whenever you wanted."

"We could share him."

"No. He's mine. I called it first. He'll be a good guard dog. I thought you were worried about my safety."

I let Bob go and he sat down, looking at me, panting heavily.

"He wouldn't scare away anyone," Daniel said. "You need a gun."

"I can't shoot."

"I'll teach you."

"I don't want to learn."

"Everyone should know."

"I want a dog, not a gun."

Daniel said, "I could take him on weekends when you go to your Saturday workshops."

"Shiny would miss him."

"I'll take her too. I won't split them up. We've got to do what's best for them."

Were we really arguing over custody of the dog? I snapped my fingers and Bob came to me, hanging his head over my shoulder.

"Come here, boy," Daniel said. But Bob just looked at him.

I slung my arms around him. "Looks like he chose me."

Bob rode to Coral Cove in the backseat of the Mustang, head hanging out the open window, stub tail wagging constantly. I was happy to have a new dog. Shiny didn't belong to me. She was Andre's. He got her at the pound before I met him. He wanted a big dog and there was a shortage at the pound. The day before his visit, all the big dogs had been shipped to the vet school in College Station to be used for experimental surgery. The van came monthly and if Shiny was still there when it returned, she'd be taken too. Andre saved her. I thought it said a lot about his character. And then he left her.

Back in Coral Cove, Daniel came in to witness the meeting of the dogs. I'm not sure if he was expecting a fight, but they were instant friends. Bob liked Shiny and Shiny liked Bob back. He followed her around, tried out her bed, sniffed her food bowl, and drank from her water bowl. We took them for a walk. I left Shiny on her own and used her leash on Bob. He would need some work. He wanted to go where he wanted.

Daniel walked on high alert, surveying the street, peering warily at shadows. "Do you always do this? Walk alone at night?"

I never worried about it before. "I have two dogs."

"It's a dangerous world."

"I try not to think about it."

"That doesn't make it go away." He stopped walking and looked at me, his musky scent washing over me. "We're getting close. I can feel it. There might be blowback."

I liked that he was worried about me, but it was unnecessary. "Blowback from whom? Rique? He's harmless. Plus he's gone."

"He could have friends. Be part of a gang. I don't like you out here alone. Let's go back. I don't have my gun."

We turned around, brushing shoulders. Just a faint touch of him electrified my skin. "I don't go far."

"I wish you wouldn't go at all."

I wished *he* wouldn't go at all. "I'll be careful."

"I don't want anything to happen to you. I could stay over."

"Go home," I said, wanting him to stay.

"If you insist."

I didn't at all.

We walked back in silence and stopped by his car. "I'll see you tomorrow." He took my hand and squeezed it.

I squeezed it back feeling sparks shoot up my spine. It took a lot, to let him go.

Chapter 25

The next afternoon he was back and we headed to Vero Beach to interview Barbie Cramer. Daniel had to work all day and I'd spent the sunny afternoon at the dog-friendly beach, letting the dogs run wild. Shiny loved the water and paddled around, but Bob hated the waves and stayed on shore and howled while Shiny leapt and bounded in the surf. By the time Daniel arrived at five, clouds were rolling in and the dogs were exhausted and sleeping side-by-side on Bob's new bed.

Barbie Cramer was working from four till ten at a gym called The Fabulous U which was on US-1 just past Route 60. Rather than take I-95, we took the main drag, hitting every light. Daniel thought the trip was a waste of time. He was convinced the kidnapper had got away. He wanted his lieutenant to issue a BOLO, a "be on the look-out" for Rique, but his lieutenant refused. Apparently the boss needed concrete evidence that Rique was a drug trafficker, and I concurred.

"I spoke to the social worker this morning," Daniel said as we stopped for another light. He pulled a slip of paper out of his pocket and passed it to me.

There was a name, Brad Abbott, and the word, Orlando. "Who's Brad?" I asked.

"The poor guy who was supposed to get Rique's baby before the girlfriend died and he nixed the adoption. Brad used to live in Miami. I hope he can shed some light on Rique. Might give us a clue on how to find him."

I tucked the note into the pocket of my jeans. "Did you call Brad?"

"I tried. I left a message. He didn't get back to me. We might do better going to Orlando than Vero."

"I want to see Barbie. Did you talk to her?"

"She hasn't returned my calls."

"How did you get her birth date?" Daniel had texted it to me earlier.

"Ciro. He got it from the employment records at J'Adore Del Mar. Boris left his birthday blank and no one ever called him out about it."

"Maybe Barbie will tell us."

"It doesn't matter." Daniel had already convicted Rique.

We drove a block and hit another light. To the west, the sky was black, bringing an early dusk. I heard the low rumble of thunder. A storm was blowing in.

I entertained myself by reviewing Barbie's chart. I could tell with Venus in Libra conjunct Jupiter and Uranus, she was lucky and likely beautiful. She had Moon and Mars in Capricorn, which would make her cold, and depending on the house, give trouble conceiving a baby. But the Capricorn planets also gave ambition and the ability to work hard.

"According to Barbie's former boss at J'Adore Del Mar, she's a paradigm of virtue," Daniel said as he drummed his fingers, waiting on another light. "She was never late, never missed work, and was real dedicated. He wanted to promote her, but that meant elevating her above other people who'd been working longer, and he thought it might start a war. Also, he was worried about

Boris. The man has a temper. He's also strong. He won some Mr. America contest. The boss said neither one would be involved in a kidnapping."

But Barbie had Mars with Saturn and Uranus. She could be impulsive, frustrated, act out.

Daniel glanced at me. "What does the chart say?"

I pointed to the light that had changed and we shot forward. "I have to see her."

Barbie wasn't beautiful, she was drop-dead gorgeous. Through a glass window, we watched her prance around as she wound down a step class. Tall and muscular, she wore a cream-colored thong leotard and white stretch shorts that showed every curve and crevice. She had red hair pulled back in a ponytail that bounced wildly as she swung her head and gyrated her hips.

The class ended, she turned off her music and stretched languidly. Daniel swept in and motioned for the students to skedaddle. He got out his badge and they did as he asked.

Barbie rubbed the back of her neck with the towel, not taking her eyes off him. "What's this about, officer? Can I call you officer?"

"You can call me Daniel. *I'm* looking into the kidnapping at J'Adore Del Mar four years ago," he said, explaining why *he* had come. I wasn't mentioned.

Barbie bent forward and lifted her foot up on a block step and gave a deep bend, stretching out her calf and lifting her derriere high in the air. "That was so sad."

"You knew Tiffany?" Daniel asked.

Barbie stood with her legs apart, raised her hands over her head and thrust her hip to one side while dipping the other. "I didn't *know* her. I read about her. You don't mind if I cool down, do you?" she said breathlessly. "I'm kind of hot." She fanned her face. I thought she smelled like stale perfume.

"Please continue," Daniel said.

"You never caught the guy?" She repeated the stretch on the other side.

"Not yet," Daniel said. "We're closing in on him."

"Or her," I said.

Barbie looked taken aback, as if I had popped in from out of thin air. "Who are you?"

"This is Morgan. She's not with the police department."

"I'm helping with the investigation," I said, giving Daniel a frosty look.

"Off the record," Daniel said, sounding apologetic.

"Where were you the night of the kidnapping?" I asked.

Barbie laughed at me. "She your bulldog?" Said with scorn and an almost imperceptible shake of her head as she dismissed me. *With my nice-looking haircut and cool glasses and all.* "When was Boris born?" I asked coldly.

"Why do you want to know?"

I narrowed my eyes and glared at her. "Why is he so secretive about it? What is he hiding? Was he born in November?"

She smiled slowly, a knowing smile. "You're an astrologer! OMG. I've never actually met one before." She threw back her head, laughing raucously.

Daniel began to laugh with her, until I shot daggers of ice at him with my eyes. He cleared his throat. "Miss Cramer. Were you working the night of the kidnapping?"

She toweled her deep cleavage. "You can call me Barbie and I was. I had an alibi. I talked to the police and the FBI and I was cleared. I don't know what the astrologer's telling you."

"We heard you wanted a baby and couldn't get pregnant," I said.

Daniel swung his head and shot me a warning look with wide-open eyes.

I refused to back down and continued staring at Barbie. "Were you treated for infertility?"

"That's none of your business."

"I'll ask the questions," Daniel said sharply.

I made a disparaging noise and ignored him. "IVF is expensive. How could you afford it?"

"I'm guessing I make more than an astrologer."

"Boris said he has kids. He's not the problem."

She put her face in mine. "You don't know anything."

"Why don't you tell me what I don't know."

"Astrology is stupid."

I opened my mouth to respond, but I didn't have a chance. Daniel raised his hands. "All right, ladies." He flashed me a deep frown. "I'll ask the questions, if you don't mind." He turned to Barbie and offered her his dimpled smile. "Do you have children?"

"No. Nor do I want any."

"Did you have infertility treatment?"

"No."

"Thank you very much for your time." He gave her his card. "Call me if you think of anything else."

Barbie dipped her head and pulled a coy smile. "You're welcome. Let me get my card. You can call me. You don't need a reason."

I rolled my eyes as she bounced away and returned with a purple card.

We left. Outside, the storm had passed, leaving puddles on the asphalt. "You should learn to take your own advice," Daniel said as we crossed the parking lot. "You catch more flies with honey."

"I didn't realize you knew you were dealing with a fly. She was deliberately trying to distract you and you let her. You trust no one, unless they swing their hips and flaunt their boobs. Then you stop thinking."

"She was cooling down. That's a strenuous workout."

"Of course it is. How could she be guilty."

He stopped walking. "You're jealous."

"No. You're not objective."

"Oh, *I'm* not," he said with a laugh.

I started walking. "I just want to find out what happened to Sierra."

He caught up to me. "Then we need to focus on finding Rique."

"Or, check out Barbie's story. Why do you think she's telling the truth?"

"My gut."

"Oh, that's your gut, is it?"

"Barbie didn't do it."

"Heavens no, can't be Barbie."

We reached the car and he got out his key and unlocked the doors. "They were both working the night of the kidnapping. I checked their work schedule. No opportunity."

"Boris had two jobs. Obviously they needed money. I bet she did want a baby and she lied about it. Here are two people with motive. They knew the layout of the place. He's foreign. I'm sure either one of them could climb the wall. They fit the profile. You should check her out."

Daniel opened my door. "Fine. I'll run her through the system and see what comes up. Happy?"

"All right."

"Feel like dinner?"

"You don't have to go help someone move? No one's sick or needs shelves built?"

He stared into my eyes. "I'm all yours."

***

We went to a small place in Vero Beach where we thought no one we knew would see us. The Ocean Grill was on the island, perched precariously on the sand and less than ten feet away from the pounding surf. The place was packed and we left our name at the front and took a seat in the back at the bar to wait for a table. The margaritas were on special and seemed especially strong. I'd taken only a few sips when our table was ready.

It was tucked in a dark corner, glowing with a bright candle that made the heavy silver gleam. The tablecloth was thick, the napkin heavy, and the waiter, old but fast. He ran through the specials, left us with wooden menus and a basket of crackers and a blue-cheese spread. From somewhere nearby oil sizzled and my stomach rumbled.

I looked around. Most of the tables were for two. The place was dark and intimate. Light classical music played in the background of soft chatter. I felt like we were out on a first date. I gulped my drink and the booze flushed my skin. I wondered how in God's name I would keep myself to myself during dinner, and beyond.

I put down my glass. Daniel was staring. He said, "This is like a real date."

I traced a bead of condensation down the glass. "I was thinking the same thing."

He rested his elbow on the table, chin in his palm. A seductive pose if there ever was one. "Hmm," he said. "Maybe I can read your mind."

"Is that right?" I didn't think so. If he could, he would know my thoughts were way past a first date.

"I called Claire's lawyer this morning. I made an appointment for Thursday. I'm going to get the ball rolling. I called Jen. Told her to expect papers."

I picked up my glass, as my heart rate picked up. That was good news.

"We're going to rush it."

I sipped my drink, the booze slid down my throat, cranking up the temperature, burning my belly. That was enough, wasn't it? The promise of a divorce. Real papers, signed by a lawyer and sent to a cheating spouse who was far away.

And just like that, all my resolutions fell away. I was done with it. Done with the waiting, the invisible lines, and boundaries that kept Daniel at bay. He had called the lawyer. The case was almost closed. It was Barbie or Boris. Once Daniel checked them out he'd see what the trainers were capable of and view Exercise Barbie in a new light. There was no reason to keep on the brakes. I threw back more of my drink and put down my glass. Daniel was still staring.

"What was going on in your head right there?" he asked.

I put my hand on the table, half way across, reaching toward his side. "I was thinking about how hard it is to wait."

"Tell me about it. It's killing me. It's something I've never done before. I don't like it much."

"Me neither." We were on the same page.

"I don't know how you do it," Daniel added. "You're so determined. You say you're going to do something and you do it. You make it look easy."

"It's not easy," I said, as I traced the salt rim on my drink, then tasted the tip of my finger in what I hoped was a provocative pose.

Daniel leaned forward. "I should never have kissed you. I crossed a line. I did something I can never undo."

He was using my words. But this was hardly the same. "You don't have to feel guilty."

"I do. I should have never tempted you. I won't do it again."

Wait! What? *No!* This wasn't how it was supposed to go.

The waiter was back to take our order. I got the special and the first choice of everything he offered, hoping to speed him up. The conversation was turning out wrong. At this stage we were supposed to agree there was no point in waiting any more. We'd waited long enough, it was time to move forward.

The waiter left, promising to be right back with the wine. Who ordered that?

"I like myself when I'm with you," Daniel said. "I feel in control. Typically, my mind checks out and I go by instinct. I like being able to rise above it. I never knew it was possible. I'm surprising myself."

I wanted to bang my head on my bread plate. How could he blow cold when I was about to boil over? "There are limits to limits," I said.

"Yes. Claire said you'd never go beyond them. I didn't believe her, but she was right. She said you had morals and ethics and you would never waver, no matter how hard it got. You dragged me with you. Made me rise to the occasion."

That wasn't the rise I wanted from him. I withdrew my hand, picked up my drink, and polished it off. It was hard to swallow. I had backed myself into a corner with my pious stance. I saw no way out.

He stared at the candle. "I like who I am when I'm with you. A better version of myself."

I looked for the waiter. I needed another drink. Make it a double. This was going all wrong.

"Let's talk about something else," Daniel said, throwing back a mouthful of ice. He didn't have any trouble swallowing. "I hear a tropical storm is coming."

In my view it had already arrived, dousing all passion.

"I won't be here," Daniel said, his words bringing more rain. "I'm going out of town for a few days."

"More work?" I asked, in a high, hollow voice.

Daniel tore the plastic wrapping off a pair of crackers. "I'll leave tomorrow after lunch."

"Are we having lunch?" I asked, scraping at crumbs.

"At my parents," he clarified. The optional weekly barbecue that none of the siblings ever skipped. "I won't be gone long."

Every day was too long. "When will you be back?"

"Tuesday."

The day of my deposition. "Morning?" I might need a pep talk.

"Evening."

"Okay." I might need an ally or consoling, depending on how the appointment transpired.

The waiter was back with the wine. Daniel looked up. "You can just pour," he said.

At least the wine was good. As it turned out, I'd ordered an excellent seafood casserole with creamed spinach and a side salad with Roquefort dressing. Daniel got a steak with mashed potatoes and green beans. If I couldn't satisfy my libido, I could at least satisfy my appetite, and by the time the plates were cleared and dessert was denied, I had made peace with the status quo. I didn't like it, but I could live with it. At least until we closed the case. I didn't think it would take long.

We were among the last to leave. I guess I drank most of the wine, which left me somewhat tipsy and wobbling on my feet. On a couple of fabricated occasions, Daniel had to grab me and hold me up and I hung on, but he set me straight and gave me space, leaving me to wonder where this cold man came from. I liked him better when he blew hot.

Chapter 26

He left me at home with a chase kiss on my forehead that nearly singed my skin and had me longing for more. As Claire aptly put it, he took the sun with him, for when he left, the rain came. It rained all day Sunday and all through the night. A tropical depression had stalled when a low pressure system refused to budge. Roads and lawns flooded.

Monday came and my roof started to leak. By Tuesday, the day of the deposition, my toilet backed up, a portent of things to come. The day began with a bang and got worse. Just before noon, as I was wrapping up my work day, my mother called.

"How could you?" she demanded when I answered, her voice dripping with anger.

I was sitting at my desk, writing out my notes from my last client. "How could I what?"

"Don't play dumb. You know what I'm talking about."

"How could I give Suzie a good time to marry? Unlike the political time you chose? How could I? Maybe because I'm a decent person and I want Suzie to be happy."

"Watch your tone. I'm trying to save you from yourself. You've been so obstinate about the wedding election I got a second opinion. I asked the president of the Astrology Association of America to compare my election chart with yours. You know whose chart she picked?"

I threw down my pen. Since when did my mother know the president of the AAA? "May 28th is way better than August 27th."

"You can't see it, can you? To think you actually do this for a living. Unbelievable."

"What did I miss?"

"Your true calling. When will you realize you're wasting your time and leave astrology to the professionals." It wasn't a question.

"There's nothing wrong with May 28th," I said, stubbornly holding on to my date.

"The president of the AAA hated it. She couldn't believe you'd suggest something so close to the eclipses."

"They're not hitting Suzie's chart."

"They hit everybody. You don't even know basic astrology. Look at the nodes and you'll see what I mean."

"The nodes?"

"Of the Moon."

"I thought they showed past lives and karma." Concepts I didn't buy into.

"They show more than that. Read the latest research. Try to keep up. Then look at the diurnal, Black Moon Lilith, Ceres, the Jupiter–Pluto midpoint, Cupido and Zeus, and maybe reconsider."

"Cupido?" I asked, wondering again if she looked at all of these things.

"A trans-Neptunian."

I knew what it was. A hypothetical planet used by symmetrical astrologers. I said, "Suzanne likes my day."

My mother actually hissed. "You leave me no choice. Persist and the AAA will censure you. They'll eject you from the organization. They'll rescind your cherished diploma. They'll remove you from their website. You'll be finished."

"You would do this?"

"*You did this*. Don't blame me. Fix it, or else." I heard a click and the dial tone.

I dropped my phone and stared into the rain, heart racing, mind fuming. I wanted to throw the phone, but I knew given my current luck, it would break. Instead I threw my sandal and left a black mark on the wall. This was the 'terrible mother' of my childhood rising up and threatening to end the world if she didn't get her way. She could make the sky fall on a whim. And she did, time after time. I'd spent my life learning how to roll with her punches, but she always got me. Effortlessly she reduced me to an insecure sniveling scared adolescent. I knew she could ruin my life and would do so to prove a point. I wanted to scream. I did scream and the dogs came running.

I hugged them both and calmness came. I opened the astrology app to see the sky. Sure enough Mars and Mercury were in the 10th house of the mother, constellating anger and attack. I was the Moon, in the 5th house of children; becoming one again. It took ten minutes of deep breathing and ten years of psychological training to coax back the inner adult.

Despite having no appetite, I ate too much lunch. Then I took a shower and dressed in the black suit I wore to defend my first master's thesis, which was not unexpectedly a little tight. I didn't like the prominence of the rapid response alarm button hanging around my neck and replaced it with a single strand of pearls. Forsaking nylons and sensible shoes, I grabbed my black huaraches. This was Florida after all. Then I stepped into my flip-flops. I wasn't going to let puddles ruin my good sandals.

There was a knock on the door and Bob started barking. Wondering if I'd forgotten to cancel a client, I hurried down the hall.

Annie. I relaxed, until I saw her face.

She came in and it was obvious she'd been crying. "Kolby's going to keep her," she wailed.

My knees buckled. I put my hand on the wall. "What happened?"

"She changed her mind," Annie yelled. "What do you think?"

I closed my eyes, summoning the horary chart. There was an opposition, signifying separation, followed by a trine. There would be difficulty that I said would end well. "Mercury's still retrograde," I said. "Kolby will change her mind. Don't do anything rash."

Annie looked at me sadly. "You can't admit when you're wrong. You always have to act like you know everything."

Striving for a calm voice, I said, "I know you're upset."

"Upset doesn't come close," Annie shouted, so loudly she spat. "You said not to worry. I didn't worry. You said to name her, make her ours, and we did. I don't know why I ever listened to you."

I'd seen the hiccup. I thought it was the health issue, but it was this. This was the meaning of the opposition: separation. "Mercury goes direct on Friday. Whatever happens now will be reversed. Wait it out."

She gave me a withering look. "I'm done. To hell with Kolby and to hell with you."

"She's just a kid. You don't know what you're asking her to do."

Annie was in my face. "And you do? As you sit on your throne and decide how the world will turn?"

That was hardly fair, but understandable.

"I'm going to sue the little bitch. She'll rue the day she picked us to screw over."

"Annie, don't. Please. Sleep on it. You'll make things worse."

"I don't give a shit." She raised her hand and for a moment I wondered if she would strike me. Instead, she slashed at the air. "To hell with both of you."

She punctuated each vibrating word. Then she whirled around, thumped open the front door, and stormed out. I watched her peel out of the drive and nearly hit a station wagon. She leaned on the horn and let out a screeching honk, as if the other driver was to blame.

I watched her go, wanting to go after her, and knowing it was no use. I had to go myself. Kevin's lawyer, Jeffery Jerrick, had an office in Stuart, a forty-minute drive if you didn't factor in the school buses, flooded streets, and rain. I was already late and there was nothing I could do but wait for the storm to pass and the transits to change.

I was heading south, driving fast in heavy traffic when I noticed the car's temperature gauge in the red zone. The car was overheating—more Mercury and Mars. I used Andre's trick and turned on the heater to cool the engine. I slowed down and managed to reach Stuart with the needle in the black, but by the time I got to the law office, I was dripping in sweat. And late.

The tall building was as a cold as an igloo. I wondered if I was getting sick as I rode a swift elevator up to the 38th floor. As instructed, I had brought my laptop and my hands were hot, even though I felt cold and clammy.

The secretary gave me a second look as she buzzed the lawyer to let him know I had come. Jeffrey Jerrick came out, hand extended and wearing a million-dollar smile. He dropped his hand before we could shake as if I might be carrying a contagious disease. "Everything okay?"

No, I wanted to yell. A friend was losing a baby, another friend was afraid of losing her house, a baby was lost, a mother was bereft, my mother was vindictive and insane, my car was breaking down, and I had to testify under oath for an astrology-hating judge… Nothing was okay.

"Are you sick?" The lawyer took a few steps back. He was short, not much taller than I, with sandy blond hair that was going gray, likely prematurely, because he didn't seem over thirty-five.

"I'm fine. Just a little hot."

"Would you like a drink? Water? Coke?"

"Water, thank you."

The lawyer motioned for my laptop and I handed it over. He passed it to the secretary. "Come on back. We're waiting on Sam Harris."

Sam was Claire's lawyer. I looked at my watch. I was five minutes late. "He's not here?"

"Not yet."

I followed Jerrick down an icy hallway layered with thick carpet that left the imprint of the soles of my huaraches. We went into a conference room. A slovenly woman in jeans and a t-shirt that didn't completely cover her belly, lifted herself almost out of her seat in greeting. Jerrick introduced the court clerk who would record the testimony. She smelled of cigarette smoke.

He pulled out my chair, laid a light hand on my shoulder, and said in a kind tone, "It shouldn't take long." The secretary came with a tall crystal glass of water that was brimming with ice and wet with condensation.

Jerrick took the chair across the table from me. "Thanks for coming. I know it's an inconvenience."

I took a sip of water and thought maybe it wouldn't be so bad. "I'm happy to help Claire."

"You know her long?"

The phone rang and Jerrick raised a finger. He answered and stared across the table at me. He ended the call and put down the phone. "That was Sam Harris. He has car trouble. He won't be able to make it." Jerrick leaned back in his chair and laced his hands behind his head. "What do you want to do? We can reschedule or proceed. Up to you."

I looked at my watch. I'd already taken off the afternoon and driven all this way. Jerrick wasn't the shark I was expecting and he already said it wouldn't take long. "We can proceed."

He lowered his hands, snapped forward, and nodded to the clerk. "We'll begin. Morgan Sterling has agreed to participate in the absence of representation." He smiled a winning smile. "The testimony is under oath, so just tell the truth and we'll be fine."

He began by asking personal information, my full name and address, and rewarded my answers with encouraging smiles. He took notes on yellow foolscap as the camera rolled and the clerk examined her nails. Then, "What is your relationship with Claire Quade?"

"We're friends."

"Just friends. Have you ever had a homosexual relationship?"

I braced myself for what was coming. "No."

"Has Claire?"

"I don't think so."

"So it's possible."

"I think she would have told me and she hasn't."

"For the record, please answer yes or no. Has Claire Quade, to your knowledge, had a homosexual relationship?"

"No."

"What's your occupation?"

We'd moved on quickly and I sensed a trap. "I have graduate degrees in clinical psychology and neurobiochemistry."

He held up his hand. The clerk stopped the camera. "I'm asking what you do for a living. Please answer the question." The camera's red light came back on, as if in warning.

"I'm an astrologer."

"Louder, please."

"I'm an astrologer."

The clerk's eyebrows shot up.

"How long have you been in your profession?"

"As a counseling astrologer, four years. But I've known astrology my whole life."

"What do people pay you for?"

"Advice."

"Of what sort? I'm curious." He flashed a smile that was no longer so winsome.

I sat up straight, my body tight. Everything I said now had to convince the judge astrology wasn't bunk. "I give advice on problems."

"Such as?"

I thought of Suzie: "When is a good time to marry?" And of Annie: "Is this a good adoption agency?" Then, of my best friend: "Should I divorce a lying, cheating deadbeat?"

Jerrick laughed without mirth. "Did Claire ask for advice in that last area?"

"I can't talk about my sessions."

"Claire has already stated for the record that you find opportune times to sign contracts and hold open houses."

"That's correct, yes."

"Did you find opportune times for her to meet with opposing counsel and the judge?"

I stared at him, swallowing with difficulty. The room was silent. I could hear his watch ticking from across the table. "Did she say that?"

"I'm asking you. Did you use astrology to set and/or alter legal appointments with the sitting judge?"

"I didn't think she got to set appointment times."

Jerrick slight smile was more of a smirk. "How success-ful are you?"

"Excuse me?" I wasn't prepared for the change in course and wondered where he was going.

"I'm talking about in real estate. Not these proceedings."

"Claire's a top agent."

"How many sales were you correctly able to predict?"

"I don't think 'predict' is the right word."

"Okay, how many sales has she closed, using your input?"

"In the last four years?" I paused and looked up at the ceiling. "Thirty? Forty?"

"How many times were you wrong?"

"I don't know. I don't get paid when I'm wrong."

"Would it surprise you to know you've been wrong thirty-eight out of seventy-two times?"

I slumped in my seat. That many? I could do the math and the numbers surprised me. I immediately felt hot, like I was back in the car with the heater running. I was a lousy astrologer and had no clue.

"That's not a good track record," Jerrick said.

It was terrible, but I wasn't going to tell him that. "Where did you get the numbers?"

"Claire."

She might lie to help her case, but she wouldn't lie to hurt it. I was quietly appalled by my performance.

"Can you explain how astrology works?"

"No."

"Excuse me? You can't explain it? Or this is privileged information and you won't explain it?"

"I don't know how it works."

"Yet you use it."

"I do. We don't know how electricity works and we use that too."

"Electricity works when electrons flow from a positive to negative pole."

"All right. Astrology works when planets circle the Sun in a counterclockwise motion around the ecliptic."

"And the planets tell you what to do."

"Not at all. That's a common misperception. The planets' position and interaction with each other show the quality of ambient energy."

"Energy now."

"All matter is energy."

"How does energy tell the stock market whether it should go up or down?"

"The planets don't tell the stock market what to do."

"Yet you advise people on when to buy and sell stock."

I wondered how he knew. "Actually, I ask experts."

"So you don't know."

"It's not my field," I said, feeling inept and idiotic. I wanted to be the one asking questions. His were ridiculous and showed an absolute ignorance of astrology.

There was a knock on the door and it opened. The secretary waltzed in with my laptop. She walked around the table and put it down in front of him. She passed him a folded piece of paper. He glanced at it and returned it. We waited, listening to the swoosh of her heels on the deep carpet as she exited. When she was gone and the door closed, he resumed.

"Do the planets circling the Sun in a counterclockwise manner tell you whether or not you've contracted an STD?"

With that question, my stomach dropped to the floor. It was part of the title of one of the charts Claire had deleted from my laptop. I looked at Jerrick and saw him looking back at me. I kept my face blank. "Perhaps."

"Show me how you'd use astrology to find out if you have an STD." He pushed my laptop across the table.

"It's complicated."

"Pretend I know astrology. Show me a chart. Any chart's fine."

I opened the laptop and brought up my astrology program. Jerrick got up and walked around the table. The clerk unscrewed the video camera from the tripod and came down the length of the table and stood behind me, filming.

Jerrick pointed to the screen. "Is that a chart?"

"Yes." It showed the current transits. Mars and Mercury were on the cusp of the 9th house of law.

"Can you save the chart?" Jerrick asked.

"Sure."

"Show me."

"It's really hard. You press save." I did so and sent him a hard stare.

"Now what happens?"

"It's saved."

"What if I want to delete it?"

"Press delete." I showed him.

"So now it's gone."

"Right."

"What if I told you, wrong?" He showed his shark smile. "The software saves the chart, but the information is saved on the hard drive." Jerrick edged me to the side with a shoulder, and with a few strokes on the keyboard, brought up the deleted horary file entitled: *Claire STD?*

"Kimberly is a computer whiz," Jeffrey said. "You thought if you deleted the file from the astrology software it would disappear. I'm afraid it doesn't work that way. Why did you delete this chart?"

I stared at the screen, feeling hot and feverish. The silence was interminable.

Jerrick strolled around the table and sat down slowly. "I'll ask you again. Why did you delete it?"

Here was the trap. I thought for a long time what I was going to say and didn't know. The ticking of his watch was suddenly loud.

He broke the silence. "What does *Claire STD* mean? Were you worried she gave you an STD? Are you lovers?"

"No," I managed to croak through a frog in my throat.

Jerrick opened his file and passed a piece of paper across the table. It was a copy of Claire's HIV test. I barely glanced at it before pushing it back.

"How did you get this?" I asked. "Medical records are confidential."

"Read the fine print. You don't seem surprised she needed a blood test."

"Is that a question?"

"Why did you think she had an STD?"

"I never thought that."

"No, you didn't have yourself checked, did you. But why would you, when you can ask the stars. Though with your record, you'd have a 50-50 chance of being wrong. You'd do as well to flip a coin as to check an astrology chart."

I closed my eyes and took a deep breath. When I exhaled, I opened my eyes and faced him. "I'm not gay. I didn't have the test because we're not lovers. Claire is my friend."

"Who's given you a lot of money over the years. How long have you accepted gifts from her?"

"I work for her. I declared the money she paid me on my taxes. You can check my returns."

"Oh, we have." Jerrick closed his file. "It's not the IRS you're in trouble with." He looked at the clerk. "We're done here."

The clerk turned off the camera.

We're done here. They sounded like final last words.

Chapter 27

Outside the office building, standing under gray threatening skies, and nearly dizzy with heat and anxiety, I called Claire. The line rang busy. I left her a simple voice message. "Call me."

I headed home at a reasonable speed and at least the needle on the temperature gauge kept to the black. Halfway home, stopped at a light, I called Claire again. This time it rang and rang and went to voice mail. I hung up, put on my turn signal, and made the left turn, heading for her house.

She lived in Sandpiper Estates, next door to the Club Med on the St. Lucie River. It was a gated community, much like J'Adore Del Mar, complete with a guard house. I knew the gate code and used the residents' access to enter. Then I drove the meandering palm-tree-lined streets to her home.

Claire wasn't there. She had a garage, but it was packed with junk and she typically parked in the drive. It was empty. I called her again. No answer.

I went to Daniel's. He was supposed to be back today and he'd know where she was. He had a tracking device on his phone that enabled him to locate her 24/7. She had the app on her phone for him as well.

I took the Boulevard to the Drive and went north. On the intracoastal, white caps were churning and close to shore, the palm tree fronds bowed in the wind. There were puddles on the grass and water had collected in the deep dips in the road that sprayed the underbelly of my car.

I got to Daniel's and saw a black Mercedes in the drive. I parked, thinking Claire had got a new car. I got out, forming my defense for my dismal performance as I headed for the door. Her lawyer didn't show up. I was on my own. She deleted the chart. She was the one who screwed around on her husband and was worried she got an STD. She asked me to pick the court dates. I did what she wanted.

The door opened before I reached the steps and Daniel emerged. He closed the door quickly and bounded down the stairs. He was dressed casually, in khaki shorts and a pale pink polo. The dimpled smile I expected was not in evidence.

I headed toward him. "Is Claire here? I need to talk to her." I heard music coming from the house. The sweat coming off him for once didn't smell like sex.

He stepped in front of me. "She's not here. What happened at the lawyer's?"

I stared at the water. I was getting a bad vibe and figured he'd already talked to her. "Her lawyer never showed and Kevin's is a shark. I should never have gone through with it."

"Kevin called her to gloat. He wants to know when he can send over an interior decorator to measure the windows."

I exhaled loudly, my body deflating as the air left me. Her worst fear was going to transpire, thanks to me.

"She'll get over it. She never stays mad for long." Daniel scratched at his five o'clock shadow. "I have bad news as well."

I looked at him sharply.

"My lieutenant got wind of what we were up to. He called me in. I've been ordered to stand down."

I almost staggered backwards. "But we're making progress. Did you tell him?"

"I'm not telling him anything. If I don't drop this case, I'm fired."

I stared at the water, whipped by the wind. "Did you tell Tiffany?"

"I tried calling her."

I shivered, feeling cold. The clouds were thick, with no sign of the sun. "How did your lieutenant find out?"

"An anonymous caller filed a complaint. It will go on my record. I'm making the force look bad by consulting an astrologer."

"Who called? A man or woman?"

"I don't know. I can't listen to it because it's about me. Apparently the major complaint was you. My lieutenant asked me if I'd lost my fucking mind. It won't help my case in Jacksonville."

"Barbie did it. She's the only one who knows what I do."

"Oh, come on. Everyone has seen your iPad and the charts. It wouldn't be too hard to figure out what you're doing."

"I bet the kidnapper made the call to get us off the case."

"If that's true, the strategy worked."

"You can't be serious. That's it? It's over? What about Tiffany?"

"My hands are tied. There's nothing I can do."

I stared up at the dark clouds and saw vultures circling. Daniel was giving up, just like that. How could he?

The screen door banged and I turned to the house. My jaw dropped. Barbie.

She came out onto the wrap-around porch looking as surprised to see me as I was to see her. She was wearing a short white dress held up with strings and holding a wine glass. "The sauce is boiling over," she told Daniel.

"Turn it off," he said, not taking his eyes off me.

I watched her go inside and close the door. I felt light-headed. Had my heart stopped? Would I faint? The world spun. The ground felt uneven. Would I fall? How could I speak? Somehow I did. "So, that's how it is."

"She called. She was in the neighborhood. She remembered she'd seen some vagrants near J'Adore Del Mar at the time of the kidnapping."

I narrowed my eyes. "Let me guess. And she overheard a name. Sounds like Ricky."

"She didn't hear a name."

I should have left right then, shut up at least, but I couldn't. Anger came spilling out on words. "And then what? The crabs crawled out of the sea and jumped into the étouffée pot? The wine bottle uncorked itself and the music turned itself on."

"It's not what you think. I didn't invite her to dinner."

"Right. Yet here she is."

He stared past me at the water. "Nothing will happen. I'll hear her out."

"While you're off the case." I nodded at the house and saw her looking out a window. A drape fell. "You better go. She's waiting for you."

I strode to my car. He jogged by my side, trying to grab my arm, making excuses, which I couldn't hear with the blood rushing through my head and my mind screaming: stupid, stupid, stupid, stupid, stupid....

I threw myself in the car and locked my door. I backed out, tires screeching.

I drove toward home, pushing the old car so fast the steering wheel shook and the temperature gauge returned to the red zone. I was sniffling hard, swallowing phlegm that tasted like tears, determined not to cry.

My phone rang. I picked it up with too much hope. Tiffany. I pulled into a parking lot and took the call.

She was crying. "I just spoke to a police lieutenant. He apologized for Daniel's insubordination. He said Daniel had no authority to reopen the case. He has to stop."

From somewhere close, a dog was barking. "I'm so sorry."

She sniffled loudly. "Daniel said this morning he was moving in on a suspect. The lieutenant called it hogwash. He said there never was new evidence."

"There is a suspect, Tiffany. *I* won't stop looking."

"What can *you* do? You're just an *astrologer*."

She said it like it was a dirty word. I stared through the mud speckled windshield at a world that looked blurry and bleak.

"I'm sorry I wasted your time," Tiffany said, sounding dead.

"Don't do anything. We'll work it out. I—"

I heard the dial tone. Tiffany had hung up. I tossed the phone across the car.

I drove home with the engine overheating and when I reached my driveway smoke billowed from the hood. I left the car, released the dogs, and sunk down on the steps. It was happening again, a world imploding. Trust betrayed, a heart crushed. *Fuck you*, I screamed at the storm clouds, as I had screamed at Andre when I learned what he'd done, and should have screamed at Daniel for the same. He was off the case. Fucking Barbie. If not now, then soon.

When I could, I dragged myself into the house. It was dark, uninviting and unfriendly. I kicked off my huaraches and fell onto the couch. It smelled stale, of wet dirty dogs, who wouldn't come near me now. They lay in Bob's bed, staring with black, accusing eyes.

I could be in financial trouble. My introductory astrology class was over and I had no new students. I hadn't given Jake his monthly stock report and he hadn't paid me. I would lose Claire's business. Like her, I could lose my house. Sierra would stay lost and who knew what Tiffany would do. If I got kicked out of the Astrology Association of America, I'd get no new referrals. If I couldn't do astrology, what could I do? I was fucked.

My throat burned, as if I was getting sick. Or maybe I'd been yelling. I stared into the dark pit of the fireplace. Once more, everything I depended on was evaporating in a cloud of smoke. I actually thought I had turned a corner. I should have known there was no hope.

I went to the kitchen and got a glass of water. It looked brown and tasted dirty. I poured it down the drain. In the bathroom, the toilet was still backed up. Shit couldn't stay buried.

I went out back and stretched out on the lounger. The dogs followed me, but kept their distance. I stared up at the darkening sky and saw no stars, no light from distant suns. Even they had given up on me.

Maybe my mother was right. I was a fraud. I couldn't do astrology. It was clearly stated in my chart, which I couldn't read. I deserved to have the AAA disbar and censure me. I couldn't read an adoption horary, couldn't tell when to market a house, and couldn't find a kidnapped baby. I hung my head. When it came to the abduction, I could be way off-base. The horary came with a warning I ignored. With Saturn affecting the 7th house, the astrologer's judgment was off. My accuracy was no better than chance. I wasn't the astrologer the *curandera* saw.

I was alone, again. An outcast of a neighbor, hated by the neighborhood. Shunned by my best and cherished friend. Thrown over in an instant by a man I fell for in an instant. How stupid could I be? I wrapped my arms around myself and shivered with cold. A front was blowing in, clearing the humidity. Air pressure was dropping; Saturn hitting Mercury could do that.

No! I screamed to myself. Stop! It was over. I was done with astrology. I was no good at it. Or it was no good. Pure bunk. I saw it in high school and left it. I should never have gone back. How could so many disbelievers be wrong? I grew up inside it and couldn't see it from the outside. It was preposterous to think that balls of gas or rock corresponded to events on earth. It was disheartening to think I'd wasted so much of my life on it.

And now what? I couldn't face another chart. I couldn't give advice on how to live when I didn't know myself. It was an ugly, senseless, stupid world. There was no fucking point. Just a series of random accidents that brought pointless misery day after day. Suffer and die. I stared sullenly at the black sky and silently screamed at the unseen planets and stars. "Let me go. I quit."

I waited and there was no response, just the shriek of a night bird and the chill of a cold wind. On the ground, lying on the detritus of winter, Bob stirred uneasily, and Shiny ran in her sleep, crying as if trapped in her own nightmare. I called her name and woke her up and we went inside.

Chapter 28

I didn't sleep all night and got up feeling physically ill. I canceled my appointments, no way I could sit through them. I went to my office, turned on my desktop, and typed a generic email to everyone on my client list, save for Claire. The message was simple: I was incapacitated and would be in contact as soon as possible. Then I fed the dogs, went back to bed, pulled the covers up over my head, and shut out the world. In the living room, I heard the phone buzz with texts, ring with calls and I let them go. I didn't get up until five and by then the phone had died.

My back ached from so much bed rest, my nose was stuffed up, and I had a throbbing headache. I plugged in my phone and checked the missed calls and messages. There were a number from Claire and Daniel and I deleted them. Ciro left a voice message informing me that Tiffany had had a nervous episode and was in the hospital and wanted me to call. I would have to do that. There was a text from Suzie. *Wedding date 8/27. Mom paid in Feb. Can't change date.* Which explained a fuck of a lot.

I went to shower. I was getting out when the phone rang. I didn't have my glasses, thought I saw a Miami area code, and answered, expecting Ciro. I heard a woman's voice.

"Is this Morgan Sterling?"

"Who is this?" I said, in my coldest tone.

A kindly voice said, "Judith Rendell. Do you remember me?"

The name seemed familiar. I wracked my brain and came up empty.

"You ran into me by accident a few weeks ago."

The dog trainer who taught intuition training. What did she want? Had she reported me to the insurance company after all? "I remember you."

"I hadn't seen you and wanted to remind you of my class. It starts at eight."

"I'm having a bad week."

"Yes. It is the resurrection after all."

We were heading into Easter and I guessed she was talking about that. "I'm sorry I can't make it. Another time."

"All right, stay home, feel sorry for yourself. Enjoy your pity party. Or, get out, learn something new, make peace with yourself. Your choice. Up to you."

I closed my eyes. It sounded like something my grandmother would say.

"There are people here you should meet," Judith added. "There's power in groups and not many like us."

"Like us how?"

"Don't be coy. You know what I'm talking about. We're going to listen to some drumming and have a nature meditation."

"I thought you did intuition training."

"Same thing."

"I don't have any intuition."

"Nonsense. Everyone does. It merely withers. Our culture kills it. What you feed grows."

"I'm sick."

"No, you reached the end of the dark night. It is always darkest before the dawn."

I sighed heavily. "I don't know what you're talking about."

"Which is your problem."

"You don't know my problem."

"Perhaps not the specifics, but the dark night is always the same. You face meaninglessness. You feel like you're dying and you are. Then comes the resurrection. Fitting timing, don't you think?"

"No."

"My point being, inevitably the sun will rise and the light will come. That's when it starts."

"What starts?"

"Living an authentic life. Seeing who you really are and knowing why you came. It's the phoenix rising from the ashes. Transformation. Pluto at work. I thought you were an astrologer."

"Not anymore."

"Check the transits. Tonight's a good night."

"Not for me."

As if I hadn't spoken, she said, "I'll save you a seat." She paused, and added. "Your radiator needs water." The phone went dead.

"Screw you, I'm not going," I said, even as I found my glasses, picked up my iPad, and opened the astrology app. The 7th house of partners was packed. Mercury, Venus, Mars, Jupiter, and Uranus were all there, with the Sun on the 8th house cusp of hidden knowledge. I was Venus, exalted in Pisces, in the last degree; signifying the omega, the end that came before zero degrees of Aries and the beginning. I was in the 7th house, with all the others. It looked like I was going.

No, forget it. I turned off the iPad and dropped it on the couch. The planets weren't going to tell me what to do.

I put on old sweat pants and a faded, stretched-out t-shirt and went to the kitchen. I put the dogs out in the back yard and made a cheese sandwich for dinner. I watched the news. The same old story was unfolding in Washington. There was too much spending. Even the government couldn't pay its bills, if you overlooked the fact it could print all the money it wanted.

I closed my eyes and shook the Magic 8 Ball. "Am I fucked?" *Signs point to yes.* "Will I lose my house?" *Better not tell you now.* "Does my car need water?" *Most likely.* "Should I go tonight?" *Yes, definitely.*

I tossed the ball on the easy chair. "Well, I'm not going," I said out loud to no one.

Nonetheless, I went to my car, opened my hood, unscrewed the radiator cap, and peered inside. No water. I got the hose and filled the tank. It must have been empty. At least one problem was solved.

I went back inside, plopped on the couch and watched *Jeopardy*. I had trouble answering the questions. I flipped through the newspaper. A fire had shut down the turnpike. A cancer doctor had been charged with giving patients without cancer, chemotherapy. A Nebraskan gal told Dear Abby she was grateful to her mother for teaching her to write thank you cards. I threw down the paper.

The overhead lights flashed, an alarm on the cable box shrieked, and the electricity cut out. Great. Had I forgotten to pay the bill? I looked out the window and saw Jake open his front door, then raise his blinds. Power must be out in the neighborhood. Perfect. Now what? I looked at my watch. Seven-thirty. What the hell. I got dressed for a resurrection.

I said goodbye to the dogs and they barely registered my departure. They were good company for each other and likely appreciated not having to share the couch, or be subjected to my dark mood. I started my car and headed west toward the sinking sun.

I reached the ranch just before 8:00 and parked on the side of the road. I wasn't going to be on time. The twilight sky had turned a royal blue. The waning full Moon was not in sight. A few bright stars were out: Regulus, Spica, and Antares. I knew Saturn, the harsh task master, was rising behind them, hidden by trees.

At 8:05 I got out of the car. I heard chatter in the backyard and walked alongside the house. The pack of dogs came running. I turned the corner, saw a circle of chairs around a roaring fire, and the talking stopped. Judith turned. A smile broke out on her face.

"We've been waiting." She pointed to an empty plastic lawn chair. "We're so glad you came. Please sit down."

I sat.

"Morgan is the astrologer," Judith said. She introduced the gang, linking names with professions: Sally did body work and muscle testing, Wendy was a dietician, Trish was a Reiki Master, Paige was a Jungian therapist, and Pam was a psychic. They were all women, all around my age.

"We're looking at Venus," Trish said, pointing to Spica. "And that's Jupiter." She pointed to Regulus.

She was wrong on both counts, but I kept it to myself. First of all, Venus could never be so far from the Sun, and second of all, Jupiter was in Aries, just below Andromeda and already out of view. Plus, stars twinkled and planets didn't.

Judith focused on me. I sat directly across the fire from her and she had a clear line of sight. "We thought you'd come the last few weeks. We tried to summon you and were disappointed when you didn't appear."

I remember I'd been thinking about it. But there was shopping, the makeover, and yoga. "I was busy."

"This week I decided on the direct approach and used the phone," Judith said.

"And here I am."

"Well, if we're all ready, we'll start the meditation."

"Great." I didn't know anything about Reiki or muscle testing, but I did guided meditation all the time in yoga.

"I'll play music," Judith said to me. "It's just drumming. Close your eyes. Focus on your breath. Clear your mind. We will invite the great spirit of the universe to fill our being and remove all negativity that separates us from our source. See what flows in. Try to keep open, no matter what happens."

Now she had piqued my curiosity.

She turned on an iPod and a drumbeat filled the air. The beat wandered around and came back, repeating itself. Boom-boom-bom, boom-boom-bom. I inhaled deeply through my nose, exhaled through my mouth, and began to feel hungry. After not eating all day, a piddly sandwich was hardly enough and my stomach was rumbling. I had to go grocery shopping. Was there enough dog food for the morning? With Bob, I went through food twice as fast. Should I stop on my way home? I had to get gas. I could buy a can of food. Did I have cash? I would have to transfer money from my savings to my checking account. No reward money. I'd never get back the book I sold. Fuck Daniel. Flirting with the enemy. "

The thought made me so mad, my eyes snapped open. Judith was looking at me. She lifted her eyebrows. I smiled and clamped my eyes shut.

Breathe in through the nose and out through the mouth. Count the drum beats: boom-boom-bom. Up to three and repeat. Boom-boom-bom. Follow the breath. I heard the hoot of an owl. Boom-boom-bom. One, two, three. The crickets were loud. The air buzzed. Sparks from the fire snapped. Boom-boom-bom. Watch the breath. Breathe from the diaphragm. Make it expand like a balloon. Exhale and let the balloon shrivel. Shrink like the gonads of a hulking steroid addict. One, two, three... boom-boom-bom. More stars came out. The moon was rising. The east horizon turned silver. And above that, a shooting star, arcing in the sky. It sped my way and Joy perfume scented the air as the light came near. It turned into a lantern held by my grandmother. She wore a dark cloak with an oversized hood she removed with a shrug. Her white hair was done up as usual in an elegant french twist. The diamond earrings she'd promised to leave to me and my mother now had, dangled by her neck. She held something in her arm, hidden beneath the cloak, out of view.

I walked toward her, effortlessly; light on my feet as if my body had no weight, drinking in the beneficence of her smile, and the comfort of her being.

The lantern was gone. She glowed in her own radiance. She lifted an elbow, cast the cloak off one shoulder and I saw what she held. I gasped.

A baby. *Holly.*

I thought the name and my daughter turned her head. She was whole, in one piece. She smiled, showing two bottom milk teeth and bright sparkling blue eyes.

I reached for her. A sob broke through my throat. "I let her die." While I went to get my hair cut, Andre went to the mall with her and his lover. The three of them were shot. The shooter aimed for Andre's heart and got Holly's head. The memory turned my skin ice-cold and brought a flood of tears.

My grandmother lifted her free hand and I went to her. "You do not hold the power of life and death in your hands. You could not stop what happened." She encircled me in her arm, Joy perfume engulfing me. She whispered in my ear, "Let go of the past. Stop wasting energy. Use your time well. Embrace the mystery. Never forget."

"Forget what?" As I said the words, I realized we were talking telepathically with our minds. "What am I supposed to remember? What happened to Holly? I'm done with men?"

My grandmother looked displeased. "Don't be obtuse. Obviously you're not done with men. Remember who you are. What you came here to do."

"What?"

"The only thing you can do." She raised her eyes and looked up at a sky full of unfamiliar stars.

"Astrology?"

She gave a ponderous nod of her head.

"I can't do it. I don't have the chart for it."

"Nonsense. You have the perfect chart for it. Believe in yourself. Believe in a universe that will help you."

"Help me?" I shrieked. "After what happened?"

Holly gurgled and I touched her cheek. I had forgotten how soft her skin was. She reached for me and cooed. She hadn't forgotten me. She curled her hand around my fingers.

I looked at my grandmother. "I hate what happened."

"I know my dear," my grandmother said sadly. "You must get past it and move on. Learn to forgive. What is, is. You could not change what must be. Stop seeking reasons." My grandmother lovingly patted Holly's head. "She served her purpose."

My next words came out in a cry "What purpose? To break my heart?"

"To bring you where you are. Try to look at it that way."

"Where am I?"

"Precisely where you are supposed to be. You are not lost. You are not off-track. And you would not be where you are, if not for her. Look at that as the reason for what happened."

"I hate that," I said in the peckish voice of a child.

"Release the past. The future needs you. Fulfill your destiny. There is no one else to take your place." She waved her hand, as if in farewell. "Let the light of your sun show you the way."

"Wait," I said, but she was already receding.

She began to glow, a bright white aura expanded around her and filled the cloak with light. In a flash she became a shooting star that retreated quickly, blending into the starlit night.

I shivered with loss and felt cold as the drumming reached a crescendo that peaked with the clang of a cymbal, and shrill startling silence.

I opened my eyes and saw Judith staring across the fire. The others opened their eyes and in silence that lasted a long while, we watched the fire and the sparks dance.

"If anyone wants to share…" Judith said after a while.

I had no words or desire to say what I had seen, but she wasn't looking at me. People shared their experiences and from the insights they gleaned, I wasn't the only one who'd been dazzled.

We ended the evening with an intention to go into the world and do our best not to elicit any negativity. We would try to be happy, which was a gift to the world. We would not forget the universe was alive and to treat her with respect. We were to show compassion for all sentient beings.

Afterwards there was food, which I declined. I had an overwhelming urge to go home and process what happened.

Judith didn't protest. She walked me to the car. "Thank you for coming."

"No. Thank you. It was amazing."

"As I mentioned, there's power in groups. The drumming opens portals between realms. We get a glimpse of what lies beyond tangible reality. May I ask you something?"

I nodded.

"Who was the old woman?"

I got goose bumps. "You saw her?"

"And the baby."

I was speechless. Judith had seen them?

The dogs began barking and Judith looked down the drive. The dogs were racing toward the barn. "I should retrieve the retrievers. See you next week?"

"Absolutely."

She kissed my forehead in the space between my eyebrows, and I saw purple. "Do what you must and you will find what you seek."

Was she talking about Sierra? Daniel? Astrology?

"The answer will be clear. All is well." She touched my shoulder, jolting me with a spark of electricity that brought shivers to my skin.

Chapter 29

I got home with my mind spinning, literally reeling. My house was alight; the power was back and the toilet flushed. The dogs sniffed my ankles and legs, as they would a stranger's. I snapped on their leashes and went for a walk, staring up at familiar stars twinkling brightly in the clear night sky. I was halfway through my walk when I realized I was being followed.

I'd been lost in euphoria. I knew I'd just experienced a Uranus awakening, or a Pluto transformation, or a Neptune enchantment, or perhaps all three. A supernova had blown the boundaries of my mind. Rationally I knew what happened was like a dream. The drumming induced altered brain waves that elicited a vision. Except it felt real. And Judith had seen it too. I didn't know how it happened, but knowing Holly was with my grandmother brought peace that had eluded me for years.

Then I turned the corner and saw the headlights. The car was moving too slowly. In an instant I was back in the real world where physical survival mattered. With my heart pounding, I picked up my pace, turning my head slightly to gauge the trolling car's speed. It matched mine, creeping along four houses behind me. I was glad for Bob and kept him close. He was happy to walk fast, but Shiny was dragging and couldn't keep up. With much relief I reached my street, turned another corner, and saw the bright lights of home.

The car sped up, coming closer. It rattled at a strained idle and I forced myself not to look. I was out of breath and breathing hard, walking at almost a run. I reached Porter's drive, nearly home, when the engine gunned and the car zoomed into his drive, blocking my way.

The driver's door flung open and a man I'd never seen before sprang out. He yanked open the back door and Boris emerged. Bob began to growl.

"Shut that dog up," he ordered.

"Bob, sit," I squeaked, and he sat. My hand went to my neck and there was nothing there. My rapid alert alarm button was on my dresser. I'd removed the pearls, but hadn't replaced the alarm. My phone was in my purse on the entrance table at home.

Boris stalked toward me until his face was in mine. He was so close, I was certain he could hear my heart jumping. "Stop asking questions about me," he spat, and spittle hit my cheek. "Don't look at my records. Don't ask about my birthday. Don't draw my chart."

His friend leaned against the car, looking bored. He lit a cigarette with a flaming lighter. He crossed his feet and stared up at the sky, inhaling deeply.

Boris grabbed my arm. "I didn't take that kid, so go sniff somewhere else with your star bullshit and birth time bull crap. Do you hear me?" he screamed in my ear.

Somehow I managed to say, "I hear you."

"I didn't want a kid. Barbie didn't either." He squeezed my muscle, letting me feel his strength. "Leave her alone. Your dickwad friend is sniffing the wrong snatch."

"Okay."

"We're going to go inside and talk. Leave the dogs." He yanked the leashes from my hand and flung them on the grass.

His friend flicked his cigarette onto Porter's lawn. Boris jerked me forward so quickly I stumbled.

The perimeter lights on Porter's lawn blazed. A moment later his front door opened, then slammed. I heard the cock of a shotgun and blinked in the sudden bright light.

Porter stalked across the unkempt grass, gripping the gun sideways with both hands. He reached the driveway and directed the barrel at the friend. "This is my property. Pick up that fucking cigarette, you freaking baboon. Move the fucking car."

"And leave," I added, as I grabbed the leashes and shuffled to Porter's side.

The driver picked up the burning butt.

"Now get the fuck off my property."

I sidled behind Porter, hoping they wouldn't get off his property by getting onto mine.

Porter raised the shotgun to his shoulder and aimed it at the friend. "You understand English, amigo?"

Boris laid his hand on his friend's shoulder. "Let's go."

Porter leveled the barrel at the car. "You heard the man."

The friend raised his hands. "I'm going."

Porter lifted the barrel and squeezed the trigger. A shot boomed, piercing the still quiet of the night.

Boris and his friend's eyes widened. They threw themselves into the car and drove off, tires burning rubber.

I was weak with relief. I turned to Porter, never so grateful to see him. "Thank you so much."

"Get the fuck off my property."

I jerked the dogs' leashes and did as he said. I reached the house when a door slammed. I whirled around. Jake's house was bright and he rushed across the street in a shuffle, dressed in slippers and striped pajamas. He hurried across my walkway and up the steps. "Are you okay? I called 911. Did Porter shoot my tree? Who were those ogres?"

I didn't answer his questions. I was so glad he was talking to me again, I dropped the leashes and threw my arms around him and hugged him tight. He hugged me back.

I heard sirens and we looked down the street. A black and white patrol car turned the corner, red and blue lights flashing. It tore up the road, bumping over the curb and parked on the lawn. Two officers jumped out.

Jake and I separated. "It was me who called 911," Jake said, when the cops reached the steps. "I heard a shot and looked out and saw Porter. He lives there." Jake paused and pointed. "He had a shotgun and Morgan was with the dogs and two ogres I didn't like the looks of at all."

One cop was young, clean shaven, and afflicted with acne. He said, "Are you all right, Miss?"

"I'm fine."

He nodded to Jake. "Go home, sir. Lock your door and good night."

Thank you, I mouthed to Jake. He gave me a quick hug before he left.

The other cop, older and bald, nodded at my house. "Let's go inside."

I opened the door and went in, followed by the dogs and the cops. As I closed the front door I heard another siren and within seconds, a red pulsing light lit up the night. With tires screeching, the Mustang roared into the drive. Daniel hopped out. In an instant, he joined us in the doorway. He glanced at me sharply and then at the bald cop. "What happened."

"Reported gun shot," said the cop. "Two ogres." He cleared his throat. "Two men. Neighbor with a shotgun."

"Two ogres?" Daniel arched his eyebrows at me.

"Boris and a friend."

"Are you okay?"

I nodded.

"I'll take it from here," Daniel said.

"Yes, Detective."

The cops left and Daniel shut the front door and turned the lock. He got down on one knee and greeted the dogs. "What did Boris want?"

"For me not to run his chart."

Daniel stood up, swamping me with the smell of his sweat. It was more sour than usual. "You didn't return my calls."

I stubbed my shoe on the pine wood floor, "You didn't tell me you invited Barbie for dinner."

"Because I didn't," he said shortly. "Do you really think something would happen?"

"It looked like something *was* happening."

Daniel ran his hand across the stubble on his chin. "Okay, she wanted it. That doesn't mean I did." He folded his arms over his heart and looked aggrieved, as if he was the one who had been wronged. "When she called, I was making dinner. She was nearby and came over to tell me about some street people who slept under the bridge near J'Adore. There was enough food, so I asked if she wanted to stay. Then you came. She ate and left.

That's all." Daniel stared across the living room at the fireplace. He slowly turned his eyes on me. "Why don't you trust me?"

I couldn't hold his glance and stared at the dogs. I had no answer. I was jealous and stupid. There was no logical reasoning behind my emotional reaction. I blamed my Scorpio Moon.

"Maybe it is Boris," Daniel said. "Maybe I wasn't fair to Rique. That doesn't make me a racist. I thought in my gut it was him. Maybe I *was* reacting to Ciro. Transferring, or whatever you call it."

He'd obviously been talking to Claire. "Transference," I said. "An inappropriate emotional response." Give me facts and I could speak.

"You did it too," Daniel said, pointing an accusing finger at me. "With Barbie. You transferred your expectation of faithlessness onto me. Like it was something *you* would do."

I considered that for a moment. "That's not how it works."

His eyes opened wide. "*Or*, someone did it to you." He snapped his fingers. "You had to deal with infidelity. So, you expect it from me."

I sighed quietly and petted Shiny who was leaning against me. He might have a point. "Maybe you're right."

He backed up into the living room and sunk down on the armrest of the easy chair. "I didn't like you leaving."

I looked at him. "I didn't like you quitting."

"I had no choice. I could lose my job."

I walked toward him, stood before him, staring him down. "You can quit if you like. I won't give up."

"Are we talking about the case, or what?" He raised his chin, gazed into my eyes.

"You could have come after me."

"Claire said to let you cool down. I was awake all night. I called you this morning. You didn't answer. I called all day."

"I was sick."

"I was in court. I came over as soon as I could. You were out. The lights were on, the TV was blaring. Where were you?"

In a different realm. "At meditation."

"You should give me a key."

"Oh a key. Sounds serious."

He took my hand. "It is serious. Past serious." He trilled his thumb across my hand.

His touch made me shiver. My heart was skipping, dancing with desire. I sunk down on his lap and put my arms around him, inhaling his scent. Heat radiated from him and the musk aroma was back.

He said, "Is this a good idea?"

I put my mouth on his and felt his tongue. His heart was racing, his jeans, straining. I rubbed myself against him as I slipped my hands under his shirt. His skin was hot. My hands began to tremble with anticipation.

He bolted upright, pinning my hands with his elbows. I almost fell to the floor. "Keep this up and I can't stop."

I nudged forward, repositioning myself and leaning toward him, brushing his jaw with my lips. "It's already too late," I whispered into his ear, before I licked it.

His muscles stiffened. He picked up my hips and shifted me to the side. "Go to bed," he said, in a low growl. He reached down and lifted the dog's blanket. "I'll sleep on the couch in case Boris comes back. I don't want you to be alone."

I grabbed the blanket from him and tossed it on the table. "Me neither." I blew in his ear, trailed more kisses down his jaw, then moved to his mouth and stared into his eyes and saw myself staring back. I readjusted my hips, rocked against him and he gasped.

"What are you doing?"

I stood up. "Come to bed."

He didn't object.

We shed shoes as we went, and shut the door to shut out the dogs. He tore off his clothes, already fully erect, his skin shining with a sheen of sweat, muscles taut, hands trembling. In a fluid motion we fell sideways on the bed, his weight pressing down hard upon me. He bent his head and nuzzled a breast and I tilted toward him. He slid into me, filling me deeply, taking my breath away. He lifted my hips, sinking deeper, pushing and pulling, pounding and receding until I exploded, sending shock waves that pulsed around him. He groaned and flexed his hips, buttocks squeezing as tension eased and he collapsed into me again and again until his body went soft and his breath slowed. While his heart hammered against mine. Or mine against him.

He lifted his head from my shoulder and looked into my eyes. He opened his mouth and I put a finger on his lips. "Don't say anything."

He pulled out of me and flopped to the side. I could see whose heart was pounding. It was jumping in his chest. I put my head on it and nestled against him, drinking in his sweat and his heat. He traced his thumb up my side and I quivered at his touch. I took his hand and soon fell into a long dreamless sleep.

Chapter 30

I awoke to the moonlight shining through the window and an arm slung over my waist. Incredible, the difference a day could make. Daniel lay on his stomach, face turned my way, covers thrown off, legs stretched out. He breathed lightly, rhythmic puffs of air exuding with each exhale. What Andre had killed, Daniel brought back to life. I felt renewed, on fire. I touched my face, my skin was scuffed. My lips were swollen and my loins ached. I wanted to kiss him but I was afraid to wake him and break the night's spell. I gently brushed hair off his face.

Daniel opened his eyes. "Are you looking at me?"

"I am."

He took my hand and kissed it. "What happened?"

"We crossed a line."

"I can't go back."

"Me neither."

"Okay. We won't tell anyone."

"Especially Claire."

"Until I'm divorced."

"And the case is closed."

"Settled." He started to kiss me, brushing my cheek with his lips and sending shivers up my spine.

I pulled away. "We need to talk to Boris and Barbie. Did you run his prints? Check her out?"

Daniel threw himself back on the pillow. "I did. Interpol is looking into him. Nothing came up on Barbie, though I didn't really check her out. And I can't. I had to return the case notes. I can't access data banks. Not with Jacksonville hanging over my head."

"We know Boris is worried about something. I'm going to go see him."

"Not alone you won't. There's also the adoption agency. Little Angels."

I climbed on top of him. "We've got work to do. We're not finished." I lowered my head and kissed him.

He came up for a breath. "You seemed finished last night."

"Today's a new day."

He pulled me to him.

And so we made love, leisurely, as the darkness leached away and the stars faded along with the planets and light hid the secrets of the night. We came together, conjuncting, in an energetic coupling that left ripples streaming into space.

Or so I thought later, as I ground coffee beans, humming. Daniel, fresh out of the shower, whipped eggs for breakfast. The dogs were under his feet. Bob was slobbering.

There was a knock at the front door. It opened and Claire swooped in. The dogs loped toward her. Daniel dropped the whisk and buttoned his shirt while I headed down the hallway. "Come on in," I said to my oldest and cherished friend.

She opened her mouth, but no words came. She lifted her arms and hugged me, and I hugged her back. As we rocked in place swaying to an unheard song, I realized why I fell so fast for Daniel. He was too much like Claire. He had her big heart, love of family, care and concern for me. They made me feel protected and safe. They were the family I never had. They possessed a *joie de vivre*, what Andre called an 'exultation of spirit' he said I sorely lacked. They were optimistic and for good reason—luck came through for them. When I was with them I felt it coming through for me.

She let me go. "I needed that," she said.

"Me too."

Daniel came out, looking domestic with a tea towel slung over his shoulder. He kissed Claire's cheek. "French toast?"

"Sure."

He returned to the kitchen.

Claire laid her purse on the shelf. "I tried to call you. You cancelled class tonight?"

"I'm celebrating the resurrection."

She looked at me with Daniel's eyes. "As in Easter?"

"Yes, today is Holy Thursday. Don't ask me what it means."

"It's the Last Supper and the betrayal of Christ."

"Scratch that. I'm celebrating Jupiter's day."

"You look happy."

"As do you," I said. Considering she could lose her house. "I blew it at the lawyer's. I'm sorry. I don't want Kevin to get your house."

Claire broke into a smile. "He won't. The judge heard your deposition and decided Kev's lawyer was heavy-handed and should have rescheduled. The judge threw out the whole thing."

"That's great news." With Mercury stationing, about to go direct, things *were* turning around.

"Only now Kev is threatening to hire his own astrologer. He wants cosmic advice too."

"Watch out. Maybe he'll find someone better than me."

313

"There's no one better than you."

My heart shrunk as an inner cloud darkened an otherwise sunny spectacular morning. "Not according to Jerrick. He gave me a success rate of 38/72. That's just over fifty percent. I can't believe I'm so bad."

Claire rubbed her chin. "Those aren't the numbers I gave him. You were 38/42. Man, he plays dirty."

My mind was stuck on the numbers. "I'm that good?"

"You're great." That came from Daniel who materialized behind me. "Breakfast is ready. Come on, you two."

"Great?" Claire said, shooting him a questioning look.

"I'm back on the case," he said.

She looked puzzled.

We sat at the counter and he plopped plates in front of us and glasses of juice and empty mugs. Claire looked at him, pursing her lips. "What's going on here?"

"We're having breakfast," Daniel said, coming with the coffee pot as my whole body stiffened.

"I mean, what are you doing here? Don't you have to be at the lawyer's?"

"I'm going."

"This isn't on the way."

Daniel and I exchanged glances.

"All right. I know you were here all night," Claire said. "I was tracking you."

"He stayed over," I said.

Claire's eyes rounded.

"There was trouble," he added. "I was worried for Morgan's safety. I offered to sleep on the couch." He pointed to the living room and Bob's green blanket, still strewn on the coffee table.

Claire followed his finger. "You made him sleep on the couch?" She looked at me, eyebrows arched high.

I was going to say, I tried, but she didn't give me a chance. "That's great. I love it. That's my brother. How can you not love him?"

How, I wondered, looking at the man standing in the morning sunlight.

We had breakfast and they left, going their separate ways. Claire had to show a house and Daniel was going to the lawyer's. "What are you going to do?" he asked, though the open window of the Mustang while Claire idled at the curb.

I was going to open a dark closet and face what I had buried. "I'm going to find the details of the book for you."

"I'll be back at 5:00," he said, "We'll go to Ocala and confront Boris."

We didn't kiss goodbye, not with Claire waiting. I waved frantically at them both, grinning stupidly, as they drove off.

I returned to the house, thinking about the night, about breaking my code. What happened was simple: I gave in to desire. And, I guess, the planets. Mars with Uranus and Pluto could mean unexpected or sudden explosive sex. I wasn't sorry about what happened. He was almost divorced and our case was almost closed, I rationalized. We were a little ahead of ourselves. Time would catch up.

I did a quick clean of the house, bracing myself for the task ahead. When I could procrastinate no longer, I went to the bedroom and pulled open the closet door. The remnants of my past fit in one small U-Haul packing box that was overly secured with tape and stuck in the back corner. With more than a bit of trepidation, I pulled it out. I got my sharpest knife and ripped the seam. I expected to see dirt and smell mildew, but what I got was a whiff of baby powder. I lifted out files of clinical notes and research, my Hook'Em Horns t-shirt, and my wedding picture. There I was with Andre standing before the Eiffel Tower smiling stupidly at the stranger who snapped the picture one gray afternoon when Saturn stood with the Sun, and the Moon stood with Pluto, and I was six months pregnant and ignorantly expecting a lifetime of marital bliss. I turned the picture upside down.

I found the manila folder with the information of "the book." The title, sub-title, sub-sub-title, and other text took half a page. A description of the text took a whole page, and a lengthy list of defects took another. There was a photocopy of the book's cover, a certificate of authenticity, a forty-year-old appraiser's report, an email from the buyer on a Netscape account, and a photocopy of the cashier's check I'd requested later from the bank. I put the folder to one side.

I saw Holly's pink baby book and paused. I went to a lot of work to make it for her. I wanted her to know when she grew up how much I loved her. I went through the pages, barely able to see the pictures and the captions through a stream of tears. There she was in the hospital in the nursery with the other babies. Our nurse said she was the best, but she probably said that to everyone. Then Holly in Andre's arms, with him smiling his goofy smile and her sleeping, as if she were safe. Then later at home, the three of us on the couch of the falling down house in the gutted living room, looking as happy as we'd ever be. And every month Holly getting bigger, sitting up, having a bottle, going to day care, eating applesauce, sitting on a young Shiny, throwing a smile that showed her first tooth, then two, and then enough blond wispy hair to hold a barrette. And then the first of June, nearly six months old and standing in a walker smiling brightly in the last picture of her life.

I closed the book and grabbed her bear that Andre named Barry and hugged it tight. I buried my face in the soft fur, smelled her scent and remembered what it was like to hold her. I saw the corner of yellowing newspaper and teased it from the book. The date was the day after the funeral: June 14th. The caption read: Baby Buried. A photo showed a crowd at the graveside squinting in blinding sunshine. Andre, temporarily released from the hospital, sat in a wheelchair, head hung. Beside him stood his parents, clasping each other for comfort. And there I was, with my newly coiffed hair, standing at a distance, on my own, arms tightly wrapped around myself.

Liv stood behind us, her arm in a sling. The lover. His student. I hadn't known then what I would soon learn, that it was no random shooting. Andre and Liv hadn't been accidentally picked out of a crowd; they were the target of Liv's boyfriend's rage. He followed her to my house, watched through the window of my bedroom as his girlfriend fucked my husband in my bed. When they went to the mall to get diapers, the boyfriend and his gun went too.

Not that it mattered now. It was gone, all of it. *Let it go*, my grandmother said. And I put it away, repacked the box, taped it up tight, and returned it to the back corner of the closet. I was repositioning shoes when I heard a knock on the door. Bob got there first and was barking. I grabbed my emergency alert alarm necklace off the dresser and went down the hall.

Annie. She let herself in and I tucked the alarm in my pocket. "I'm so sorry," she called from the door.

The past was gone. My future was calling. Full of goodwill and forgiveness, I went to her and hugged her hard. When we stepped apart, I apologized.

"It's my fault. I should never have been so emphatic." For this I blamed my mother's bad influence. "I don't know what's going to happen in the future. No one knows."

"You do! You were right. Kolby changed her mind. She called the social worker yesterday. She wanted to know if we still want her baby. We're meeting with her next week."

"That's fantastic." We hugged again.

Annie went on. "I took your advice. I went home and slept on it. Yesterday I called the social worker and said we'd work with Kolby. She could take her time paying us back. That made all the difference in the world."

"Repay you?" I asked.

"Yes, the money we gave her. If she reneged on the deal she had to pay us back."

That was an ah-ha moment, streaming in with a ray of bright sunlight that fell across us.

Annie was talking about Kolby's change of heart and I forced myself to pay attention. "Kolby thinks we'll do a better job of raising the baby than she. Kolby wants us to have her. She loves her baby and wants what's best for her."

"I always said you'd make good parents. I wish you were my parents."

Annie chuckled as if I was joking. She knew nothing of my history. "Well, I just wanted to tell you," she said. "I have to get back to work."

After she left, I rushed to the bathroom, dumped my laundry hamper on the floor, and tore through the dirty clothes looking for the jeans I'd worn to Vero. I found the slip of paper in the pocket that had the name and number of the adopted family who were originally going to get Isabella.

I went to my office and grabbed my phone. Brad Abbott answered on the third ring. It sounded like he was in a hurry.

Whereas I was at a loss for words, unsure of how much I should say. "I'm… uh… calling about the adoption agency… um…"

He stopped me. "Little Angels. Right. Look, I'm heading out the door, but I'll be back around six. You could come then."

I figured at some point Daniel had called him. He may have been way ahead of me the whole time. "That would be perfect."

"The gate code is 157." Brad hung up and I wrote down the code that went with an address I didn't have.

Daniel appeared at the end of the day. I kissed his warm generous lips and got lost in his arms. It took a while to ask about the lawyer.

Daniel kicked off his shoes. "The divorce could take six months."

A hiss of air escaped my throat. I'd been thinking a month at most.

Daniel ripped off his socks. "The clock doesn't start ticking until the request is filed."

I stared at the fireplace, wondering how on earth we'd be able to keep our secret that long.

He unbuttoned his shirt. "Time will go fast. We'll keep busy." He nodded at the bedroom. "We could go to Ocala tomorrow,"

"Only the Abbotts are expecting us at 6:00 in Orlando."

He dropped his hands. "Were they the adoptive parents who were supposed to get Rique's daughter?"

"Yes, Isabella. Exactly."

"You made an appointment to talk to them?'

"I did."

"You're no fun, you know."

"That's not what you said earlier."

He looked at his fancy watch. "All right. We better go if we're going. Traffic will be a nightmare."

"Unless you're a cop."

He smiled. "A detective."

Chapter 31

We were in Orlando by 6:30, without using the lights or siren. The Abbotts lived in a gated community near Disney World. The gate keypad wasn't working, and we had to sign in at the guard house. The Abbotts were called and when our entry was approved, Daniel got directions to the house. "Follow the main street back to the lake. First house on the left with the for-sale sign on the lawn."

We found it easily. The house was massive, though dimly lit. The grass was nicely manicured, but the paint on the front door was peeling. "Selling 'as is,' no doubt," Daniel said, repeating a phrase he must have learned from Claire, who used it a lot. He rang a buzzer that didn't buzz and then rapped the door with his knuckles.

The door opened quickly. A thin, emaciated man with graying hair and dark hooded eyes said, "Come in." Brad Abbott shook our hands. He took us to the living room where a television blared. A chubby dark-haired girl of about three was watching Snow White. "Shelly, go watch in your room, okay sweetheart? Daddy has to talk to these people."

The child surprised me. Still, I guessed once one adoption fell through, there were other unhappily pregnant mothers in need of adoptive parents.

Shelly grabbed her doll and sent us a sidelong look as she left. She had dark hair that was wired in tight curls. Her head looked rather large, she had jet black eyes, and a wide down-turned mouth. She didn't look happy, despite her cute dress and silver sparkly slippers.

Brad turned off the television and sunk down on the loveseat. Daniel and I sat down on opposite ends of the couch. "Is your wife here?" I asked.

Brad looked pained. "Jane's in a nursing home. She has Lou Gehrig's disease." He took out a hanky and blew his nose, wiped his eyes. "She's dying."

"I'm so sorry. Does Shelly know?" I wondered if that explained her dour look.

"She knows her mother is sick. She doesn't know how bad."

I nodded with sympathy. As soon as I had Holly, dying became my biggest worry. I didn't realize that me dying wasn't the worst thing that could happen. I said, "Is that why you didn't have your own children? Jane has a genetic disease?"

Brad nodded. "It was also why we were picked over at the agency. We had to disclose our health issues. What pregnant mother would give her child to a woman who might die? Is dying."

"Yet someone did," I said. "Even if the first adoption fell through, one worked out."

"For a price, yes." Brad sighed sadly. "We used to have money. Not to brag, but I was one of the top real estate agents in the area. In the height of the boom, I was closing three to four houses a month. These were million dollar homes." He shook his head as if in wonder at the memory of it. "So we kept upping the stipend that we would pay any expectant mother who selected us. It got to the point where it was ridiculous." He paused and wiped his nose with a hanky. "But it worked. Finally we were picked."

While Brad spoke, I was staring at a row of pictures on the wall by the staircase. Most were taken in a professional studio with a dark-haired woman I took to be Jane, looking frail, but happy with her baby, growing with the years.

Brad was talking about the real estate bust and medical bills and not having a job, when I tuned back in. Now, the real estate market had crashed, his wife was in a nursing home, and the house was in foreclosure. He had taken out a third mortgage to pay for promising treatment in Germany that hadn't worked. He didn't know how he would pay off his debt, or pay the nursing home to keep Jane. He didn't know how he would raise Shelly as a single dad.

"How did you find the adoption agency?" Daniel asked.

"Through our lawyer," Brad said. "It was a small private agency with a good ratio of expectant mothers to adoptive parents. We thought that gave us the best shot of getting a baby. We could have gone to China, but we wanted a newborn."

"Did you meet any of the other adopting parents?" Daniel asked.

"No. We met privately with a social worker."

"Did you meet all the pregnant women?"

"Not until we were selected. Then we only met her."

While Brad explained the process, I went back to looking at the pictures on the wall. There weren't any photos of Shelly as a newborn. I interrupted. "When is Shelly's birthday?"

"January 11th."

"Is she three?"

"Four."

"How old was she when you got her?"

"Four months."

"Then you didn't get a newborn," Daniel said.

"No," Brad said. "As you know, the first adoption didn't work out. A few months later the agency contacted us and asked if we'd be interested in an older baby. Shelly had been placed with parents who got pregnant themselves. Before the adoption was finalized, they decided they couldn't afford two babies. We agreed to reimburse the expenses they'd paid to the birth mother and that's how we got Shelly."

I got out my phone and scrolled through my emails, looking for the time-progressed picture that Tiffany had emailed me of Sierra at four. She was smiling, with straight auburn hair, brown eyes, and looking more like Tiffany than Ciro. But what if she looked more like her father? I went to the wall and stared at a professional photo of Shelly holding a doll and smiling sweetly. I squinted my eyes, blurring my focus. A chill went through me.

Behind me, Daniel was listening to Brad explain how adoptions were finalized. A judge had to sign off on the paperwork that was verified by a notary public. When he finished, I said, "Daniel, can I speak to you outside?"

"In a minute."

"Now, please." I went to the front door and opened it.

Daniel excused himself and we went outside. "What?"

"It's her. Shelly is Sierra. She doesn't look like Tiffany, she looks like Ciro."

From nearby, a mockingbird shrieked, as if at the news.

Daniel blinked, eyes open wide as he stared at the house.

"The computer got it wrong." I didn't add that I should have known the progressed photograph was off. Astrology explained why second children looked more like their father. In a natal chart, the 5th house showed the first child, while the 7th house, the house of the husband, showed the second. There was an affinity between second children and their father, and Sierra was Tiffany's second child. The software that progressed the picture had favored the looks of the mother, when it should have favored the looks of the father.

Daniel scratched his head. "Shelly does look like Ciro, but her birthday is wrong."

"Sierra was premature. She was due in January and born in November. According to Tiffany, the pediatrician went by Sierra's gestational age, not her actual age. Brad thought he was getting a four-month-old baby, but she was six months old. I don't think he knows."

Daniel exhaled slowly and stared at the house. "This is going to be tough."

"Brad has to be told."

We went back inside and resumed our places. I couldn't maintain eye contact and was glad I wasn't the one who had to relay the news.

"When did you adopt Shelly?" Daniel asked, in a sad, soothing voice.

"It was early May," Brad said. "Why?" Already he sounded suspicious as if he knew something was wrong.

"Four years ago in May a baby girl was kidnapped in South Beach in Miami. Did you hear about it?" Daniel asked.

"Is it relevant?" Brad stopped talking abruptly, his mouth and eyes opening wide. "You don't think …"

"Did you go to the agency office and pick Shelly up?"

"They brought her here. A man from the agency delivered her. When was the kidnapped baby born?"

"In November."

"There you go. Shelly was born January 11th."

"Do you have her adoption papers?" Daniel asked.

"Of course. And her birth certificate. Shelly's too young. She's not the same baby. It's not possible." He went to the bookshelf, pulled out a family Bible, then an envelope, and passed it to Daniel. He said, "The ages don't match. You're way off base."

Daniel and I studied a certificate of birth registration. The mother was listed as Jane Abbott and the father was Brad. The date of birth Shelly Jean Abbott was January 11th. There was more information on the certificate of adoption. The natural mother was listed as Graciella Horton; the father as Ronald Egan. The baby girl was born in Miami Hospital at 4.05 p.m. exactly ten days later than Rique's daughter Isabella.

Daniel scowled at the adoption certificate. It looked authentic, but how hard would it be to change January 1st to January 11th, or Gabriella to Graciella, or Hortez to Horton, and add a father, when the real father was a forger? Daniel's gut was right. Rique was the kidnapper.

Brad looked desperate. "Shelly's too young. The pediatrician never once said Shelly was older than we thought. Her development was spot on. She hit the milestones on target. Your theory is all wrong."

"Sierra was born premature," I said.

"Could we get a sample of DNA?" Daniel asked. "We'll swab her gum. Run a simple test."

Brad didn't answer. He looked upstairs and wiped a tear from his eye.

"I have a DNA kit in the car," Daniel said. "I'll be right back." He rushed out.

Brad got up slowly. "I'll get her. But I'm telling you you're wrong. It's not her."

Even so, he climbed the stairs wearily, like an old man.

I got out my phone and went to the staircase. I took a picture of the most recent portrait of Shelly at about age three holding the doll. There was no mistaking Ciro's olive complexion and dark eyes staring out of the small face. This was his child. There would be no good ending.

Daniel returned with a plastic bag and a few minutes later, Brad came down holding Shelly's hand.

"I'm going to stick a little swab in your mouth," Daniel said.

"Why, Daddy?" Shelly said in a small voice as she looked up at her father.

"To make sure you're healthy," he said after a beat, in a voice that broke.

"It won't hurt," Daniel said, as he unscrewed the cap and pulled out a DNA swab. A spongy end protruded from a stick attached to the cap. "Open your mouth and this will just take a second."

Shelly did as she was told.

Daniel ran the swab across Shelly's inner cheek. He replaced the swab in the tube, screwed on the lid, and mixed the sample, coating the DNA with buffer.

"Can I go, Daddy?" Shelly asked.

"Sure honey," Brad said. And when she was gone, he asked, "How long will it take?"

"Two to three days," Daniel said. "I'll call you as soon as I know."

We left Brad on the couch, head resting in his hands, and let ourselves out.

Daniel closed the front door and we walked to the car. Before we reached it, he leapt in the air, issuing a silent whoop. He picked me up and twirled me around in a circle and then dipped me in a swoon. He caught me and set me upright on my feet and bowed. "We did it! We found her." He squeezed me in a bear hug.

I let myself be hugged, filled with mixed feelings. One part of me felt for Tiffany and was full of joy. The other part felt for Brad and was deeply saddened.

Daniel released me and danced in circles. "My lieutenant won't believe this. He told me I was consorting with a kook, the case was closed, Sierra was dead, and to stop giving the poor parents undeserved hope. And look who's right? Look, look!"

"Who's the kook?"

He stopped dancing. "What's wrong?"

I looked at the crumbling house. "He'll lose his daughter." I knew how he felt.

"Only she's not his daughter. Shelly doesn't belong to him. Right is right, Morgan. The law is the law."

"Brad is listed as the father on the birth certificate. If we're right, I think we can expect legal action."

Daniel rubbed his chin. "It's not like we can cut Sierra in half and give each family a piece. I know Tiff won't keep Sierra from him. And Shelly won't lose a mom, she'll gain one. And Ciro has what Brad needs. Money." Daniel lifted a shoulder. "It could work out."

I hoped he was right.

His moment of seriousness ended and he cracked a smile. "And who knew it all along?" He thumped his mid-section. "I trust my gut. It's always right. Who called it? Me. The detective."

"Why not go ahead and gloat."

"The detective called it," he said, with his hands in the air and his fingers waving. His eyes were bright and his face was beaming. "The detective got it."

"Congratulations."

He picked me up again. "I couldn't have done it without you." He kissed me long and hard, then put me down, spun around, kicked out his feet, and danced a jig while he punched the air.

When he paused to catch his breath, I said, "Not to rain on your parade, but you act like you've never solved a case before."

He looked sober, thoughtful. "What are you saying? I'm going to break my arm patting myself on the back?"

"You are flying pretty close to the sun." It was a Leo short-coming. "Don't let your wings melt."

He stared off into the distance. "I'm going to call Tiff."

I suspected the news might immediately heal her nervous upset. She didn't answer. Daniel hung up without leaving a message.

"Call Ciro," I said.

"I don't have his number."

I scrolled through my phone contacts and pulled up the private number.

"I can be humble," Daniel said, as he took out his phone. He dialed and put his phone on speaker. Ciro answered on the first ring in a sharp cold tone. "Who is this?"

"Daniel Kane. I think we've located Sierra. She's alive and well and living in Orlando."

There was a long silence. Around us crickets buzzed. I was impressed by how fast Daniel grounded himself.

He went on. "I took a DNA sample and I'll get it tested. I believe we have your DNA profile on file."

"You found her?" Ciro sounded small, hollow; all vestige of his personal power and might, gone.

I pulled up the photo on my phone and held it up. Daniel said, "Morgan will send you a picture. Sierra looks like you."

"She looks like me?" Ciro voice was full of wonder, like a little boy's.

I opened a new text message to Ciro, attached the photo, and pushed send. A few moments later I heard the beep when the text arrived on his phone.

There was more silence. I listened to the crickets chirp loudly. Then Ciro said through what sounded like a sob, "She does look like me."

"We have to confirm with DNA," Daniel said. "But I wanted you to know. And Tiffany. How is she?"

"In the hospital. But I think she's going to be fine. Just fine. Daniel, how can I ever thank you?"

"I'm just doing my job."

They exchanged congratulations for a few more moments and then Daniel hung up. A few minutes later we were on our way back to Coral Cove.

We got on the Turnpike and Daniel turned off the radio. "So, this is what happened. Rique's girlfriend died, he needed money, and he kidnapped Sierra. There was no ransom note because he got money from Brad. I wonder what he did with the money."

"Or, what about this?" I knew how a private adoption worked, thanks to Annie. "Brad paid Rique's girlfriend, Gabriella, a monthly stipend when she was pregnant with Isabella. When Gabriella died and there was no adoption, Brad had to be repaid. Rique was on the hook. He needed money. He kidnapped Sierra and gave her to Brad. Brad then reimbursed Rique for Sierra's birth expenses. Rique used this money to repay Brad."

Daniel tapped his fingers on the steering wheel and frowned. "I'm confused."

I went into more detail. "Okay, prospective parents put together a package to introduce themselves to expectant mothers. From these packages, an expectant mother chooses who gets her baby. Brad and Jane put a package together and waited. No one chose them because of her health issue. So, they kept increasing the stipend and finally Gabriella went for it. Only when Isabella was born, Gabriela died before she could sign the adoption forms. That nullified everything. Rique suddenly had rights. Only, since he was keeping Isabella, he had to repay Brad. So—"

Daniel took over. "So, Rique took Sierra. He used his own daughter's birth certificate to pass Sierra off as Isabella. But he changed the date by ten days, turning the one into an eleven. He altered the parents' names."

"I think that's what happened. The money Brad paid for Sierra, he got back from Rique to settle the debt owed for Isabella. Basically, the same money changed hands twice."

Daniel nodded at the road. He moved his hand from the gear shift to my thigh. A shiver shot up my leg. I put my hand on his.

We drove on in silence. We reached my house by eleven and Daniel dropped me off. He was going to the station, going to get started on the paperwork to get the DNA tested. He didn't want to waste any time. He'd come back when he was through.

He left and I let the dogs out. I turned on the porch light, got out my phone, and sat on the steps looking at the event chart of the kidnapping. The answer was there, of course, and always so obvious in hindsight.

The mutual reception wasn't between two kidnappers, but between two infants. One had been switched for another. They changed places.

I called my mother. I didn't bother figuring out the time change. She'd roused me from sleep enough times.

She wasn't asleep and answered on the first ring. "I've been thinking about you."

"We did it! We found the baby."

"What baby?"

"The kidnapped baby, *Mother*. The baby the police and FBI couldn't find in four years. We found her."

"Oh. Congratulations. Did you get your invitation?"

That was it? That was all she had to say? I shouldn't have been surprised. "What invitation?"

"To Suzanne's wedding."

"Yes, I know. She's getting married August 27th," I said, with too much petulance. "She'll be the August political news story. Sylvia rented the club in February and the date's locked in. Who cares if Jupiter's stationing retrograde and their luck will change."

"Don't be so pessimistic. Maybe the priest will mess up the ceremony and they'll have to repeat their vows. It doesn't have to be something bad. There's a lot of good stuff going on that day."

"Why didn't you just tell me the date was fixed?"

"Because I know you. You would never do anything I asked."

I wondered if she had a point. If I was as much to blame for our messed up relationship as she was.

She said, "If that's all, good night. I'll see you later."

Wait. "What?" Was she talking literally or figuratively?

"In August. At the wedding. If you haven't got your invitation, you will soon."

"You can't go."

"I very much assure you I can."

My voice sounded frail when I said, "But you can't come back to the States."

"You didn't hear? I've been absolved. I'm out of the woods. I'm cleared."

A lump the size of a rock settled in the back of my throat. My next words came out in a thick rasp. "What happened?" I thought she was gone forever, would be arrested the second she returned.

"Pluto in the 1st in a Moon *dasa* and Jupiter *bhukti*. I've got power and the prosecutor threw out the case. Tom was absolved of all wrong-doing. Ergo, I can return. I'm coming in July."

And just like that, my world was turned upside down. "So early?"

"You don't sound happy. I have business in DC."

I almost gasped.

"I'm going to sell some books. The market will dive in August and I want capital to buy at the bottom. I'll come see you. See the little house you bought."

My heart was racing and I broke out in a cold sweat. "Florida?" I croaked.

"Is something wrong?"

"No." I said, staring at the shadows shifting on the dark lawn. She was coming to sell the book I'd sold already. And she could never come to Florida! She could never meet Daniel, I thought, as he drove down the street. I stood up, my heart pounding hard, as he pulled into the drive. "I have to go."

"Me too." She hung up first.

I closed my phone as Daniel jumped out of the car looking as worried as I felt. "Everything okay?" he asked.

"Fine. And you?"

"Dandy. If you overlook the fact my lieutenant's furious. He told me to get the hell out of the precinct. I'm on paid leave until he figures out what to do with me."

"You found Sierra."

"He doesn't believe it. He thinks there's no way in hell we did what the FBI couldn't."

Chapter 32

B ut we did. Though it was Easter weekend, the analysis was rushed and by Saturday two independent labs confirmed the DNA match. The evening news led with the story of the recovery of four-year-old Sierra Rossario, the kidnapped daughter of the Good Food tycoon. The segment showed simultaneous screen shots of old and new clips of the parents. In the dated video, the distraught couple clung to each other before an array of microphones, begging the world for news of their baby. The recent footage showed a beaming couple, waving joyfully, as they left the hospital in a forest-green Ferrari and drove off into the sunset. A company spokeswoman said the Rossarios weren't speaking to the press. The reporter explained police had issued a warrant of arrest for Enrique Garcia and Interpol was looking for him in Mexico.

That story was followed by a short segment featuring Boris Shanksky's arrest in Ocala. The surly body builder was shown with his hands cuffed behind his back as he was marched to a police cruiser. According to an on-scene reporter, an unnamed detective working one case, cracked open another involving an illegal prescription drug ring with roots in Ukraine. Boris allegedly had been supplying national sports figures and Olympians with banned steroids for years. There was no mention of Exercise Barbie.

***

On Monday, Daniel called me at lunch time. "The police chief wants to see you. Can you come to the station after work? Say 5:30?"

My throat seized up. I barely managed to croak, "The chief knows about me?"

"Apparently."

"Are you in trouble?"

"We'll see."

And so, when my last client left after an endless, worried afternoon, I put on my court clothes and headed to my car. I drove to the precinct, trying to manage my trepidation. The meeting didn't bode well for Daniel.

He met me in the parking lot and kept his distance. "We've got to be cool," he said, as if he expected me to kiss him out in the open.

"I know," I said.

He turned his back on the ugly rectangular building that housed the Coral Cove Police Department. "I'm supposed to let my superiors know if I get involved in a serious relationship. It has nothing to do with astrology. It's my undercover work. They would have to check you out."

I mopped my brow, feeling sweaty and hot. The last thing I needed was Daniel's boss snooping into my past.

"We should go." He waved at the building.

Feeling like I was walking into hell, we entered the building, where I was immediately assaulted by freezing air. Daniel signed me in, swiped a card, and unlocked a door. We climbed a steep set of stairs and went down a bright hallway. Daniel knocked on a door at the end. A guff voice barked "Come in."

The chief of police had a dark complexion. His brown hair was going gray and he had eyes of cold steel. He stood up, tall and imposing. My heart thudded with anxiety. I pegged him as a mixture of Scorpio and Capricorn. Someone who pulled no punches. He thrust out his hand and we shook. My palms were sweating. His hand was cool. I was surprised by his light gentle touch, indicative of a softer influence of Libra or Cancer. It muted my apprehension, a little.

"Thank you for coming, Ms. Sterling." He waved me into a chair.

Daniel sat down beside me. I sat forward, on the edge of my seat, arms tightly wrapped around myself, shoulder to Daniel's face so I couldn't see him and wouldn't give myself away.

The chief sat down, rolled his chair to the desk and rested his elbows on a stack of manila folders. It was a cramped office and the walls were filled with framed awards and commendations. The chief said, "You come highly recommended. Ciro Rossario thinks the world of you. He is extremely grateful for your help."

My heart calmed down. Was this why he called us in? To thank us?

"The two sets of parents are working out custody details. It would be a legal mess if the primary concern wasn't the child's well-being. Luckily it is."

That was good to hear.

"Sierra was seen by a child psychologist," the chief said. "She hasn't suffered any trauma."

"What about Enrique Garcia?" Daniel asked, and I forced myself to keep my eyes on the chief.

"We've notified the Mexican police. I'm not sure they'll be much help."

"He needs to be brought to book," Daniel said. From the corner of my eye, I saw him thump his fist on his thigh.

"If Garcia returns to the country, we'll get him," the chief said. "I doubt he'll come. Either way, a criminal is off our streets. A baby is home where she belongs." He pulled a benefic smile. "Well done."

We both said thank you, in unison.

The chief turned back to me. "Many years ago, soon after I was promoted to detective grade, I worked a bloody triple homicide that seemed a perfect crime. There were no clues. Not a fingerprint, nor splash of blood. I was in over my head and my lieutenant knew it. I think he put me on the case to weed me out. Or perhaps to put me in my place. He didn't think I deserved my promotion and maybe he was right. I wasn't sure I deserved it either. Then I met an astonishing woman in Georgetown and everything changed."

The name of the DC suburb snagged my attention immediately.

The chief gazed across the desk with a penetrating look. "You probably don't remember me, but we met long ago. I knew your grandmother and your mother. You were a child, three or four."

I blinked. I can't say I almost fell off my chair, but figuratively I did.

The chief went on. "I was astonished when Ciro told me your name. I could not believe my good fortune. Tell me, how is Viviane? Did she retire?"

I was flabbergasted he knew my family. Somehow I managed to say, "I'm afraid she died."

The chief tapped a finger on the desk. "I'm sorry. I suppose that explains why the DC success rate in solving crimes has plummeted. I hear your mother left the country."

"She may come back," I said, and the words twisted my stomach in knots. "To DC."

The phone rang. The chief didn't answer. He pushed a button and the ringing stopped. "Up north we used astrologers routinely. Of course nothing could be said publicly, but I never underestimated the help. Here, though, it's frowned upon. I tried to put out feelers, see if anyone in the PD used a service such as yours, and all I got were blank stares."

I nodded with him in commiseration, relieved he'd been looking for help, not to chastise open-minded officers.

The chief cracked a knuckle and nodded in Daniel's direction. "How did you two meet?"

Keep it cool and distant I told myself. "Daniel's sister is my best friend. She's taken my classes."

The chief cocked his head and fixed a steady gaze on Daniel. "I have to hand it to you. Given your history, your current predicament, and the limited understanding of your lieutenant, you have surprised me. I wish I had more detectives like you."

"Thank you, sir." Daniel said in a flat tone as if the praise meant nothing, as if he routinely closed unsolvable cases.

The ponderous stare swung back to me. "If we need help in the future, can I call on you? Quietly of course."

I paused and turned, looking at Daniel, looking stoic. He wasn't giving anything away. And this could be his get-out-of-jail card. "Daniel knows where to find me."

The phone rang again and the chief looked at the blinking light. "I have to get this." Nonetheless, he punched the button to silence it. "Morgan, if I may call you Morgan, I appreciate your discretion and your help." He stood up and offered me his hand.

I jumped to my feet and held out my hand. He held it lightly with both of his. "You'll never know how many times I begged the universe to send me someone like Viviane or Faye and here you are." He released my hand. "How did you end up in Coral Cove?"

"I threw a dart at a map."

"A dart." The chief laughed heartily as the phone rang again. "From God's ear to your hand." He reached for the receiver. "Take care of her, Detective."

"Yes sir," Daniel said in the same bland tone.

Daniel and I left his office and I don't recall leaving the building. We hadn't been called in to be lambasted, but congratulated. I felt as if I were floating on air, sailing up in the stratosphere. Now Daniel was smiling and sailing along with me. He'd never had the endorsement of a police lieutenant, let alone a chief. His childhood dream was coming true; he was gaining a reputation for being a good cop. As for me, in the tradition of my blood line, I'd used astrology to solve a crime. Forget my mother—I heard the sky speak.

***

On Friday, it was back to Miami to celebrate Sierra's home-coming. This time I was ready and dressed up in a turquoise Victoria's Secret sundress that Suzie insisted was made for me. When Daniel came to pick me up he had me out of it in seconds.

I was too eager, too excited, and I had no idea how we'd sur-vive the next six months while we awaited a divorce and kept our secret. One look, I thought, and anyone would see the desire of my Scorpio Moon.

As we re-dressed, Daniel said, "Tiff was asking about you."

I turned my back so he could zip me up. "Asking about what?"

"You and me. She wondered if we were a couple."

I turned around. "Why would she think that?"

He kissed my neck. "Maybe because we are?"

I stared into his eyes. "I told Ciro you were my client. Nothing could happen."

Daniel lifted his eyebrows and smiled wickedly. "Oops. Something happened."

I poked his ribs with my finger. "We have to keep it quiet."

He kissed my temple. "I know. He's too close to the chief."

Because of the delay, we were late getting to Miami. The sun was heading for the trees and a line of clouds had built by the horizon. We signed in at the gate and drove toward the ocean and buzzed the bell. The gate opened slowly, as did the big glass front doors. And there, bathed in the hall light stood the golden family. Ciro looked dapper in a blue pastel suit with a matching shirt, open at the neck. Tiffany, tall and blond, looked resplendent in a pale violet gown and appeared happier than I'd ever seen her. The reason stood between them. In a pink party dress, wearing white patent leather shoes, with her hair tied in pink bows, was Sierra, safely back home.

We parked and went up the stairs. Ciro, tearing up, hugged me tightly and kissed me thrice, leaving my cheeks wet. I bent down and shook hands with Sierra. Before I could say anything, he said, "This is Shelly."

I was surprised by the name. "We met in Orlando."

Kathy T. Kale

Sierra looked at me with Ciro's eyes. "I remember you," she said in a high voice.

With his face glistening with tears, Ciro watched Tiffany and Daniel hug. When they finished, Ciro enclosed Daniel in his arms, thumping his back, holding him tight. When Daniel was finally released, Ciro said, "I owe you forever."

"You don't," Daniel said.

"What do you owe him?" Sierra asked in her sweet soprano voice.

"My happiness," Ciro said.

He waved at the house and we went inside. The change in atmosphere was immediately apparent. The air was lighter and less dense, as if a heavy cloud had lifted.

"Do you want to see my room?" Shelly asked.

"Sure." Tiffany and I went upstairs with her, leaving the men together. The bedroom had been redone in a Snow White motif. Gone were the crib and stuffed toys. Now there was a single bed with a Snow White quilt, white bookshelves, and a small table set for tea. The windows were open and Seven Dwarves curtains billowed, slapping the security bars. Outside, the waves pounded and lights flickered on the ocean.

I sat on a small chair and Shelly introduced me to her dolls. "I'm going to get a cat," she said.

"That's nice."

"He'll live here."

"Great."

"Mommy and Daddy live down the street."

"Oh." I looked to Tiffany.

"Her parents are moving here," she said aloud, and then mouthed to me: *I'll tell you later.*

Shelly picked up the remote control. "Can I watch TV?"

342

"Sure sweetheart," Tiffany said. "I'll call you when it's time for dinner."

Tiffany and I went downstairs and joined the men on the back porch. Ciro uncorked a bottle of champagne and poured four glasses. I stood on the far side of Tiffany, keeping my distance from Daniel.

"We're going to share her with Brad and Jane," Tiffany said, cupping her flute. "Ciro bought them a townhouse down the road and gave Brad a job in the head office. He moved Jane out of rehab and we hired a nurse so she can stay home. Shelly will go to a nearby preschool in September. We're working with a therapist who will tell us how to break the news about who we are. Right now Shelly thinks we're old friends of her parents. Jane doesn't have long to live and I think she's relieved Brad won't be left alone to raise Shelly. I think he's relieved, too."

Wow, I thought, remembering Judith's outrageous statement that "all was well." She was right.

"I'm grateful to the Abbotts for giving Sierra a good home," Tiffany said. "I'm forever in their debt."

"Which reminds me," Ciro said. He reached into his breast pocket and passed me a check.

I could see the name and numbers without my glasses. It was made out to me for one hundred thousand dollars. I looked at Daniel. "We'll split it."

"I told Ciro to make it out to you."

"You reopened the case," I said. "You knew long before me who was guilty."

"Yes," he said, hanging his head, with none of his Leo braggadocio in evidence. "I got the spotlight. You can have the money. I don't need it."

I looked at the check. I did need it. With my mother coming, if I couldn't return her book, at least I could give her money.

"You heard him," Ciro said. "It's yours. A win-win for everyone."

He had no idea. I slipped the check into my purse.

Ciro nodded his approval. He lifted his glass. "To the *curandera*, who saw the future."

We clinked glasses.

Daniel and Tiffany exchanged glances. Daniel said, "What are you talking about?"

"Magic," Ciro said. He sipped his champagne. "Speaking of serendipity. I hear you killed two birds with one stone."

"Excuse me?" Daniel said.

"You caught a drug smuggler. How did you swing that?"

Daniel spoke into his glass in a flat, matter-of-fact tone. "Boris is a false name. The man is really Konstantin Filatov. He stole the ID of a dead man. He was in the country illegally and very protective about his birth date. Morgan got his fingerprints. Interpol has been looking for him for years."

"What about his wife?" Tiffany asked.

"She says she didn't know what he was doing," Daniel said.

I stared at the water and rolled my eyes.

Daniel leaned on the balcony railing and changed the subject. "Would you consider hiring a bounty hunter to find Rique Garcia?"

Ciro studied his flute. "As far as I am concerned, this is over. My daughter is home. I want nothing more."

"A bounty hunter could find him in no time," Daniel said.

"Let him go," Tiffany said. "I feel bad for him. He almost lost his daughter. He had no say."

"He deserves no sympathy," Daniel said. "He's guilty. He has to pay."

Ciro disagreed. "He'll pay with karma. We don't need human laws to punish him. His own deeds will dog him the rest of his life. As for me, I shall hear no more of this. I will press no charges. Not now, not ever." He raised his glass to the darkening sky. "To the end and a new beginning."

Daniel caught my eye and winked. We all touched glasses and imbibed as champagne bubbles popped, stars came out, and the ocean shimmered in reflected starlight. The night breeze blew, a seagull shrieked, and waves rolled as we drank to Sierra and a girl who came back from the dead.

www.ingramcontent.com/pod-product-compliance
Lightning Source LLC
Chambersburg PA
CBHW051947240626
47153CB00005B/1653